Resurrection of Liberty

Resurrection of Liberty

Michael L. Wentz

Novalibre Publishing, LLC
Phoenix, Arizona

© 2006 Michael L. Wentz. Printed and bound in the United States of America. All rights reserved. No part of this book may be reproduced or transmitted in any form or by any means, electronic or mechanical, including photocopying, recording, or by any information storage and retrieval system without written permission from the author, except for the inclusion of brief quotations in a review.

This is an original work of science fiction. All of the characters, incidents, and dialogue are imaginary—products of the author's imagination. Any similarities to actual persons or events are purely coincidental. Incidental references to products, services, entities, or persons are also fictitious and are not intended to disparage any product, service, entity, company or person.

ISBN-10: 0-9767973-2-1

ISBN-13: 978-0-9767973-2-6

LCCN: 2005903249

First Edition

This book is printed on acid-free paper.

To those men and women
who have dedicated their lives
to the cause of liberty and freedom.
Let their deeds echo throughout history.

Acknowledgments

Resurrection of Liberty is a novel that took countless hours and the help of many people to get it to the point where the story now rests on the printed page. I would like to thank those who have been so important to the realization of this project.

First, my loving wife, Wendy, who encouraged me from the very beginning of this journey—her constant love and support helped me through the ups and downs every author experiences when penning a new work. She listened to me babble about story lines and characters and was right there when I wanted to share a new passage or plot twist. She has the patience of a saint, and I cannot thank her enough.

My parents, Michael and Lenore, who read through revisions, provided candid opinions, and kept pushing me forward—their support has been instrumental to me my entire life and was invaluable in the creation of *Resurrection of Liberty*. My mother, a tried-and-true fan of science fiction, spent many hours editing the first revision of the novel, and my father, a former marine and salesman extraordinaire, gave me invaluable advice on business.

To my in-laws, Donald and Phyllis Josephson, who, along with their support, provided a nice place for me to stay during Book

Expo America—I am glad they enjoyed the brunch at the Ritz, which was meager compensation for having to put up with me for a week.

For Tom Kurtz, whose perspective on life helped give me the courage to share my stories with the world—his assistance was invaluable.

I also want to thank two people who had to deal with my endless array of questions and without whose help I could not have completed the novel. Beverly McGuire did an excellent job of editing the book. I learned a great deal from her and appreciated her indulgence concerning all my queries about style. Michele DeFilippo at 1106 Design designed the cover and did all the typesetting, along with providing me with instant access to her years of expertise in the publishing world. Both of these artists helped craft this book well beyond my expectations.

And finally, to you—I thank you for reading *Resurrection of Liberty*. Enjoy the story.

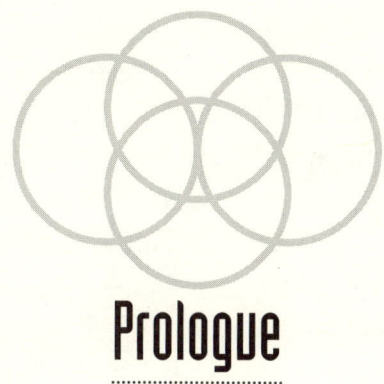

Prologue

A PLASMA TORPEDO SLAMMED INTO THE SHIP, buckling the hull and slamming Captain Meikre Jostak onto the deck of the bridge, his forehead absorbing the full impact. The captain fought the waves of pain, grabbing his head, his hair drenched with blood. Commander Detrina rushed over.

"Captain, you all right?"

Dazed and in shock, the words muddled in his ears as the young captain slowly rose to his feet with the assistance of his first officer. Explosions continued to pummel the ship, making it difficult for him to return to his seat. Bracing himself on the arms, Captain Jostak was able to maneuver into position, blood continuing to cascade down his forehead and into his eyes. A medical technician rushed over and placed a cloth on his head to slow the bleeding.

"Sir, you're injured!" exclaimed Commander Detrina, looking at the horrific gash on his captain's head.

"Dooen't matter. Did we lift off?"

"Yes, sir, but not before they were able to get a few hits. We have taken major damage. Shield generators are offline. I have—"

"What?" asked the captain with disbelief. Without shields they would be sitting ducks. "How long?"

"Ten minutes," responded the commander.

"We don't have ten minutes."

"Sir!" barked the tactical officer. "We have fighters coming in!"

"Arm the belt guns! Don't let any get through."

The tactical officer's fingers flew across his terminal as he brought to life the many small weapons that ringed the great ship. They began to fire automatically, targeting the small craft that were bearing down on them.

"Commander, damage report."

"Hull breaches on several decks, shields out, reactors down to 38 percent …"

The color disappeared from Captain Jostak's face. "We won't have enough power to slide." He turned away from the commander to a young woman standing only a few feet away. "What about it, Doctor?"

Doctor Jetr Tyl was leaning over the engineering officer, trying to help her juggle the ever-increasing power problem. "It's never been tested. You know that."

"No choice. It's our only option, unless you have another."

The doctor huffed, her head shaking.

"Commander, when will we clear the atmosphere?"

"Sixty-three seconds."

The captain punched up the intercom. "This is the captain. We will be engaging Doctor Tyl's prototype device in less than a minute. Shields are out, and we cannot slide. It will be our only chance of running the blockade. Secure your stations!"

Tyl and the engineering officer worked feverishly, trying to prepare by routing power away from damaged sections of the ship, the engines, and anywhere they could find it.

"Captain! Four marauders moving to intercept us once we leave the atmosphere," announced the helmsman.

Prologue

"Stay on course," he ordered. "Doctor? Doctor?" There was no response as Tyl continued to work.

Commander Detrina was standing with the tactical officer, tracking their exit from the planet. "Sir, we will breach the atmosphere in twenty-four seconds. Marauders will be in range in twenty-seven seconds."

Captain Jostak sat in his chair, staring at the viewscreen, watching the blue of the sky darken as the ship moved out into the emptiness of space. Off in the distance he could see the four enemy craft that were waiting for them patiently, moving to intercept their escape vector.

"Twenty seconds … fifteen … ten …"

"Doctor?"

"Nine …"

"Doctor?"

"Eight …"

"Power down to 20 percent!" screamed Tyl. "We just don't have enough!"

"Six …"

"Sir, gun ports opening on the marauders!" yelled Commander Detrina.

"Five … four …"

"Tyl!" barked the captain. "No more time! Arm it, or we're dead!"

The doctor turned, face beet red from the stress. "Actuator transferred to your command."

The captain looked down at the blinking button embedded in the arm of his chair.

"Two … one … we have cleared the planet!"

Doctor Tyl closed her eyes as the stern-faced captain firmly pressed the button to arm the device.

Outside the great ship, the enemy marauders targeted what was left of the heavily damaged vessel as she shrieked out of the atmosphere. Guns trained in on her fire-damaged hull when all of a sudden, in a shimmer, she was gone.

A New Toy

NOT EVERY VISIT TO GRANDPA'S HOUSE was this much fun. Most of the time there were oodles of family members milling about, visiting with one another, and trying to squeeze Danny's cute four-year-old cheeks. Danny hated this part the most. Why couldn't they just shake hands with him like an adult? No, they had to grab, squeeze, poke, and pinch. Later in life one could probably look on the back of any phonebook and get help for this kind of treatment from some less than scrupulous attorney, but at four-years old, it was just part of any large family gathering.

But this day was free of such horrors—no cousins, aunts, uncles, or distant relatives from Cleveland who talked way too much about the Browns. It was only Danny—well, Danny and his grandma.

It was Danny's fourth birthday, and as was tradition in the Foster family, he could request to do whatever he wanted, within reason and, of course, in the confines of the family budget. Danny chose, as he did the previous year, to spend this special day over at his grandparents' home. The lure of the expansive backyard, cable TV with endless cartoons bursting from the screen, an old but fully functional swing set, and, oh yes, his grandmother's baking was much more than any child could resist.

"More cookies, Danny?" asked his grandma from the kitchen.

"No, thank you," responded Danny politely. He had already eaten five, and if he attempted one more, it would be the end of the living room carpet. This boy knew his limit, yet the temptation of just one more challenged his will.

"Where's Grandpa?"

"He went to pick up the new car," responded Grandma.

"A new car!" Danny was extremely excited. His dad was a big car nut and had instilled this passion in his son from the moment he rode home from the nursery. Even at four, Danny could identify most of the cars on the road, even though he could not really read yet. As he and his parents drove about, Danny would blurt out, "Ford!" "Chrysler!" "Chevy!"

Danny raced into the kitchen and stopped abruptly at his grandma's feet. "What kind of car is it?" he asked, looking up at her with his brilliant green eyes.

"Now, Danny, I don't know those things. You ask me about food, politics, clothing, or even any Hollywood gossip, and I could help ... but cars, well, you will have to see when it gets here."

"What is Hollyw ..." Danny's voice trailed off before he finished his thought. His grandma knew a lot of things, but he was in no mood today for a lecture on some new soap opera saga or this Hollywood place. So succumbing to his will, he quickly grabbed that sixth cookie and trotted off to the window to wait for the new car.

As four-year-olds have the attention span of a golden retriever, Danny's vigil didn't last long. He stumbled off the window seat and made a beeline for the backyard to play on the swing set. It was the same one his mom had played on as a little girl. Old and a bit rusty from the upstate New York weather, it still did the job—even though it grunted and squeaked while it did.

The metallic symphony of the swing set was joined by a rumble coming up the long driveway. Danny leaped off the swing in midoscillation and fell face first onto the grass. Lifting his head and wiping the greenery from his teeth, he saw it. Covered in the purest white paint and accented by miles of chrome, the car emanated a luminescent glow in the afternoon sun. Danny hoisted himself up and stood staring at the magnificence of this marriage of paint, rubber, and steel. So glorious was its presence that he half expected angels to burst forth from the trunk.

Breaking himself from the trance, Danny sped across the yard and positioned himself by the driver's side door to greet his grandpa. The car came to a stop, and the door cracked open.

"Happy birthday, kiddo!" exclaimed Grandpa, as he climbed out of his new chariot.

Danny responded with a hug to his leg, but then quickly turned his attention back to the car as that open driver's door now revealed the inner world of this marvel. Luxurious gray leather lined the seats; wood-grained accents and a generous portion of chrome adorned the dash.

"Now hold on, sport. I have something for you."

Grandpa pulled a wrapped box out of the backseat and handed it to Danny. "Now what type of grandpa would I be to bring home a car on your birthday, but not have one for you?"

Danny dropped to his knees on the asphalt and proceeded to tear off the paper.

"Thank you, Grandpa!"

It was a model of the very car that was sitting in the driveway.

"I can be just like you!" Danny exclaimed as he rolled the car back and forth on the driveway. "I'll give you a ride in mine, if you give me a ride in yours."

"I tell you what," responded Grandpa. "Give me some time to do some work, and I will take you out for ice cream."

Score! A ride in the new car and more sweets; this was the best birthday ever!

Clutching his new car, Danny got up and bounded after his grandpa, sticking close to his heels as the two entered the side door into the house, leaving Grandma out in the driveway picking up the odd pieces of wrapping paper that were blowing about.

Danny's grandfather, Henry Rittenhouse, was a hulk of a man. Standing six feet four inches tall, his sixty-two-year-old body was in better shape than those of many men half his age. He ran seven miles every day and had even participated in the New York City Marathon on five separate occasions. The last being on his sixty-first birthday! To keep his muscles strong and limber, he had the most bizarre sixty-minute exercise routine—it looked like a combination of yoga, jujitsu, and gymnastics. But as funny as it appeared, it kept him in tiptop shape. In fact, his health was so good that no one could remember him ever seeing a doctor.

They made it to Grandpa's office. He fumbled about in his pocket for the key and, upon finding it, unlocked the door. Danny loved to come in here and look at all the neat gadgets, but his grandpa kept it locked, and not even Grandma had access. In fact, even hovering around in the hallway outside the locked door was a no-no, as Danny discovered on one unfortunate occasion. So the only time the young man could enter the room was when his grandpa was working.

What Grandpa did in this room he called work, but Danny saw it as play. With all the funny electronics, radios, star charts, and maps, it was a neat place for any kid.

"Now remember, Danny, the deal is that you can sit here with me as long as you are quiet and do not touch anything."

"Okay," said Danny shyly, because he would try, but with all the temptations littered about the room, it was tough for a four-year-old to maintain his composure.

Danny's grandpa worked hard. He had his own company, which made electronics for everything from factory automation equipment to this new gadget he called a "fax machine." He seemed to always have something to do, and Danny took any opportunity to spend time with him, even if it just meant sitting quietly and watching.

"What are you doing?"

"I need to talk with some friends about business."

"What type of business?" asked Danny.

"Oh, nothing for a young man like yourself to worry about. Go back to playing with your car, and when I am finished, we will go get you that ice cream."

A consummate salesman, Grandpa knew that kids were easily sold on lines like that, and on cue Danny went back to playing with his car while Grandpa fired up the ham radio.

Different voices crackled over the air. Their words seemed almost incomprehensible, and Danny had no idea what was being discussed. What he did observe was that when his grandpa talked, everyone else seemed to quiet down. It may have been his booming voice, but when he spoke, the others on the radio seemed to listen intently and acknowledge with a "yes, sir" or "no, sir."

This was not a surprise to Danny. His grandpa was a leader in every respect, whether in business or in the community. It wasn't only his physical presence that made people sit up and listen, but also his commanding voice and unique ability to understand people. His company had one of the highest employee satisfaction ratings in the industry, and 60 percent of his workforce had been there twenty-plus years. Not many Fortune 500 companies could claim that accomplishment.

"Darn bugs!" exclaimed Grandpa. He hated bugs and kept a can of bug spray in every room of the house. Snatching the one on the desk, he quickly dispatched the offending fly. His obsession with a bug-free home drove Grandma nuts, but she tolerated it. Plus, he kept most of the exterminators in town busy.

He put the can down and went back to the radio.

As Grandpa was talking, he would grab for lists, maps, star charts, and the like. Danny didn't care. He just wanted his grandpa to finish up so they could go for a ride in that new car and get that ice cream.

"All finished," said Grandpa, as he switched off the radio and other machines.

Danny popped up from his chair and followed his grandpa out of the room. Grandpa locked the door and secured the deadbolt. The two headed toward the kitchen.

"Grandpa?" uttered Danny, tugging at his grandpa's pant leg.

"Yes?"

"When I grow up, can I have the big car?"

His grandfather laughed, paused for a minute, stooped down, and started to look very serious. He put his head down, eyes to the floor, and sighed. This startled Danny, because he thought it was a simple question and did not know why his grandpa looked so upset. Danny felt relieved when he finally raised his head, now exposing a slight grin. He whispered under his breath, "*Metaliate dretis dakh.*"

"What?" asked Danny, confused by the strange muttered words.

"Danny, never judge a book by its cover. What may seem like a simple responsibility may be much more. For now, your car there is the book whose story you can handle. When you are older, and I think you are ready, we will discuss another story."

Danny stood there for a minute looking at the toy car and smiled. He figured he'd better not push it. This was the perfect day, and for now, he had his car, and that was just fine.

Danny looked back at Grandpa, who slowly stood up.

"Let's go get that ice cream!"

End of an Era

THE RADIO SPRUNG TO LIFE, projecting soothing sounds of the best easy listening from the sixties and seventies throughout the room. A shoe was lifted from the floor and immediately launched with violent intent across the room, smashing into the clock radio and ending its serenade of faded pop classics. Dan had strategically located his alarm far away from his bed and set it to the station that would annoy him the most. This was designed to guarantee that he would have to wake up and lurch across the room to stop the madness. Unfortunately, he had discovered that a shoe moving at high velocity did the trick, and that allowed him to flop back on his pillow to catch a few more winks, defeating the entire purpose.

"Dan!" *Pound, pound, pound.* "Dan! Are you awake?" frantically asked his father.

"Yeah, sort of."

"Get up. Your mom is on the phone with her sister. Grandma is in the hospital."

"What! Uh … uh … hold on." Dan was unnerved. His grandfather had died several years ago, which devastated him. Now his grandma was in the hospital. He was feeling a cascade of emotions from grief, to anger, to hopelessness, all wrapped up in a knot in his stomach.

Quickly Dan pulled on some sweatpants and a t-shirt, then bolted out of the room and down the stairs. He heard sobbing from the kitchen, so he darted in that direction. His mom was seated at the table, elbows propping up her head. His father stood over her, resting his hands on her shoulders. Tears, red eyes, and smeared mascara covered up his mother's normally strikingly beautiful face. Dan stood there feeling helpless. He did not like to see his mom cry.

She reached to her right to grab a tissue out of the box resting on the table and wiped her tears in an attempt to compose herself.

"Danny?"

"Yes, Mom."

"Sit down." Dan grabbed a chair across from her. They sat there for a minute holding hands and staring at one another.

"Grandma got a severe headache last night. She called Aunt Jean when the pain got increasingly worse. Jean went over her house, picked her up, and took her to the hospital." She started to cry again and broke her grip from Dan's hands to grab another tissue.

After wiping her eyes, Dan's mother took a deep breath and regained her composure. "They … they admitted her and began running some tests. While Jean waited in the exam room, Mom … she … had a stroke."

Dan turned bright red, and he could feel his eyes welling up.

"Son, your grandma passed away." She began crying again. His father bent down and hugged her to try to absorb some of the pain.

Dan didn't know how to react. He felt more anger than sorrow. *Why couldn't they save her? Isn't that what hospitals are for?* He tried to push all those thoughts from his mind as he looked across the table at his sobbing mother. He had to be strong. He needed to act like a grownup; after all, he was sixteen. He wasn't a baby anymore.

Reaching out for his mother's hands, he grasped them consolingly and peered into her teary eyes and said, "I'm sorry."

For the first time that day, he actually saw his mom smile. Dan had reacted a lot like her father would have, with strength and courage. Her little boy was growing up.

Six years ago, Dan's grandpa had died after being very ill for several months. Despite his wife's urging, he vehemently refused to go see a doctor. Grandma tried to enlist Dan's mother's help in getting Grandpa to go see a physician, and Dan could clearly remember the multitude of frantic phone calls. Yet in the end, nothing worked; this man was set in his ways, and there was no budging him when he had his mind made up. One day he collapsed at work and died of an unknown cause at sixty-eight years of age. He left explicit instructions that there was to be no autopsy and that his body was to be cremated. The family never knew exactly what took him. Even the doctor who signed his death certificate was unsure and simply chose "undetermined" as the official reason for his demise.

After Grandpa passed away, Grandma dealt with the loss by keeping his belongings undisturbed around their home. The door to his office remained locked, as it was when he was alive; she never entered the room, even though she could have. The business was sold to the trust Grandpa had set up. This trust was structured to give the workers ownership of the plant, a promise he had made to those who started the business with him many years before.

Grandma also kept Grandpa's beloved car locked away in the garage. It was the same car that he had brought home on Dan's fourth birthday, and it had remained stored away for the past six years.

When Dan was eleven he asked if he could buy it when he was old enough, pledging to give it the best of care. His grandma grasped his hand tightly and looked him square in the eye, saying, "You don't want the type of responsibility that comes with that thing." Needless to say, after a reaction like that, Dan never brought forth the question again.

That was all in the past; now, Dan had to focus on the present and be strong for his family. After he spent time consoling his mother, he rose from the table, hugged her, and went upstairs to get showered and dressed. It was a long drive from Boston to Albany, where his grandma lived, so he had to hurry.

Dan headed straight into the bathroom; did a less than perfect job of shaving, although he wasn't bleeding as much as normal; brushed his teeth; and took a lightning-fast shower. His parents, who had been up most of the night, had already packed a bag for the trip. Dan, wrapped in a towel, dripped his way back to his room and spotted his backpack. Picking it up, he dumped out the books on the floor and proceeded to stuff in some clothes to take along. Two nice polo-style shirts and jeans would have to do. Anything more formal could be picked up from the mall or borrowed from a relative. He zipped up the bag, donned some clothes over his still damp body, and headed downstairs.

His mom was waiting in the living room; he heard his dad speaking on the phone in the kitchen to some relatives, sharing their travel plan. His mom looked much better. Her hair was brushed, and the smeared mascara was gone. What was left was the mom he knew—blonde hair, fair complexion, and remarkable green eyes. His friends would joke that Mrs. Maria Foster was the best-looking mom in the neighborhood.

Dan plopped down in the easy chair opposite her. "You look much better."

"Thanks. You helped a lot."

"How?" Dan asked, giving her a confused glance, brow furrowed under his soggy blonde hair.

"You reminded me of my dad. I saw you about to cry, but then you pushed your own feelings aside and focused on me. You worried about how I felt. That's the way your grandpa always used to be. You showed me that you are all grown up."

"Thanks, but I'm not grown up yet. I haven't even finished high school."

"You still showed me that you're not a little boy anymore."

Little? One look at Dan, and anyone with two eyes could see that wasn't the case. He rose six feet, three inches from his feet to the top of his head. His hair was a striking blonde, like his mother's, and he had her brilliant green eyes. Dan was not a jock by any means, but liked to run and bike and keep in good shape. He even tried to copy his grandpa's exercise routine, which he performed diligently every day. Not that he was capable of every move, but it still helped him build some rather uncommon strength. A little boy he was no more.

"Thanks ... I guess. Can we change the subject?"

"Sure," his mom laughed. "You were never very good at taking a compliment. Anyway, we should get going. It's a long drive back to Albany, and with the summer traffic going to the Berkshires, we're sure to get behind our share of slowpokes. Hey, Michael, are you off the phone yet?"

Michael Foster was Dan's father. With his brown hair and eyes, he looked nothing like his wife or son. Dan's parents had met during their undergraduate years at Rensselaer Technical Institute in Troy, New York. When Michael graduated, he decided to go to law school at Union University in Albany. With the scores he got on his LSAT and his 3.9 GPA from Rensselaer, he could have gone to Yale, Columbia, Harvard, or Stanford for law, but he wanted to stay close to his future wife. Michael's expertise and focus were corporate law. He began his litigious career with a small manufacturing company in Albany, but a few years ago he was presented with an offer from John Hancock. This precipitated the family's move to Boston.

"Just hang on a minute," a voice declared from the kitchen. "I'm having problems getting us a hotel."

"Call Jean! We can stay at her place!"

Oh, no ... no ... no! This was not what Dan wanted to hear.

Aunt Jean—Jeanne Torres, to be specific—was his mom's sister. She was married to Antonio Torres, the diner magnate of upstate New York. They had two kids—Martin, the youngest at two years old, and Stacey, at the bubbling age of five. Both children had behavior "issues," and staying overnight at their house was akin to a carnival meets a full-scale riot. No doubt the somber occasion would dispel some of the usual craziness, but still, it was not the place Dan wanted to be. He needed some peace and quiet to deal with the loss of his grandma. Aunt Jean's was not the place to do this.

"Already called her," responded Michael. "She said that the guestroom is getting remodeled."

Dan suppressed the smile that was forming on his face.

"She said we should just stay at your mom's house if we can't find a room." His voice moved from a shout to a normal tone as he walked from the kitchen into the living room and stood in the doorway.

"I guess that would be all right," his mom said tentatively. "I could start to clean up and organize things. It will be hard, but I can do it." She threw a smile in Dan's direction.

Dan's father grabbed his car keys. "Let's go then."

The drive to Albany down the MassPike was long, but scenic. The amount of greenery in this part of the country was always amazing, as was the amount of traffic in August. Refugees from the coastal heat and humidity used this four-lane highway to take them to the cool Berkshires, the majestic Adirondacks, or anyplace in between. At least the roadway was littered with those East Coast-style turnpike rest stops where travelers could grab a greasy burger or some burned coffee if they needed a little break from the traffic.

It was a beautiful day, and the turnpike was bursting at the seams. It was a big weekend at Tanglewood, the summer home of the Boston Symphony. Also, Bernadette Peters was appearing as a guest artist at some big summer stock festival in northern

Connecticut, and it was race weekend in Saratoga. These events and all other goings on in the region contributed to the lack of available hotel rooms, so the Foster family headed to the grandparents' former home. It lay on the far west side of the city of Albany in a semirural area. This location allowed Grandpa to have his huge ham radio antenna and two full acres of land. That was why Dan used to enjoy going there as a boy. He could run and play in the big yard, on the swing set, and not worry about city traffic or any of the urban dangers that could befall modern-day youngsters.

Dan fell asleep in the back of the car. He usually didn't sleep in cars, planes, trains, or just about any other form of movable transportation, but the events of the morning had definitely wiped him out. A large pothole jostled the car and ripped him from his slumber only a few blocks from the Rittenhouse homestead. The neighborhood was dotted with classic postwar era homes on two-acre plots. Their winding driveways and well-manicured yards hearkened back to another era. Driving through here was like traveling back in time. Only the modern-day cars gave away the fact that they were very much in the present.

As they approached their destination, Dan could see the huge ham radio antenna, which towered above the trees. It rose out of the backyard like an unfinished suspension bridge. Grandma didn't take it down after Grandpa died, even though she hated the gargantuan structure. As ugly as it was to her, it still was a reminder of her loving husband.

The house itself was a large ranch that sat perched atop a lush green hill. The driveway circled up from the street and skirted the yard, dancing up the incline toward the right side of the house, eventually ending up in the back. The driveway terminated at a small circular parking area in front of the two-car garage.

Michael Foster stopped the car right in front of the garage and jammed the transmission into park triumphantly, after making the trip in only three hours and twenty minutes. Dan immediately freed himself from the clutches of the seatbelt and sprang out of the car so the blood could return to his gluteus maximus.

The sunshine from the morning yielded to a light overcast. Dan peered toward the side door, which functioned as the "real" front entrance used by friends and family alike. He remembered his grandparents coming out to greet them, and this was the first time that the door remained closed. No one came out; there was only an eerie stillness made all the more foreboding by the gray clouds and calm wind. Dan looked over at his mom, who was obviously experiencing the same uncomfortable mix of sentiment. She simply stared at the house, expressionless. His father occupied himself by pulling the bags from the trunk.

"Hey!" Dan turned around and looked at his father just in time to catch his backpack. "Maria, do you have the key?" asked Michael.

"Yes." She started for the door. Dan grabbed another bag from the trunk and followed. The screen door was half closed, just resting against the latch, obviously as a result of the quick exit of Aunt Jean and Grandma. Dan realized that they would be the first to step into the house since Grandma had passed.

Maria opened the door, and the three stepped inside to the mudroom. Long and narrow, it was the first stop for any people entering the house so they could politely shed their muddy boots and wet jackets. Michael and Dan dropped their bags and followed Maria into the kitchen. It was spotless, because Grandma had firmly believed that all sicknesses started somehow from a dirty kitchen. An old black-and-white tile floor grounded the "modern" metal cabinets. The sink and main workspace were to the right, with a window facing the expansive backyard. A large oven was on the opposite wall next to a refrigerator. Dan remembered the myriad of muffins and cookies that had been pulled from that oven, but just as the rest of the house that day, it sat quiet and ignored.

Maria continued on, and Dan went to follow. Michael grabbed him on the back of the shirt. "Better give Mom some time alone."

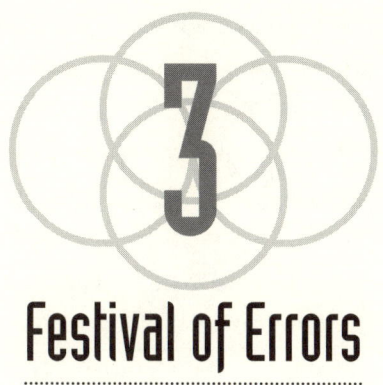

Festival of Errors

THE FUNERAL THE NEXT DAY was very respectful. The large turnout gave Dan and his mother an opportunity to meet with some of Grandma's friends so they could hear the stories about her youth, learn what she was like as a friend, and see the impact she had on so many. If one can refer to "closure," then this day accomplished that for both daughter and grandson.

The Fosters quietly drove back to the house, giving each time to reflect on the day's events. Dan's mom wanted to visit a few of her old haunts in town to help clear her head, but Dan just needed to rest and have some time alone. They dropped him off at the Rittenhouse homestead and went on their way. Dan had the place to himself.

Grabbing a soda from the fridge, he planted himself in front of the TV. The large screen he remembered from childhood was a mere twenty-five inches, but it still worked fine. Surfing the channels only briefly held his attention, and boredom quickly set in. He started to wander about the house.

As Dan passed Grandpa's locked office, he paused and looked around to ensure that he was truly alone. Even after Grandpa passed away, Grandma kept everyone clear of the room and would not even succumb to the incessant whining of Aunt Jean to be allowed access. Entering this office without Grandpa, or even standing alone outside the locked door, had always been taboo.

Dan reached out carefully with his hand and allowed his fingers to gently grasp the cold brass knob. Taking a deep breath, he turned the knob to the right, but it did not move. *Locked.* A scowl dashed across his face, but it began to fade when he realized that Grandma kept all of her keys in a drawer next to the sink in the kitchen. She would never throw out a key, and the drawer held hundreds, even if they no longer had a lock to open. In her mind, doing this meant that she could never lose one. If the key was anywhere, it would be in that drawer.

Dan sped into the kitchen and began to rummage through the drawer for any key that looked like it might work. *Nothing!* He kept searching anyway and found a small box toward the rear. It was so far back that he had to fish with his arm to retrieve it. Pulling the box out, he carefully placed it on the counter and slowly closed the drawer, his eyes affixed to what he had discovered. He paused, continuing to stare at the old gray jewelry box, as he knew instinctively what was inside. He opened the top, and there they were—Grandpa's keys!

Dan peered out the kitchen window over the sink, surveying the area just to ensure his parents were not back early. Satisfied he was truly alone, Dan sprinted back to the door and started fumbling with every key. Finally one fit! As he turned the key, a shock of giddy excitement pulsed through his body. Not only would he be the first to discover this room's secrets, but also he would have a chance to learn more about his grandfather.

The room was pitch black, as it was absent of any windows. The faint glow of sunlight that streamed down the hallway provided very little illumination. Dan fished on the wall for a light switch, and he found one that powered a dim desk lamp.

The room was extremely small. Ahead was a black rectangular table with a few radios along with associated broadcast equipment.

All the paper was put away except for a few small pieces attached to a clipboard. Running along the sides of the room were six filing cabinets—three on one wall and three on another. All around the room the walls were papered with maps and star charts dotted with multicolor pushpins, apparently marking certain areas of significance. On one of the filing cabinets was a can of bug spray for eliminating those insects that drove his grandfather crazy.

Dan took a few tentative steps forward and noticed two drawers under the table. The one drawer contained only some random papers and receipts, but the second held something much more significant and sentimental to Dan. Contained within were the keys to his grandpa's car—the same car that he had brought home on Dan's fourth birthday.

Dan's eyes lit up. He knew that the car was in the garage. Maybe he would be allowed to take care of it. With the keys were some repair papers, all from the same shop, and miscellaneous gas receipts. Dan shoved the keys into his pocket.

He grabbed the clipboard and examined it. The handwritten pages were covered with names alongside a series of numbers after each. Frustration set in. *What could these mean? Who are these people? Maybe the answer is in those filing cabinets.* Dan carefully placed the clipboard on top of one and fished out a key that seemed appropriate for the style and size of lock. He inserted and rotated it in the mechanism until he felt a satisfying click. The smile that began to form on his face was cut short midgrin by the piercing screech of a siren so loud that it was like getting an auditory baseball stitch driven into his skull. Dan backed away and attempted to remove the key, but it was too late. A flash occurred in each cabinet, one after another, followed by the smell of burned paper.

Dan stood there in shock, eyes wide and mouth open with jaw to the ground. *What just happened? What did I do?*

The siren mercifully stopped its wail, and Dan took in a breath of air for the first time in over a minute. It was too soon to relax, as the silence was short lived, disturbed by the beeping of the house smoke alarm. Dan flew down the hall, frantically trying to open some windows in order to ventilate the smoke. Next he turned his attention to the smoke alarm, running toward it, and in one movement he wrenched it from the wall and removed the batteries to end the noise. The sound of the smoke alarm was replaced not with silence, but with the sound of cars turning off the street and climbing the driveway.

Dan put the smoke detector back on the wall and darted into the living room to look out the big picture window. He saw his parents' car, along with the Torres' minivan. *Oh, no!*

Dan ran as quickly as he could back to the office. At this point the smoke had cleared. He put the car keys back in the drawer and the clipboard on the desk. He noticed that the papers on the clipboard were singed, probably as a result of the flash from the filing cabinets. He pulled off the papers and quickly folded them and shoved them into his pocket. Dan took one more quick survey of the room to make sure everything was in order before he shut off the light and locked the door.

At top speed Dan bolted into the kitchen and put the keys to the office back into the little box, which was still on the counter. He then crammed it back into the drawer and closed it just as the door to the mudroom opened. In bounded Martin and Stacey, who made right for the refrigerator. Aunt Jean and Uncle Tony were straight behind, barking out the usual orders to the children—"Don't!" "Stop!" "Wait!" "You better ..."

Michael and Maria stepped into the kitchen. "Dan, Jean called me on my cell phone. She changed her mind and decided to come by."

"Yeah, Mom never let us go into Dad's old office," grumbled Jean. "I want to get in there. I've wanted to get into that office my entire life and only could when Dad was in there. And when he did allow me in, all I could do was sit there and not touch anything."

A dark cloud of doom began to develop over Dan's head. This was the worst-case scenario, and it was playing out right in front of him. His sweaty palms were by his side, and he subtly gave himself a pinch just to see if it was a dream. *Nope, it wasn't.*

"Cool. I always wanted to get in there myself," Dan said innocently, attempting to hide his previous activities.

Tony barked out, "Jean, I think your mom kept the keys in that drawer by the sink."

"Of course she did!" responded an obviously annoyed Jean. "How long have we been married, and how long did we date before that? You know that Mom always kept her keys in there!"

"Yeah, whatever. Hold on a minute." Tony went to the drawer and started fishing around. Sure enough, he came upon the box. "I think I found something that may have those keys in it."

He pulled the box out and put it on the counter, almost the same place it had sat just a few minutes before.

"Hey, kids, why don't you go out and play?" Tony waved to Martin and Stacey, who bounded out the door to the backyard carrying the sodas they had plundered from the refrigerator.

Tony turned his attention back to the box and opened the lid. Jean and Maria moved closer to peer in.

"Sis! Those are the keys!" exclaimed Maria.

Jean yanked them out of the box and started down the hall for the office, followed closely by Maria, Tony, and Michael. Dan simply stood in the kitchen covered with the heaviest veil of fear he had ever experienced. He stared out into space; every muscle in his body lay still. He even thought his heart had stopped. Time didn't exist, for if it did, its passing would only hasten his doom once they opened that door.

Dan could hear them going through the keys, trying to get the door open. This roused him from the trance, and he slowly made the march toward the office. He turned into the hall just as they successfully gained access.

"Turn on the light, Maria," ordered Jean.

"I don't remember where it is … hold on … ah, there." Maria switched on the light.

At this point Dan had made it to the open door and was standing right behind his father. Jean and Maria examined the desk and of course saw nothing. They looked over the maps and star charts, but could make no sense of them. Next came the drawers. The first, with the receipts, did not impress them. The second created a moderate reaction.

"Jean, Dad's car keys!"

"Oh, that piece of garbage," whined Tony. He had never liked that car. "That piece of junk is still in the garage. Probably doesn't even start. Who would want it?"

Dan saw his opportunity. "Hey, I'll take it." All four looked at him, startled at his boldness. Jean and Maria gave each other conferring glances.

"I'm okay with it," responded Jean. Maria nodded in agreement.

"Well, I guess you got yourself a car, mister sixteen-year-old," responded Dan's father, who gave him a pat on the back.

How could this disaster have worked out in his favor? Dan was not sure, but he was not out of the woods yet. The filing cabinets remained. Jean took the filing cabinet key and went to open the lock. Dan turned into one tight ball. He could almost hear every pin hitting the key as if it were happening in slow motion. Jean finished turning the lock, but there was no siren. There was no sound at all.

Jean yanked open the top drawer. "Empty!" She went from drawer to drawer with the same result—empty. There were not even any ashes or remnants of the combustion that had burned the contents only a few minutes before.

"Well, Jean, much ado about nothing." Maria looked relieved, but Jean was clearly frustrated.

"Come on, hon," said Tony. "Let's go. Nothing here except some old radio equipment and keys to a busted-up old car—no offense, kid." Tony was nothing if not a diplomat.

The four adults walked out of the room, turned off the lights, and shut the door. No need to lock it, as there was nothing of value in there. As they proceeded down the hall, Dan just stood by the old office. He knew that there had been something of great importance in those cabinets that he had accidentally destroyed, something so precious that his grandpa would go to such lengths to protect it. Now, no one would ever know. He felt awful. At least the car was left. He was entrusted with its care, and he would hold on to it as the last piece of whatever his grandfather had held precious.

4

Just a Weekend by the Lake

IT HAD BEEN TWO MONTHS since Dan brought home his grandfather's Cadillac Fleetwood. When he first saw it in the garage, it was layered in six years of dust and grime. Just starting it up took considerable time, as he needed to put in a fresh new battery and labor with Uncle Tony to siphon the six-year-old gas out of the tank to replace it with fresh and combustible petrol. The tires were good, and all the electrical components worked fine.

What seemed strange was the rather small trunk. It had no full-size spare and could hold only one suitcase. The rest was covered by metal and carpet. The same was true of the engine compartment. The V8 that sat in there was small and not typical of a big, luxurious cruiser. Areas around the engine and over the wheel wells were also covered.

Dan had no desire to unfurl this mystery; he was just happy to have some wheels. The car ran well, held his friends for trips to the mall and the movies, and was a nostalgic head turner. He just wished that it had a CD player instead of its old eight-track, which was yet another irregularity about the car. Eight-tracks had gone out years before, making this archaic piece of technology stand out like a sore thumb.

Dan could have used that upgraded stereo, especially for this weekend, as he was taking his friends Janet and Tom up to Tom's parents' cabin on Lake Winnipesaukee in New Hampshire. This would be the longest drive he had taken with the car since he brought it back from Albany. He could not believe that his parents were allowing him to drive up with his friends. This was a big step for him.

Dan was in his room packing his bag. His bedroom, like those of most teenagers, was littered with items that interested him—awards, posters, model cars, and so on. Dan was a very accomplished student. He had a 3.7 GPA, and his wall held several certificates of academic accomplishment. What were absent were school trophies, especially surprising for someone who was so athletic. Dan had tried school sports, but was more interested in martial arts, running, mountain biking, and general fitness than in having a letterman jacket. Instead he had awards for moving up the rank to black belt in jujitsu and bib numbers from his runs and mountain bike races neatly tacked on to the wall. This suited Dan just fine. He never went with the crowd.

Dan kissed his mom goodbye and headed out to the driveway. He put his duffle in the trunk and fired up the old white boat. The headlights flickered to life, as it was now October and getting dark earlier, and at 6:30 on this Friday night, the rays of daylight had already been replaced by the shadows of dusk. Mercifully, he and the rest of his school had a long weekend. It was the first long weekend with the car and without his parents. Dan wanted to be sure to play it straight so he could gain their trust for future excursions, and he fully intended on being home by 10:00 Monday night as promised. Pointing the old Caddy toward the street, he drove off toward Tom's house.

Tom was an interesting character. His full name was Thomas F. Hunt, and he was the son of a Japanese mother and German father. His parents moved to the United States from Japan a few months before he was born. He was a smart kid with an affinity for bugs, which he voraciously collected.

As Tom lived in the same neighborhood, Dan's drive was short. He pulled up in front of Tom's house, turned off the car, got out, and walked toward the front door. A ring of the doorbell was followed by the sound of Tom bounding down the stairs. The door swung open.

"Hey, man, you gotta check this out!"

"Tom, are you ready to roll, or are we gonna look at bugs all night?" griped Dan.

"Don't be such a jerk! Just come upstairs with me while I grab my bag, and you can see this."

Dan reluctantly followed Tom upstairs. Tom's bedroom was a shrine for bugs. The reason the Hunt house did not have an insect problem was that they all found refuge in Tom's room. Rome and Athens, his two aquarium-sized ant farms, stood like two prominent museum display cases almost in the center of everything. Decorating the walls were frames holding hundreds of different bugs mounted on pins. He had the inevitable tarantula and books upon books relating to his bug passion. Otherwise, the room was spotless. Tom was very meticulous about keeping clean. His locker at school was more sanitary than most hospital operating rooms—all this from a bug guy.

Tom motioned to Dan. "Come check out Athens."

"Wow, ants ... what am I looking at?"

"Dan, I put some ants from Rome into Athens to see what would happen. Do you know what they did?"

"Uh ... they made them late for a road trip?"

Tom flashed a scowl. "No, even worse. They're making them work as slaves. Check it out!"

Dan really wasn't sure what he was seeing, but he humored his friend just the same.

"So what motivated you to do this?" Dan was hoping for a sane answer, as he did not want to spend the weekend with a crazy person.

"Well, I've been doing a ton of research on different bugs that use other bugs or animals for labor, food, and even to take care of their young."

"Wow, bug daycare," smirked Dan.

"No, seriously, people underestimate the organizational power of these things. Look at how a tiny fire ant or Africanized bee can kill a person."

"Yeah, you need a boatload of ants and bees—"

"Working together. Exactly my point!"

Dan muddled the thought. "Nice, but ... what does that have to do with us going to the lake?"

"Fine, let's go."

The two headed out to the car.

Next stop was Janet Whitley's house. She lived a few miles away in an old turn-of-the-century neighborhood lined with grand Victorian homes. Her dad, Romley Whitley, came from a wealthy and well-established New England family. His company, Global Investments, continued building on the family fortune, specializing in opportunities in Eastern Europe.

This unlikely trio had met five years ago, right after Dan moved to the area. At the beginning of the sixth grade there was a class trip to Washington, D.C. On the agenda were the Lincoln Memorial, the Washington Monument, the National Zoo, and the Museum of American History. Several members of the class were disappointed to learn that the Museum of Natural History was not on their sightseeing itinerary, as it held that which fixated many ten- to eleven-year-olds—dinosaurs.

Dan took it in stride, but one very outspoken young lady did not. Her name was Janet, and she tried everything from a note from her father to giving a speech in front of the class to somehow sway political sentiment to her cause. Of course nothing worked, so the class headed off on its preordained schedule, but Dan had a feeling that Janet had not given up her fight.

The field trip for Dan was his opportunity to meet new friends after just moving from Albany. He took the time to try to talk with as many different people as he could on the buses, at the rest stops, and at meals. This outgoing attitude was awkward, especially for the new kid, but many of his classmates appreciated the fact that he did not seem to act like a snob.

The day came when they visited the Museum of American History. Situated on the Mall between the Washington Monument and Capitol Building, the museum was just one of the many Smithsonian buildings that lined the long grassy promenade. Tantalizingly close this day was the Museum of Natural History, which held the dinosaurs.

During lunch outside, Dan saw Janet sitting off in a corner by herself, the wind blowing through her long brown hair. All the other students were busy munching on their turkey sandwiches. He decided to be friendly, and anyway he was at the age when boys first start discovering that girls are not that icky, and this one seemed to be even less icky than the others.

"Hi," Dan said with a smile to cover his nervousness.

"You're the new kid," responded Janet, still chewing on her red delicious apple from the box lunch.

"Yeah ... I—"

"Hey, you wanna do something fun?"

Dan was a little shocked. "Okay ..."

"I'm gonna go see the dinosaurs," she said with a smug grin. "They're right over there." She pointed over her shoulder to the museum just down the street.

"Uh ... did you get permission?"

"That's the best part! I decided to give myself permission."

Dan chuckled. "You can't just give yourself permission."

"Yeah, I can, and I just did. You wanna come?"

During the early stages of puberty, the male mind begins to lose some of its judgment, especially around attractive women. One look at Janet, and common sense flew out the window. *See dinosaurs and hang out with this cute girl ... hmmm ...* "I'm in."

Janet winked at Dan, put down her apple, and in one movement jumped over the hedge. Dan had to clamber to follow her. The two scurried down the street, looking over their shoulders to make sure they weren't being followed.

"We're gonna get busted."

"No, we won't," answered Janet confidently. "Look, we have one hour for lunch. It's only 12:15. By the time everyone finishes and they get people lined up for the buses, it will be 1:10 at the earliest, which means if we're back by 12:55, no one will know the difference. We have forty minutes to get in and get out."

Sounded reasonable to Dan, and anyhow it seemed worth the risk.

They climbed the museum stairs, entered, and took a right past the huge African elephant that was the centerpiece of the lobby. They made it to the hall of dinosaurs, and it was only 12:21. They had plenty of time if Janet was correct.

The two wandered the hall with their mouths wide open in wonder, silently trying to take in all that they were seeing. The eighty-seven-foot-long *Diplodocus longus* sitting on the center podium with an *Allosaurus* was both strange and terrifying. Dan grabbed Janet by the shoulder and pointed to the *Tyrannosaurus rex*, his favorite. They quietly walked over, eyes affixed on the huge creature, not even seeing the kid they plowed into.

"Hey!" protested the young man.

"Sorry," Dan apologized. He studied the kid a little more closely. "Hey, aren't you in my class?"

Janet pointed. "Yeah, you're Tom Hunt—and you're not supposed to be here either."

"Wow, you kids from Boston don't seem to have much respect for authority," poked Dan.

"Bugs."

"Huh?" inquired Janet and Dan in unison.

"I came here to see the bugs. The O. Orkin Insect Zoo is upstairs. It's really cool."

Dan looked down at his watch. "Uh, we should really get back to—"

"Cool! Can you show us?" bubbled Janet.

"Yeah, let's go!"

The two bounded off, leaving Dan with a decision to make: go with these rebels or head back. One look at Janet's flowing hair as she and Tom scurried toward the insect zoo made up his mind for him. "Wait up!"

The O. Orkin Insect Zoo was amazing, as was how knowledgeable this Tom kid was about the myriad of creatures on display. As one would expect, they lost track of time.

Janet looked down at her watch. "Oh, no!" It read 1:37.

Tom and Dan did the same and shared her reaction. Without saying a word, they careened out of the exhibit and down the escalator, pushing past many startled museumgoers, and launched themselves toward the door. They were stopped dead in their tracks by their teacher, Mrs. Summers, and two of the chaperones.

"Thought you three might be in here!" she barked.

"Yeah ... uh ... we got lost ... and ..." Dan gave Tom a shove to shut him up.

"Well, not only do you have to sit on the bus the rest of the trip, but you all have detention for the next month. I should suspend you, but I think the extra two hours of school everyday would be good for three knowledge-hungry students."

Not only did they have to suffer that punishment, but their parents, upon being informed by Mrs. Summers of their little adventure, grounded them for the duration of the school detention.

For the next four weeks, the only faces Dan saw were of Janet and Tom. This type of incarceration can precipitate a relatively tight bond, as it did with this trio.

Dan rolled the white boat up the semicircular driveway in front of the grand Whitley house and honked the horn. Janet made her way out and jumped into the backseat.

Janet did not look like a rich snob, nor did she act like one. Standing about five feet six inches tall, with long straight brown hair, she was always well groomed, but preferred jeans and t-shirts to the day's designer fads. One could have even referred to her as having the slightest tomboyish tendencies. Like her two companions, Janet did exceptionally well in her scholastics and was very popular with the students and teachers. Currently holding the office of junior class president, she was very busy, and any time that she could spend with her two best friends was cherished.

Her real passion was science fiction. From a very early age her mother had sat her down in front of the TV, exposing her to *Godzilla*, *Dr. Who*, *Star Trek*, and the *Twilight Zone*. This early indoctrination gave her an insatiable appetite for anything having to do with space and the future. From *Star Trek* to *Babylon Five*, from *Lost in Space* to the *X Files*, and, of course, *Stargate SG-1*, Janet was awash in sci-fi trivia. She once wore a Klingon costume to a *Star Trek* convention and was the best-looking Klingon female that most people had ever seen.

"Hey, guys!" she exclaimed as she clicked on her seatbelt.

"Hey, Janet, what's up?"

"Dan, I got a surprise for our trip, but let's get going before I give it to you."

"Cool." Dan started driving.

They were taking the back roads to the highway. The car was so large that Dan got nervous driving where there were a lot of turning traffic and pedestrians. This back way was almost always deserted and made for a stress-free, if indirect, way to the interstate.

Tom sat quietly, which was a bit unusual for him. Mr. Hunt's jaw was always humming away talking about something, but he just sat in the passenger seat, silently looking out the window.

Dan tried to snap him out of it. "Hey, you all right?"

"Guys, I have a confession," he mumbled, still staring out the window, not wanting to see his friends' reaction. "My parents aren't up at the cabin; they're actually in Toronto visiting relatives. I didn't want to trick you guys, but I knew your parents would freak if they knew we were going up there all alone."

Janet lurched forward from the backseat. "What? We have the cabin on the lake to ourselves for the whole weekend? Whoohoo!"

"Wait … wait … ," Dan said nervously. "I had to beg my parents to let me go on this trip. Now we'll be up there alone, with no parents, in a house all by ourselves on the lake."

"Duh?" responded Janet as she reached over and pinched his cheek. "You need to live a little. Just keep driving … and here … here's my surprise. Maybe it'll calm you down."

Janet pulled out an eight-track tape. Tom took a look at the label. "Hey, *Dark Side of the Moon* … Pink Floyd—cool! Put it in the deck, Dan."

Dan took the old eight-track and jammed the tape into the dash. He had never played a tape like this before, so he was just guessing at how it operated. He powered on the player, and there was nothing—just static.

"Sounds good," joked Tom.

"Stuff it, bug boy!" barked Dan. He was not in the mood for jokes about his car or his ability to operate it.

Dan started pressing buttons randomly—first two, then three at a time, and some weird combinations just out of frustration. Then all of a sudden something finally resonated from the speakers: "*Fret tuyaly cuuratioon malassea, Fret tuyaly cuuratioon malassea.*"

"Oh, sorry. The tape's all messed up," Janet said, dejected that her gift was a flop. "It just sounds like gibberish."

Dan yanked the tape out, but the female voice continued: "*Taylate contissawqy—Bah, tret, friey, dahle, pret—Treyalit pretave yewitey.*"

The three friends looked at each other, confused, as a loud humming sound now emanated from the trunk.

"Do we have a flat?" asked Tom.

"I'm not sure. I'll stop and check." Dan quickly pulled off the road into an abandoned gas station. He tried to open his door, but could not. "I can't open my door!" Janet and Tom both tried theirs, tugging on the handles and thrusting themselves against the doors, but they didn't budge.

"What's going on?" shrieked Janet.

A suctiony sound ripped through the car, and the three grabbed their ears.

"Ow!" exclaimed Dan.

"We're pressurizing!"

"What, Janet? What do you mean—pressurizing?"

The humming that began from the trunk now resounded throughout the car and shook the three like a massage chair, pulsating waves through the old leather seats. The steering wheel split on the top and bottom, with the parts telescoping into what appeared to be a flight yoke. The brake pedal flipped vertically and moved to the left.

No one could speak, but Janet was able to utter a few trembling words. "Dan … Dan … what exactly did your grandfather do for a living?"

The three screamed as the car lurched upward. The wheels tucked themselves up into the wells; vents opened on the front and rear quarter panels. The car was now hovering. A handle appeared out of the dash. The voice began again: *"Meiynie ya, meiynie ya—Bah, tret, friey, dahle, pret."* The car started to rise—ten feet, twenty feet, fifty feet. They were now floating above the abandoned gas station. Dan tried the controls.

"The controls don't work!" he screamed.

"Well, shut off the car!" advised Tom.

"What? We're fifty feet in the air! I am not shutting this car off!" Dan turned to Janet. "Hey, Mrs. Spock, any suggestions?"

They both turned to see Janet totally frozen, staring off into space, with her jaw open and eyes wide.

The humming now modulated to a higher pitch; the hood angled upward; and the car quickly accelerated, banking and yawing until the moon appeared directly in the front window. Dan looked back to see the gas station shrinking in size as they rocketed away.

Their speed continued to increase, taking them higher and higher. The historic city of Boston was now viewable in its entirety. The glistening lights began to shrink away as the seconds passed and the car shrieked into the heavens.

Tom started scrounging through his pockets. "Look, I have my cell phone. We can call 911."

"And what, tell them that we're in a car that's turned into an airplane? 'Hello, Ms. 911 Person, we were sneaking off to the lake, and the car we're in turned into an airplane. Please help us.'"

"Well, I'm just trying to think of something!" snapped Tom. "I mean, anyway, we're in major airspace. Someone has to see us in this airplane thing."

"Make that a spaceship." Janet finally broke from her stupor. "Look." The three peered out the window to see the curvature of the planet, complete with the faint glow of the hemisphere still lighted by the sun.

"Forget it! I'm dialing!" Tom frantically punched in 9-1-1 on his phone and put it to his ear, ripping it away just a moment later. "I guess no service at this altitude."

The voice started again: "*Talayta mescatre.*" The vents on the side of the car closed, and there was a sudden rapid acceleration. The car began to pull away from Earth at an incredible rate, still pointed squarely at the moon.

"Janet, do you have any idea what's happening here?" asked Dan.

"What do you mean? Are you blind? Your car has turned into a spaceship; we've left Earth's atmosphere and are apparently speeding out into space! Does that about sum it up, Einstein?"

Dan took a moment before carefully responding. "Okay, I don't think freaking out at the driver is helping here. We need to think."

"Driver? Try pilot?"

"Janet—okay, pilot—happy?"

"Fine."

"Dan, how 'bout *you* telling us about what's going on?" snapped Tom.

"What … what do you mean?"

"It's your grandfather's old car. Come on. You must know something."

Dan slumped down in his seat and sighed. He knew nothing other than always being infatuated with the car from the time he was a boy and fondly remembering the day his grandfather brought it home and took him for ice cream.

"No, I … I was too young. I don't—"

"Great."

Dan took a deep breath and tried again. "We need to focus. We need to work the problem. First, does anyone recognize that voice or the language from the stereo lady?"

"No clue," offered Tom. "Sounds like an Italian trying to speak Russian. Other than that, I have no idea."

Janet shook her head.

"Then let's go back to the beginning. Apparently I triggered something when trying to get the tape to play. If we can recreate the sequences, maybe we can go home." Dan began to randomly push buttons on the tape player again—first one, then two, then three, and so on. There was no reaction.

"Let's try the tape again." Tom handed the eight-track to Dan, who put it back into the deck. Dan powered up the tape player, and all of a sudden they started to hear music.

"Well, at least we know the eight-track works." Dan's attempt at levity was met with scowls from his friends. He looked into the rearview mirror and could now see Earth in its entirety. "Look!" The three turned around to see their home planet, moving farther away. They were obviously moving extremely quickly.

"I'm strong enough to admit that I am totally freaked out," confessed Tom.

"Tom, we're all scared," said Janet, as she consolingly patted him on the shoulder.

Dan sat staring forward, brow furrowed, thinking about how to get out of this situation. This experience further compounded the conundrum surrounding his grandfather. The mysterious office, the papers, the star charts, and the high-security cabinets—they all related in some way to what was happening, but Dan was sure there was more.

The moon was getting larger as they continued flying straight toward it.

"Hey, there was a *Stargate* episode where Colonel O'Neill and Teal'c were aboard this modified Goa'uld spaceship, and they got pulled out into space with this funny autopilot that had the ship head toward its home base." Janet was trying to pull something from the vast science fiction library locked away in her brain.

"Great! How did they get out of it?" Dan asked hopefully.

"They were rescued by another ship," she answered.

"Well, I don't think that's going to happen, but keep thinking. Maybe all your knowledge about science fiction can get us out of this," said Dan, trying to encourage Janet, while hoping to himself that she could.

Change of Plans

As they shrieked along, every second moving further away from Earth, Dan and Tom helped Janet run through her vast knowledge of science fiction. They discussed several decades of *Dr. Who*; rambled through the three seasons of the original *Star Trek* series; and tossed about plots from *The Time Tunnel*, *Lost in Space*, *Farscape*, and *Buck Rogers*. They were coming up dry at every turn, yet the quest brought a ray of hope that the answer was close and kept their attention away from their continuing encroachment into deep space.

Dan sighed and wiped his hands across his face. "Janet, I don't want to be negative here, but I don't think we're getting anywhere. I think the only chance we have is if someone, the government or whoever, saw us racing out of the atmosphere."

The hope that still somewhat sparkled in Janet's eyes grew increasingly dim. "Dan, only problem with that is what would they rescue us with? The only spacecraft they have is a thirty-year-old space plane that doesn't even leave orbit!"

As the three sank into their seats, a stiff silence took over from the optimism that had been so dominant only moments before.

"She has a point," mumbled Tom, careful not to disturb the dark veil that now enshrouded the trio.

As Earth diminished in size, the moon continued to grow, now almost filling the width of the front windshield. Since they had left the ground, the car had been pointed squarely at their planet's rocky satellite, not straying from course even once.

"*Trestai kamolize dab.*" Their speed now began to slow, the mysterious female voice announcing the apparent next leg of their journey.

"Speak English!" The words just exploded from Dan's lips in pure frustration, but what happened next was truly unexpected.

"English confirmed. Accepting voice input. Slowing to high moon orbit."

"Cool! Tell it we want to go home," babbled Tom with unabashed excitement.

"Home." There was no response. "Earth." The voice remained silent. Dan continued, trying his home address, the name of his high school, city, state, and even his zip code—all with the same result—nothing.

"Well, at least we're slowing down."

Tom and Dan turned around, and both shot Janet quizzical looks.

"Janet, look out the back window," said Tom, as he turned and pointed. "That is where we should be. Now let's look out the front window. Hmm … that is the moon. Not good in my book, and I don't even have a winter jacket with me."

Dan gave him a shove. "All right, cool it. We're all in this together. No need to lay it on so thick."

The car entered a high orbit and traveled counterclockwise toward the dark side of the moon. For the first time Earth was starting to be shadowed by the dusty gray rock, last visited by humans over thirty years ago.

"Sending order to decloak and begin automated docking procedure. Emergency authorization protocol."

"Decloak what?" asked Tom.

"I think that there's another ship out there somewhere," answered Janet, as she searched the horizon. "At least that's what it sounds like."

"Are you serious?" queried Dan.

Earth was now completely obscured by the shadow of the moon.

"Emergency protocol accepted. Prepare for autodocking sequence."

Off in the distance, a shimmer materialized out of the darkness. Waves of shapeless energy cascaded over an enormous object that moment by moment arose out of the cold void of space. The waves ceased their dance to reveal their destination.

"See, I was right!" squealed Janet with glee.

Floating in space before them was a massive structure like nothing any of the three had ever seen before. Stretching the length of several modern aircraft carriers, the flowing lines were intoxicating with their beauty. Curving from a rounded point in the front, the hull swooped up toward the rear of the craft, ending in a dramatic tower. Forward of this high structure, the hull majestically curved both port and starboard, creating two bulbous "wings." Behind the main section projected four round cones, most likely functioning as the engines.

Dan, Tom, and Janet remained silent as they attempted to absorb what they were seeing. Their eyes scanned the huge craft in a desperate struggle to grasp the enormity of what lay before them.

As the car hastened closer, the damage they had not noticed from afar began to reveal itself. Burn marks, missing pieces of hull, and evidence of explosions pockmarked the vessel and smeared the once-beautiful ship.

"This thing looks all busted up. Janet, could that be battle damage?"

"Sure looks like it, Dan. These folks were slugging it out with someone."

Tom scowled. "Nice. Well, let's hope we don't meet up with those folks. I don't think a Cadillac would do well in a space battle."

As they closed in on the strange vessel, the car lined itself up with the port "wing." At this distance, a shimmering force field was visible, protecting the entrance to an apparent landing area from the vacuum of space. The car effortlessly passed through into a vast hangar deck. Climbing up the left wall were four-story banks of cubicles, some still holding a few small spacecraft. On the right, a two-story structure held others that were bulkier, possibly shuttles or transports. Both banks of ships were raised and lowered via cranes that hung from the ceiling, looking eager to grasp an awaiting customer. Littered across the deck of the hangar were remnants of partially damaged and destroyed craft, debris, and evidence of the mayhem this ship had experienced.

Their car came to rest on the deck. The familiar humming that had accompanied the trio since they left Earth ceased as the car shut itself down. Dan and Tom went for the doors.

"Wait!" Janet grabbed Dan to prevent him from getting out. "What if they don't have the same atmosphere that we do?"

"Janet, we've been breathing the whole time. Obviously if this car is intended as a ship to come here, the atmosphere will be the same." Dan smiled at her, hoping to get an affirmative from the sci-fi groupie, but she just looked blankly back at him as Tom responded.

"I hope you're right."

Dan shot him a glance as he grasped the door handle and pulled. It opened effortlessly and allowed in a blast of cool air. He stuck his head out and took a deep breath. "Well, seems okay." Dan climbed out of the car with the other two looking on intently. He put one foot on the deck and then the next and stood up, propping himself up by the door as he stood.

"Well, seems okay."

Tom looked over at Janet. "Hey, you're the space lady."

After giving Tom the appropriate scowl, Janet opened her door and got out of the car. Tom soon followed.

"Where's the welcome party?" asked Tom.

"I don't know if there will be one," said Dan, while looking up at the cranes overhead.

"Why not?"

"Well, you saw all of that damage. Look around; most of the ships are gone, and there are only a few left. I think that this place was abandoned."

Janet nodded. "If we can't figure out how to get the car to work, we could always use one of the remaining ships to get out of here, but then, of course, we would have to learn how to fly it."

"Nice, but right now we have no clue how to do either." Dan looked down at the ground while he vocalized his thoughts. "This was my grandfather's car. It had all these weird things about it that we could never figure out, and here we are, aboard some spaceship. There has to be some connection."

"I agree, but we're not going to find out anything standing here." Janet's eyes started to beam with excitement. "I've always dreamed of having an opportunity like this someday, and here we are! We're aboard a spacecraft, possibly alien, but definitely cool!"

"Where do we start?" asked Tom.

"In the movies most of the time they go to the bridge, right, Janet?" She nodded back at Dan. "Let's find a way out of this docking bay."

The three quietly, carefully, and nervously walked away from the car along the length of the hangar deck, looking for a way to get to another part of the great ship. The battered and half-destroyed craft that covered the deck were like a maze, their charred hulls not revealing any of the secrets to their demise. Step by step they continued, eyes scanning all directions. The cavernous room was eerily still, and even the distant sound of recirculated air did nothing to disturb the uncomfortable silence.

Several minutes into their steady promenade, they came upon what appeared to be a bank of approximately ten elevators at the far end of the deck. Four looked to be destroyed or damaged, four others were scarred with burn marks, and another was blocked by a fallen piece of debris. They approached the only one that appeared undamaged. As they neared it, the door slid open, and they stepped inside.

Dan looked at Janet. "Any suggestions?'

She motioned to a panel to the right of the door. It was decorated with several strange markings. At the top were three distinctively colored buttons—one blue, one green, and one yellow. "Let's go with blue," she said, as her index finger zeroed in on the button, but she was abruptly stopped by Dan's quick grasp.

"Why blue?"

"It's my favorite color," Janet announced as she finally pressed the button.

The elevator began to move. A panel above the door commenced to flash with different symbols, presumably indicating the various levels through which they were passing. The seconds ticked away as the symbols continued to parade across the panel, each one exponentially increasing the stress level as they moved deeper into the ship and farther away from the car that had brought them there. What seemed like an eternity later, the elevator slowed, and the door finally slid open.

Dan was the first to step out into a small lobby area. Four elevators, two on each side, flanked the room. To their left hung an elaborate sculpture embedded into the wall, and to the right the small lobby opened into a much grander space. They walked over to a railing overlooking the area; two stairways ran from the landing on either side. There was a theater-sized viewscreen directly in front of them. Lining the walls of the room were two levels of workstations and terminals. Directly below the landing on which they were standing was what appeared to be the captain's chair, and directly in front of it were two stations, separated by several feet. Farther down was a reclined chair in what resembled a great Plexiglas bubble.

"Good call on the blue button. I would assume this is the bridge." Dan looked over at his friend to see her bubbling with enthusiasm.

Janet looked like a kid at Christmastime. Her eyes were wide and sparkling; the grin on her face was evidence of her wonder at the sight in front of her. She cheerily ran down the stairs and onto the landing with the commander's chair. "This must be where the captain sits ... and those terminals are most likely navigation or tactical. Now that's cool!" She pointed at the reclined chair in the bubble. "That must be the helm. What a great idea! It probably projects a 360-degree view around the ship."

"Glad she's having a good time," whispered Tom as he and Dan walked down the sweeping stairway to join Janet on the landing.

"Uh, Janet?" asked Dan. "How do you know so much about—"

"Duh, silly! This is set up just like so many fictional ships that it just makes sense!"

Flanking either side of the captain's chair were two open doorways. "Hey, check it out." Dan began to walk through one. It opened into a conference room, probably used by the command staff. Screens dotted the walls; a long table filled the center of the room, encircled by swooping black leather-looking chairs. In front of each, embedded into the table, were small terminals used for the staff to access the computers while in meetings. Tom and Janet joined Dan in the room.

"This must be where the command staff had its meetings." Dan's hands rested on one of the chairs as he stroked the leather-like texture.

"Dan, Janet, what's through those doors?" asked Tom.

On the far wall were two more doorways on either side, but unlike the ones that led into the conference room, these were closed. Dan stepped toward the one on the right, and as he approached, it acknowledged his presence and slid open. The doorway led into a dimly lit office. The room was circular, with bookshelves and cabinets lining the walls. In the center were two opposing couches flanking a long coffee table. At the far end of the room, floor-to-ceiling windows looked out into the blackness of space. Standing in front was a beautiful desk with one chair behind and two in front.

"This must be the captain's office," said Janet confidently, still bubbling with excitement. She sped toward the desk and plopped down in the chair. "Now this is cool. I could see myself as Captain Whitley, commander extraordinaire. Yeoman Tom, can you get me a soda?"

"Hey, Janet, maybe you should chill out for a minute." Tom was not in any mood for humor, especially at his expense.

Something caught Janet's eye, and she leaned forward. She reached for a picture frame sitting on the desk. "Wow, this guy's cute!" Dan and Tom rushed over to look at the picture, the sight of which froze Dan in his tracks and drained the color from his face. His friends were startled by his reaction.

"Yo, Danny ... you all right?" asked Tom.

Dan said nothing, but picked up the picture and continued to stare at it, his face blank and pale. Janet grew more unnerved; she rushed up from the chair and grabbed him by the arm. "Dan, what is it, buddy?"

He didn't respond.

Janet started tugging on him. "Dan, you're scaring me. What is it?"

Dan's mouth began to move. "It's him ... I can't believe it ... it's him ..."

"It's who?" asked Janet, still awash in concern.

"I saw pictures before of him as a young man ... and ... this is him. This is all starting to make sense. Janet, Tom." He turned the picture around for them both to see. "This is my grandfather."

The words shot through the room like lightning. Amazement, concern, and surprise all jumbled through Janet's and Tom's minds as they attempted to grasp the reality of what Dan was telling them. Their experiences had, up until this point, been overwhelming, and this notion that the man in the picture was Dan's grandfather was the first moment at which everything began, at least in some small part, to come together.

In the picture stood a tall and muscular gentleman, dressed in a royal blue uniform decorated with golden accents. His blonde hair and sharp green eyes were distinctive. On either side were two others many years older, one man and one woman, beaming with pride at the uniformed officer.

"Those must be my great-grandparents," Dan said, as he pointed to the two clearly proud figures behind his grandfather. Color now started to return to his face, and he began to smile.

Janet examined the picture more closely and then turned her inquisitive eye toward Dan. "You really do look like him. I can also see your mother with the same hair and eyes."

Dan, as if awakened from a long sleep, now began to be a little more aware of his surroundings in the office. The awards and certificates that lined the walls popped into view. A display case resting on a shelf held several gleaming medals protected by a glass cover, and several other pictures were displayed throughout.

Overwhelmed with emotion, Dan moved slowly toward the chair behind the desk and sat down. He placed the picture on the smooth black surface and ran his hands across it, attempting to grasp the enormous irony of his discovery. "This was my grandfather's ship. This was his!" He paused to look at the astonishment on his friends' faces. "We need to find out more. Why did they come here? Why did they abandon the ship? Where are the other members of the crew? From the damage we saw outside, they were in a great battle, but with whom?" Dan had determination and purpose boiling inside of him. He was finally starting to make some connections; the pieces of the puzzle were not exactly coming together, but he knew at least where some of the pieces were.

"I understand what you're feeling, but we need to find a way to get home. That's our first priority," remarked Tom.

"Wait, Tom. I think answering some of those questions is paramount to our getting out of here," responded Janet. "In order to find our way home, we need to discover more about this ship and how things work. In the process, we're going to learn more about Dan's grandfather."

"Thanks, Janet. But listen. I don't want to bog you guys down with this. This is my mystery, but I got you here, and I need to get you home. First—"

All of a sudden the lights in the room changed from a dim white to a pulsating red. A siren began to blare—*buzz buzz, buzz buzz*—followed by a frantic announcement in the alien tongue being broadcast throughout the room: "*Ratitaue Pakt, Ratitaue Pakt! Ratitaue Pakt, Ratitaue Pakt!*"

Tom gritted his teeth. "Okay, that sounds like a bad thing."

New Friends

Dan and Tom threw Janet a startled look, expecting her to know what was going on. She shrugged her shoulders and shook her head.

"Don't look at me. I have no idea what's going on … but …"

"But what?" asked Dan.

"It could be a red alert," she answered.

"What?"

"Tom's right. This could be a bad thing. We should get back to the bridge."

The three ran full speed out of the office, through the conference room, and onto the bridge. Red lights were pulsing all around, and a red band encircled the large viewscreen. Dan, Janet, and Tom made their way onto the landing. Tom continued toward the console on the right, drawn by flashing lights that were not there before.

"Hey, I'm just guessing, but this looks like a radar screen, and if we're in the middle, those red blips are coming this way." As Tom was speaking, Janet and Dan moved down to get a closer look.

"Maybe we could recloak the ship," said Janet, "or maybe we have shields."

Dan threw his hands up. "We're in a room the size of a basketball court filled with buttons and terminals. Do you know where we could start?"

Janet looked at the console on the left and saw a silhouette of the ship. "Here. This is my best guess." She pressed the three buttons below the silhouette, and an outline drew around it. Out the viewscreen they could see a momentary shimmer.

"You rock, Janet!" Dan exclaimed. "Shields are up … I think. Now we need to figure out what's next. If you were right before, Tom is sitting at tactical, and I bet the station on the left is engineering."

Janet nodded in agreement. "And that's the helm." She pointed to the chair in the bubble and made her way down to it.

Tom grew more agitated as he watched the radarlike screen. "Whatever they are, they're getting closer."

Dan sat down at the engineering terminal. "Let me guess. We need to turn on the engines and weapons."

"Good call," responded Janet from the helm. They could hear her clearly even though she was sitting almost fully enclosed in the bubble.

"Tom, you look for something to turn on the guns, and I'll work on the engines."

"Hey, Dan, how do you know this thing has guns?"

"Dude, it's a freaking spaceship! They all have guns!"

Tom looked at the console. The markings made no sense, and there were more buttons than he knew what to do with. Dan was having a bit more luck.

"Uh, I found four circles with bars next to them. There are two buttons below each one. I'm going to venture a guess." Dan pressed the red button, but nothing happened. Then he chose a green button under one of the circles, and it began to come to life. They heard a humming course through the ship, and the circle began to fill with an orange glow.

"Bingo!" responded Janet from her bubble. "Something's happening here. I'm getting funny markings on the interior of the globe. Keep going!"

Dan pressed the other three green buttons. There was a corresponding vibration in the ship as each engine reactor started.

"We have power!" Dan said triumphantly. "Try moving the controls, Janet."

Janet's feet were on two pedals, and her hands grasped two joysticks. She moved her right foot, and the ship turned to the right. She pulled up on the right stick, and it began to bank upward.

"I think I know what all of these do. I just need to know how to move forward." Janet noticed a slider on the left joystick in easy reach of her thumb. She pushed it forward.

Tom blurted out, "Look at the viewscreen! We're moving!" Their static position behind the moon began to change as the ship slowly inched forward.

"Okay, Janet?" asked Dan.

"Yeah?"

"At this point, just pretend you're playing a video game. Keep us moving and away from those blips."

"Aye aye, Captain."

Dan liked the way that sounded and smiled a bit.

Tom turned to Dan and shrugged his shoulders. "Heck, I don't want the job," he remarked before saluting his friend.

Janet moved the throttle directing the spacecraft out of the moon's orbit and into open space. She turned the right joystick and put slight pressure on the right pedal to turn the ship so that the oncoming "blips" were to their rear. The bubble projected the entire exterior and tactical situation of the ship, making it easy to maneuver.

"Good, just keep that up." Tom sounded much calmer as the blips moved toward the rear of the ship.

"Tom, any luck with the weapons?" Dan got up and stood behind his friend.

"No ... I mean ... heck, I don't wanna press the self-destruct."

"Don't be such a chicken. Try this one." Dan leaned over and pressed a button, and the sirens turned off, but the red lights remained. "Well, at least that's an improvement." Janet echoed that sentiment with a solid "thank you" enunciated from the helm.

"Hey, I had a thought," added Janet. "How do we know they're hostile? How do we even know if they are a *they* anyway?"

This was not something the trio had considered. The approaching ships could be friendly. They could even be the crew of this ship coming back from an exploration mission. There was no way to be sure.

"Well," Dan added, "I don't know. I think the blinky red lights and siren put the odds against them being friendly, but I don't think it matters, because we're having zero luck with the weapons. This terminal is really complicated."

"Then we continue to run, is that it?" asked Janet.

"Well, we need to do a better job of running. Look!" Tom pointed toward the screen. "They're catching up!"

"I have the throttle, or whatever it is, all the way forward," Janet said. "What are your orders, Captain?"

"Whoa, hey, hold on a minute. We're in this together," Dan said nervously.

Tom's agitation bubbled to the surface. "Listen, space boy, you got us here, this is your family's spaceship or something, and about five minutes ago you pledged to get us home! Whether you like it or not, you're the captain. So what do we do?"

Dan's heart sank. He felt responsible for getting his friends into this perilous situation, and now he realized that it was truly up to him to get them through this so that they could return home. He needed to be strong and push his own feelings and fear aside for his friends' sake. Just as he had supported his mother so many months ago after Grandma's death, he now had to do the same for his friends. He needed to be their rock.

Dan walked toward the captain's chair—the place where his grandfather once sat. Dan thought of Grandpa sitting there, shouldering the burden of command and ensuring the safety of the hundreds or thousands who once crewed the great ship. Dan's current predicament probably paled in comparison to what his grandfather had had to deal with every day.

The thought of his grandfather's smile, strong voice, and bounding confidence gave Dan the boost he needed. He turned and lowered himself into the captain's chair. Closing his eyes, he took a deep breath and pushed his fear deep inside. The concern that painted his face only minutes before melted away and revealed a stoic confidence that this bridge had not seen for many years.

"Let's find out their intentions. Janet, slow to a stop and rotate the ship toward the approaching objects. Tom, I need you to announce their approach. We can't run, so might as well see what we're up against."

Janet slowed the ship and turned it toward the oncoming objects. Tom started to call out their position. "They're getting closer and are now in the smallest square on the—"

"I can see them!" interrupted Janet.

Projected up on the enormous viewscreen was a line of spacecraft moving toward them. There were four in all, square shaped, with engine nacelles protruding from all four points. The harsh lines were a sharp contrast to the ship that the three friends occupied.

"The design doesn't look anything like this ship," noted Janet. "I would venture a guess that they're not from the same folks who built this thing."

"Do you think they have hostile intentions?" asked Dan.

"We'll find out in a few moments," responded Tom. The four ships spread out in an arc. The detail was now easier to see. The jet-black hulls were broken into three distinct segments. The first segment was small and may have functioned as the command deck. The second segment was progressively larger and bristled with projections that pointed menacingly forward, appearing ready to jab whatever the ship approached. From the third and largest segment, four engine nacelles burst from all four corners.

Bright flashes emanated from the four ships at the second segment. Janet screamed, "They're firing at us!"

"Helm, evasive maneuvers! Get us out of here fast!" Dan gripped the arms of the captain's chair as Janet rotated the ship and began to accelerate away, but the move was too late. As the great ship turned, one of the missiles impacted the starboard landing wing, disintegrating in a violent explosion that rocked the ship. The shields appeared to deflect most of the damage, even though the lights flickered, and the jolt threw everyone off balance for a brief moment, but as they caught their breaths, second and third missiles rammed into the engine nozzles in quick succession. Dan was knocked forward out of his chair, and several terminals on the bridge showered sparks from the energy overload. The four hostile ships were now right on the tail of the larger craft, bombarding it with a river of energy projectiles.

A frantic buzzing emanated from the engineer's console. Dan picked himself up to investigate. The console was covered with red flickering indicators.

"Janet, the lines around the silhouette of the ship are fading. What does that mean?"

"We're losing the shields!" yelled Janet. "They, whoever they are, are trying to kill us!"

Dan went back to his chair. "Nope, dying wasn't on my to-do list today. We'll get out of this!"

The engineer's console buzzed again, prompting Tom to take a look this time. "Uh, one of the circley thingies just turned red ... ah ... now it went dark."

"I think we lost an engine," Janet pointed out from the helm.

Something caught Dan's eye. "Janet, do you see that red handle just to your right?"

"Yes ... yes, I do, but normally red handles are bad."

"I don't think we have a lot of choices. Pull it!"

Janet grasped the lever and pulled hard, but nothing happened. The weapons from their pursuers continued to rattle the ship.

"Nothing!" said Janet, visibly frustrated.

Dan, who was leaning forward, sat back in his chair. As he sighed, he noticed one of the buttons on the right arm of the captain's chair. It was blinking now. It had not been blinking before Janet pulled that lever.

"Hold on. I don't know what's going to happen next." Dan could see Janet and Tom stiffen as he pressed the blinking red button.

The female voice they had heard before now reemerged, saying, "*Yuilata frets.*" Everything got very still, as if the universe were holding its breath; all the ambient sounds ceased, muted by a deep rumbling. Dan could feel himself growing heavier and sinking deeper into the chair, which he was clutching with white knuckles. On the viewscreen the stars appeared to shower past more and more quickly, until they joined each other in continuous beams of light. A blinding flash wiped these sticks of light from the sky, replacing them with a luminescent blue-green shimmer.

The trio sat silent and motionless, overwhelmed with wonder and fear at what they saw projected on the viewscreen, hoping time would help them comprehend the strange sight. Then the screen flashed again, and the stars streaked by and slowed, until once more they could be seen as pinpoints of light. Appearing in front of the ship now was something even more strange and wondrous—a huge orange planet, encircled by rings.

The lever near Janet snapped itself back into position.

"What just happened?" Tom muttered in a barely audible whisper.

"We either jumped, warped, went through hyperspace, or something," replied Janet, still staring at the orange planet filling the viewscreen.

"Tom, do you see those ships anywhere?" asked Dan calmly.

"No, the screen's clear, and the red lights are out. Must be a good thing—for once."

"Cool. Now that doesn't look like the moon." Dan motioned to the viewscreen. "Where are we?"

"I would guess Saturn. It didn't seem to take too long to get here," Janet noted.

"But are you sure?" asked Dan.

"No ... sorry ... I'm doing my best."

Dan could sense the trepidation in her voice. "Actually, you're doing great," he said encouragingly. "We all did great."

There were no hurrahs, no celebration, just silence as the three stared at Saturn projected on the viewscreen. The luminescent orange color and sweeping series of rings were breathtaking. Pictures from the various probes from Earth that had surveyed the planet did not aptly recreate the intense beauty of the orange jewel. As mesmerizing as this sight was, there were still other issues at hand.

Dan was the first to break the stillness. "Okay, folks. We need to figure out what's next. I recommend we try to get the cloak back online, just in case."

"Agreed," responded Janet. "Who knows if those ships could follow us? This ship has probably been sitting cloaked and undisturbed for years." She climbed out of the bubble and went over to the engineering terminal. The silhouette that earlier indicated shields protecting the ship was now dark. "The shields must have disengaged when we went through warp, or hyperspace, or whatever. I'm thinking that the controls for the cloak are probably around somewhere near this." She started pressing buttons, but nothing seemed to work. "Could it be that simple?" she asked herself as she pressed the silhouette itself. The image disappeared as a blue band of light appeared around the viewscreen. "I think that was it."

"How can we tell?" asked Tom.

"We can't," responded Dan, speaking before Janet could react. "Until we learn more, we can't be sure of anything." Janet and Tom looked back at Dan. He could see from their expressions and the dark circles under their eyes that they were exhausted. "Tom, what time is it?" he asked.

"According to my watch, it's 1:00 a.m."

"We should try to get some shuteye." Janet and Tom nodded. "Let's head back to the captain's office."

The trio wandered from the bridge, through the main conference room, and into the captain's office. Dan motioned to Janet and Tom to take the couches. He would opt for the floor and seized a pillow to rest his head.

"I'll set my alarm for 5:00 a.m," said Dan, while fiddling with his watch. "It's only a few hours, but I don't think the situation warrants sleeping in." Janet and Tom agreed and lay down to go to sleep.

As Dan's head hit the pillow, he could not empty his mind of all the questions racing through it. Exhilaration and fright, coupled with exhaustion, were clouding his judgment. He would need to try to rest and recuperate before he made any more decisions. He was not even sure that he could fall asleep, but he at least had to try.

Discovery

TOM OPENED HIS EYES. He had the reaction that most people do when they wake in a strange place from a deep sleep—the memory is fuzzy, and the first few seconds of the waking day begin with confusion and panic, then realization and acceptance. He sat up and looked over at the desk. Dan was sitting there, evidently in very deep thought.

"Dan, you all right? What time is it?"

"Six thirty by my watch."

"What?" Tom's outburst awoke Janet.

"Hey, Tom, modulate the tone," said Janet, grabbing her head and sitting up.

"How long have you been sitting there?" asked Tom, looking a little annoyed at Dan.

"Uh, three or more hours. I was wide awake after about two hours of shuteye."

"Why didn't you wake us?"

"You're going to need your full strength if we're going to get out of this." Dan had an intensely serious look on his face. "I've been doing a lot of thinking. Do you realize that no one we know or have ever met has been in a situation like this before? We'll need to think innovatively and come up with solutions to problems that are hundreds of years in our technological future. If you sit and think for a minute about what we've been through in the past twelve hours, you'll realize that what we've done already is unprecedented. We flew to the dark side of the moon, boarded an alien ship, engaged in battle with some other alien ships, and are now waking up on Saturday morning in orbit around Saturn."

Janet and Tom mulled this thought around; they knew he had a point. For all of their lives they had been able to count on the wisdom of others, whether it be their parents, teachers, friends, coaches, or even books; there was always a place to turn where they could leverage someone's outside experience for any of life's problems. But this situation was different—there were no classes, self-help books, counselors, or even television shows about how to survive when stranded on an alien ship. They would have to figure out everything on their own.

"Dan the philosopher," remarked Janet, rustling her long brown hair in lieu of a comb. "Let's break some ground scrounging up some food."

"Hold on." Tom dug into the pockets of his cargo pants. "I have energy bars—two, actually."

"Tom, you da man! I will never make fun of your propensity to carry around snacks!" Dan hungrily walked over to see what flavors he had.

"Thank you, sir, but having only two, we'll need to ration. Let's start with the chocolate chip—the breakfast of champions—mmm." Tom opened the package and broke the bar into three pieces and distributed them to his friends.

Janet began to speak as she chewed. "So, Dan, you've been up most of the night. What have you come up with?"

"Just some theories, but hopefully they'll give us some ideas." Dan began to pace back and forth, as if to help his mind collect his thoughts from the past several hours. "If my grandfather went to Earth, and there's no crew left on this ship, I would bet money on the fact that there are others down there like him. Unless there's another space station or something hovering around out here, I say that when the crew left this ship, they went to Earth." He took a bite out of his energy bar before continuing. "Now, no one in my family had any clue about my grandfather's true identity. Yeah, he had some strange habits, but nothing that even made any of us suspect he was some alien captain."

"I don't follow you," remarked Tom.

"Tom, check it out. He would have had to learn to blend in somehow—learn the language, customs—don't you see?"

Janet's eyes got wide. She could not contain her excitement. "And if they had to learn English, maybe we can use the systems to learn their language, or at least decipher enough to help."

"Bingo!"

Tom got up from the couch, scrunching the empty energy bar wrapper in his hand. "How do we get started?"

Dan was thrilled. His friends understood his logic, and now they had agreed unanimously on their next steps. "Conference room," Dan said, as he stood up from behind the desk and started walking out of the office. Janet followed, but Tom paused to shove the empty wrapper into his pocket before continuing.

Instead of joining his two friends at the table, Tom's curiosity got the best of him. He walked toward the closed door opposite the office where they had spent the past several hours.

"It's locked," said Dan. "I already checked while you guys were sleeping. I got curious too. Don't bother playing around with the panel on the right—no matter what I did, the door refused to open."

Tom scowled and grabbed a chair from the conference table. "That's all right. Probably just some green flesh-eating monster in there."

"Okay, I think this conference room is a great place to start. The senior staff probably met in here to discuss command situations, have staff meetings, etcetera. So—"

"So in theory," interrupted Janet, "they should have all types of access to various systems so they can make proper decisions. Whoohoo! Let's play with buttons."

Janet enthusiastically began manipulating the panel that lay embedded in the conference table directly in front of her. As she pressed various buttons at random, strange alien text flashed in front of her, expanded to fill the table, flashed on the many screens surrounding the room, and generally illustrated to anyone who was present that she had no idea what she was doing.

"Janet? Janet?" Dan snapped his fingers, trying to get her attention.

"What?" she said, still pressing away at buttons. "So I'm clueless! Does Flash Foster have any suggestions?" Tom snickered momentarily at that comment.

Dan, ignoring the jab, leaned over Janet's shoulder and pressed one of the buttons toward the lower right of the panel. A schematic of the ship appeared, projected both on the table and on the screens surrounding the room. "I told you I couldn't sleep."

Janet stood up and looked intently at the schematic, walking around the table to get the best angle possible. The other two let her mumble to herself for a minute before Tom spoke up.

"Well? Ahem ... Janet? Earth to Ms. Whitley?"

"Oh, sorry. I'm just so shocked. I think I can make this out. All those years reading those goofy fake sci-fi technical manuals seem to have finally paid off. Look, here's the engine room, there's the docking bay we landed in—and here, you can even see the elevator path we took to the bridge."

"Now check this out," said Dan with a smirk as he pressed yet another button on the panel. The ship rose out of the table, forming a three-dimensional holographic projection.

"Oh, now, that's cool." Even Tom was impressed.

Janet, in a burst of excitement, climbed up on the table to get a closer look. Her hand passed through the projection as she attempted to orient herself.

Tom, the usual skeptic, had to at least drizzle on the parade. "Okay, now that we have a map, how do we bring it with us? I don't have any paper on me."

Dan smiled knowingly. "Well, remember all those buttons in the elevator and those consoles we were sitting at on the bridge?" Tom nodded. "Well, they all have the same symbol as the one I pressed to bring up this image. It made some sense to me that they would have to have some sort of easily accessible map system on the ship so that people could get around. Do you remember John Davis's older brother who went into the navy? He was stationed onboard the USS *Nimitz*. That ship was so big, they actually gave him a map so he could find his way around. Well, since this thing is easily five times that size, chances are that any hapless recruit would need some way to navigate."

"Dan, I take back everything I said about you," said Tom with a smile.

"Janet, can you find any sort of room that may be for training?"

"Well, look here. There are some big spaces that could be training rooms, but I can't read the language, and unless we explore I would just be guessing." She hopped down from the table. "Shall we, gents?"

Janet skipped her way out of the room. Tom chuckled sarcastically and muttered, "Glad she's excited." They laughed and followed her to the elevator landing overlooking the bridge.

"Just one complication," added Dan. "This ship had its literal butt kicked, and there are parts that are completely destroyed. We have to be careful. We don't want to open a door to space or have stuff fall and crush us—that sort of thing."

"The hologram had several sections marked in red. Call me crazy, but I'm sure those are the places we shouldn't go," Janet pointed out confidently.

"Hey, there's that symbol!" Tom said triumphantly, as he pressed the panel next to one of the elevators. A schematic of the ship appeared.

Janet walked up behind Tom and tapped him gently on the shoulder; he backed away, knowing this was her department.

"Now, I'm hoping that if I press one of these areas, the elevator will take us there." Janet searched the map for a good place to start. "Look here—there are three big areas that are very similar to each other. I say we try the closest." She pressed a large area several levels down that had smaller rooms jutting off to the sides. As she had noted, there were two other identical sections, all situated in the heart of the big ship. Her selection changed to blue, and there was a pleasant *bing* followed by an opening elevator.

Janet, with her usual bravado, leaped in, followed by Dan and Tom. The door closed, and as before, the symbols above the door changed to coincide with their movement through the large spacecraft. A few brief moments later and the door opened onto a balcony overlooking a grand open space. Four stories tall, it was ringed with walkways leading into many smaller rooms. The center section was open and airy; stairways led down to a common area on the first level. As the three friends walked toward the railing, they could see that all four levels were identical.

"Crew quarters?" asked Dan, as the layout looked a lot like that of a hotel with a center atrium.

"Only one way to find out," answered Janet, as she made a move to the closest open door.

One look inside confirmed Dan's theory. Two bunks were built into opposite facing walls. The furnishings were simple, but looked comfortable enough. There were a couch and coffee table, two workstations, two closets, and two dressers. The room was extremely neat and well made up, but devoid of any personal belongings.

Tom milled about through the drawers and under the table. "Nothing."

To the left was a door that opened into a common bath/shower area shared with the room immediately down the hall. They assumed that the shared area was a bathroom, as the function of the fixtures seemed to be similar to what they were familiar with on Earth. Timing was critical here, as they all had to go. They hadn't had the opportunity to use such facilities since they left home.

"Looks clean," Tom pointed out. He was a stickler for a spotless bathroom.

"All right, I'll go first." Dan ducked into the small room and closed the door. A disturbing whooshing sound followed a few minutes later as Dan opened the door. "That was weird, but it did the trick. Mr. Hunt?"

Tom went next and came out not much later, his brow furrowed. "I've had my adventure for the day."

After Janet's turn she remarked, "If we get out of this, I want to patent the function of that thing on Earth. We could make millions!"

"Stop saying 'if,'" responded Dan, who was outwardly annoyed. Positive thinking was critical to their staying on task. He would not allow any dark clouds of doubt to move in, even when covered in shades of sarcasm.

"Sorry, sorry," said Janet, with hands in the air in surrender.

"Let's see what we can find."

The three began to explore room to room. Some of the quarters were just as empty as the first, whereas others had been torn apart in the crew's haste to get off the ship.

Tom asked, "Why do you think that some of the quarters are so neat, while others—"

"Maybe they didn't have a full complement of crew. Or maybe they didn't need everyone." Dan tossed the thought around in his head. *Why would they only have a partial crew?*

They continued down the stairs to the third level, then to the second, and finally to the first. There was nothing of significance—uniforms, some personal effects, and journals written in a language they still could not decipher. After well over an hour of searching, they came up with nothing of use to help them get home.

On the ground floor of the dormitory structure was a common area with couches and various furniture pieces that could be games or other forms of diversion used by the crew. Tom plopped himself down onto one of the overstuffed couches.

"We just spent the past—wow, this couch is comfy! Sorry. Anyway, we spent the past few hours going through room after room, and other than knowing where the bathroom is, I'm not sure we're any better off."

Dan agreed in his heart, but did not want to communicate this to his companions; he needed to keep them motivated and quickly looked around the large room for anything to keep them moving. His eyes scanned until he saw a large door that did not appear to be an entrance to a standard crew domicile.

"Hey, look over there." Dan quickly walked toward the door, hoping his friends would follow, and they did. He stepped through the double doors into a room the same size as the common area, neatly lined with long rectangular tables with chairs tucked properly underneath them.

"Looks like a cafeteria—and a cafeteria usually has—"

"Food!" shouted Janet, her enthusiasm regenerated. She scoured the room hungrily, searching for alien vending machines or anything that might have something to eat.

Against the far wall were two doors. "You know, I can't read the symbols over there, but that barks kitchen in any language," said Tom, as he bounded after Janet. Dan was close behind.

Discovery

They went into the kitchen, which remarkably appeared like many cafeteria kitchens on Earth, albeit with much more exotic appliances. There were cabinets, a flat area that functioned as the grill, doors that opened into ovens, and refrigerators and freezers.

The three eagerly began opening the cabinets and searching for anything edible.

"I found some boxes ... hold on ... there are some things wrapped in ... hey, it looks like foil." Dan pulled one of the foil packages out of the box and opened it. "Sure as heck looks like crackers." He crunched into one. "Sure tastes like crackers too," he said impolitely with his mouth full.

Tom and Janet came over and pulled their own foil-wrapped packages out of the box. The three munched through them. Partially stale or not, it was good to have something other than bits of an energy bar.

"Mwk."

"Tom, I can't understand what you're saying, and would you please not talk with your mouth full?" Dan requested, with a hint of annoyance in his voice. "You're spewing cracker everywhere."

"Milk!"

"Yeah, right. We're lucky we can eat these. Who knows if these people even have cows where they come from?"

"Duh, but I'm still thirsty," grumbled Tom.

"Look for anything that may be a faucet," said Janet. "Over there!" Janet ran over to what could only be described as a sink with a faucet. She put her hand underneath, and cold water flowed out. "Look, just like in the bathroom at school. Put your hand underneath, and it runs."

Dan looked a bit alarmed. "Wait, how do we know we can drink it? This ship has been floating abandoned for longer than we've been alive."

"Dude, you just ate ancient alien crackers!" Tom's wisdom was unmistakable, even with his mouth full.

Succumbing to Tom's logic, Dan walked over to the sink, cupped his hands, put them under the faucet, and took a drink. Tom and Janet watched him intently, just to see if anything dire would happen.

Dan smiled. "That's some darn tasty water." With that, Janet and Tom smiled widely and fought for room at the sink to get their own drinks. Dan reached up into a cabinet to pull down three glasses and passed them out, so they wouldn't have their dirty fingers ruining the taste of the water.

"Check this out," said Janet, after taking another gulp. "We're the first people from Earth to drink water from an alien planet. NASA keeps searching for water on the moon, Mars, and other places, and here we are, pulling alien water from the tap."

"Okay, enough irony." Dan wanted to get the group back on track. "Tom, stuff some crackers in your cargo pants in case we get hungry. We can always come back here, and I'm sure there are more cafeterias onboard. We now have food and water, which means we can survive—"

"Don't forget bathroom," Janet snickered.

"And yes, Janet, we now know how to use the alien potty," Dan continued. "We're in much better shape than we were several hours ago, but we still need to find where they oriented the crew to Earth culture. I suggest we go back to the elevator to pull up the schematic again."

Tom stuffed two of the foil cracker packets into his pocket, and the trio made their way back into the cafeteria and to the common room. Locating an elevator, they pulled up the schematic to review.

Janet studiously searched the map. "Well, now we know that these three areas are the crew's quarters, so we don't have to continue to search them, but where would the training rooms be?"

"Janet, how about this?" asked Dan. "If we can rule out areas of the ship that are obviously utilitarian, meaning the engine room, docking bays, etcetera, I think we can narrow it down."

"Excellent suggestion, Captain." Janet smiled sarcastically. "Look, there are a series of rooms two levels down of good size that don't appear to be near any critical system, at least as far as I can make out."

"Let's go," said Dan, as he saw Janet press the area on the schematic.

The door to the elevator opened, and they stepped in. A few moments later they stepped out onto the new level.

"Much better," remarked Dan. "This looks like the conference area at the Holiday Inn."

In front of them was a lengthy hallway, which was nondescript except for doors that were spaced farther apart than those by the crew's quarters. Picking the closest door, they entered the room. It was filled with long rows of terminals, all facing one end of the space, where there was a podium placed purposefully in front of a huge screen.

"This place reeks of college lecture hall," said Tom. "I think we found one of your training rooms, Captain."

Dan walked up to the closest terminal and started to play around with the buttons. The main screen came to life, and a movie began to play. It showed scenes from Earth. There was narration, complete with subtitles.

"Bingo! Our orientation film." Dan, Janet, and Tom sat and watched. They tried to match up the subtitles with what was happening on the screen.

There were everyday scenes of cars, markets, schools, how to dress, and even a five-minute excerpt on the handshake. This went on for at least an hour; then a scene came on that stood out.

"That can't be Earth," said Janet. "Look at their uniforms. They're like the ones we saw in the crew's quarters."

Two men were escorting a crewman into a room with a reclined chair. This appeared to be a medical facility, as there were two others waiting inside, dressed in long white coats. The crewman who was the subject sat on an intimidating-looking chair. Obviously for some medical purpose, it was menacing, with straps to hold down the subject and a really scary-looking mechanism directly behind the headrest.

The crewman was strapped in. A few moments later there was a loud popping sound, which not only made the crewman jerk, but also startled Janet right out of her seat. The men in the white coats undid the strap on the subject's head, and he stood up. The camera zoomed in on his face as he said, "Hi, my name is David. I am a plumber."

"That's English!" screamed Tom.

"That's what we need," said Dan. "We need to find that chair."

The three, almost in unison, burst out of the room and back to the elevator to pull up the map of the ship.

"Medical … where would medical be?"

Janet's eyes scanned the schematic. Her expression hardened. "Look here. This must be the hospital area, but most of the rooms are in red, which means they're damaged or destroyed. Plus, if you see," her finger followed the elevator shaft, "the elevators are destroyed down below this level."

"Stairs?" asked Tom.

"Good thinking! Janet, how can we get down to that level to at least access the intact rooms? Are there any ladders or stairs?"

Janet continued to intently study the map. "There are several air shafts throughout the ship. Down this hall there's one, but I have no idea if we can access it or even climb down. One more thing—the shaft will be about fifteen stories tall."

Tom gulped. "You mean we need to go to a fifteen-story air shaft and climb down to a damaged level of the ship?"

Dan looked right into Tom's eyes. "Let's go." Dan patted Tom on the back and started walking. Janet and Tom exchanged glances and then followed.

At the far end of the hall was a grate. Dan stopped in front of it and waited for his two companions to catch up.

"I assume this is it?" he asked, as he looked at Janet, who acknowledged with a nod. Dan grabbed the corners of the grate and pulled it off. The entire opening was only about two feet square.

"Does it look like we can open the grates once we're in the shaft?" asked Tom, clearly concerned with this course of action.

Dan could not hear, as his head was poking through the opening. "Tom, did you say something?" he asked, as he pulled his head back into the hall.

"No, never mind."

"All right, then. We have about two levels above us and a whole bunch below. If Janet's right, that's a good twelve stories down, but there's no bottom."

Tom really started to change color now. "What do you mean no bottom?"

"The shaft seems to turn about forty-five degrees and continue on."

Janet piped up. "Hey, these air vents have to go somewhere. According to that schematic, the vents terminate toward the back of the ship near the engine room."

Tom's hands flew up in the air. "What? Now the long drop is even longer, because it ends probably at some huge fan back near engineering, just the right size to chop up, oh, let's see, some unsuspecting teenager! Has anyone besides me seen this movie?"

"We'll be right there with you," responded Dan in an attempt to console his friend. "Do you think we're psyched to go down there?" He looked over at Janet. "Okay, besides Janet." That coaxed a laugh out of Tom.

Seizing the moment, Dan started through the opening. Sliding through backward, he grasped the ladder with his left hand, followed by his right. With both hands secure, he used them to climb up the rungs of the ladder, all the while pulling the rest of his torso through the opening, allowing him to rest his feet on the lip. His hands climbed up two more rungs for better leverage, and then he swung his left, then right foot onto the ladder. "See, no problem!"

Tom followed, and despite his fear a few moments before executed a much smoother mount of the ladder. With Janet the only one left, Tom climbed higher and Dan lower to make room for her in between them. Janet began the same as Dan, putting both hands on the ladder.

"You're looking good, girl!" encouraged Tom.

"Of course I do!"

Janet now began to pull herself into the shaft. She put one foot on the lip of the opening and then the next, but her right foot slipped, taking her left with it. Her grip on the ladder loosened all at once, and she began to tumble down the shaft. A haunting scream erupted from her lungs as she fell.

Dan quickly reached out and grabbed Janet's arm as she fell past him and in one quick motion swung her over to the ladder. Janet scrambled to get her feet secured on a rung. She was desperately trying to catch her breath.

Tom shouted from above, "Janet, you okay?"

Janet responded with a weak and startled, "Yes."

Dan still held on tightly to her left arm. "You all right?" She nodded, eyes closed, still shaking. "Now I need you to focus for a minute. I'm going to guide your left hand to a rung. Grab it." Dan maneuvered her arm so she could grasp a rung with her left hand. "Now take your right hand and grab onto another." She reached over and grabbed a rung in front of Dan's hip.

"Now I'm going to move to the side to make room for you. I want you to climb past me on the ladder. You're doing great." Dan swung over to the side, with only one foot supporting him to allow

Janet to slowly and nervously climb up the ladder. She was terribly shaken, and her eyes were welling up with tears. Dan and Tom gave her some time to compose herself.

A few tense minutes passed as they watched her breathing ease. "I'm okay. Thanks, Dan. You saved my life. I guess we're even now."

Tom started chuckling, causing Janet and Dan to break into giggles, the moment of levity relieving the tension. One thing about Janet—she could always bring a little light to any dark situation, even one as potentially dark as what had just occurred.

Now that they were all in the shaft, they cautiously climbed down the ladder. The return air rushing by made the metal feel icy. Each hand movement on the rungs seemed to suck more body heat from their fingers. By the time they made it down eleven levels, their extremities were nearly numb. Dan maneuvered himself parallel with the grating and kicked it with his right foot until it popped out and fell to the hallway floor. Then he reversed his movements from when he entered the shaft until he found himself standing in the medical corridor. He immediately assisted Janet and Tom. Once they were all safely in the hallway, he turned his attention to their new surroundings.

The hall was similar in structure to the one several levels up, but the dim lights and copious amounts of debris littering the floor made it evident that they were near some very severe damage. The lights, which fortunately still functioned, flickered as if they were expelling their last drop of illumination. The corridor to the right was completely collapsed, the ceiling and floor meeting in a pile of rubble. At the far end of the hall a mess of debris completely obscured the elevator door.

Dan started down the hall. He moved passed the first room, as the ceiling had collapsed, past the second room, as the door was jammed shut, but further down on the left was a small hallway mercifully devoid of damage. Dan passed through to a seemingly intact door at the end; it opened to reveal the chair that they had seen in the training video several minutes before.

"Well, now, that doesn't look comfortable," Dan said, as he pointed to the cold metal chair with several straps for arms, legs, feet, and—most disturbing—a strap for the head.

Janet forged forward to investigate. "Uh, there's a hole right where you put your head. It's a small hole. Hold on." Her hand moved to the area behind the headrest. "There's a mechanism back here."

"Let me guess," began Dan. "You're supposed to strap yourself in there, and they inject something in your head that allows you to identify yourself as a plumber."

"You are unfortunately correct," Janet said, as she emerged from her examination of the device. "There's a big needle back here that does the job. Kinda medieval looking, if you ask me."

Tom spotted a control panel that rose out of the floor. "Well, let's give it a try. I'm going to press the big green button ... because green means go ... I guess." Janet and Dan backed away as Tom pressed the button on the control panel. A loud pop echoed through the room, prompting all three to grab their ears.

"Did it work?" asked Dan.

Janet timidly walked over to the chair and leaned toward the headrest. "Not sure."

Thoughts of the video they had watched rolled through Dan's head—*the man lying in the chair, the loud pop.* The realization that someone would have to sit and endure whatever tortures that device held frightened Dan to the core. He still felt responsible for everything his friends had gone through up until this point, including, most horribly, one's near death in the airshaft. He would not put them in further peril. He would have to be the first one to take the risks needed to help get them home.

Sighing deeply, Dan studied the barbaric-looking machine; fear tumbled through his body in anticipation of what lay before him. "Strap me in."

"Whoa, whoa, wait a minute!" Janet trembled with concern. "You don't know what this thing does. It may kill you. How do—"

"Janet, my grandfather was an alien, which makes me one-quarter alien. Looks like I'm the most compatible, and if you can come up with a better suggestion … then I'm listening."

Janet turned bleach white. She had no ideas and instinctively knew that this had to happen—Dan had to go through this. Her eyes began to tear. Dan leaned forward and grabbed her hand.

"Listen, don't you cry," he ordered. "Just don't. Please." He sat down in the chair and laid his head back on the mechanism.

Janet, still sniffling, strapped Dan's arms, legs, feet, and head into the ominous-looking device. After securing the final strap around his scalp, she rested her hand on his forehead and looked at him, hoping this would not be the last time she could touch his warm face. Pushing back tears, she stepped away to the console behind Tom.

"Let her rip!" commanded Dan, brandishing some hard-won confidence.

Tom closed his eyes tight and pressed the big green button. There was a loud pop, and they could see Dan lurch in the straps and let out a deep grunt. Janet ran over and quickly freed him from his bindings.

Dan's eyes were closed, and he lay motionless, but still breathing. He collected his strength and then gradually leaned forward while holding the back of his head.

"*Tyulaitoc frek!*"

"What was that?" asked Janet and Tom, almost in unison.

"I said that hurt," responded Dan.

"No, try again," said Janet, grabbing his hand.

Dan opened his eyes, surveyed his friends' concerned glances, smiled, and parted his lips to say, "*Tyulaitoc frek.*"

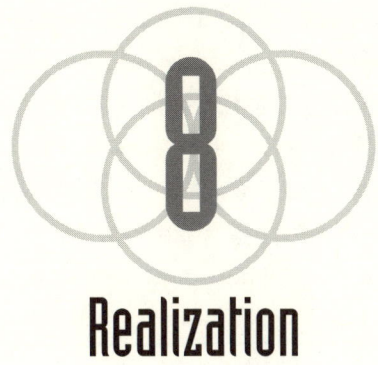

Realization

Unfortunately it had worked—unfortunately for Janet and Tom, who now had to have their own one-on-one experiences with the chair. The tactile experience was not as overwhelming as the aural sensation of the loud pop, which accompanied the long needle as it entered the back of the skull to deposit its cargo. What cargo? They did not know, but could theorize that it was some sort of translator. For Dan, Tom, and Janet, the needle injected a device in the back of the brain that gave them the ability to understand this alien language, which they could now read and speak fluently. A funny side effect was their vastly expanded command of the English language, along with fluency in all other major Earth dialects.

"I think I can speak Chinese," said Tom in amazement, "and Portuguese, and … I think Russian … and I bet my German is even better. I could impress my dad!"

Janet was babbling in the alien language. "*Tuet Jautuo maletek rustokek dahk.*"

"Nice … you just learned an alien language, and all you can say is, 'My name is Janet, and I am happy to meet you,'" taunted Dan.

"*Daktistratae menetstrai bart fr—*"

"English, please. I can understand, but let's control our temptation to speak in seventy-five different languages." Dan was in no mood to get scolded in an alien tongue.

"Fine! I was just thinking that we may want to brush up on our skills just in case we meet E.T., for Pete's sake!" Janet spat back.

She had a point, but what were the chances they were actually going to meet anyone? Their main objective was getting home, hopefully before Monday, when they were due to return from the lake. An alien encounter was not on the itinerary.

"Let's focus here, you two," Tom muttered, trying to jerk his friends back into the present. "We know the language now. I suggest we go back up to that training room and do some studying. There have to be some tutorials, or maybe—even better—a simulator."

Dan perked up. "Now, that would be cool! I could definitely go for something like that."

Janet was looking down at the ground. The smile was gone from her face, and she looked embarrassed.

"What's up?" asked Dan.

She sighed, face still pointed toward the floor. "I ... I don't think I can deal with that shaft again." Janet looked up to gauge her companion's reactions. "I don't want to be a wimp, but ... I just—"

"Don't sweat it," said Dan, interrupting her thought. "We can now read and speak this language, so it will be easier to find another way out of here."

Janet threw Dan a quick appreciative grin. "Thank you, but I couldn't find any other way. Do you think I would have suggested the shaft if there were one?"

"This section of the ship is damaged," remarked Dan.

"Yeah, and where have you been?" queried Tom with a dash of sarcasm.

Ignoring the comment, Dan continued, "If this part of the ship is damaged, doesn't it show up on the map?"

Janet nodded, "It shows up as red boxes."

"Right, but it doesn't show *what* the damage is." Dan's friends appeared puzzled. "Guys, there may be a hole in the wall or something somewhere. Let's think creatively. If we can get over to another corridor, or find a crawlspace, or even kick a hole in the wall, I say we go for it!"

Janet's smile was back. She went over to one of the workstations and pulled up the map one more time.

"Wow, that button we've been pressing for the map—it says map," Tom said, proud of his discovery.

"Here we are." Janet pointed to the room where they were located. "This part of the ship is really messed up. Most of the medical level is destroyed, and the hallways are collapsed. There's even a hull breach about twenty-five yards that way, but it looks like there's a seal in place—good thing." Her eyes, aided by her index finger, continued to search.

"Here!" Dan directed their attention to a small closet off the hallway. "Take a look at that."

The three peered at the map, but could not make out what Dan saw.

"Folks, look—right there! It appears to be a small utility closet. It's damaged, as well as the one just above it on the next level. Maybe there's a hole in the floor or something that will get us up to the next level."

Janet examined the level just above. "And that area looks fine."

"Let's go," said Dan, as he made his way out the door to the utility closet, which stood near the damaged elevator. The other two followed.

The door was stuck halfway open, and even from the hall they could see it was filled floor to ceiling with debris. Dan slid his head through the opening and looked up to see a small hole that would be just the right size to allow them to pass up to the next level. Conveniently, all the damaged material was situated in such a way that a person could climb up and shimmy through the small opening.

Dan squeezed himself into the closet and began to climb. He hoisted his body through the small gap in the ceiling until he found himself standing on the upper level.

"Next!"

Janet made her way through, followed by Tom. In just a few moments they were all on the next level above in an undamaged hallway and, more importantly, in front of a working elevator.

Dan selected the training level on the schematic and turned to his companions. "Let's go to school."

Close Encounters

MAJOR DAVID JENSEN LOVED HIS JOB. While growing up in Key West, Florida, he had always dreamed of being a scientist, explorer, astronaut, fighter pilot, and baseball player. Strong ambitions even for the imaginative, yet his choices in life did make his dreams come true. Entering the Air Force Academy fresh out of high school, he immediately became the star on the baseball squad. A major in astrophysics, he graduated second in his class, prompting the military to send him to the Massachusetts Institute of Technology for graduate school—on their bill. His skills in the cockpit and educational achievements made him a natural for the space program, which he was invited to join at the young age of twenty-seven. Now thirty-four, Major Jensen was mission commander aboard the International Space Station. Being brand new and not even near to completion, the station, with its small crew and scientific experiments, was a perfect proving ground for this young leader. Both the U.S. Air Force and NASA had a lot invested in him, and they were hoping this stint aboard the ISS would test his leadership skills.

David reflected on the amazement of being in orbit above Earth as he gazed out the window, finishing his afternoon snack. The station began to pass toward the dark side of the planet. Being a Floridian, David preferred the sunshine to the dark, but the view of Earth shrouded by nightfall was a treat for only the very few who were privileged enough to trek into space. The twinkle of the world's major cities sparkled like Christmas lights, and David liked to imagine what the people were doing as they moved about their evening. They were living in the present, and he was living in the future. Someday, everyone down there would have the opportunity to visit space as he did, and his efforts were helping that day come to fruition.

A buzzing siren ripped him from his thoughts. He reached over and hit the intercom. "Proximity alarm! Vodnikov, what do you see?"

Major Sofiya Vodnikov was an astronomer from Russia and a member of the current crew. It was her job to monitor operations, which usually was a very quiet task, except when a piece of space debris came too close to the station; then things would get interesting.

Major Vodnikov checked the radar. "Four objects ... very large ... moving ... wait ... they ... that is—"

"Spit it out, Major."

"Sir, they appear to be ... in formation. Commander, better get up here."

In zero gravity, nothing moves quickly, but David did his best to get to command and control as quickly as possible. He floated over to Major Vodnikov's station and looked at the scope. "What in the world? I need to contact Houston."

Saturday afternoon at the Houston Space Center was routinely quiet. Mission Control, normally the stress capital of the planet during a shuttle launch or reentry, was calm and peaceful. The technicians who were on duty paged through magazines and books, occasionally glancing over at their monitors. A few worked away like busy beavers, but for the most part Saturday was relaxed and casual.

A voice boomed over the intercom, interrupting the tranquility. "Houston, this is commander ISS. We are getting a proximity warning. Objects unidentified."

The mission commander on duty, Mark Walters, put on his headset. "Commander ISS, this is Houston. We observe your proximity warning. Please state status."

"Four objects, large and evenly spaced, are moving toward ISS."

"Evenly spaced? Please explain, Commander."

"Houston, acknowledged. Four large objects are moving in unison, as if in formation, toward the ISS. No direct visual contact at this time."

"Do you perceive any danger to the ISS?"

Those words sent a chill through everyone at Mission Control and squashed the last bit of calm that was present in the room. Those who were reading put down their books and looked up at Mark Walters, who stared straight ahead, dreading the response.

"Houston, objects are unidentified and moving at a high rate of speed. On current course they will collide with the ISS in approximately five minutes. Anticipate catastrophic structural failure of station if collision occurs."

Walters froze; he knew that this was a grave situation. People from Earth were relatively new to space and had very few contingencies for situations like this. He felt helpless. Standing in a room with some of the most advanced technology on the planet, he could press no button, flip no switch that would make those objects stop or move the station out of the way in such little time.

"Houston … Houston, you won't believe this. They're moving apart into an arc and slowing down. These objects are definitely not space debris!"

Questions spun through Walters's mind—*What are they? What could they be?* It was clear to him that things were about to spiral out of control very quickly. Surveying his staff, he knew that they were struggling with the same disbelief and hopelessness. This was out of their hands. It was no longer a simple scientific mission—it was now much more.

Walters looked over at his assistant, who rushed up toward him. "Get me the president."

"Commander ISS, this is Houston. As there is an imminent threat, we are notifying the president and going to Code Alpha. This mission will now be coordinated by Near Earth Threat Operations, Cheyenne Mountain. Prepare station for Code Alpha. Houston out."

Near Earth Threat Operations was a secretive command of the air force established several years ago by presidential order. There had been much concern in the scientific community that there was no coordinated effort to monitor or deal with any near space dangers, whether they be asteroids, falling satellites, wayward comets, or—at the less likely end—alien incursions of Earth. A small but vocal delegation in Congress also grew anxious, as many of these scientists were wealthy contributing constituents. Several low-key meetings with the president were held, and he ultimately saw no problem with creating a separate command in the air force to specifically monitor the space situation around Earth. It was good politics, and, as the Roswell incident illustrated sixty years before, it is better to be prepared than surprised.

NETO was housed in a new section built just for them in the Cheyenne Mountain complex located outside of Colorado Springs. Constructed very deep in the ground, this new part of the installation was hopefully well encased enough to handle a direct hit by an asteroid, a nuke, or any other space nasties. NETO kept an eye on the space near Earth with coordinated links from the ground-based Electro-Optical Deep Space Surveillance System, four geosynchronous satellites, the Passive Space Surveillance System, and links to the radio antennas of SETI (Search for Extra-Terrestrial Intelligence), supplemented by phased-array and mechanical radars to provide the current holistic view of space. This was some of the most advanced equipment on the planet, all in the hands of this small unit of one hundred personnel.

The commanding officer was General Frank Peters. A decorated war veteran of both Vietnam and the Gulf, he took the assignment for several personal reasons. For one, it was located near his alma mater—the Air Force Academy. He loved Colorado and the area around where he went to school so many years before. Having the chance to settle here for his last assignment and ultimate retirement was the best gift his grateful nation could give to him. Second, NETO was, as his grandson would call it, a cakewalk. Since it was an autonomous command reporting directly to the chief of staff and the president, he did not have to deal with the usual bureaucracy and had the freedom to run things as he saw fit. The staff was small, which made it very easy to get to know everyone by name, which he liked to do, and the personnel were all highly skilled and intelligent. They had to be, as they worked with technology that was at the far end of humanity's knowledge envelope. Peters's final reason for taking the assignment was the peace and quiet that came with it. NETO watched the skies and occasionally linked up with NASA or SETI on some weird asteroid, comet, or radio signal, but otherwise this was as low stress a position as a highly decorated general could get in the military.

This was Saturday, and General Peters liked to come into the office just to keep people on their toes and clean up long ignored e-mails from the previous week. He sat at his desk going through the list when, almost simultaneously, both phones in his office rang—including the seldom used red phone, which had a direct link to the White House. He quickly pressed the speaker on the internal phone. "The president is calling. Please stand by." He picked up the red phone. "Yes, sir."

Peters's expression hardened as he listened to the president. "Yes, sir, we'll take care of this. Count on it." He hung up the red phone and picked up the other one.

The officer on duty, Captain Janet Dillings, responded, "Sir, we have a situation. I have Mission Commander Walters from Houston. They are transferring command to this facility."

"I have it," he said as he heard a click and then the voice of Mark Walters.

"General, no doubt you just got off the phone with the president, but in case he hasn't already told you, we have four unidentified craft moving toward the ISS. We are initiating Code Alpha and transferring command to you. The craft will be on top of the ISS in just a few minutes."

"Acknowledged," responded General Peters. "Assuming command. We will link you with our systems. Officer on duty, Captain Dillings, will initiate the link."

General Peters hung up the phone and walked out of his office into the NETO Operations Center, which was set up very similarly to NASA's Mission Control. Three tiers arranged stadium style were crowded with terminals and staff, all facing a theater-sized screen flanked on either side by four smaller viewers. Many other flat-panel monitors hung suspended from the ceiling around the room.

"Captain Dillings, we are going to Code Alpha. Please proceed with systems link."

Almost in unison, the officers on duty at their workstations turned and looked at the general. They had trained for Code Alpha, but everyone thought it was a joke. One of the prerogatives, however absurd, of NETO was to protect Earth from attack from space. There were two experimental "communication satellites" in orbit that had small lasers on them. Powerful for the time, they could do no more than break up a small rogue satellite. Their more powerful option was to coordinate with Air Force Space Command to reprogram and launch intercontinental ballistic missiles into space if needed. This option was put in place mainly to deal with an asteroid or a comet. A final option was to invoke a treaty between Russia and China to coordinate efforts to repel a threat to the planet. This was a loose treaty, chock full of more political intent than anything else, but it was at least something the three countries could agree upon.

Code Alpha was reserved for "possible alien threat," which is why no one took it seriously, but the stern look on the general's face showed everyone in the room that this was for real.

"Systems link successful," announced Captain Dillings.

"Good," responded the general. "Ops, tactical Earth view, if you please."

A moment later a tactical view of Earth, with its hundreds of artificial satellites, was up on the main screen. This view was a compilation of information from several of NETO's monitoring systems and provided an overall picture of the objects near the planet.

"Zoom into ISS."

The screen zoomed until they could see the space station, with four blips moving toward it in an arc. Everyone in the room seemed to gasp at once.

"ISS, this is General Peters, Air Force Near Earth Threat Operations. We have assumed mission control. Please acknowledge."

"This is Major David Jensen, station commander. We have secured Code Alpha. Science team has been moved to the emergency capsule. Command team remains in C&C."

"What's your situation?"

"Four unidentified objects moving toward ISS. Behavior denotes intelligent control. What are your orders?"

"Who's with you in C&C?"

"Major Vodnikov and myself, sir. All other personnel are aboard emergency escape capsule."

General Peters covered his mouthpiece and turned to Captain Dillings. "Do we have any of the lasers close by?" She shook her head.

Peters removed his hand from the mouthpiece. "Major Jensen, if you deem situation to be hostile, I want you and everyone else out of there. Acknowledge?"

"Yes, sir," responded the voice from space.

The tactical screen showed the objects inching closer to the station, all the while continuing to slow.

"General, we have a visual," crackled the voice of Major Jensen. "I see four … oh, my … four spacecraft!" Those words made everyone in the operations center gasp in shock and amazement. "Very angular … wait. One is breaking away and moving closer."

General Peters turned to Captain Dillings with a questioning glance, but she again responded, "Sorry, sir. We do not have any hardware to deal with this. It is up to Major Jensen."

The general looked angry. He had a potentially explosive situation here and could only respond with two weak lasers that were nowhere near the ISS at this point in their orbit. An ICBM would be useless with small objects that could change their speed and position, plus the blast would be too close to the ISS. Anyway, he did not have time to make the arrangements to get an ICBM targeted and launched.

The intercom crackled again. "General, I have a visual on the craft. Switching on external cameras."

The general snapped to indicate his team to link up with the images; they popped up on the big screen.

Major Jensen continued, "Three sections—front could be for the pilot. General, I would swear those look like weapons protruding from the second section."

General Peters was quick to bark, "Abandon the station! Get to that escape pod and get out of there!"

There were only a few seconds of silence, but it felt like an eternity to everyone. Then the response came from Major Jensen, "No time, sir. That thing is right on top of us. I'm ejecting the pod now."

The general called out, "Tactical!" The viewscreen changed to the overall picture and showed the escape capsule separating from the station. What they witnessed next was truly horrifying.

"General! Unidentified craft moving toward escape pod! We're seeing flashes of light. Oh … oh, no! Oh, capsule has been destroyed! Sir, they're all gone. General …"

General Peters just stared at the tactical view, as he witnessed the craft race toward the blip that was the escape capsule. He saw the flashes of light and watched the indicator for the capsule fade away, along with the lives of the four astronauts who were aboard.

The invading craft rejoined the other three and quickly accelerated into space. They were gone.

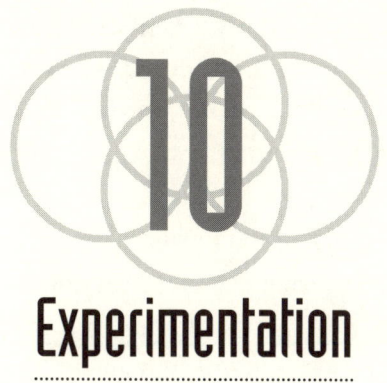

Experimentation

WHEN THE TRIO FIRST RETURNED to the training room, they again watched the video that had given them the clue about the chair that implanted their translators. The format was not much better than that of a 1950s public service short, with terrible acting, fake sets, and goofy plot lines, but just knowing that they were watching an alien movie was enough to hold their attention. The film discussed conforming to Earth social standards, which Dan, Janet, and Tom already knew as well as any sixteen-year-old could. Yet by watching, they were able to discover more about the devices that now resided in their skulls. The chair implanted a chip at the base of the brain that allowed comprehension of many languages, both from Earth and from other alien worlds. It used the current vocabulary and linguistic knowledge of the subject as a base, then linked the learned cognitive abilities of the subject to allow that subject to understand a myriad of languages.

The hours ticked by as Dan, Janet, and Tom pored over the information in the training room. Working each at their own terminal, they were able to fill their young minds with critical information to help them on their quest to get home. The terminals were strictly for training; there was no direct access to information such as ship's systems, crew logs, or anything other than the nuts and bolts of learning. Evidently the instructors on this ship had the wherewithal to restrict student access to keep them focused on task. This was unlike their computer class in high school, which had everyone checking e-mail and surfing the Internet, much to the chagrin of the teacher.

The three friends studied basic tutorials on navigation, piloting, weapons, and bridge station functions. The material was clearly targeted for new recruits and did not go into any depth, but that was fine for these three. All they needed was enough knowledge to be able to return to Earth.

"Janet, do you think there are any simulators onboard?" asked Dan.

Janet punched up the ship's map on her terminal. "Yes, there it is right there," she said, pointing to an area several decks down. "Unfortunately, it's in red."

"That means it's toast, right?" asked Tom.

"You got it," replied Janet.

Dan thought for a moment. If they did not have a simulator that functioned, they would have to do the next best thing. "Team, let's go to the bridge. There we can try out what we've learned and hopefully not kill ourselves."

"I agree, plus I'm eager to get home. These crackers, or whatever they are, don't beat a good old-fashioned cheeseburger," said Tom, as he crunched away on some of the stale crackers he'd lifted from the cafeteria.

Tom's two friends nodded in full agreement, then headed out of the room, down the hall to the elevator, and then ultimately up to the bridge.

Dan stepped out onto the landing first and looked over to the sculpture hanging on the wall in the lobby area. "It says *Liberty*. That must be the name of the ship—*Liberty*."

Experimentation

Janet went over and touched the sculpture and ran her fingers over the alien lettering. The sculpture hung in a cylindrical alcove, cast in bronze with beautiful gold accents. A meticulously detailed globe sat floating above an irregular trapezoidal shape, with vertical sides sweeping down in an arc, terminating at sharp points on the base. *Liberty* was scrolled across the globe on a raised ribbon. Three arrowlike objects created sweeping lines that met above the equator, twisting back upon themselves to form three circles of diminishing size until ultimately separating above the north pole and moving off into space. Two final distinctive markings were a five-pointed star in the upper-left hemisphere and what may have been a small silhouette of a moon in the upper right.

"Do you know what this means?" asked Janet, still caressing the sculpture. "This means that this culture held liberty in the same regard as we do. Why else would they name a ship *Liberty*?"

Tom looked over at Dan. "Now that's cool. At least we know they aren't a bunch of fascists."

"Freedom's the universal language. I remember my grandfather was always so frustrated with the fact that many of the peoples of Earth were not free. I recall him yelling at the nightly news." Dan paused, allowing the memory to grow more vivid. "Kinda fills in the blanks a bit more."

"C'mon, I wanna blow stuff up!" snapped Tom, giving Dan a shove to break him from his nostalgia.

The two walked toward the stairs, and Janet eventually caught up after she broke her fascination with the sculpture.

Dan sat in the captain's chair, Tom took the tactical station, and Janet made her way down to the helm. Dan fidgeted with the buttons on the arm of the chair, because now, thanks to the training, he knew exactly what they did. A small screen emerged, allowing him to access data from any of the terminals on the bridge. Not that he was familiar with all the intricacies of their functions, but at least he wasn't afraid of his curiosity either. He punched up the engineer's terminal. The schema gave him a summarized view that allowed him to manipulate all the major functions.

Dan's eyes scanned through the data. Three of the reactors were running—two at 100 percent, one at 80 percent, with the fourth offline from the damage of the battle they had been in near the moon. Most of the critical systems had power, and life support was functioning normally.

"Helm, we have power. Three reactors functional, and maneuvering thrusters at your discretion."

"Aye, Captain."

"Helm, move us forward at your pleasure. Let's see how well you can drive."

Janet gripped the controls and nudged the throttle forward, and they began to move. She made some basic turns to get a feel for the response of the enormous ship and was surprised at how relatively nimble it was. The planet Saturn danced in and out of the viewscreen as Janet banked and rolled the *Liberty*, all the while increasing her self-assurance that she could actually fly the ship. She pushed the throttle a little more to pick up speed and pointed the nose of the *Liberty* toward Saturn's north pole. Projected around Janet in the bubble was the entire exterior of the ship, including a tactical view of the planet, complete with its gravity and magnetic field, making it easy to avoid trouble.

The *Liberty* crested Saturn's north pole and began to dive toward the planet's equator.

"Nice," said Tom, duly impressed.

With a slight pull of the controls, Janet adjusted the course toward those famous rings. Consisting of a compilation of ice and rock, they were not something through which one would want to pilot a spacecraft.

"Janet." Tom tried to get her attention, feeling a bit nervous about their rapid approach to the rings. "Janet ... hey, Janet!"

Concern crept up the bridge to Dan. "Janet, stop being a cowboy ... or cowgirl ... cowperson ... whatever, just slow up a bit!"

This request was met with silence and a little giggle from the helmsman. Janet had her own agenda, and unfortunately, neither Dan nor Tom could snap her out of it. The ship continued to accelerate.

"Janet, come on, don't wreck the thing," babbled Dan, his concern growing by the moment. He knew that she had a lot of experience with video games, but this was a *real* spaceship. Five thousand feet worth of alien metal not only was careening toward the rings, but also was in the hands of a sixteen-year-old girl who just got her driver's license two weeks prior.

Tom turned around in panic, his face red with emotion. "I think she's crazy! Can I shoot her?"

Dan knew that Tom was joking, but scowled at him anyway for even suggesting it. Tom wiped the sweat from his brow and grabbed his console.

Janet rolled the ship 180 degrees; the rings still grew closer, and the larger particles were now more distinctive.

"Janet!" shouted Dan.

Janet pressed hard on the *Liberty*'s controls. The rings began to disappear, falling away at the top of the viewscreen, replaced by the blackness of open space. A full press of the throttle, and the ship moved quickly off into infinity.

Tom stood up, waving his arms and shouting loud enough for Janet hopefully to hear in the bubble, "What was that about?"

"Man, you have to get your head out of the bug world and watch some TV," she answered, bristling with confidence. "Anytime that you have anyone on your tail, that's the best maneuver, because more often than not, they crash as you fly safely away."

"What? What? How did you know that we wouldn't crash?"

"Because I wouldn't let it happen."

Tom huffed and just sat back down. He was not going to win this conversation.

Dan hit the reverse view on the screen. Saturn was now well in the distance. Even with only a little less than three engines, the *Liberty* was one fast ship.

"Full stop. This is good enough."

Janet acknowledged and slowed the ship until it hovered motionless.

Dan studied his summarized view of the engineer's console, checking weapons status and ensuring there was adequate power.

"Tom, your turn to play. Power up the weapons."

A grin the size of Texas dashed across Tom's face as he pressed a button on his console. A screen emerged with which he was able to see the status of all the weapons, including targeting information. Outside, on the anterior of the ship, four outer doors opened. Two large turrets, reminiscent of old World War II-type battleships, exposed themselves, rifled barrels telescoping outward. One turret was farther forward and lower than the other so that they would not cross fire. On opposite sides of the outer hull two long doors, running the length of the ship, opened to reveal large fixed guns.

"You know, it was cool when we learned about it in training, but it's way cooler now to see it in action," said Tom, overtly tickled with the awesome display of weaponry. "Wait, I'm getting an error in the starboard side main gun. The door is damaged and will not open. System is taking the gun offline." Tom pressed a few buttons on the terminal and looked over his readouts. "Everything else looks good to go. Can I shoot something?"

"Try a test fire of the port fixed gun," ordered Dan.

"You got it, Captain." Tom pressed the appropriate button to fire the weapon.

Experimentation

The *Liberty* shook, prompting Dan to check the power systems. Massive amounts of energy were being sucked from the engines. "It's draining lots of power!" he shouted, as all of a sudden the gun fired.

The shock of the recoil, even with the ship's inertial dampers, gave everyone a good jolt. A large red beam of light was thrust from the front of the *Liberty*. It continued for several seconds and then stopped.

Janet applauded in celebration as Dan and Tom checked their terminals.

"Captain, test fire of weapon successful. Looks like gun is offline to recharge."

"Tom, that thing whacked a whole mess of power from the engines. I wonder what firing both of those would be like?"

"Yeah, check that out," added Janet. "I can see the drain in here. Those things must be used for last resort. I'm down to about 50 percent available power."

"But it was still awesome!" Tom jumped out of his chair in excitement.

"Calm down, Rambo," requested Dan. "Janet, can you take us back toward those rings? We could do a little target practice."

"Aye, sir," she said, directing the *Liberty* back toward Saturn.

"Tom, let's try the main turrets. If we get into trouble, I say we use those over the big guns. I don't want to drain away our power. Speed is sometimes the best defense."

"You got it, Cap." Tom played around with the console. He selected some of the larger asteroids, painted them as targets, and locked them into the system. The turrets rotated until they were pointed in the appropriate direction. Tom had purposely chosen two objects to hit, since the guns were supposedly capable of targeting and firing on multiple enemies.

"Dan, I've targeted two separate asteroids."

"Good! That way we can practice hitting multiple bad guys. Just tell me when we're in range."

Saturn again began to fill the viewscreen as they approached. Dan brought up the tactical schema on his chair so he could observe Tom's shooting ability. The targets had a flashing red line around them, indicating they were out of range. When encircled in green, they were ready to be engaged.

"In range," eagerly announced Tom.

"Fire!"

Tom pressed the commit button, bringing the forward guns to life. They expelled several rapid bursts of energy, which pummeled the asteroids, breaking them apart. The trio cheered. They could now control the weapons and maneuver the craft. This was a huge achievement and brought them closer to getting home.

A beeping interrupted their celebration. Dan looked over to his console and saw that it was an incoming message. He brought up the communications schema.

"Uh, someone's calling," he said, staring in amazement at the incoming message.

"Maybe E.T.'s phoning home," joked Tom.

"That's what I'm worried about."

Janet emerged from the helm and joined Tom, who just stared blankly at Dan as he intently studied the communication.

"Oh, this is not good. When it rains—"

"What?" asked Janet and Tom in unison.

Dan chuckled, more in nervousness than humor. "Uh … it's a distress call. No kidding."

"Wait, we're the ones in distress," said Tom. "Where do people get off?"

Janet gestured to Dan. "Well, answer it."

Dan pressed the receive button, and a voice speaking in the alien tongue broadcast over the bridge speaker system. With their implants, they could understand and comprehend it clearly.

"Mayday! Mayday! Request assistance. This is cargo vessel *Stoic 2*. We are carrying over one hundred passengers. Our engines have failed. Our reactor core began to overheat, and we had to shut it down. We are in hostile space. We require assistance." The message just repeated over and over. Back on the navigation console, there was a blinking on the display. Tom looked over and studied it.

"The message just repeats," said Dan, as he tried to press buttons to acknowledge. "Nothing. Could be automated."

Tom kept studying the blinking blip on the navigation display. "Hey, look at this. Bet you this is where the message is coming from." Janet looked over his shoulder, and Dan came down from the captain's chair.

The navigation console showed what appeared to be a large tactical view of their location in the galaxy relative to where the message was being broadcast.

"That isn't even in our solar system, is it, Janet?" asked Dan.

Janet leaned over Tom and began manipulating the screen to get a better idea of what they were looking at. "No, it's very close in stellar terms, but that is *not* our solar system."

They listened to the message repeat over and over again. Panic was evident in the voice, very clearly communicating a grave sense of urgency. If those who sent this message did not get help soon, they would cease to be.

Dan stepped back toward the captain's chair to sit and think. Tom added some more information. "It looks like ... wait a minute ... uh, I have an option to plot a course to the ... blip."

Dan continued to listen to the frantic message as he mulled over what Tom was telling him. "If you plotted a course, what next? What would we do?"

"We would have to use the hyperdrive," added Janet.

"Which would mean what—we'd warp there?"

"Actually, warp is incorrect. In our training they alluded to faster than light travel as sliding."

"Please explain," requested Dan.

"Sliding, which comes across as a slang term, is a way to move from point A to point B by creating a wormhole through hyperspace."

"Lost me," said Tom.

"With a warp, you'd warp space-time to move faster than light. This can be done by creating a warp bubble around the ship or by folding space. Both are sound theories. With traveling in hyperspace, you wouldn't have to warp space-time, but since hyperspace exists above and outside of normal space, you'd need a way to safely enter and traverse it."

"Janet, is this fact or your science fiction theory?" asked Dan.

"Actually, a little of both. It's theory back on Earth, but these folks have put it into practice. When the *Liberty* travels faster than light, it must precalculate its destination. The ship then opens a portal into hyperspace and creates an artificial tunnel to the destination, called a wormhole. Then we effectively slide through hyperspace in this wormhole to our destination. Without the wormhole, there's no telling where we would exit from hyperspace, if at all."

"I think I get it," noted Dan. "So if Tom is able to plot a course, how do we activate the hyperdrive?"

Janet looked at the panel where Tom was sitting. Her finger moved along the console, reading every little bit of information. She studied the map that showed the location of the *Stoic 2*. They could almost see the light bulb appear over her head as she bolted over to the engineer's panel. Her finger ran across it like she was using her tactile senses to discover how to activate the hyperdrive. "Yes," was all she could mutter as her legs lifted her out of the chair and down the stairs, back to the helm. She poked her head in, studied the controls, and triumphantly stated, "I got it!"

"Great!" Dan replied. "Can you fill us in?"

Janet leaped up the stairs and stood before Dan, who was still seated in the captain's chair. "Basically, it's a three-step process. A course is plotted on the navigation/tactical control panel at which Mr. Tom is sitting. Tom, can you wave at the nice man?" Tom waved, playing into her little game.

"Funny. Now can you get on with it?" asked Dan.

Janet chuckled and then continued. "The engineer then needs to route power and activate the drive. The hyperdrive is not always on and takes considerable juice, so if the ship is damaged, other systems would need to be diverted—for example, the shields, weapons, etcetera."

"I follow you so far."

"Good. Next, the engineer gives control to the helmsman, who can activate the drive using that red handle that we used before to get here."

"But you pulled the handle, and then I initiated the slide."

"I would assume that's an emergency fail-safe. If the helm pulls the slide lever before a course is plotted or power is assigned, then the captain can override, which you did. That's what brought us to Saturn. An emergency slide—how cool is that?"

"So what you're saying is that we could slide the *Liberty* back to Earth?"

"Yes, sir, that is exactly what ... I ..." Janet's speech trailed off as they could still hear the distress call echoing throughout the bridge.

Dan sighed and put his face down into his hands. He and his friends kept an eerie silence as they focused on the pleadings of the *Stoic 2*'s captain. They were all contemplating the same thing. The final piece was in place for their return to Earth and their families. A few buttons were all that now separated them from going home.

Dan ran his hands through his hair and looked up at Tom and Janet, who had not moved a muscle. The blank expressions on their faces told the story; the decision would be up to him. Their desire to return home was so strong, but they were also good people who would always help out someone in need, and judging from the voice emanating from the *Stoic 2*, there was someone in need.

But they had also barely escaped the encounter with those other craft near the moon. Who was to say they would be any use on a rescue mission? They had just learned how to operate the ship—a severely damaged ship that had been sitting idle for fifty or more years. What if the *Stoic 2* saw them as a threat and blew them out of the sky? What if it was a trap?

Dan stood up. "I need a minute alone." He walked behind the captain's chair and into the conference room. He ran his hand across each one of the chairs as he somberly walked by. *What would they have done? How would they have handled this?* Walking into the captain's office, Dan sat down at his grandfather's old desk. He grabbed the picture of his grandfather and great-grandparents and studied it closely. For minutes he merely stared at the picture with no thought in his mind, just absorbing the experience of seeing his grandfather so young.

Delicately placing the picture back on the desk, Dan looked around the office. There was more to this story than what he had learned so far. There was a reason these alien peoples came to Earth, and that reason was larger than Dan or his two friends. Dan could not just go back home and walk into high school on Tuesday. He had changed, as had Janet and Tom. They had discovered something so groundbreaking it would tear apart the perceptions of so many people on Earth. Not only would *he* not be the same anymore; *nothing* would be the same anymore. They were no longer alone in the universe—they knew now that there were people like them in other parts of the galaxy.

Dan's eyes lowered to bring the picture into view once more. "I know what you would do," he muttered as he stood up and made his way quickly back to the bridge.

Panic

MAJOR JENSEN SLAMMED HARD into the bulkhead of the ISS, his head rebounding like a basketball, the skin splitting to reveal several drops of blood, which floated away in the abyss of zero gravity. He grabbed onto a handrail for leverage and peered out the window, looking for any sign of the escape module. All he could see was debris. The shockwave from the explosion was so close to the space station that it knocked it very hard and jostled the two remaining crew like rag dolls.

"Stabilizing thrusters firing automatically, sir," announced Major Vodnikov. Hearing her voice meant that she was okay. It was also comforting to hear that the thrusters were attempting to stabilize the ISS, which began to rotate and list due to the explosion.

"Do you have any indications of damage?" asked Jensen.

"Communications seem to be out, we had a hull breach near the escape area, and it is showing that several of the solar panels are damaged."

"We need to get communications back as soon as we can. See what you can do."

Vodnikov paused and looked at Jensen. "They … they are gone—"

"And we may be gone too if we don't get to work," indicated Jensen. He did not want to give himself time to grasp what had just happened. That would come later. Right now he needed to ensure the safety of his last remaining crewmate, and having her wallow in the loss of their comrades at this moment would only put their safety at risk.

"Yes, sir," said Vodnikov, visibly holding back the cascade of emotions that were building up deep in her stomach. She pulled the panel from the communications terminal and began to work.

"What just happened?" barked General Peters.

Ops coordinator Seaford, who was sitting in front of the general, blurted out, "Sir, the escape capsule is no longer visible, and we can't pick up its signal. The four bogies have disappeared. Communications with the ISS seem to be out."

"Get them back! Captain?" Peters turned to Captain Dillings. "Until we know what happened here, this room is locked down. No one comes or goes. All external phone calls are to be screened by you or me. Sever communications link with NASA. Tell them we're having systems problems. Get whomever you can to block their ability to get anything through to the ISS. If word of this gets out, we'll have not only an international incident with the Chinese and Russians, but panic from our own citizens as well."

"Yes, sir," responded Dillings as she walked away to execute the general's orders.

Peters went into his office and shut the door. A red-and-orange flashing light appeared on the black phone, indicating that external communications were being shut down. He sat behind the desk and looked at the red phone. He had no choice. He had to notify the president.

General Peters grabbed the red phone and put it to his ear as he sighed. After a few clicks and several seconds of waiting, he began to speak. "Sir, we have a grave situation on our hands."

12

Action

Dan appeared from the conference room and returned to the captain's chair. Janet and Tom, who were talking, stopped and walked up to him.

"I'm sorry, but we have to help them. I can't listen to that voice and turn away and go home." The other two just responded with muted smiles, as they knew it was the right decision. "We've found out that we're not alone in the universe. We are not it. Earth isn't the one rock where people like us live. There are other places—other worlds. Now that we know what we know, could we go home?" This was a rhetorical question. Janet and Tom knew the answer.

Tom turned toward the navigation console. "Plotting a course to distressed ship."

In turn, Janet leaned over the engineer's console. "Routing adequate power to hyperdrive reactors." She walked down to the helm and stepped in. "On your order, sir."

Dan pulled up the engineer's schema. "Tom, as soon as we exit hyperspace, I want you to power up weapons and get ready to shoot anything that looks scary. I'll take care of the shields. You got it?"

"Aye, Captain."

"Helm … slide!"

Janet pulled the lever. The stillness they experienced before the last slide returned. There was no vibration or feeling of motion, only a silence and sensation of heaviness, as if one's pockets were filling with quarters. The ship began to accelerate toward the speed of light, making the stars appear to streak by. A white flash indicated their open window into hyperspace, and as they passed through, what greeted them was the shimmering beauty of the wormhole itself as they slid towards their destination.

Dan looked around. He lifted his right hand and examined it. He could move his fingers and still make a fist. He tried the other hand and got the same result. "Well ... I feel okay. How you guys doing?"

Tom stood up, jumped up and down, and did a few jumping jacks. "I feel fine, besides being hungry, tired, lost, and now traveling in a different dimension."

"Good, you're still surly. Janet, how 'bout you?"

"Just peachy," she answered.

Tom sat back down. "We have about two hours until our destination. At least that's what I think this means. Either that, or I hit the self-destruct, and that's how long we have to live."

"Two hours?" asked Dan. "It took less than a minute to slide from the moon to Saturn. How far will two hours of this take us?"

Tom turned around, holding an index finger from each hand up in the air spaced several inches apart. "According to the screen, about this far."

"Funny." Yes, it was funny, but Dan wasn't amused. They were already far from home, and now this escapade was only going to take them farther. Plus, they had no idea what to expect at the end of the two-hour journey.

Survival

"I THINK I HAVE SOMETHING." Major Sofiya Vodnikov had spent the last hour attempting to get the communications with Earth functional again. The external antenna was destroyed, and the area where the escape pod docked with the station had a hull breach and was venting atmosphere. As the spacewalk equipment lay in that part of the International Space Station, there was no way for them to go outside to make the necessary repairs. The situation warranted improvisation. Vodnikov had the idea of using the station's water pipes as an antenna. They twisted throughout the structure and were possibly the best chance for a makeshift repair.

"I tied in the radio with the water pipes and am getting a weak message."

"Great job!" Major Jensen was impressed. Even with the Cold War long over, there was always a sense of competition between the Americans and the Russians. This passion to outdo one another sometimes manifested itself in very creative solutions to problems, as exemplified by Vodnikov's ingenious repair. "Turn it up."

Vodnikov adjusted the volume until they could faintly hear an incoming voice. "ISS, this is NETO. Please respond. ISS, this is NETO. Please respond." The weak message repeated itself over and over. Major Jensen put on his headset.

"This is Major David Jensen, commander ISS."

"This is NETO, Major. You are coming in very weak. Please boost your signal."

"Not possible. Station has taken damage, and external broadcast antenna destroyed. We had to rig," he looked over and smiled at Sofiya, "a creative solution. This is the best we can do."

"Acknowledged, ISS. Please stand by."

Back at NETO, deep within Cheyenne Mountain, Lieutenant Seaford adjusted the communication equipment and motioned to Captain Dillings. "Captain, I have commander ISS on the line. Station has taken damage to the communication system."

"I'll get the general."

"Also, Captain, NASA keeps asking for a better explanation. They're not buying the story about systems problems."

"Are you jamming the frequency so that NASA doesn't pick up our chatter with the ISS?"

"Yes, I'm using some of our communications satellites to generate enough electronic traffic that no one else besides us should be able to cut through."

"That is the best we can do for now. Keep stalling them, and I will see where the general is with our lockdown procedures." Captain Dillings walked toward General Peters's office and knocked on the door. She heard the click of the secure lock release and walked into the room.

"General, we have the ISS back."

The general glanced up from his computer terminal. "What about our NASA problem?"

"Sir, they are still looking for a better explanation. They saw the same things we did, and they know we are giving them a snow job … sir."

Peters sighed. "I didn't want to do this."

"Do what, sir?"

Without responding, the general turned his attention back to his computer. His fingers began flying across the keyboard as he composed a short message, pressing the Enter key to send it on its way. A few moments later there was a beep indicating a reply. His order had been received and acknowledged. "It's done."

"What's done, sir?"

General Peters adjusted his gaze from the computer screen to Captain Dillings. The concern on his face was apparent, and his response was only one word. "Quarantine."

No Leaving Early Today

"I DON'T CARE WHAT HE'S DOING, you just get him on the line!" barked an agitated Mark Walters, rising from his chair to coincide with his rise in blood pressure. "No … no … you listen here, mister. We saw the same things that you did, and … No! No! I won't hold for the captain! I want to talk to General Peters right now!" The line went dead.

"Betty! Betty!" screamed Walters, grabbing the attention of his assistant, Betty Tedesci. "Get them back, and I want to talk to the general, no pipsqueak lieutenants!"

"No problem."

"Any luck getting hold of the president?"

"No, they said he's busy."

"What do you mean busy? That is a red phone! The red phone means something! He can't just be busy!" Walters continued to rant and rave. He knew that something had happened, and then all of a sudden Houston was shoved in the dark. No one would talk with them, and their link to Near Earth Threat Operations was severed right after they lost contact with the ISS.

The din in the control room was deafening. A sense of urgency and the unmistakable sound of panic boomed throughout the large space as technicians yelled across its expanse at one another, trying to get communications reestablished with the International Space Station. They had witnessed the disturbing events—watched the escape module disappear and four possibly alien craft move aggressively toward the station. Without communications they could not confirm exactly what had happened or if any of their astronauts were still alive.

Mark Walters burst out of his office and walked up to some of his most senior techs. "Do we have any way to reestablish contact with the station?"

One of the engineers turned and responded. "Sorry, Mark, we don't. We've been trying everything. It's almost like we're being jammed. We've tried different broadcast stations, satellites, you name it—nothing's working."

Mark breathed a frustrated sigh, took his glasses off, and wiped his face with his hand in disgust. This confirmed his paranoia. They were deliberately being kept in the dark. Whatever had happened was bad enough to pull the plug on NASA.

How could this get worse? Putting his glasses back on, Mark peered out the window to see several Blackhawk helicopters landing on the lawn outside. *I think this will do the trick.*

Commandos in full garb poured of the helicopters. Next came the screams as soldiers dressed in jet-black combat attire entered the room with guns at the ready. Several positioned themselves to block the exits. Three came toward Mark.

"Are you Mark Walters?" asked a tall, well-armed man, sporting a buzz cut and arms the size of tree trunks.

"Yes, I am. Who are you people, and where do you get off barging in here like a bunch of Neanderthals?"

"I'm Agent Wachovic of the National Security Agency. We have a situation and require this facility and all its personnel to be quarantined until further notice. No one may leave the building or contact anyone outside of this facility. Am I clear?"

"You just wait a minute here! You can't—"

"Sir, yes, we can. We're the guys with the guns. Can we go to your office?"

Mark did not respond but simply walked away to his office, followed by Agent Wachovic. He booted his trash bin across the room before sitting down in the chair behind his desk. Agent Wachovic quietly shut the door and pulled the blinds on the windows.

"Mr. Walters, I understand your situation here, but—"

"You don't understand boo, mister! I am responsible for those people up on that station. I have followed procedure only to be cut off and held hostage in my own facility."

"Sir, authorization for this mission came directly from the president," said Agent Wachovic in a stoutly stern voice. "Not to sound cocky, but my unit does not get called out for anything unless it is of grave international severity, where the security of this country, meaning you," he pointed at Mark, "and me and those people out there are in danger. Now I am asking for your cooperation. We will make sure everyone is comfortable and will get food and water, magazines, or whatever. I need your support and leadership, Mr. Walters. Can I count on you?"

Mark slumped in his chair and gazed off into the room. He did not have a choice; the president had apparently made it for him. With the weapons these agents were brandishing, it was clear that he was no longer in charge of this facility.

"I'll go talk to my people." Without glancing at Agent Wachovic, Mark Walters stood up and walked into the control room to talk with his staff. As he crossed the threshold of his office, he turned to Agent Wachovic and said, "You can count on me."

In The Deep End

CONVENTIONAL WISDOM WOULD SAY that if you put three teenagers on an alien spacecraft and shot them past the speed of light, there would be no possibility of boredom rearing its ugly head. That would have been the theory, but it definitely wasn't the reality. Dan, Janet, and Tom were bored, not in the traditional not knowing what to do on a rainy Saturday sort of boredom, but the kind that comes before a significant event, like before Christmas morning, a big game, or the night before the SATs. This boredom comes from knowing not only that was there nothing to do in the entertainment sense, but also that all known preparations had been made, and the only task left was to simply sit and wait. Idleness caused the worst-case scenarios to play out in their minds. Horrors that could happen were so tangible that their hearts elevated their rhythm, sweat began to bead on their brows, and fingers held in the air revealed a slight quiver.

The three friends had almost two hours just to sit and wait—wait until they traveled faster than the speed of light, through hyperspace, to an area of the galaxy no Earthling had ever been, to meet and rescue an alien ship. Of course they played with their consoles to see what the buttons did and explored some more of the ship's info, but most of all they just sat. Tom even fell asleep, which was made evident by the unearthly sound that erupted from his lungs.

"Uh ... you know ... uh ... never mind," muttered Janet timidly, still seated at the helm.

"What, Janet?" asked Dan.

"No ... forget it."

"What? Don't do that. Speak up."

"Well, what if we get in over our heads?"

"Janet, we've been in over our heads for a while now. Look around you."

"I know ... I know ... just ... what if we screw this up? What if we do something to get these people, or whoever they are, killed?"

Dan needed to craft his answer carefully; this could not be a flippant response. Janet had a valid point. They did not really know how to run this ship, and it was only their principles that thrust them forward to help the *Stoic 2*. Good sense would have had them turn home. "Janet, you heard that voice. If we do nothing, there's a good chance that they'll die anyway. Plus, just think for a minute." The thought rolled into Dan's mind. "We could use their help too."

Tom broke from his slumber and pointed at his captain. "And that's why you're the boss."

The response made Dan feel good. He had their confidence, and he needed to maintain it.

"All right, guys," said Dan, trying to focus the team in order to keep them from dwelling on the negative, "we have about five minutes until we slide into normal space. Janet, do like you did back at Saturn. Think of it as a video game. If we meet any nasties, fly this ship like you mean it, and don't be shy. The inertial dampers should keep us from puking. Just keep moving. A moving target is harder to hit."

"Aye, Captain!" Janet exclaimed.

"Tom, you arm those weapons and look for anything that may want to kill us."

"Dan, I also found, while we were sitting here, that there's a defensive perimeter we can arm. There are smaller automated guns all over the ship."

"Good man! Remind me to recommend you for a promotion," Dan responded, prompting a momentary chuckle from the team. "Turn everything on as soon as we—"

"Counterpoint, Captain," interrupted Janet.

"What's up?"

"I've had time to think this through. If we slide in there with guns ready to go, they may see it as a hostile move."

Dan thought for a moment. "You know, you're right. Tom, change of plans. I'll arm shields, but do not arm the weapons until we see something, and only on my order. Let's go with Janet's instincts, which have been spot on. I don't wanna pick a fight if we don't have to."

"I'm all for that," agreed Tom, pecking away at his console.

The bridge again got quiet as the three looked over their stations to make sure that they were ready and knew exactly which buttons to push. They didn't want to eject an engine or hit the windshield wipers by accident.

"Just one more thing," announced Dan. "This is our *second* space battle."

They all chuckled, but it was true. They had already survived one battle back when they knew nothing about the ship. They knew so much more now. This was an instant confidence builder.

"Thirty seconds!" called Janet.

"Everyone get ready," ordered Dan.

The countdown clock went to zero. A flash filled the screen as a window into normal space was opened. They passed through. Stars streaked by like comets. As the ship slowed, the streaks turned back into the infinite points of light that filled the depth of space. They had arrived.

"Raising shields," said Dan, as he pressed the proper button. "We have power to sublight engines, except for the one that was blown up, of course."

"Thanks for pointing that out," bellyached Tom.

Dan pulled up the communications view on his console. "Okay, I have the phone ready. Does anyone see anything?"

Tom punched away at the panel in front of him for what seemed like an eternity. "There! There it is!"

Janet moved her head around in the helm control, searching space around the *Liberty*, hoping to catch a glimpse of the *Stoic 2*. "Where is it? I don't see anything."

"Uh, it's a blip. Oh, I bet we slid in close, but we still need to navigate toward it."

"Probably," said Janet. "I can't see it anywhere near the ship. At least in visual range."

"Can you drive toward the blip?" asked Tom half joking.

"I would, but I don't see any blip."

Dan was getting a little annoyed at this exchange. "Janet, check in there. There has to be something to bring up a long-range view so you can fly to it."

"Hold on," Janet said. They could see her trying different levers and switches. After several seconds of experimentation she exclaimed, "Found it! I see a blip and hope that's our ship in distress. I'll start to fly toward it. Tom, just tell me if we're getting closer."

"You bet."

Janet turned the *Liberty* until the "blip" was directly in front of her. She slid the throttle a quarter of the way forward, and they began to move.

Dan looked over the communications controls. "I have no idea how this works. I'm going to try a few things." He attempted button after button, but he had no clue how to contact the other ship. "We have a problem here."

"What?" asked Janet.

"Unless someone else can figure this thing out, I don't think we'll be contacting anyone."

"Communications may be down," Tom pointed out. "I mean, the *Liberty* is trashed. I wouldn't be surprised if the phone's busted too."

Janet spoke up. "I would just wait for them to contact us. Maybe then you'll get some type of option to answer."

Tom kept his eyes fixed on the image of the ship moving toward the blip on his console. "Janet, you're doing good. Keep going."

"I see it!" Janet exclaimed. "Look!"

On the viewscreen they could see a shape growing larger—it was the *Stoic 2*. Only the second large spacecraft they had ever seen, it lacked the flowing lines of the *Liberty*. Long and rectangular, it looked like the alien equivalent of a tractor-trailer. A tower rose out of the main hull toward the rear of the ship, probably holding the crew's quarters and the bridge. On the back were two cones that acted as the main thrusters for the sublight engines.

Dan glanced down at his panel, and sure enough there was a blinking light indicating an incoming transition. "Janet, you made the right call. I have a communication incoming. Slow the ship and hold position here."

"Yes, sir," Janet acknowledged.

Dan pressed the receive button. He heard a voice crackle across, "This is the *Stoic 2*. Please identify yourself. Are you here to assist?"

"Uh, yes ... yes, we're here to help," responded Dan, a little unsure of his galactic radio technique.

"My name is Captain Deshin. Who are you? What is your ship? We cannot read your ident signal."

Dan cleared his throat and sat up straighter in his chair. "This is ... uh ... this is Dan."

"Dan? Dan who? What is your ship's name?"

"My name is ... Captain Dan ... Captain Dan Foster of the *Liberty*."

"Are you joking? What are you saying? This is not funny!"

"What do you—"

"Dan!" Tom screamed in alarm. "Two ... holy ... oh ... two freaking ... uh ..." Tom strained to get the words out.

"Tom? What—"

Janet interrupted, her voice quivering. "Captain, two really big ugly ships headed this way. They just exited hyperspace. They're huge!"

Dan's stomach churned as he saw what was projected on the viewscreen. They were enormous, even from this distance. Both identical, the two ships were a compilation of right angles and boxy sections, a sharp contrast to the graceful lines of the *Liberty*. Dan's eyes were affixed to the closest vessel. The oily black hull was diamond shaped, flaring out toward the aft section. A tower in the form of a three-sided pyramid protruded from about three-quarters toward the rear of the menacing ship. Below, what could only be described loosely as wings extended out both the port and starboard sides of the hull. They were several decks thick and arced aggressively toward the front of the craft. At the rear, a single diamond engine nozzle finished out the terrifying look.

"Uh, they look like they could be from the same friendly people we met near the moon," said Janet after looking at their oily color and unfriendly design.

Yes, this is the worst-case scenario? Dan had to think quickly. This was way more than they had bargained for, and neither he nor his friends had anticipated being met by two ships that were larger and more powerful. One of these monsters would have been a force to reckon with, but two—the odds were firmly against them. Dan did not have years of experience commanding a spaceship to draw from, and his crewmates were just as innocent. He had better open his mouth and say something before fear caused his friends to panic.

"Helm, move us in between those ships and the *Stoic 2*. Tom, let's get those weapons fired up. Give me a targeting solution on both ships." Janet and Tom acknowledged with a quick "aye."

Dan forgot that he still had a channel open to the *Stoic 2*. A terrified Captain Deshin began to plead, "Captain Foster, you must help us! Those are Gaarich marauders, and they will capture this vessel, take its cargo, and kill all of us!"

"Gaarich?"

"Captain? Stop taunting us and help!"

Dan pulled up the engineer's view to make sure the shields were online as Janet positioned the *Liberty* between the marauders and the *Stoic 2*. Tom armed the weapons and targeted each of the large ships with one of the *Liberty*'s turrets.

"Ugh!" grunted Dan.

"What?" asked Janet.

"I think I hung up on that guy … I mean Captain Deshin."

"Dan, look out the window. We've got bigger issues right now than being rude to some alien dude," growled Tom. "This stinks! I was supposed to be partying at the lake this weekend; now I'm gonna get all blown up!"

"No one is going to die here today, all right!" Dan was getting a little miffed from the defeatist attitudes of his friends. Yes, this was a hopeless situation, and the odds were stacked smartly against them, but sitting and whining about it were not going to help them.

"If they're going to capture the *Stoic 2*, that gives us some information that we may use to our advantage," offered Janet.

"What do you mean?" asked Dan.

"Well, if they want the cargo ship, they may not want us."

"Good point. They may just want to blow us up," grumbled Tom.

Dan paused and thought for a moment after his friend's flippant remark. If the Gaarich wanted to capture the *Stoic 2*, then they did not want to simply destroy it. "This makes it a much more complex operation for them. They need to capture the vessel, and we're the pains in the butts in the way. So, all we need to do is be annoying—a pain in their side—like a fly buzzing around you on a hot, muggy summer day."

"Let's not get swatted," added Tom.

"We still have to win somehow," noted Janet. "Apparently the cargo ship can't fly away and can't repair itself. It would have done that by now."

"Even with David, there was only one Goliath, not two," snapped Tom.

Dan's agitation reached its peak. He jumped out of his chair. "Listen! We are going to kick their alien butts! I didn't get this far only to be totally whacked by some interplanetary bullies. Now cut the cute comments, and let's go kick some booty! Got it?"

"Yes, sir!" shouted Janet and Tom. That may not have been the most inspiring speech, but it seemed to do the trick.

"Janet, quick question. If I arm the cloak, will the shields drop?"

"Without having a degree in off-world engineering, I would have to say yes. The shields use a ton of power, as does the cloak. I doubt you can use them both at the same time. Let's at least assume this for the purposes of this exercise."

"Good, Janet, let's use speed to our advanta …" Dan stopped as he saw many small objects careening out of both marauders. "What are those?"

There was no response as the three gazed at the viewscreen to see a swarm of smaller craft bursting out of the sides of each Gaarich marauder. Very tiny and fast, they began to speed toward the *Liberty*.

"Not sure, but they don't look friendly," said Tom.

"Fighters ... they're small, look fast, and there are a bunch of them," added Janet, speaking softy, as if afraid they could hear.

Instead of being frightened, this only made Dan angrier. Just as he was attempting to formulate a plan, the Gaarich threw this at him. Frustration was the order of the day, not fright. Seeing those ships launch only made Dan more determined. They were taunting a rattlesnake that was getting ready to strike.

"Janet, on my command I want you to fly full speed toward the ship on the right. Keep zigzagging to avoid its fire. Get as close as you can, right below the apex of its starboard hull. The closer we are to it, the harder it will be to target us, and we could sock that thing in the gut a few times."

"What about the fighters, or whatever they are?" Janet asked. "We would be flying right toward them!"

"Just the way I want it. I want you to fly right into them and make them follow us." Dan could anticipate the verbal objections. "Listen, just trust me. This will work."

"Tom, I want you to start shooting everything on my command as we move toward the ships. Aim for stuff that looks important—and take out some of those fighters if you want to. Now hit it!"

The *Liberty* lurched forward and headed straight for the Gaarich marauders, her weapons firing at both ships. The shots impacted the enemies' shields but did not produce any noticeable damage. Both of the marauders opened fire as the *Liberty* closed; every impact rocked the ship. The shields held, but because of the hefty amount of damage she already had incurred, the relentless bombardment was tearing apart the thin glue that still held her together.

The smaller ships now met up with the *Liberty*, their small size and nimble maneuvering confirming Janet's assertion that they were fighters. As Tom fired the main guns at the larger ships, the automated belt guns that bristled along the sides of the *Liberty* chipped away at the fighters.

Janet zigged and zagged using her skills from years of playing flight simulators to try to avoid the fire from the marauders. Piloting the *Liberty* toward the vessel on the right, she skimmed over the threshold of the enemy's hull, prompting the other ship to cease firing or risk damaging its partner. Their target also stopped its assault, as the large guns could not deal with something flying only meters above their hull.

The fighters now led the bombardment of the *Liberty*, rocking her violently as she paralleled very close to the marauder's hull. Salvo after salvo crushed away at the shields, overloading power systems, causing lights and control panels to blow out. A beam ripped from the ceiling, crashing into the stations on the upper level of the bridge.

Dan braced himself on the captain's chair, his hands firmly grabbing the arms as he watched Tom intently focused on his task. He was firing burst after burst at the closer enemy vessel while still maintaining a continuous barrage against the other ship. The *Liberty* was now so close to the marauder's hull that its guns were able to penetrate the shields of the marauder, being rewarded with brilliant explosions that lit up the main screen.

"Janet," ordered Dan, "I want you to pick up speed and fly right at the top of the tower as fast as you can. Head straight for it, and just as we're about to hit, pull up hard, just like you did back at Saturn. Shout when you're about to pull up. *This is very important.* I need to have a verbal indicator when you're going to pull up."

"Aye!" responded Janet, as she nudged the throttle forward and pointed the ship toward the top of the tower, with the pursuing ships close on the tail of the *Liberty*.

Dan's finger hovered just above the engineer's console. He had to wait for the right time. He could not rush this—it was their only chance. The top of the tower closed in quickly.

"Now!" shouted Janet, as the muscles in her arms began to flex to pull the *Liberty* up and over the tower to avoid a collision.

Dan allowed his finger to contact the button he had been preparing to press upon Janet's notice. His index finger touched the cold panel, the cloaking indicator dimmed, and the *Liberty* vanished.

The pursuing ships, caught by surprise, slammed into the bridge of the marauder one after another. They were following so closely in a swarm that they had no time to react. One by one they disappeared into a cloud of fire, as the tower reciprocated by collapsing into the back of the ship. The huge vessel commenced to list starboard and crash into the other marauder. Their hulls began to fail and buckle. Explosions glistened down their sides, blowing out large sections of structure. Their engines went dim, and a few seconds later the two exploded in a bright nuclear flash, followed by stillness. They were gone.

Dan disabled the cloak, and the *Liberty* was again visible in space. The three friends jumped up out of their seats and cheered. Janet ran up and gave Dan and Tom a big hug.

"We did it!" shouted Tom. "We really did it! We beat them. You said we would, and you were right. You were right on!"

Dan savored this moment. They had done it—three teenagers from a planet whose dreams of deep space exploration were still just that. It was not the power of positive thinking—it was strategy and action that got them through this. The determination to survive and save those people on the *Stoic 2* was what drove them to this victory—not years of training at an academy or a certification in space combat, but simply the human desire to survive. Dan's emotions almost overtook him as he looked up at the viewscreen to see the *Stoic 2* in the distance, still there, all its passengers alive and well.

There was a beeping to indicate an incoming transmission. Dan sat down in the captain's chair and pressed the correct commands to acknowledge. "This is the *Liberty*."

Dan could hear cheers in the background as he heard the voice of Captain Deshin saying, "*Liberty*, this is the *Stoic 2*. Thank you! I have never seen anything like that. You *must* be the *Liberty*! The time has come. We have all been waiting for your return."

Another series of beeps came from Tom's console. He sat back down to look, and his eyes grew wide. "Captain, we have company!"

Dan looked up at viewscreen and could not believe what he saw. "It just keeps getting weirder."

Call to Action

"This is Near Earth Threat Operations to International Space Station. Please acknowledge," sounded General Peters.

A voice began to crackle across the loudspeakers. "This is Major Jensen, commander ISS."

"What's your status? What happened?"

"Sir, this station was attacked by four unidentified craft. Escape module was destroyed with Captain Hou, Major Pascal, Captain Chang, and Lieutenant Davis all onboard. Ships attacked without provocation. Sir … there were no survivors."

The command center at NETO was silent. They had feared that this was the case, and now they had the verbal proof to back it up. Four scientists—four astronauts—were dead, attacked by a craft that was unlike anything they had ever seen. *Could there be more? Could they come back? Would they come back?* Just the thought of these questions sent a shockwave of fear through the command center.

Here lay the problem—this same fear would grip the people of Earth. This event would confirm that there was life on other planets, but would feed the paranoid notion that this alien life was hostile, and in this instance it most assuredly was. Earth was unprepared and had no response. Fear would grip the populace and tear down any unity they could muster to deal with this new threat.

It was up to General Peters now. He quarantined NASA in Houston to ensure that they had time to react before the rumor mill made it to CNN, Fox News, and the Drudge Report. The next few hours were critical. They could not keep this a secret for long. The Chinese, French, and Russians all had crew aboard the station and would be wondering about their well-being. As the seconds ticked by, inaction would surely usher in chaos; only decisive haste could bring about resolution. So much for a quiet retirement job for the general.

"Major, I am sorry to hear of the losses. What is your condition?"

"Both myself and Major Vodnikov are a little battered and bruised, but we'll be fine. The ISS is in worse shape. The explosion damaged the section where we have the airlocks and spacesuits. The long-range antenna is broken, and we're concerned about the overall structural integrity. We can't space walk to do any inspections."

This was what the general feared the most; the ISS was damaged from the residual explosion, and who was to know if a structural failure was only moments away. He could not mount a rescue. None of the shuttles were ready, and the preparations for an emergency launch would take at least two weeks.

"Major, you are going to have to do what you can up there. We don't have any hardware in place to mount a rescue. Earliest we can do is fourteen days."

"Understood. Docking port is in damaged section. We would have to come up with alternatives anyway, and we're prepared to do that."

This the general was happy to hear. Major Jensen's strength impressed him. He was showing the qualities of a true leader in this difficult time. "Good to hear that, Major. You also need to understand the global significance of the situation that we are in. Cool heads need to prevail here. You must understand that this is a military mission now. We have been attacked and need to act appropriately—as soldiers. Your line of communication is to me and this facility, no others. Do you understand?"

"Yes, sir," crackled the major's voice.

"Keep this channel open. We will require a check-in with status every thirty minutes. Is that clear?"

"Yes, sir. Commander ISS setting communications to standby—next contact in thirty. Major Jensen out."

General Peters marched back toward his office and motioned Captain Dillings to follow. He walked behind his desk and sat down. The captain closed the door.

"At ease, Captain. Take a seat."

Captain Dillings sat down in front of the general.

"Now, I need to know our situational status."

"General, NASA command center in Houston has been locked down by the NSA. All communications to the ISS are being jammed. We cannot jam telescopes, but I am hoping that if we move within the window of opportunity, no one will get that curious."

"And what is our window?" asked the general.

"I estimate six to eight hours. The Chinese, Russians, and French were all involved in this mission. They will want to be informed and will get curious. Pressure on the president will mount over the coming hours to tell them something."

The general looked down at his desk, the gears of his brain beginning to turn. Unique situations called for unique solutions. What may seem superfluous may in reality be the key to success.

"Global Defense Pact," he muttered.

"Sir?"

He looked up at the captain. "The Global Defense Pact—it may be the key."

"Sir, if I may?" The general motioned for her to proceed. "The pact was nothing but political shine. Something that the Russians, Chinese, and we could show our people to give the impression that the three of us could actually work together on something."

"True, but we need to give the world some confidence. Confidence comes in preparation and determination. If we give the people of the world the impression that we're prepared for this, then they're less likely to panic."

The captain looked confused. "But sir, we are not prepared for this."

General Peters leaned across the table and looked into Captain Dillings's eyes. "But yet we are, Captain. We're more prepared than we think." He turned around to the small safe behind his desk and punched up the combination, followed by a thumbprint confirmation. He opened the door and pulled out the procedures for engaging the Global Defense Pact.

Putting on his reading glasses, the general began to scan through the document. It was very thin, just a few pages—a hastily put-together plan that was more political fodder than operational substance.

"The president, Joint Chiefs, and military all have roles here. We kick this thing off." The general tossed the book over to the captain, who caught it, the confusion on her face still clear. "Let's get it going. I'll call the president. We're going to invoke the Global Defense Pact."

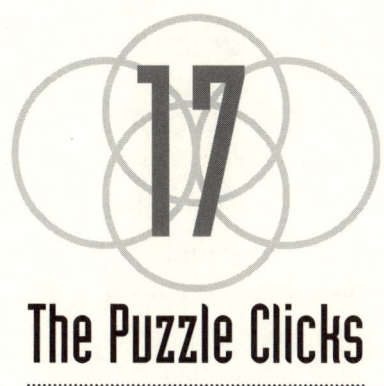

The Puzzle Clicks

DAN AND HIS COMPANIONS STOOD STONE FACED, looking out at three ships that were identical to the *Liberty*, albeit in much better condition. They had come out of hyperspace toward the end of the battle and surprised not only the *Liberty*, but also the *Stoic 2*.

"We have another incoming communication."

"This is Captain Demenar of the corvette *Defiance*. Please identify yourself."

"Oh, now they're gonna know we stole this ship. Wait, did we steal it? I'm freaking out a bit, aren't I?" Yes, Tom was freaking out, but they had no time to calm him down.

Dan mustered enough confidence to respond, "This is Captain Foster of the *Liberty*. We … uh …"

"The *Liberty*? Please confirm."

"Well, we think this is the *Liberty*."

"What do you mean *think*?"

"Uh, we're from Earth, and … well … we—"

"No time for explanations. We need to evacuate the *Stoic 2*. I will come over to your ship. Can you have a delegation meet me in the starboard docking bay?"

"Uh, no. I mean, there are only three of us. Oh, and by the way, the starboard docking bay has been destroyed, but we didn't do it. Just so you know."

"Whoever you are, stop playing games. We will be over there in fifteen minutes. *Defiance* out."

A slight panic crossed through the bridge as the three friends realized that they would be meeting an alien, possibly more than one, in just a few minutes. Dan ran his fingers through his hair in an attempt at grooming. Janet stepped out of the helm and examined her reflection using the Plexiglas-like material as a mirror, but Tom just sat with his face in his hands, making no attempt to clean himself up.

Still clutching his head, Tom asked a question of his captain. "Any clue how to roll out the welcome wagon?"

"None. Let's just be ourselves and be friendly. I'll just have to explain that my grandfather used to be the captain of this ship and we were taking his car to your parent's lake house when an incident with an eight-track tape had us flying toward the moon and this ship. A few wacky scenarios later, we got into two battles with those Gaarich whatevers, and here we are."

Tom pulled his face away from his hands and looked at Dan. "I'm sure they had similar problems with eight-track tapes." His eyes targeted Janet, who continued to primp herself. "Hey, glamour girl. You look great. Your grooming's making me nervous!" She simply responded by sticking her tongue out at him.

"We should probably go meet them," Dan recommended as he rose out of his chair. Janet and Tom followed him to the elevator as they made their way to the port docking bay.

A small shuttle left the *Defiance* and headed toward the *Liberty*. Captain Demenar ordered a close pass of the ship. As they closed in, it was easy to see the horrific level of damage; the hull was blackened with scars. The door to one of the main guns was stuck partway open, the area around it pockmarked with buckled metal. The starboard docking bay's hull was breached, and toward the back he could see right through to the other side. What the captain was looking for most intently were markings—any markings that could indicate the origin of the ship. The starboard side was so severely damaged that he could not make out the lettering indicating the ship's name. Making a pass by the engines, he saw that one of the four was completely obliterated, leaving only a part of its nozzle still attached to the ship. As they rounded the rear of the craft toward the port side, the name came clearly into view—*Liberty*. This was the *Liberty*—Captain Dan was not lying! Demenar ordered his shuttle to land.

Already in the docking bay, the trio nervously stood waiting for their visitors. They watched the small craft pass through the force field, travel forward slowly, and come to rest about ten yards away from them. The side hatch opened, and out stepped three men. They definitely appeared human. No obvious differences—no third leg, antennas, or green skin. Two were dressed in gray suits with black boots; insignias decorated their arms and chests, seemingly to denote rank.

The man in the center wore a handsome blue uniform with well-tailored pants, black boots, and a three-quarter-length mandarin coat emblazoned with gold. This was Captain Demenar. He towered above the others and was built like a tank. Even with the uniform, it was clear that his arms were thick with well-developed muscles. If he lived on Earth there would be no question that he would have been a professional wrestler.

Demenar paused to look at the extensive damage in the landing bay, whispering something to his companions as his eyes trailed through the expansive space. Then, with brow furrowed, he directed his attention to Dan and his friends, slowly walking forward and stopping about five feet from them.

"Hello. Is Captain Foster onboard?"

"Yes. I am Captain Foster," announced Dan, prompting chuckles from Demenar and his two officers.

"With all the damage this ship has, it is amazing how you all can maintain your sense of humor. Now, really—where is Captain Foster?"

In a fit of instinct, Dan grabbed his wallet out of his pocket and handed his driver's license to Captain Demenar, who took it reluctantly. "No, look. That's me, Daniel Foster. I'm not joking."

Demenar's eyes got wide. He turned to his assistants to show them this driver's license. Janet, who knew something about first contact situations from her science fiction studies, cupped her hand and leaned into Dan's ear. "They can't read English. Guaranteed you just freaked them out."

Demenar handed the license back to Dan. "I do not recognize the language. Where are you from?"

Dan took a deep breath and sighed. It was time for the truth. It was the only way he could ask for and hopefully get their assistance to go home. So he started—started to tell his incredible story about his grandfather, the car, the fateful trip where they discovered the *Liberty*, and the skirmishes with the Gaarich. He showed them the car, which still rested in the docking bay, as proof. They listened, in either disbelief or amazement—it was difficult to tell.

"And we only wish to go home. That is the 100 percent truth, Captain." Dan looked at Demenar to gauge his reaction.

Demenar smiled and chuckled. "So the three of you were responsible for taking out two Gaarich marauders with a beaten and battered corvette that's been sitting idle for over fifty of your years." He burst into laughter, joined nervously by Dan, Tom, and Janet. "I believe you. This ship, the *Liberty*, was sent to Earth many years ago on an important mission—important to you, to me, and to the whole galaxy. Your grandfather is very famous, and there is a lot more to tell you, but time is not on our side. We need to get back to a safe quadrant." Demenar turned to his assistants. "Radio back to the *Defiance* that we will need a salvage crew to take the *Liberty* to safety. Once the crew, passengers, and cargo of the *Stoic 2* are secured, destroy it. Let's not leave anything for the Gaarich."

Demenar turned back toward the trio. "Have you eaten?"

"No, sir," replied Dan. "We haven't. And we've been here for almost two days."

"We did find crackers," said Tom triumphantly, as he grabbed some out of his cargo pants.

"We will take you back to the *Defiance* and get you some good food and much-needed rest." Captain Demenar motioned for them to follow him back to the shuttle. They stepped inside. It was very small. There was a seat for the pilot up front, and benches ran along both walls, with only enough room to hold about eight people, albeit not that comfortably. The three friends each found a place to sit. Captain Demenar poked his head out of the opening. "Zenmet, Tramier, wait for the shuttles from the salvage crew and coordinate. Remain aboard. Tramier, you will be in command of the *Liberty*."

Demenar's order caused a shock to run through Dan. He knew that he was not a real captain, but with everything they had been through the past several days, he felt as if the ship were his own. It had been his grandfather's, and he felt tied to it, but hunger and fatigue quickly wiped away the negative feeling. He looked over at Janet and Tom, who both had bags under their eyes from lack of sleep; the two projected the appearance of having been through a physically and emotionally challenging ordeal.

Captain Demenar sat in the pilot's seat and powered up the shuttle. He lifted off the deck and rotated it toward the force shield that led into space. "*Defiance*, this is *Shuttle 01*, leaving *Liberty* and heading home."

A response crackled over the radio. "*Defiance*, acknowledged *Shuttle 01*."

Demenar turned around and surveyed the three very exhausted teenagers. "Hey, by the way, you did great protecting the *Stoic 2*. It actually was quite unbelievable. I've never known one ship, let alone a severely damaged craft such as this, piloted by three so young as you, ever able to take on two Gaarich marauders."

Dan smiled and nodded as a gesture of a thank you. He was too tired to speak. He wanted to ask about the Gaarich—who they were and what they wanted. He wanted to ask about his grandfather and this very important mission that the *Liberty* was on, but fatigue clouded his thoughts, and he did not have the emotional stamina to handle the answers to his questions. Instead, he and his companions took a moment to rest in silence as the shuttle exited the *Liberty* and headed toward the *Defiance*.

The *Defiance* floated in space not far from their ship, flanked by two other identical corvettes. They appeared factory new, devoid of the *Liberty*'s battle scars. Lights shone from just about every visible deck. It was incredible to realize that they were teeming with life, just as the *Liberty* once had been.

"*Shuttle 01*, you are cleared to land."

Dan looked out the window as they flew past the starboard hull of the *Defiance*. The name and insignia were clear on the smooth, flowing hull. The beauty of its sculpted shape was emotionally breathtaking. As the shuttle skimmed toward the rear of the ship, Captain Demenar lined up with the starboard docking bay. He passed through the force shield into an area vibrant with life, a sharp contrast to the broken and battered landing area of the *Liberty*. All the fighters were tucked neatly into their launching cubicles. On the left were several shuttles being lowered by cranes for the awaiting salvage crews to board for the journey to the *Liberty*. The neatly arranged deck was alive with mechanics servicing varying ships. All the activity was exciting to see.

The Puzzle Clicks

The captain set the shuttle down gently and opened the door. He stepped out of the pilot's chair and walked back to where Dan, Janet, and Tom were sitting.

"Now, listen," said the captain. "You are my guests, but this is a military craft. Do not go wandering about without escort. The *Liberty* and its mission are central to our people's hope for salvation, and I do not want you bombarded with questions." This generated a confused reaction from all three teenagers. The captain responded, "In due time I will tell you everything, but now let us get you cleaned up." He motioned for them to step out of the shuttle.

As they emerged, three people waited for them—two men and one woman. Captain Demenar introduced them. "These three officers are your escorts. They will take you to your quarters so you can get cleaned up and fed. Afterward, I will sit with you in the main conference room, and we can talk. All right?" The three nodded in agreement.

"Tom, you will go with Lieutenant Kertich. Janet, you will go with Lieutenant Yerit, and Dan, you are with Commander Teitrik. I need to go back to the bridge to supervise the evacuation of the *Stoic 2* and salvage crew on the *Liberty*." The captain turned and walked toward the elevators.

"Well, welcome aboard the *Defiance*," said Commander Teitrik. "Those are very strange clothes. Well, no matter. We will get you fresh garments. Come with us."

As Janet, Tom, and Dan followed the commander to the elevators, they were greeted with confused glances and curious stares from the crew, who continued to look busy while examining their new passengers.

Janet, who hadn't said much since they met Captain Demenar, had a wonderful grin on her face. Her head rotated as she tried to take in all that was around her. This was much more than the lonely ship they had come from. It was alive with activity, and with people—not people from Earth, but *people* nonetheless.

As they approached the elevators, each pair took a different one. Dan stepped into his with the commander, who punched up their destination. As the doors closed, Dan realized that this was the first time after leaving Earth that he would not have his friends by his side. Although he knew nothing about these people he had just met, his instincts allowed him to trust them. They flew ships identical to his grandfather's, seemed to be from the same planet, and even had information about the *Liberty*'s mission.

Dan's escort, Commander Teitrik, was quiet and just stared blankly forward toward the elevator doors. Dan glanced over and gave him an awkward smile, reminiscent of those that strangers exchange when in an elevator. That did not seem to break the ice, so he tried conversation.

"So, where are we going?"

"I'm taking you to the guest quarters."

The discussion lasted a few seconds and did nothing to make Dan feel more at ease. Nothing was really going to make him feel better. This was a strange and awkward situation. He did not know how to act or even if he could shake hands with these people. There was no protocol that he could muster to assist him.

The door to the elevator opened, and the two stepped into the hall. From the map that Dan saw, he noticed that he was very near the bridge. Four rooms were accessible from the small hallway. Commander Teitrik ushered Dan into the nearest quarters on the right. The door opened into a well-equipped compartment, diminutive in size, but with everything a guest on the ship might need. On the left were a table with four chairs and a doorway leading to a private bathroom. Straight ahead was a cozy sitting area, separated from the sleeping quarters on the right by a small partition.

"There are clothes in the closet, and feel free to bathe, if you desire. If you need anything, just press the green button on the table, and someone will get it for you. I will be back in about two hours. That is how long it will take before we can leave this part of space. Rest up." The commander quickly walked out of the room, leaving Dan by himself.

The door slid closed, and Dan stood there in the middle of the room. The realization that he was alone for the first time since leaving Earth rattled through his head. The stillness and isolation, which should have been refreshing, were unpleasant. He looked at the bed, made his way over to it, and sat down. The softness felt good. He lay back, letting his body sink into the mattress as he gazed up at the ceiling. Dan and his friends were in pretty deep at this point, and he had no idea when he would see home again. He should have felt happy that they had made it this far and were alive, but he could not. The exhaustion was sweeping over him like a wave. He succumbed to the weight of his eyelids, allowing them to slide shut. A few moments later, he was asleep.

Call to Arms

P RESIDENT THOMPSON GOT THE CALL on the hotline just as he was meeting with the secretary of defense and the chairman of the Joint Chiefs on the situation with the International Space Station. General Peters had decided to invoke the Global Defense Pact. Near Earth Threat Operations had full discretion to use the pact if they deemed the situation to be of just consequence, and the president, along with the leaders of Russia and China, were to follow through with their respective tasks. When this pact was originally drafted, no one ever thought it would be used, but that was about to change.

"Bunk! Do I need to listen to this garbage?" asked the president.

Secretary of Defense Sandra Jackson turned to the commander in chief. "Not unless you want to anger the Russians and the Chinese. We agreed to this silly thing, and now we're stuck with it. Plus, I think General Peters may have a good idea here. At least it gives us some structure to deal with the situation at hand."

"Agreed," growled Admiral Lenny Davis, chairman of the Joint Chiefs. "They'll be wrapped up in the process, and it will help them deal with the blow. Heck, it will help me—all this alien bunk."

"Thank you," interrupted the president. "It's alien bunk, but we're stuck with it nonetheless. This could blow up big, and not only from the panic when people find out, but what if these things come back with bigger and stronger ships? Well, what then?"

"This is what I mean," added the admiral. "If they come back, what in the world do I throw at them? We have the strongest military force on Earth, and I have no piece of hardware that can go up against some flying green men."

"But you will mobilize everything we have and make it look like we do."

"Sir?"

"A show of force by us and our allies in this treaty will give our people confidence. This will give us the needed time to figure this thing out. It's all we have and is the best we can do, so we might as well do it." The president pressed the intercom on the phone. "Dave, bring me the action sheet for the Global Defense Pact." There was a slight chuckle as a response. "Don't laugh! This is serious. Get me the stupid action sheet and cut the comedy."

A few moments later the president's assistant quickly walked into the office with the action sheet and dropped it on his desk, leaving the room with haste. The president put on his glasses and examined the document, his lips moving slightly as he read.

Putting down the papers, he ripped the glasses from his head and looked over at the admiral. "Looks like I'm going to wake the Russian president and the Chinese premier out of bed on a conference call. Then you are going to go to Defcon 2 coordinated with our allies."

Admiral Davis reacted with a frustrated smirk. "Yes … sir. I will be awaiting your call." He stood up, acknowledged the secretary of defense, and left the room.

The president activated his intercom once again. "Dave, get me the secretary of state in here pronto—and I mean fifteen minutes from wherever he is in Washington. Send a copter or whatever. Just get it done."

"What else did it say?" asked Sandra Jackson.

"The three leaders are to make coordinated speeches to their nations on the situation. The lid is going to get blown wide open on this thing. I hope we know what we're doing."

Frustration

MARK WALTERS'S SPEECH TO HIS STAFF went over like a lead balloon. These scientists and technicians did not take it well when jackbooted thugs came storming into their workplace and took them hostage. Now they apparently were in control of the head guy, who gave a nice love-in speech about cooperating. What they didn't know was that this was part of Mark's strategy. He wanted his staff to get frustrated. Giving them this "just calm down" pep talk ensured that they would do the exact opposite, but moreover, they would be very secretive about it. Creativity would always win out against brute force.

Mark sat in his office trying to hack his way out through his computer. The Internet and all e-mail were disabled. The phones were out, and cellular calls were being blocked. Mark watched the activity from his office window and could see the NSA agents standing guard, ensuring that no one could come or go.

There was a knock at the office door. It was Betty Tedesci, a senior project manager and his technical assistant. She walked in clutching her signature clipboard. "Mark, nice speech out there, but you know that nerds and black helicopters don't mix. You watched the *X Files*."

Mark chuckled and motioned for her to shut the door. "That's what I'm countin' on. They're so ticked off right now that they'll do just about anything to get back in contact with the ISS. Just take a look."

Betty peered out the office window and was now able to understand what Mark was talking about. There was a carnival of activity out on the floor, but to the untrained eye, it did not look any more like casual conversations and innocuous systems diagnostics. A smile crept across her face as she realized what was happening. The staff were resisting in their own passive-aggressive way, eager to show these NSA types, and even the boss, that if they wanted to know what was going on, they sure as heck were going to find out.

"So, do you think our *escorts* will notice anything?"

"Ah, doubtful. Did they ever watch the *X Files*?" They both snickered. Mark continued, "Betty, I want you to keep an eye on what's going on. If someone gets something, I want you to send them in here right away, but don't make it look too suspicious. Also, if any of our new friends out there get curious, distract them."

She sighed. "All right, but I hate being the middle man. Our technicians don't know that we know ... and the NSA doesn't know ... but we're supposed to keep them both confused. I think I've got it ... sort of."

"Good. I'll do my part and thin out the herd a bit."

"What do you mean? You aren't going to shoot any—"

"No ... no, just send in Agent Wachovic. I have a little request."

Betty looked at Mark with a puzzled glance. "Fine. I'll page the goon squad for you." She walked out of the room.

A few moments later Agent Wachovic appeared from the main control room. "Mr. Walters, what can I do for you?"

"Well, you said that you could get us anything we needed to be comfortable. Correct?"

"Yes, you are not hostages. What would you like?"

Mark threw a pad and pen across the desk. "Better write this down. We have a lot of hungry technicians out there, and I bet you guys could use something to eat also."

"We should be fine, but thank you." Agent Wachovic took the pad and pen.

Mark began, "We'll need about ten dozen donuts—make sure you mix and match; we have a lot of varied tastes—four buckets of fried chicken, some hot wings from Mrs. Dees downtown, and twelve pizzas from Maroneys. We have pop and stuff in the break room, but why don't you bring back a couple of six packs too?"

Agent Wachovic stopped writing after the donuts. "Sir, we are not a delivery service."

Mark stood up and pointed an angry finger at the agent. "Listen, you said you would make us comfortable and get us what we needed. At this point I have cooperated and got my staff to do the same. Now you are giving me grief about food! What, do you expect those folks out there to starve? Have you ever seen a starved tech? Well, you don't want to. So I suggest you get a couple of your goons to go out and pick this stuff up."

Agent Wachovic slowly rose from his chair, locking on to Mark's eyes. The two merely stared at each other. Wachovic had a stern and angry look, seemingly trying to intimidate Walters, who didn't flinch. Frustration at the boiling point, the agent picked up the pad and wrote down the rest of the request from memory. He turned and walked out of Mark's office, slamming the door upon his retreat.

The corners of Mark's mouth slowly turned upward in a smile as he sat back down in his chair, putting his hands behind his head in relaxation and triumph. He had gotten rid of some of the agents on their little mission—a few less eyes prying at his staff. It was now up to them.

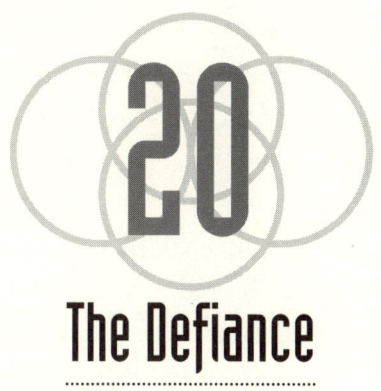

The Defiance

Dan's footsteps echoed through the hall as he ran. His sneakers drummed a distinctive sound as they impacted the cold tile floor, the noise bounding against the metal school lockers. He could not believe that he'd forgotten; he had been gone so long. Slowing his pace enough to grab the doorknob to the classroom, Dan gave it a slight turn and pulled it open to reveal a class well in the middle of their midterm exam. This was physics, and Dan desperately needed to study, but he forgot. Sweat poured down his brow as he made his way inside. His classmates shot him a myriad of surprised glances as an angry teacher glared at him from behind her desk.

Dan could hear the echo of every single breath rattle through his skull. The clock read 11:00 a.m.—only one hour to complete a two-hour exam. He turned to see the teacher handing him his test and silently pointing at the time with a judgmental frown.

Dan clutched the paper and moved quickly to an open desk. He sat down and wiped his damp forehead. With dread and anticipation, he opened the exam, but it was blank. He turned one page, then the next, then the next—nothing. He glanced over at the girl sitting next to him. She was feverishly writing, but no ink was coming out of the end of her pen. The page was blank, and she was writing nothing. He looked over and saw the same on the paper of the boy to his left.

Then there was a beeping—a constant beeping. Where could …

Dan opened his eyes; a rush of adrenaline surged through his body. The beeping was someone at the door. He must have fallen asleep. He was still on the *Defiance* and dressed in the clothes he came aboard with. The beeping was incessant.

"You all right in there?" asked a muffled voice from the hall.

"Uh, yeah," answered Dan.

"Are you ready? We are going to meet your friends to get something to eat."

No, Dan wasn't ready. He had been sleeping and now would have to scramble. His hair was greasy, as he hadn't bathed in quite a while.

"Just … um … just give me a minute." Dan quickly undressed and scurried into the bathroom. As he walked in, the lights turned themselves on and presented him with fixtures very similar to those he had seen in the crew's quarters back on the *Liberty*. He knew how to use the toilet, but not the shower, and he desperately needed a shower. There was a small enclosure that looked like it might fulfill the purpose. Dan stepped inside and shut the door. He only saw one button—this had to be easy. He took a deep breath, closed his eyes, and pressed it. A blast of warm air surrounded him. He kept his eyes closed as he felt small particles hitting his body, like someone blowing talcum powder through a leaf blower. Next was a blast of steam. This got him damp enough that he used his hands to rub his face and body. Another blast of steam was followed by a bright glow that quickly evaporated the moisture from his skin.

Well, that wasn't so bad. Dan stepped out of the shower. As strange as it was, he felt better and cleaner. The only problem appeared when he looked into the mirror; his hair was standing straight up. Frantically he rummaged around for anything that would do as a comb. Plenty of grooming gadgets were available, but unrecognizable as anything resembling what he needed. Instead, Dan wetted his palms and tried the old finger grooming technique. It was not perfect but would have to do.

The beeping at the door started again, followed by the muffled voice, now sounding more agitated. "Listen, we need to go. Are you ready?"

"Just one more minute," answered Dan as he sped out of the bathroom and over to the closet. As he opened the door, a very neatly arranged wardrobe of clothes greeted him. Hanging up were several pairs of pants in the uniform gray color with a corresponding tuniclike shirt. Dan found some that seemed to be the right size and put them on. The fabric felt good, and the neatly tailored lines made him look very nice. He found some boots in the closet of the appropriate size and pulled them on over a pair of clean socks.

Dan finally opened the door. Waiting anxiously outside was Commander Teitrik. "Okay, I'm ready."

The commander looked him over. "You smell better, and those clothes don't look as strange as yours. You almost blend in ... but what is wrong with your hair?"

Dan quickly ran his hands through it to try to improve the look. "Well, just a bad hair day, I guess."

"No matter. Come with me. We will be meeting your friends in a private dining room for some food. Afterward you can come up to the bridge and observe the jump from there."

Dan looked puzzled. "Maybe this translator thing isn't working, but did you say jump? I thought it was referred to as slide."

The commander chuckled. "Let's get going, and I will explain." The two walked toward the elevator, boarded it, and headed toward their destination. Commander Teitrik continued, "There have been many advancements since the *Liberty* went on its mission. The old ships slid through a wormhole, as you apparently already know.

There was no way to get a reference from hyperspace to normal space. Without precalculating the 'slide,' there was no safe way to enter or exit. A ship would simply get lost and risk exiting at any random point in space—even inside an object like a star or planet. Since then we've developed tracking technology that uses discrepancies in natural radio and magnetic forces in normal space as, well, beacons. We can use these as references in hyperspace so we know exactly where we are at all times. Therefore, our ships now simply jump into hyperspace and can freely navigate in complete safety. Plus, it gives us a great tactical advantage."

"You and the captain keep referring to the *Liberty*'s great mission. What's that all about?"

"Let's get some food in you. Once we jump out of here, the captain will explain everything."

The elevator deposited Dan into a small reception area. Beyond, double doors opened into an ornate dining room. The main table was rectangular and could easily seat ten or more people. A large window faced Dan as he entered. It shone out into space, where he could see the *Liberty* floating off in the distance. Tom and Janet were already there, dressed in the same outfit as Dan, with hair no more neatly groomed than his.

"Looks like you guys found the shower," Dan joked.

"You too, buddy," said Tom. "Nice hair."

"But, hey, aren't these clothes comfortable?" queried Janet. "They're smooth as silk. I wonder if they would let us take them home."

Dan looked around. "Where did our handlers go?"

"I don't know. Dhashti just told us to wait here," said Janet.

"Who's Dhashti?" asked Dan, a little puzzled.

"Oh, that's Lieutenant Yerit—my handler, as you said. She's really neat."

Dan frowned. "Great ... you're on a first-name basis. My guy dumped me in the room, and that's about it. I would like the cute alien next time."

"Did you talk about anything?" asked Tom.

"Yeah, we don't slide anymore—we jump, or something."

"Wow!" exclaimed Janet. "You have to tell us."

Dan sighed and looked up at the ceiling. "Listen, I am so sick of talking tech stuff."

"Yeah, well, that tech stuff saved our butts."

"I know, but I wouldn't mind a break from it for just a few minutes."

"Too bad," said Tom. "Cough it up. We get a break when we get home."

Dan did not like getting lectured, especially from Tom, but looking at the eager and inquisitive Janet, he began his tale. He spoke word for word about jumping as Commander Teitrik had told him. When he finished, Janet reacted with her trademark enthusiasm.

"Awesome! So they have even newer stuff!"

Janet was interrupted by one of the crew entering the room with three bowls. The trio sat down, and the crewman put a bowl in front of each of them. The bread was placed in the center of the table, and water filled their glasses. They each reached for a spoon and started to eat.

"Whoa, this is really really good!" exclaimed Tom.

"It's white, like chowder, but tastes like tomato soup. Only better," added Dan.

They slurped through the bowls of soup like ravenous puppies after an afternoon of gallivanting around the yard. They tore at the bread and chugged through the water. For the first time in days, they felt full.

Commander Teitrik entered the room. "Well, I hope you feel better." The trio nodded. "Please follow me up to the bridge."

They followed the commander to the elevator and up to the reception area near the bridge. An opulent insignia scrolled with the name of the *Defiance* hung proudly on the wall by the four elevators, just as on the *Liberty*. Walking toward the overlook, they were greeted with a bridge very similar to the one where they had spent so many of the past few hours, but this one was different. It hummed with activity and was bursting with crew engrossed in their assigned tasks. The two levels lining the walls were filled with officers attending to their stations. Just below, they could see Captain Demenar seated in his chair. Both consoles in front of him were manned, as was the helm lower down. He turned and waved for his guests to join him. They walked down the stairs and stood near the hub of all the activity.

"Now, that looks better," said the captain, commenting on their wardrobe. "Are your quarters adequate?"

"Yes," said Dan, answering for his crew. "And the food was really good." Tom and Janet gave agreeable nods.

"Fine, then. If you would excuse me." Captain Demenar turned his attention to the tactical officer. "Is the *Liberty* ready to slide yet?"

"Yes, sir. They are powered up and ready to go."

"Bring her up on the screen and open a channel," said the captain.

The tactical officer executed the order. The *Liberty* could now be seen up on the screen. Even though they had only been aboard the ship for a brief time, for Dan, Janet, and Tom it felt strange to see someone else piloting her.

"*Liberty*, this is the *Defiance*—you are cleared to slide."

"*Liberty* acknowledged."

The Defiance

A glow appeared from the *Liberty*'s aft section. She accelerated away in a streak of light and disappeared. A distant flash indicated her entrance into hyperspace.

"Weapons, fire one missile to destroy the *Stoic 2*," ordered the captain.

The officer at the tactical station answered with an affirmative and launched a single missile toward the *Stoic 2*, which lay dead in space. The viewscreen focused on the awkward ship as it broke apart and disintegrated in a flare of white light.

"Helm, let's get out of here."

Dan watched to see if the jump procedure was anything like what they did on the *Liberty*. It was not. The captain simply had to give the order. The helmsman was in complete control as the ship accelerated toward the speed of light. The stars streaked by as the *Defiance* opened her window into hyperspace with a colorless flash. When they passed through the event horizon, they were greeted not by the shimmer of a wormhole, but only by strange blackness. No stars sparkled in the black depths, and the only luminance came from blue and green misty gases that swirled freely in the dark void. This was hyperspace.

Captain Demenar stood up. "We are on our way now. Let's go into the conference room to talk, as there is so much to talk about."

The captain, Commander Teitrik, and the teenage trio headed into the executive conference room behind the bridge. This again looked very similar to the one on the *Liberty*, but there were minor differences in the equipment that dotted the space. This was to be expected, considering this ship's technological innovations over the past several decades.

Captain Demenar sat at the head of the table near the entrance to his office, with the commander to his right. Dan grabbed a chair to his left, with Tom and Janet taking opposite facing seats. The captain motioned to a security officer who had entered the room. "Secure the doors and stand outside. We will be here a while." The officer left, and the captain turned to the teenagers and smiled.

"Earth. Incredible. You are the first Earthlings I have met. I'm sorry I could not be so forthcoming before. The *Liberty* is a legend and a symbol of hope for my people. She was not to return as she did, but she has returned, and the fact that you were onboard was also very unexpected."

Dan thought he should say something. "Listen, I can assure you that—"

Captain Demenar interrupted. "You have said enough, my young friend. I believe your story. Now I have one to tell, and I wish you to extend to me the same faith I have offered you."

The three nodded.

"The experiences you have had over the past several days cannot have prepared you for what I am about to reveal, but you must know. I am sorry that I may change your view of your planet and your people. The perception you Earthlings have of the universe is so small. You are just taking your first steps and should not be expected to run, but run you must. There is a peril that is greater than anything you could envision. This peril brought the *Liberty* to your world and us to this meeting.

"We are from a planet called Daemerik. It is the fifth planet from our sun in a solar system about seventy light years from yours. We are human, like you—in fact, exactly like you, but our lifespan is longer. Our ancient history speaks of the universe being seeded with 'bones of the elders.' My people have long held the belief that humans and humanoid creatures evolved from this seed that was cast across the universe. Several centuries ago we began to explore space in search of others like us. What we found was fascinating. We met several worlds with humans—some more advanced than us, and some less. But what was truly inspiring was the other intelligent life that also evolved from this seed. They were humanlike but had other characteristics due to their unique evolution, but yet were still related. We fought some wars, as you may imagine, made friends, enemies, as the story goes; yet for the most part we were at peace. Then, about 150 years ago, our people started to hear rumors about an invading force spreading across our section of the galaxy. One by one we lost contact with several worlds. We would send ships to investigate, never to return.

"Then one day, on a joint exploratory mission with the Votraxain, we met them for the first time. They were fast and vicious. Our ships barely escaped, and both of the Votraxain vessels were destroyed. This race—the Gaarich—were insect-based life forms that had no interest in peace, only conquest. They spread over the galaxy like a plague, taking over world after world and enslaving the inhabitants to work for them, looting the planets they conquered of all available resources."

Dan and Tom glanced at each other. They were both sharing the identical vision—Tom's little experiment with his ant farms, Rome and Athens.

Captain Demenar continued, "We fought side by side with the Votraxain when their world was invaded, but we were no match. We lost many ships, and the entire Votraxain battle fleet was destroyed. We had to fall back to Daemerik. We had time until they came for us, but no allies to help. All of our friends, even our enemies were overrun. The Gaarich established a firm foothold on a planet before they moved to another. So we built up our fleet and put all of our efforts into defending our homeworld. Then they came. Relentless and brutal, they destroyed ship after ship—outpost after outpost. We fought and held the line for some time, but we could not hold out against their seemingly unlimited resources.

"This takes us to fifty years ago. Your grandfather, whom we knew as Commander Meikre Jostak, was the captain of a small frigate called the *Horot*. He and four others were escorting a damaged corvette back to Daemerik. The corvette had a damaged hyperdrive and could not sustain a wormhole for more than three light years. The ship needed to stop to cool its engines before sliding again. They emerged out of their second slide in a remote part of space right in the middle of the main Gaarich battle fleet. The vicious enemy pounced on them immediately. Your grandfather quickly ordered the other ships to surround the corvette. In an unheard-of feat of resourcefulness, he linked the systems of all the frigates and the corvette together, pulling the collective strength of the smaller ships into the firepower of a much larger craft. In addition, the ring of frigates around the corvette acted as an additional shield to protect the beleaguered craft. With great bravery and aggression, this mass of ships leaped directly for the largest concentration of vessels, hoping to cause as much confusion and chaos as possible. All that your grandfather needed was enough time for the corvette to cool down so they could slide out. The bombardment was terrible, and two of the frigates were quickly destroyed, leaving the *Horot*, the *Nitrae*, the *Detri*, and the damaged corvette. Adequate time had finally passed for the corvette to cool enough for a short jump. Your grandfather ordered the others to slide. He and the *Horot* would remain to ensure their escape was successful. The surviving ships quickly slid away and eventually made it back to Daemerik, but there was no sign of the *Horot*.

"The news of the rallying Gaarich fleet was critical information, delivered to our forces weeks before the attack would begin, giving needed time to prepare. The word of Commander Jostak's heroic actions spread throughout Daemerik. In this time of gloom, our world desperately needed heroes, and your grandfather definitely earned that mark. Days and weeks passed, but the *Horot* was not heard from. The ship and its crew were officially pronounced lost in action.

"The fleet that ringed our home planet was preparing for the great battle, which all knew would be the final fight before invasion.

As the ships were getting ready, the *Horot* appeared out of hyperspace to the surprise and delight of all. The frigate could barely fly and had sustained horrible casualties, but yet, under Jostak's command, it came home. The fact they had returned alive was a miracle.

"Celebration was short, as the menace of the Gaarich approached. Your grandfather was quickly summoned to the capital in front of the Magnicieat—our great council. The words that would then touch his ears must have torn at his soul.

"The Magnicieat had decided that there was no point in fighting the Gaarich. In their minds, Daemerik had already been beaten. The invasion was not much more than a formality, as the fleet was decimated, and what remained would have been no match for the full Gaarich invasion force. It was more important to evacuate as many people as they could and move what remained of the once grand fleet out of the area. For them, the war was over.

"But for him—for now *Captain* Meikre Jostak, the war would go on. He was to take some of the top scientists with him on a new experimental corvette called the *Liberty*. His mission was to seek out our only hope and only possible remaining allies—you—Earthlings. He was to take this ship, along with all of our knowledge, to Earth, integrate into your society, and determine what would be necessary to bring your technological and social consciousness to a level where you could not only defend yourselves, but also hopefully come to our aid and the aid of our other brothers in the cosmos.

"The *Liberty* had a prototype cloaking device to hide itself from the Gaarich. It was developed by Jetr Tyl, daughter of one of our most famous scientists, Romatt Tyl. This was the only one of its kind.

"Your grandfather was to head to the ship immediately and prepare it for departure. It was already loaded with most of the equipment and a good cross-section of the planned passengers.

His mission was to leave in two days for Earth, cloak the ship behind the moon, and take the crew down to Earth.

"He immediately made for the *Liberty*, which was still in the shipyards down on the surface of Daemerik. The next day, as he was preparing the ship, the invasion started. The Gaarich invasion fleet was so enormous that it created shadows like clouds on the surface of our planet. Without haste, the bombardment began.

"The *Liberty* was caught defenseless on the ground. Under Captain Jostak's command they raced to power up the reactors and break the *Liberty* from her moorings, but it was too late. An orbital strike began to rip her hull apart as she lay helpless on the ground. Not all the scientists were aboard, and they only had a skeleton crew, yet they were able to get the *Liberty* free. She sped toward the heavens, getting struck by salvo after salvo, her shields inoperative. Most of the damage you saw occurred as she was leaving the atmosphere. Once the *Liberty* got out into space, the cloaking device was engaged, and she disappeared."

Dan had been holding his breath for the entire story. He remembered his grandfather, the way he looked, the way he moved, even the sound of his voice, but he could not quite grasp the awesome importance of his mission and legendary status to his people. To Dan he was always Grandpa, but to Captain Demenar and the people of Daemerik he was their last hope. Their very survival as a people rested upon him, his mission, and an untested ship. Dan could feel the waves of emotion creating goose pimples all up and down his body. He did not look to see his friends' reactions; he just sat there in awe. Dan had already had great respect for his grandfather, but now the profound depth of the respect was unequaled.

It had not only been him. The whole room was silent. Captain Demenar and Commander Teitrik were holding back their own emotional reactions, and the three teenagers were each containing their own feelings. The story meant something different for each of them. For the Daemerae it described the end of their world and their greatest hope for salvation. For Dan, the story told an aspect of his grandfather that he could never imagine, and for Tom and Janet, the tale woke their young minds up to the fact that they were not alone in the universe—not alone and definitely not secure.

Up until now, Dan, Tom, and Janet had simply been trying to get home, but home was a place they could no longer go. They'd found out that the galaxy is filled with other humans and humanoid species, people who were no longer free and were under the rule of a terrible insect-based race—the Gaarich. It was only a matter of time before they came to Earth, before they would enslave and conquer their friends and family. Their concerns from only two days ago now seemed so small—good grades, sports scores, who was dating whom, and so on. It all was so trivial compared to what experiences had introduced themselves into their lives, and moreover, what knowledge and wisdom they had attained.

Dan directed his attention to the captain. "Sir, I'm honored and humbled to be related to someone like my grandfather. He told me nothing of this, and my family knows nothing. He … he died before he could tell us."

"Dan, I am sorry for your—for our loss," responded Demenar. "He was a great man, but there is no time for sadness. The Gaarich had previously been to Earth, according to our intelligence, but did not denote your planet as a threat. Rest assured, they would come when the time was right, but they had plenty of resources from our home planet and the others they had conquered. Those Gaarich you encountered were scouts. Now that they have seen a Daemerik corvette near Earth, they will attack to neutralize any threat."

"So, when we decloaked the ship, we attracted these Gaarich, and now that they've seen the *Liberty*, they think that Earth is a possible threat?" asked Janet.

"Unfortunately, yes," answered Commander Teitrik. "By awakening the *Liberty*, you have put your planet at risk, and we don't have the forces to mount a defense against Earth. We only have one fully functional battle cruiser, with the other still suffering severe battle damage she incurred fifty years ago."

"Well, we need to do something," implored Dan. "Earth is our home!"

Captain Demenar leaned across the table. "Listen, we have been fighting these last fifty years just to stay alive. We have been living in space, on small outposts, and running to keep one step ahead of the Gaarich. We are in no shape to stand up to them. Anyway, it is not up to me. I cannot make the decision. We will have to discuss this once we make it home." He snickered, "Home, for what it is."

With that the captain stood up, acknowledged the three friends, and headed back to the bridge, followed by Commander Teitrik. He left Dan, Janet, and Tom to sit and absorb what they had heard.

The air in the room was heavy. The realization that their world was in danger, and knowing it was partially their fault, was much more than the three teenagers could handle. Everything else they had heard was enough to overwhelm anyone, but this additional bit of data added a terrible dimension to their predicament.

"How screwed are we?" asked Tom.

"Well, you see the technology these Daemerae have? It's way more advanced than anything on Earth," said Dan, "and if they got their butts kicked by these Gaarich, well, you do the math."

"The math stinks!" exclaimed Janet.

"But the heck with the math!" Dan shouted. "I mean, just think for a minute. Look at the impossible odds we had to deal with to get this far. Not too long ago we were in the car, totally freaked out, but we figured it out. We pulled our heads together and figured it out. We may be far from home, but we're alive, and that says something."

"You do have a point," added Janet, her lips curling up in a smile.

"Could say we're lucky," countered Tom.

Dan responded, "I don't think so. We were way more than lucky. We used our brains and took chances. Think about it. Every great person in history took a great risk against incredible odds. Some made it out, and others didn't, but that effort said something about the person and also about the people of Earth. We don't stand and take it, and I won't now."

Janet and Tom nodded to themselves as they contemplated Dan's words.

"Just give me some time," said Dan softly. "Let's keep our minds open to the opportunities that may present themselves."

21
Preparation

AMERICAN MILITARY FACILITIES AROUND THE GLOBE received the order to go to Defense Condition 2 and wait for additional instructions. Bombers lifted off from the ground, fighter planes began their patrols, missile silos hunkered down, and nuclear submarines went to their designated firing points. The initial emotional reaction from all U.S. forces was confusion. The threat of global nuclear war had waned with the end of the Cold War between the former Soviet Union and the United States, and the regional conflicts regarding the current war on terrorism would not warrant such a strong response. The next orders transmitted were the most puzzling and continued to fuel rumor and speculation. These orders required that all missiles have their targeting coordinates reset and that firing solutions would be given, if launch was deemed imminent, by Near Earth Threat Operations, Cheyenne Mountain. Because this effectively erased the missiles' preprogrammed attack coordinates, they would, if launched, simply fly off into space and float away into the cosmos once they expired of fuel. Why would NETO, a secretive arm of the air force that was more political joke than serious command, have the authority to determine missile firing targets? This response was anticipated, and the queries from commanders around the globe were given the same response—this was an invocation of the Global Defense Pact, and they would have to wait for the speech by the commander in chief.

Back inside Cheyenne Mountain, General Peters was very busy. Since he had requested the implementation of the Global Defense Pact, he had spoken to practically every superior officer at the Pentagon; each one of the Joint Chiefs; and even the commander of NORAD, with which NETO shared the Cheyenne Mountain Facility. He also had to coordinate with the Russian and Chinese space agencies to share information and together monitor the situation in orbit. Captain Dillings was in charge of making sure the three operations were communicating. The Russian and Chinese agencies had English-speaking leaders, making the task of sharing information much easier.

Captain Dillings entered the general's office while he was on the phone.

"No," grumbled the general into the mouthpiece. "No, listen, did you ... no ... wait ... hold on a minute! Did you read the action sheet? Good! So now you know that I only deal with the president directly and my counterparts in China and Russia. That is it ... no ... no ... all right, fine, but if he gets in the way, I'm going to shoot him as a threat to national security." He slammed down the phone and looked up at the captain.

"That putz General Davidson from NORAD wants to send one of his colonels down as an observer. Tell you what—put him at a terminal and tell him to shut up and stay out of the way. We have way too much going on to have some hot shot asking questions."

"Yes, sir," Dillings responded. "Pentagon has reported that we are at Defcon 2. The EA is in flight and is codenamed Alice. That is your contact for adjusting force locations and communicating firing solutions. President will have to give the launch codes."

"Good. How are Majors Jensen and Vodnikov?"

PREPARATION

"They are fine and have been reporting in every thirty or so minutes. They are making minor repairs to the ISS, just trying to keep busy. I think that given a few quiet moments to think about their predicament ... I would lose it in that situation."

"Bull! You're a tough lady, Captain!" exclaimed Peters, prompting Dillings to blush. "Anyway, I need you here, not on some space science station."

"Thank you. Sir, have you had any luck with the Russians? Do they have a rocket with which they could mount a rescue?"

"No, they are fourteen days out from having one fueled and ready to go."

"I am concerned about the condition of the station. We don't have the tools here to diagnose if there are any major structural problems."

"No, I'm not getting those NASA folks involved just yet. They love to go to the press, and we have to keep the lid on this until the president speaks in a few hours. After that, I don't care. Give them what they need for access, but not until then."

"Yes, sir." Captain Dillings expected that answer, but still needed to express her concern at NETO's lack of system support access to the station.

"What have the forces been told exactly about moving to Defcon 2?"

"Nothing, really. They have been told it is regarding the Global Defense Pact and that there is no impending action against any specific country," answered the captain.

"That has to be driving them nuts. I know that NORAD is all over my butt about it. I can only imagine what games the Joint Chiefs are playing. We are not as good at rumor maintenance as the Russians and Chinese."

"Speaking about rumors, several reports about going to Defcon 2 have surfaced in the media. The cover story is about a drill. Hopefully it will hold out," added the captain. "Regarding our *allies*, they have provided us with a link to their systems, and we have a rather good tactical view of the near space situation. We will be able to see if anything large is approaching."

"What about small ships, like those that attacked the ISS?" asked the general.

"That is the main concern right now. Until we are allowed to pull more people into this officially, we do not have the comprehensive network a coordinated effort with the civilian agencies can offer."

General Peters sat in his chair, his brow crinkled in thought. He wanted to get assistance. He would have loved to get the help of NASA or the European Space Agency. No doubt they would have the minds to help. They might have even had aliens working on their staffs, for all he knew. Yet he realized the best thing to ensure that there was some measured control over the operation required the restraint he was employing.

"Captain." The general looked up at her. "For now, just keep them clueless, and let's hope our friends at the NSA are keeping a tight lid on Houston."

22

Issues

IT ACTUALLY WORKED. Mark Walters got Agent Wachovic to send out some of his NSA team for the food he had requested. The NSA was apparently in a tight situation. Normally these black helicopter types would simply gas the room and knock everyone out for a few hours, but there must have been a whole boatload of political baggage on the order to lock down NASA, and this Mark could use to his advantage.

His computer was useless, completely blocked from any outside access. So Mark just looked out his office window into the command center, watching his staff ever so subtly trying to hack the blocks in the hopes of finding out the International Space Station's status.

Betty had herself positioned in such a way as to observe the goings on. If she caught any brief expression of joy or accomplishment from anyone in the command center, she would act. Her gaze moved from across the room to the agents standing watch. The NSA types did not look threatened at all. They probably thought that they could hold this room of pocket protector-clad scientists with a stick and some stern words. So they relaxed, joked with one another, and all but ignored the defiance and deception occurring right under their noses.

Betty kept a particular eye on Marcus Washington. He was the youngest and probably most brilliant member of the team. Fresh out of the Massachusetts Institute of Technology, Marcus grew up in a tough neighborhood in Washington, D.C. His father was a cab driver whose only dream was to have his son go to a good school. Marcus made his dad proud, earning a scholarship to MIT, where he did his undergraduate and graduate work. He interned at NASA in his junior year, and ever since then the agency planned to hire him right after he finished school. Marcus had an offer in hand months before graduation, but he did not rest on his laurels. He finished at the top of his class.

Marcus loved music—all types of music, made evident by the headphones to his digital music player, which seemed to be permanently attached to his ears. When he was close to a breakthrough or any significant discovery, he had a propensity to *groove* to the music. This head bopping was what Betty was waiting for.

It didn't take long. From her angle, Betty could see Marcus's head starting to move and a slight grin emerge on his face. This was her cue. She stood up only to see one of the NSA agents heading straight for him.

Argh! Betty made her way quickly over to his station.

"Hey." The agent tapped Marcus on the shoulder. "Hey, what are you listening to?"

The agent's touch ripped Marcus from his concentration. He turned and looked up nervously at the agent, hoping the gun-toting goon would not see what he was doing at his terminal. "What?" Marcus asked as he pulled an earphone away from his ear, the music now slightly more audible to those in close vicinity.

"What are you listening to?" asked the agent again.

"Uh, just some Tower of Power. Good seventies funk always keeps me awake on the weekends."

The agent snickered. "What? That's way before your time."

This annoyed Marcus, who pulled the headphones off completely. "What do you mean? Are you saying I can't appreciate a good slap bass line because I wasn't around when bellbottoms were popular—the first time?"

"No, I was just trying to make conversation," defended the agent.

Betty interrupted the two and shot the agent a quick sarcastic smile. "I'm sorry." She looked down at Marcus. "Listen, Mr. Washington, we told you about wearing headphones at work, but you continue to do it."

Marcus looked puzzled. "Wait wait wait ... what? You never—"

"Get up," ordered Betty. "We're going to speak to Mark about this once and for all!" She grabbed Marcus by the arm and hoisted him out of the chair. She again smiled at the agent as she escorted a confused Marcus Washington into Mark Walters's office.

The two entered the office, Marcus's face still wrought with confusion. Betty motioned for him to take a seat in front of Mark's desk. He did so as she closed the door.

"Now, listen, what's this about?" asked Marcus in agitation. "Betty, you never said anything about my headphones until now. What—"

"Calm down, son," interrupted Walters. "Just tell us what you found."

Marcus's eyes got big. "Nothing. I found nothing ... okay?"

"Bull!" said Mark. "Spill it!"

Marcus paused and wet his lips, looking over Mark and Betty one more time just to make sure that they were sincere in their request. "Well, it's not much, but I was able to get a systems diagnostic from the ISS."

"Good man!" exclaimed Walters in muffled excitement.

"Well, don't get too happy. The entry/exit module is damaged. I'm getting red on multiple systems in that area, including enough data to indicate structural damage."

Mark shook his head. "Oh, no. How bad?"

"Don't know. Officer tough guy out there came over just as I was digging deeper, but what I did see didn't look all that great."

Mark slumped back into his chair, mulling what to do next. He could not send Marcus back out onto the floor and have him constantly coming into the office with updates. It would be too obvious. There had to be another way.

"Betty, time to get distracting," said Walters. "I need you to go out there and keep those agents from looking over this way. I don't want to shut the shades, as it would be too obvious that we're being sneaky. Just keep them occupied."

Betty was a little miffed. "What, do you want me to show them some leg or French kiss them?"

"Listen, I'm not asking you to go out there and make out with them," Mark grumbled. "I just want you to keep them from looking in here while Mr. Whiz Kid," he winked at Marcus, "finishes the diags on my computer. Got it?"

Betty shook her finger at Mark and strained to get the answer out. "Fine ... fine, but you owe me lattes for a year." She opened the office door and marched out into the command center.

"Now, Mr. Washington, get over here and finish your diagnostics."

Marcus stood up and went behind Walters's desk. Mark yielded his chair so the tech wiz could get to work.

Walters turned his gaze to the NSA agents. Betty struck up a conversation with them, and based on how bored they had appeared for the last few hours, this distraction seemed a welcome event. Betty had a genuinely outgoing personality, and she easily got three of the agents drawn into her discussion. The fourth was at an angle where he could not see directly into Mark's office—mission accomplished.

Marcus pecked away at the keyboard, brought up a remote of his terminal, and motioned Walters over.

"Hey, you're not supposed to be able to remote into your station," said Walters with a smile on his face.

Marcus was too busy to pay any attention to the joke; he just pored over the data. The look of concern grew as his eyes scanned the monitor.

"Whoa," he said, while his gaze remained locked on the screen.

"What?" asked Walters.

"Well, do you want the good news or the bad news?"

"Cut the clichés!" barked Walters. "What's up?"

"The good news is I see Major Vodnikov's and Major Jensen's vitals. They're alive. I have no data on the condition of the escape module and zero telemetry history or flight data. It cuts off after we saw the blip disappear."

Walters already knew they were gone. It was the only event that could have precipitated such a paranoid response as the NSA locking down Mission Control. It was nonetheless hard to hear.

"What's the condition of the station?" asked Walters.

"It got banged up pretty bad. Like I said before, the entry/exit module that allows the crew access to space walks and supply craft is heavily damaged. The whole section is losing air. From the looks of it, they have it isolated from the rest of the station, but there's a problem."

Mark motioned with his hands for him to continue.

"You know those solar panels that they've been experimenting with on the station?"

"Yeah, how can I forget? It took three spacewalks to get those things attached and secured."

"Well, they're only four feet square, but just two of them can provide more than enough power for the ISS. If they work, it will be a boon for both the solar industry and the space agency. We wouldn't have to have gargantuan panels extending all over the place."

"And the point is?"

"The tremendous amount of power has been fusing the relays. They've been juggling with this for several weeks now. Normally, this isn't a big deal. They're simply able to manually disconnect them from the power grid to avoid an overload. Our problem is that the scientists were in the middle of an experiment with the panels, but they evacuated the station before disconnecting them from the grid. When the ISS passed around to the light side of the planet, the relays fused again, but the manual release is in the section that's venting air."

"What's going to happen—worst case?"

"It's not worst case, Mark. It *will* happen. A couple more passes around Earth, and the panels are going to overload and feed an immense surge directly into the station's power grid. That thing will go up like a Roman candle."

"Do they know this?" Mark asked with a concerned tone.

"Doubtful. Since it's just an experiment, status is not routed through C&C. We never planned on any redundancy. They're not going to know until it's too late."

For Mark, the worst-case scenarios kept flooding in. He had been deeply concerned that the structural damage would tear the station apart, but it seemed an experiment would do it one better by blowing the whole structure out of the sky. They had to get a message up there.

"Marcus, who do you trust in communications? I need someone who knows his stuff but can keep quiet about it."

Marcus thought for a moment. "Daniels—he's a little strange, but he keeps to himself, and I can trust him."

"Excellent. Get out there and tell him to get me a channel to the ISS, in here. Link it to my phone. We have to make this thing discreet."

"Yes, sir," replied Marcus. "Once we get everything ready to go, I will stand up and stretch. Look for the sign."

23
Emerging Opportunities

After that meeting with the captain, Dan desperately wanted to go back to his room aboard the *Defiance*, his head splitting with pain from the words that filled his ears during that conversation. He needed some time alone so he could internalize all that he had learned. He could understand why the Daemerae were not willing to risk their remaining ships. They held on to their civilization by a thread. They could not worry about Earth, as they had their hands full defending their own people, but Dan had to. It was his home. His family was there, and if Captain Demenar was right, Earth was the last remaining planet with any hope of standing up to the Gaarich.

Dan's mind wandered as he thought about his home planet. People back there were concerned about having a low-interest mortgage, good schools for their children, owning a flashy car, and living in a good neighborhood. They had no clue that where they lived on Earth was inconsequential, as the Milky Way galaxy was a rough neighborhood in itself, and no gate or security system could protect them from the oncoming menace. They were completely oblivious to the danger that was about to befall them. An attack on Earth, even one to soften it up, would be devastating. Earthlings were still so concerned with their personal affairs and the affairs of those around the block that they had no emotional or mental preparedness for what was about to happen.

Dan also thought of his parents. *What would become of them?* He wanted to tell his mom all that he had learned about her father—that he was even a greater man than anyone knew. *Would he have the chance?*

Dan's thoughts were interrupted by Commander Teitrik, who knocked on his door. Dan opened it to greet him.

"Thought you could use some exercise," the commander said. "Put this on." Teitrik handed Dan a jump suit and some soft booties. Dan took them reluctantly. "I will wait out here."

Dan changed into the suit. The fabric was incredibly comfortable, and the booties, although light, had a remarkably good grip on the bottoms. He glanced at himself in the mirror; the outfit was not flattering. The jet-black suit, devoid of any creases or pleats, made him look like an unemployed mime. Dan wasn't sure if this was a joke. He walked back to the door and opened it to reveal the commander, who, he now noticed, was in the exact same ridiculous garb.

"Come on," said the commander, motioning for Dan to follow.

As before, the two stood in the elevator in awkward silence. It opened and deposited them on a deck several levels deep into the ship. Dan followed Teitrik down the hall and into a large domed room. It had padded floors and what appeared to be exercise equipment lining the walls. This was clearly a gym, and Dan and the commander were the only two inside.

"When I need to think I come in here," said Teitrik, finally breaking the awkward silence. "At this time of day it is always empty and quiet. You can hear your thoughts better."

Dan kept looking around the room, trying to make out the strange equipment that it held.

"But when I am angry, I usually like to have a sparring partner. You know—to work out the frustration."

EMERGING OPPORTUNITIES

This got Dan's attention. He looked over at the commander, who was not much taller than him, but was older and in considerably better condition. Teitrik could easily wipe the floor with him.

"Uh ... sorry you're angry," said Dan timidly.

The commander laughed. "I am not the one who is angry!"

Dan smiled a bit. The commander was doing this for his benefit.

"Did your grandfather ever teach you these moves?" Commander Teitrik started to do the exercises that Dan used to see his grandpa perform.

"No, but I've tried them myself." Dan's feet left the floor. He let his body fly forward until his hands and toes simultaneously contacted the soft gym floor, landing in a position like one prepared to do a pushup. Dan pushed off with his feet and launched into a handstand, holding his legs over his head. He then tumbled to the side, landing on one leg, then the other, until he was again standing straight, arms to his side.

The commander clapped. "Not bad. You need some work, but not bad for an alien." He stepped closer to Dan. "Now let's see the hand movements."

These had always made Dan wonder. The movements looked a lot like tai chi, but were much more aggressive, with sharp gestures, not free flowing like the Chinese equivalent.

Dan started to go into the movement—right hand out, now the left, pulling both back, hands wrapped in a tight fist slapping against his chest, elbows snapping sideways. When he thrust out with the right elbow, the move was met with a response from the commander, who smacked it away with his open hand. Dan now understood these moves. They were for fighting—Daemerik martial arts. He kept running through the routine he had copied from his grandfather, and the commander answered every move with a counter. After several minutes of repetition with increasing speed, Teitrik threw in some curves. He went for Dan's head, but Dan responded by smacking the attacking hand away with an open palm. Then the commander extended his foot to trip Dan, who instead tumbled backward, hitting the commander in the jaw while somersaulting into a standing position several feet away.

The commander grabbed his wounded chin and smiled proudly—the same way an older brother would do upon learning that his sibling was not as clueless as he seemed. He made a run for Dan, who stood still until Teitrik's fist almost impacted his jaw; then Dan bent like a feather and snapped his left elbow into the awaiting gut of the commander, who hit the floor hard.

Teitrik lay there laughing and grabbing his stomach. Dan extended a hand to help him up.

"You know," added the commander, as he hoisted himself from the gym floor with Dan's assistance, "I was born in space. I have never set foot on my home world. I don't know how the birds sound, how the water tastes, or how the sun would feel on my skin. This," he motioned at the room and the structure of the vessel surrounding them, "is all I know."

"Well, I know how the birds sound on Earth and how the sun burns my skin if I spend too much time at the beach in the summer. I know all these things," said Dan passionately. "And now I know they will all end someday—unless I do something about it."

"What will you do? You and your young friends are hardly an army."

"I understand that," Dan said angrily, his voice taut with dismay. "We aren't even supposed to be here. It was all an accident!"

"Tell the passengers and crew of the *Stoic 2* that it was an accident."

Dan gave the commander a puzzled glance. "What do you mean?"

"Even if we had gotten to them in time, we would have been no match for those Gaarich ships. They would have quickly secured the area and established superiority. The *Stoic 2* would have had no chance. It was your quick action that saved those people."

Emerging Opportunities

Dan blushed a bit, but then thought about what the commander had said. If they had not made the mistake in the car and taken the actions that led them to the *Stoic 2*, those people would have been at the mercy of the Gaarich. Their bumbling had led to the salvation of over one hundred souls.

"Whether you like it our not, my young alien friend, you are a hero—just like your grandfather—and heroes get certain privileges."

"What do you mean?"

Commander Teitrik took a couple steps closer to Dan and lowered his voice. "I have spoken with the captain. We are going to get you an audience with the Magnicieat. The rest is up to you."

24

Plan B

WALTERS SAT STARING OUT HIS OFFICE WINDOW at Marcus Washington for what seemed like an eternity, looking for the stretch that was to signal him to pick up the phone, but it had not come, and as the minutes passed he was wondering if it ever would. He so wanted to march into that command center and bark out a few orders to get the answers he needed, but with the current circumstances, it would not be a good move. He paged Betty into the office.

She stepped in with a scowl on her face, glaring at Walters with fiery eyes.

"What's your problem? Why do you look so peeved?"

"Because I had to play nicey nice with the SS out there. I found out way more about those punks than I wanted to know. But you asked, and I did. By the way, do you see the big one out there?" Mark nodded. "He's into knitting—not so tough after all, huh?"

Mark chuckled. "We have Daniels working on getting a line with the station."

"So what do you need me for?" Betty asked.

"Just go out there discretely and find out what the holdup is."

Giving Mark one more dirty look, Betty headed back into the command center. Casually she sauntered over to Daniels's station. Mark was able to observe the two chatting from the vantage point of his office window. Daniels looked stressed, but he always looked stressed—it was his nature. After about thirty seconds she tapped the nervous engineer on the shoulder and went back to Mark's office.

"Well?"

"Get this. NETO's calling the shots, and I bet they're behind our little incarceration."

"What?" Mark exploded. "What do those military hotheads know about space missions? Zero! That's right! Zero! We were to work together per Code Alpha protocol! So all of this is a result of them!" He was fuming so overtly that Betty could almost see steam erupt from his ears.

"If you calm down for a minute, I'll tell you the rest," Betty requested. Mark's face was so beet red that she was afraid he would pop.

Walters took a deep breath and braced himself on the desk with both hands. "Fine, tell me more," he said, trying to sound calm, faking it for her benefit.

"The good news from all of this is that Daniels has tapped into the frequency being used by NETO. It's coded, but with the help of Marcus he was able to break it. He's just a few minutes away from being able to broadcast, but he's trying to make sure that NETO doesn't hear your transmission. That's the hard part."

Mark was proud of his staff. Most ordinary citizens didn't realize the cerebral power of NASA employees. Some of the best and brightest scientists and technicians in the world worked at the agency in various capacities. They did so all with the common goal of advancing mankind through the exploration of space. They were all very committed to their jobs, and this passion for excellence was being demonstrated during this crisis by the industrious folks out on the floor of the command center.

"Fine staff we've got out there," remarked Walters. Betty nodded.

All of a sudden, out of the corner of his eye, Walters saw movement. Mr. Washington stood up and stretched. "That's the sign!" Mark hit the speakerphone. "ISS, this is Houston. ISS, this is Houston." There was no response.

Betty shrugged her shoulders as a voice came over the speaker. "Houston, this is ISS. Operational directives are under Cheyenne Mountain. We must end communication."

"Wait, you have a situation!"

"Houston, this is ISS—out."

"Major? Major?" There was no acknowledgment. "Great ... now what?"

"If they're working with NETO, then ..." Betty's voice trailed off as Mark projected a dead stare out his office window. The agents, docile a moment before, were talking into their headsets and glancing toward the office, their level of agitation clear.

"I think someone told the teacher," Mark said half jokingly, as two rushed toward his office and burst in, holding weapons at the ready.

"Mr. Walters, you must cease what you are doing," they ordered.

Through his office window, Mark saw the remaining agents rounding up the staff members, ordering them away from their stations with hands in the air. They had been caught. Agent Wachovic appeared from the hallway and headed toward the office. He stepped in with a level of purpose Mark had not seen since the NSA originally stormed the facility.

"Walters," barked Wachovic, "that stunt you just attempted cost you and your staff your privileges. We will be securing you in the cafeteria. You will remain there until I am otherwise ordered. Now let's move!"

Mark and Betty stood up and were ushered out of the office to join the group of staffers. They were herded from the command center and down the hall to the cafeteria. One by one they entered the room, which was designed to hold about three hundred people. The doors to the kitchen were locked, so they only had access to the main dining area. Two of Agent Wachovic's men brought in the food Mark had ordered. Once they were all inside, Agent Wachovic began to speak.

"You are not under arrest, but understand that you are not to leave this room. We will have agents posted all around. Just don't try it," Wachovic said sternly. He turned and walked out, followed by his men. The door was closed and locked, leaving Mark and his staff inside.

Marcus Washington walked over to Walters and Betty. "Well, did you get a hold of them?"

"Yes," replied Walters. "It worked fine; you did great."

"Thank you," replied Marcus. "I'm just glad they know. Knowing is half the battle."

"Now, he didn't say they knew," added Betty. "They wouldn't listen. They're taking orders directly from the air force. They just hung up."

"What do you mean? Aww!" Marcus groaned.

"That's why we are in here, Mr. Washington, and is the reason we lost our only access to the systems," Walters lamented. "We have no way of getting in touch with them now." He looked curiously at Betty, who was walking toward the far wall, the place where diners put their trays after eating. She stood there contemplating the garbage chute.

Betty turned around. "Marcus, you look about the right size."

Marcus knew what she wanted, and there was no way he was up for that. "Nah, I'm way too buff. Just check out my arms. Ooh, and my shoulders are just too broad for what you're thinkin'. That's why the ladies are always lookin' up Mr. Washington's number!"

"And exactly what are you thinking, Betty?" Walters inquired.

"This would be a nice exit for anyone small, young, and limber enough to make the trip." She smiled and batted her eyelashes at Marcus.

"Lady, I am not goin' down a garbage chute! Mark?" Marcus turned to Walters, looking for a reprieve.

Walters just took a moment to form a muted grin. "Mr. Washington, be sure to expense the replacement for that shirt, as I don't think you'll be able to get the smell out."

"Fine, but I just have one word—bonus. Just remember that word—bonus. Can we say it together? Now, once I make it down the chute, then what? The NSA are all over this place."

Walters deferred to Betty. "Well, this is your plan."

Betty again expressed her annoyance at her boss with a creative facial expression. He was going to let her work out the details. This was the way Walters liked to reward initiative. "Marcus, you'll have to think on your feet. You need to make it to the third floor training room. It's the only place that has all the equipment you need. You'll have to cross-link systems and use the training equipment to contact the ISS. Get them the message. I don't care what you have to do—just get it to them."

"No problem," Marcus answered. "You can count on me." He moved toward the garbage chute. "Ugh! Must have been taco day," he said, flinching from the strong odor. He hoisted himself through the small opening and disappeared down the shaft. It was now up to him.

Entering Mahtri

DRENCHED WITH SWEAT, Dan went back to his room for a much-needed shower. The workout Teitrik had run him through was grueling for both mind and body. It was going to feel good to clean up and put on some fresh clothes. His aching muscles helped temper the pangs of fear in his stomach. The commander had given him a lot to think about, along with a needed boost of confidence.

Before parting, Teitrik gave Dan the directions to Janet's room. He desperately needed to talk with his friends and share some of the commander's perspectives. It might help, and anyway, he could use their company.

All cleaned up and freshly dressed, Dan traveled down one deck to where Janet was staying. He rang the doorbell.

"Come in," Janet acknowledged as the door slid open. "Hey, Danny boy! Good to see you. I was getting bored going through the computer. Do you know there's an animal almost identical to a cat on Daemerik that they keep as a pet, but it has six legs?"

"I'm glad you can keep your mind occupied."

"I had to. There's no TV, so I've just been looking through information about Daemerik and its history. It's kinda cool when the science fiction movie is real and you're in it."

Science fiction movie? Dan couldn't believe his ears. It may have been like the movies or books that his friend had obsessed over for years, but this experience was intensely real. Plus, it seemed to be going down the path of ending badly for them. Dan decided to brush off the comment and continue with his train of thought. "Have you thought any more about what the captain said—about Earth being attacked?"

Janet switched off the terminal. The joy that painted her face a moment before began to fade as Dan ripped her back to reality. "Every minute since. I can only imagine what Tom's going through. He's such a freakazoid anyway."

"Well, I spoke with Teitrik."

"I thought he was cold and standoffish. How did you get to actually talk with him?" Janet asked.

"I had to fight him."

Janet's jaw dropped, and her eyebrows cascaded down toward her nose in disgust. "I can't believe what a load of male garbage that is. Well, it seems that testosterone is infecting these aliens too." She huffed. "Forget it. I don't want to know the details. So you had your little male ritual, and that's all. What did you find out?"

After absorbing the full brunt of Janet's stinging opinions, Dan pulled up a chair from the dining table and sat down. "A lot, actually—he helped me put things into perspective. I found out that we're more than we seem, just like that car of mine."

"O … k … I don't know if I like being compared to a car."

"Janet, give me a minute." Dan reached out and gently grasped her hand, looking into her deep brown eyes. "We knew nothing of space travel or any of this a few days ago, but look at what we've done. We learned to pilot an alien ship, learned to speak a new language, and saved a hundred-plus people's lives. We even fought these Gaarich things twice—the second time destroying two of their capital ships. I don't know if you noticed, but those things were huge, and we did it with a busted-up ship that we barely learned how to fly."

Janet smiled, turning her eyes to the floor, letting the words sink in. "Yeah, they were pretty big, weren't they?" she said as she raised her head, revealing a slight grin. A moment later the happiness began to fade. She pulled her hand away from Dan, stood up, and turned away in an attempt to hide her fear from him. "But those were just two ships, and we were very lucky. They're going to send a fleet of ships to Earth."

A pounding at the door interrupted their conversation. The guest apparently did not want to use the doorbell, but preferred his foot as a method for possibly gaining entry. It could only be Tom. "Yo, I heard voices through the wall; let me in." Janet released the door, and in bounded Mr. Hunt. "You know, you'd expect that as advanced as these folks are, they'd do better with the soundproofing. These walls are paper thin. What are you guys talking about? I couldn't make it all out with my ear to the wall." Before they could answer, he remarked, "Let me guess—the end of the world?"

"You're always so astute, Mr. Hunt," Dan said. "Now sit down and listen."

"Yes, sir, Captain," Tom said, saluting while plopping himself down onto the couch.

"Remember how I said to keep your minds open to any emerging opportunities? Well, check it out! Commander Teitrik and Captain Demenar are going to get us an audience with the Magnicieat. It's sort of payback for helping the *Stoic 2*. We can officially ask for their help."

"And how do you know they'll give it?" asked Janet.

"They have to," answered Dan, enthusiastically trying to make his point. "Well … they could say no … but we must convince them. The Gaarich are coming, and we're going to need the help of the Daemerae, or it's game over. If we screw this meeting up, it could be the end of our world, as Tom so put it."

"Wow, don't put too much pressure on yourself," scoffed Tom. "We don't know these people and aren't sure if they care about what happens to Earth. They seem to be rather concerned with their own problems."

"We still have to give it a shot, unless either of you have another suggestion."

Janet and Tom did not.

"Why don't we go try and talk to the captain," recommended Janet. "He seemed very personable. We could use his advice on how best to address the Magnicieat."

"Good suggestion, and I could use the walk," said Tom, as he rose and pointed himself toward the door.

"Fine." Dan got up from the chair, and the three made their way to the bridge.

Upon exiting the elevator and walking toward the overlook, they couldn't ignore the buzz on the bridge. The crew were busy at their stations, and several officers were running back and forth between areas trying to coordinate operations. As they leaned over the railing, they noticed that Captain Demenar was right in the midst of all the activity.

"Helm, get ready," the captain ordered. "Baret, signal the other two ships that we go in single file—standard approach formation. Engineering, get those shields up as soon as we pass through the hyperspace window. Let's go to red alert, people—brace for reentry."

Dan interrupted the chaos. "Captain?" The red alert siren began to sound.

Captain Demenar turned to the three standing above him. "Hurry! Take a seat over there and brace yourselves. This is always a little rough—and dangerous."

Janet, Tom, and Dan quickly moved to their left and found three jump seats against the wall that one of the deck officers kindly opened for them. Confusion and stress were written all over their faces. After buckling them in, the officer explained what was happening. "We're going to jump into the Mahtri nebula. It's where most of our exiled population lives. There's a small planet, more like an asteroid, in the center of the nebula. The star cruiser *Atera* is there. The *Atera* is the oldest of the star cruisers and one of only two left in existence. The *Atera* was almost completely destroyed in the battle of Daemerik, and only quick thinking got her here."

Janet leaned over Dan to ask a question of the officer. "Why is this so dangerous—I mean, jumping into the nebula?"

"Interference makes it almost impossible to navigate, for one. Many years ago a defense grid was set up to protect the *Atera* and other ships from the Gaarich. It uses the gases in the Mahtri nebula to form a protective shield—basically, a really large sphere. The only way to penetrate it is when in transition, which is only hundredths of a second. We've set up coded beacons to assist. If we're off by only a little, the ship will slam at near the speed of light into the barrier and disintegrate."

Tom turned to the officer. "Just how effective is this shield?"

"The Gaarich have all but left us alone. First, they don't know we're here, as the protective sphere itself is deep inside the nebula, and the interference from all the gases keeps any deep scan out. We jump inside the nebula, so it won't be picked up by any patrols. Even if they do get in, the shield will hold them off."

"Have any ships been lost going through the shield?" asked Janet.

"Only about twenty-five in the past ten years that I know of. It's been better since they improved the beacons."

Tom was going to make some fatalistic crack, but Dan's piercing glance was all that was needed to prevent the words from being uttered.

Janet pointed toward the viewscreen to a large tube visible in hyperspace. She turned to ask the deck officer, "What's that?"

"That's the wormhole created by the *Liberty*. She will slide out of hyperspace only moments before us. There," he motioned to the screen as the wormhole seemed to dissipate, "she must have transitioned into normal space." One of the crew called the officer over for assistance, so he needed to step away from his three guests.

The helmsman announced the countdown. "Sixty seconds until reentry."

Dan leaned toward Janet's ear and whispered, "So, you gonna give me the short version of what he said?"

"When we transition out of hyperspace, for a split second we exist as energy in normal space. This goes about with the theory that if you actually could travel beyond the speed of light in normal space, you would have to do it as energy."

"Thirty seconds," announced the helm.

"So, as we exit the hyperspace window, as energy, we can pass through the shield. Got it?" she asked.

"No, but I guess I'll get the practical lesson," Dan said, as he listened to the helm call out the status.

"Ten seconds—locking on beacons. Five ... four ... three ... window opening ... jumping ... now!" A flash filled the screen as the *Defiance* passed out of hyperspace, through the shield, and into the protective sphere inside the Mahtri nebula. The two other corvettes followed only moments behind.

The nebula was a wonderful luminescent green and yellow. The wisps made by the gases danced around the ship as it decelerated from light speed and slowly navigated its way to the center of the sphere. They had to move carefully. Vision was almost nonexistent and sensors fluctuated wildly. The navigator used the coded beacons to help define the path through the cosmic fog.

When the teenage trio could breathe again, after realizing they were alive, they noticed Captain Demenar standing before them with a smile on his face. "How did you like our precision flying?"

"Just fine, sir," answered Dan.

"Nah, he was scared," joked Tom.

"Well, you are safe now. The Gaarich do not know that we are here, and if they did, well, they would have a tough time trying to get through that barrier," said the captain with clear confidence. "We have to move very slowly through the nebula. It gives us time to talk. Can we move to the conference room?" He turned to Teitrik. "Commander, you have the conn," ordered Demenar, putting his first officer in charge so that he could speak with the trio alone.

Getting up from their jump seats, Dan, Tom, and Janet followed the captain into the conference room.

Sitting down at the long table, Dan was the first to speak. "Commander Teitrik said you got us an audience with the Magnicieat. I want to thank you."

"Don't have it yet, but it shouldn't be a problem," clarified the captain. "We sent word ahead, but we keep communications brief and one way, not only because of the problems with interference from the nebula, but also because we don't want the Gaarich picking up on our transmissions. Anyway, you are heroes after the incident with the *Stoic 2*—and you are from Earth. It will not be a problem."

"Well, I'm going to ask for their help—with defending Earth," said Dan.

"I would expect no less, but do not be disappointed if they say no. Our existence is barely that. The bulk of our people are here, although we have others scattered about. It has been so long since we have lived on our home planet that many have forgotten. Most who are aboard this ship were born in space—right here. They see this place as their home. Some may not have the passion to fight, only the will to survive."

"And what of your will, Captain?" asked Dan.

Janet and Tom rustled uncomfortably in their chairs. They couldn't believe what came out of their friend's mouth.

"Make no mistake about my resolve. I was born on Daemerik. I was a very small boy, but I remember. I remember enough to want that back for myself and my grandchildren," the captain said sternly, his voice trembling with emotion. "But I serve my people and the Magnicieat, and if they do not wish to help Earth, then I must abide by their wishes, although to the displeasure of my heart."

Dan felt guilty. "I ... am sorry if I—"

"Don't apologize. You have passion and conviction. That is good. Plus you care about your people. That is better. You can do great things—Captain Foster," said Demenar with a smile. "Don't ever turn away from your heart. It will guide you in the dark times. It has guided me."

Stealth Merv

MARCUS CAREENED DOWN THE CHUTE and into the dumpster, quickly sinking into the discarded scraps of food and paper from the cafeteria. Bits of tortilla and seasoned ground beef from the weekend "taco fiesta," along with a myriad of other half-eaten selections, found their way into every crevice of his clothing; it got in his shoes, down his pants, and all over his shirt. He stood up and brushed off as much of the smelly muck as he could, but as his boss had said, his shirt did not survive the journey. Wiping a tomato from his forehead, he glanced back up the long aluminum chute to see Betty flashing a thumbs up. He just ignored her.

Marcus found himself in the basement utility room. Facilities used this as a shipping and receiving area for everything from foodstuffs, to recyclables, to office equipment. A ramp led up to a metal garage door that opened to the outside. Marcus spied a jumpsuit hanging against a bank of six lockers; he studied it and wondered if the utilitarian garb would be less odiferous than the clothes he currently had on. Quietly he slinked across the room and approached the jumpsuit, giving it a brief whiff. Although desperately in need of a cleaning, the outfit was far less offensive than what he was wearing. Marcus took off his smelly clothes and put on the jumpsuit. It was a little generous in size and had the name "Merv" stitched into it, but would do the trick. He fished out his wallet and access cards from his pants and shoved them into the pocket of his new clothes, then discarded his smelly couture into the dumpster and made for the door that opened into the hallway.

Marcus nervously swiped his badge and waited for the light to indicate that it was okay to proceed. With the blink of green, Marcus cracked the door slightly. As he peered through, he could see that the hallway was completely devoid of any activity. Hastily he opened the door and snuck in, staying very close to the wall. The lights were off, except for a few lit for weekend and after-hours workers to navigate by. This level contained most of the work areas for the facilities personnel. Farther down to the left was a door that led to their break room and lockers; to the right were the offices. At the far end, well enough away from Marcus, was the elevator. Initially he remained still and let his ears canvass the area for any noise. Marcus wanted to be sure that he was alone down in the basement, as he was in no mood for surprises from Wachovic's goon squad.

As Marcus slinked along the wall, he kept his senses alert to any possible movement other than his own. He skirted past the door to the break room, which was fully open, yet thankfully there was no one inside. Next he came upon the double doors that marked the entrance to the office cubicles. They were shut, but Marcus paused before passing and pressed his ear against the door. There was no sound; so he crept toward the elevator landing.

Feeling good about his clandestine moves, Marcus glanced back down the hallway, proudly reviewing the area he had just traversed. It was a breeze compared to the problem before him. Two options presented themselves—one would mean going up the elevator, if it were actually still enabled, which he doubted, and anyway doing so would most assuredly guarantee capture. Option two, which was not much better, was to traverse the emergency stairway.

This was a secure building, and it was policy that the staff members were to use the elevators. If emergency access to the stairs was required, it could be used, but a loud buzzer along with a corresponding alert at security ensured any access was closely monitored.

The options rolled through Marcus's brain as he looked first at the elevator, then to the secure door to his left, which led to the stairway. Only a few minutes into his mission, and he was already stuck. Frustrated, he sat down against the wall and let out an audible sigh. He ran through what he knew about the security system. The door was triggered by a simple electronic connector that was severed when the door was opened. This, in turn, activated the buzzer and illuminated a small light on the security console two floors above. If he opened the door, he would not have enough time to evade the NSA, who would quickly pour into the stairwell. The smash-and-dash method would not work.

The alarm mechanism would have to be disabled. Searching his memory for anything that might be useful, Marcus came up with a simple solution. He stood up and silently jogged toward the break room he had just passed. Confident it was empty, he entered and searched for the refrigerator. It was against the far wall. He walked over to it and opened the door. A smile dashed across his face as he pulled out a tray with some aluminum foil over it. He was interested not in the food, but in the foil itself, which he tore off and put into his pocket.

A loud buzz from the hallway jolted Marcus from his plan. An uncomfortable rush of adrenaline pumped through his veins as he heard voices coming down the hall. He quickly searched the room for a place to hide. A new soda machine had been installed several days before and was about two feet from the wall. It would have to do.

Marcus quickly and quietly ran behind the soda machine and hid, his slim body making it no problem to be completely concealed. His heart pounded as he heard the two men enter the room.

"And then she hung up."

"Did you call her back?"

This was very bad. Two agents had come down to the break room. *Did they know he had slipped out of the cafeteria? Had they just come down for something to eat? When would they leave?* Paranoid delusions began to fill the mind of the brilliant engineer, causing his pulse to race and sweat to bead on his cheeks.

"No, I didn't call her back. I mean, seriously—"

"Wait," interrupted one of the agents. "I think we have a problem here."

Marcus started to shake. Had they found him?

"The thing looks unplugged, and I'm thirsty."

Marcus quickly realized that the machine he was standing behind had no power. Palms drenched with sweat, he reached down and quickly plugged it into an outlet. The compressor buzzed to life.

"Huh, that's funny. It just turned on."

"Ah, you never know how these dweebs have this stuff rigged. Just get your soda, and let's get back upstairs before Wachovic freaks."

A thud rumbled through the machine as two sodas were dispensed for the NSA agents. They quickly left the room. Marcus remained still until he heard the buzz of the stairway door opening. Allowing plenty of time for his heart to slow, he peered out from around the machine—the room was clear.

Returning to the door leading to the secure stairway, Marcus fished out the foil from his pocket and tore off a small piece, which he quickly folded into a rectangle. Fortunately he could easily see where the sensor was mounted at the top of the door. Next, he carefully slid the foil between the two contacts and bent it around to ensure that it would remain in place.

Marcus took a deep breath, closed his eyes, and pushed. When no buzzer sounded, he opened his eyes again, smiled, and made his way quickly through the now open door. He ensured that it closed silently behind him. Next, he peered up the stairwell, again using his hearing to detect any signs of movement. Since he was in the basement, he would have four flights of stairs to traverse before making it to the third floor. He lightly leaped from stair to stair until he was at his destination.

Repeating his foil trick, Marcus was able to slip through the door into the third-floor hallway without setting off the alarm. Like in the basement, most of the lights were off, except for a few to dimly light the area. The training room he needed was halfway down. It had windows that looked out into the hallway, so Marcus peeked through to ensure the room was empty before entering.

Marcus sat down at one of the terminals and commenced hacking. The training computers were not linked to the main NASA network. This was standard procedure, as it allowed learning on real equipment in real scenarios without affecting any actual missions. However, in truth, every technician who builds a network always puts in a back door—just in case. He was trying to find that back door so he could link up with the space station.

Marcus pecked away at the keyboard. Minutes ticked by as he tried command after command to access the elusive back door—and then—there it was. He had access to the production network and connected remotely to his station down in the main command center.

Before Marcus enabled the communication link to Walters's office, he had made sure to route access through his workstation. That forethought came in handy now, and in no time he had reestablished communications with the ISS. NETO had changed the coded frequency after NASA got caught eavesdropping, but this was a breeze for Marcus to cut through.

Simply contacting command and control aboard the station was not an option. They would most likely react in the same way as before—not listen—and the NSA would be all over the building in just a few moments looking for him. He had to find a way to make them pay attention without having the option of "hanging up."

The proverbial light bulb appeared over Marcus's head as he accessed the emergency systems protocol screen. This plan might just work, but it would definitely scare the heck out of the crew of the ISS—but he had no choice. He had to get the message through, or there would be no ISS.

27

The Atera

GRADUALLY THE LUMINESCENT FOG of the Mahtri nebula began to dissipate. At the center of the protective sphere lay the asteroid Daerderus, whose mere presence created a clearing within the nebula's dense gases. The asteroid lacked an atmosphere and had very little gravity. Wrinkled with rocks and dust, it measured over five hundred miles in diameter. Its size and location made it an adequate makeshift planet where the refugees from Daemerik could hide.

As the *Defiance* crossed the threshold of this clearing, Dan and his friends stood on the bridge gawking at the viewscreen with stunned amazement. The green and yellow whips disintegrated to reveal wonders they could have never expected. Daerderus and the domed enclaves that covered its surface were not the most impressive sights. It was the immense ship orbiting the small world that dominated their attention.

"Wholly buckets!" shouted Dan. "What's that?"

Teitrik walked over to explain. "That is the star cruiser *Atera*. She's more than fifty times the size of the *Defiance*. There were once ten, and now only two remain."

For its size the *Atera* was elegant. Following the artistic design of the corvettes, the hull seemed to flow out of space, every inch of the ship's massive structure appearing to have been sculpted by a master artisan. The scalloped hull began with a flowing point, as with the *Liberty*, and spanned out port and starboard. Each subsequent section was scalloped, allowing for rotating maneuvering thrusters to be subtly positioned, their purpose to help direct the immense craft through space. A wide tower swooped up from amidships, providing whoever was inside a total view of the vast expanse. At the rear, the gargantuan engines seemed to organically grow out of the aft hull.

A voice boomed over the loudspeaker. "*Defiance*, this is *Atera*. You are cleared to dock. We have already secured the *Liberty*. Welcome home."

"Thank you, *Atera*," responded Captain Demenar. "Helm, initiate link and engage autodocking sequence."

"Aye, sir."

The *Defiance* made its way slowly toward an opening in the port side of the star cruiser. As it approached, the enormous hull of the *Atera* increasingly filled the *Defiance*'s viewscreen, until all else was obscured. Their destination lay in the center, a docking bay that did justice to the size of the star cruiser. The great space allowed the mooring of no less than twelve corvettes.

The *Defiance* crept through the force shield. Dan could see the *Liberty* already docked farther down the bay, her battle damage clearly distinguishing her from the rest of the ships. The docking computer rotated the *Defiance* and backed her into her moorings. Umbilicallike tentacles grasped onto the ship, and like a cruise ship returning from port, long ramps reached out to merge with the hull.

The docking bay was alive with activity. The entire area spanned the width of the *Atera*, measuring over ten miles. The cavernous opening swallowed the corvettes like toys. Technicians and mechanics moved about the bay using antigravity packs and platforms to work on the externals of the craft securely moored inside.

Huge cranes hung from the ceiling, able to pick off large parts of the hull for movement to another area of the hangar for repair.

Captain Demenar walked over to the three teenagers, whose attention was still firmly affixed to the viewscreen. "Welcome to the *Atera*."

"Thanks ... and wow," muttered Dan, still trying to believe what he was seeing.

"How many crew are onboard?" asked Janet.

"The star cruisers were designed for deep space exploration and defense, grand enough to hold an entire fleet. You have a ship with all the comforts of a city. Docking bays large and small line the ship to accommodate craft of varying dimensions. As for crew, a star cruiser will have around one million, but in a pinch, it can hold up to three," proudly answered the captain.

Demenar motioned for the trio to follow two security guards who were awaiting them. Dan shot him a confused look.

"Are we prisoners?" he asked.

"No," said Demenar stoutly. "You are not prisoners, but we need to ensure your safety. The myth of the *Liberty* is very strong for our people. There will be many questions. Plus, in a ship as large as the *Atera*, you will need an escort. Please." He again extended his hand for the three to follow the guards.

Up until this point Demenar had been completely open and trustworthy, so the three felt no qualms about following the security officers up to the elevator landing. They rode down several decks to one of the embarkation hatches. The area was abuzz with crew eager to leave the ship. Janet, Dan, and Tom followed the guards through the mass of people and down the long ramp, which led into the *Atera* itself.

The reception area was as grand and welcoming as a modern railway station, its size equaling the length of the bay where the corvettes were docked. The Daemerae made this area a proper place for a homecoming, showing to crew and visitor alike just how valued their service was to their people. Escalators whisked the crew down to a lower level, where trains picked up their passengers for destinations around the star cruiser.

"Hey, look, they even have a subway on this beast. I hope I don't get mugged." One of the security officers turned around and gave Tom a funny look.

Tom, Dan, Janet, and the two security guards rode down the escalator to the awaiting trains. The teenagers wore the clothes that they were given on the *Defiance*, so they blended in nicely, although appearing slightly younger than most of the crew exiting the ship.

The cars were perfectly round and fit snugly in the tubes that ran through the *Atera*. Stepping onto one of the trains, they took their seats. The doors closed, and the cars sped off through the ship, stopping several times to pick up and drop off passengers. Their journey was long, stopping at station after station for more than twenty minutes.

"Either this is an enormous ship or we're going around in circles," whispered Dan.

"Yeah, I thought the *Liberty* was big, but I just can't believe this thing," responded Tom. "And to believe they had ten of these ships—just crazy."

"What's more crazy is that they only have two left," said Janet, as she gave a nervous smile to the security guards.

The train stopped, and the guards motioned for the three to disembark. They stepped out into a small station, not much larger than two high school classrooms. A set of doors led them into a far-reaching hallway that disappeared in both directions, appearing to run for miles. An awaiting elevator hoisted them several levels more, the double doors opening to reveal a regal lobby.

White marble laced with gold covered the floor, so smooth and shinny it was devoid of seams, as if cut from a single stone.

Ornate sculptures stood proudly along the walls and depicted everything from people, to planets, to ancient battles. The walls themselves swept upward to a ceiling one hundred feet above. Like everything they had seen so far, the size of the space was immense, projecting a grandeur and formality that seemed appropriate for such an important ship in the Daemerik fleet. In the very center of the cavern was a tower of elevators surrounded by guards dressed in ceremonial uniforms with golden capes.

The security officers from the *Defiance* directed Dan, Tom, and Janet into a chamber connected to the lobby. It looked like a room one would see in the United Nations or British Parliament. A table sat in the center, long enough to hold well over one hundred people. A three-tiered observation gallery lined the walls, where spectators could watch the goings on. As with the lobby, the area was elegant. Deep red walls were dotted with gold-etched paintings. All the furniture was a lustrous red cherry, shining like it had just been polished.

The taller of the two security officers spoke. "Wait here. Grand Admiral Retenik would like to speak with you. He will be down from the bridge in several minutes. He is ensuring the *Liberty* is secured and there is adequate protection around the ship."

Their escorts walked out of the conference room, leaving the three teenagers on their own.

"Grand admiral, huh," snickered Tom. "Couldn't just be Admiral Retenik. No, had to be grand admiral." Janet giggled along with him.

"Cut it out," said Dan, who didn't share in the joke. "This Retenik might be able to help us—help Earth."

Janet looked over at Dan as she sat down in one of the chairs at the conference table. "Listen, did you see the size of this ship, buddy boy? They had ten of these ... ten star cruisers that were fifty miles long. That's five hundred more miles of space hardware than we have back at Earth, and guess what? They got their butts kicked, losing eight of these monsters in the process. Don't you get it? They couldn't help themselves; what gives you the notion that they can help us?"

Janet was right. Maybe Dan was fooling himself. The Gaarich were more powerful than the Daemerae, and if they had the strength to fight, they probably would have taken back their own planet years ago. Dan pulled out a chair and sat down. "We have to at least ask. We have nothing back home to stand up to these things—"

"And they obviously don't either! And neither did any of their allies—no one in the galaxy could stand up to the Gaarich."

Dan softened his voice. "Janet, we have to try. I can't ... I can't just ... anyway, what else do we have?"

The room got eerily silent. The teenage trio were tired and had had much more mental and physical stimulation than most people had in their entire lives, packed into a short forty-eight hours—topped off with the notions that they might never go home and that the home they knew might be destroyed.

Tom, seeing his friends driven to the depths of despair, took a seat at the table and tried to snap them out of it. "Look, you're both right, which stinks. But remember—the Daemerae had all this technology, but they didn't have one thing—make that three things."

Janet gave him an inquisitive glance. "Okay, what didn't they have?"

"Us," announced Tom, the notion getting a chuckle and helping to lighten the mood. "No, wait—I'm serious! Dan, you pointed out not long ago how we've been up against just crazy odds over the past two days, and we made it through. Well, I think we can do whatever we set our minds to. I say we'll find a way to save Earth—because we have to."

Dan reached over and patted Tom on the back, a proud smile forming across his face. "You know, you're totally full of garbage sometimes, but I'm with you."

"Me too," added Janet. "Sorry, I get all defeatist sometimes."

Tom leaped out of his seat, startled as the door behind him burst open. In walked a tall and strikingly handsome man—older but handsome nonetheless. He was dressed in a very well-tailored deep blue uniform with a long, ornate coat adorned with gold frill. A contingent of personnel, about ten in total, flanked him as he entered. The old man extended his aged hand to Tom.

"I am Grand Admiral Retenik. I want to welcome you aboard the *Atera*. I do believe this is how you greet someone from your planet," the man said, with his hand still outstretched.

Dan and Janet stood up in unison. "Uh, yes, sir," answered Dan. "Tom, shake his hand already." Tom responded by nervously grasping the admiral's hand. Afterward Retenik took his place at the end of the table.

"Please, sit up near me." He motioned to the three Earthlings to move closer. They sat and waited while the rest of the admiral's contingent grabbed places farther down the table. "I never thought I would live to see the day when I could lay my eyes upon my brothers and sisters from Earth. I have dreamed of this day, as have our people. And to have the *Liberty* back—this is assuredly one of the high points in our recent history."

"Thank you," uttered Dan, his voice sounding more confident.

"You are welcome, my young friend," answered Retenik with a smile. "I read Captain Demenar's report and found it very intriguing, but also troubling, and I have many questions." As if on cue, his entourage opened their electronic tablets and activated their recording machines. "The *Liberty*'s mission was to go to Earth and prepare the planet for the Gaarich by infusing our technology and knowledge into your culture to help you advance more quickly. The *Liberty* was to return when you had reached a point of either adequate advancement or appropriate cultural awareness so that our integration into Earth would be possible or in the event that Earth was in imminent danger of attack from the Gaarich. Now, my first question is about your advancement. Tell me about your space travel technology."

Dan motioned to Janet, as she was the expert on the subject. "We don't have anything near what you do. We haven't left Earth's orbit in over thirty years. We have a space station, which is just a series of tubes—like a hamster's habit trail." Tom snickered at the analogy.

"So you have no way to jump into hyperspace or travel beyond your solar system?"

"No, sir. We only went as far as the moon, and that was a long time before the three of us were born." Janet blushed, because just the mention of it was pretty pathetic.

"I see," voiced the admiral. "How about other technologies."

"We've made a lot of advancements in computers and junk like that," answered Tom, wanting to get in on the conversation.

"Ah, that is good. Microelectronics is always the first step," the admiral said, looking more pleased. "How about culture?"

"I'll take this one," volunteered Dan. "Forget it. We still fight each other over land, religion, myth, who to marry and who not to marry, and crime is one of the planet's biggest industries. I don't see how the people of my planet would be ready to integrate with an alien culture. They would freak."

"Freak?"

"Yeah, I mean, I just found out that my grandfather was an alien, and heck—I'm part alien. That was tough for me, and I tend to be a pretty level-headed guy," Dan said, as he saw Janet roll her eyes, responding to the level-headed comment. "We might seem well adjusted to all of this, but trust me, this Daemerik, Gaarich, huge spaceship stuff is way more than Earthlings can stomach. Like I said, they'll freak."

The admiral sat back in his chair, thinking through what Dan had said. "This is most distressing. It seems that the *Liberty*'s mission has failed. Its captain, your grandfather, is dead, and the crew has not impacted society or technology as it was supposed to."

"Wait just a minute," Dan reacted, allowing his newfound confidence, rather than proper judgment, to dictate his words. "First off, if you think that we Earthlings are so easy to manipulate, well, you have another think coming. Sure, we're up for new gadgets, as the computer advancements have shown, but trying to manipulate a people as diverse and strong willed as the humans of Earth—you'd better adjust your expectations!"

After Dan said that, he regretted the words—they had simply erupted from his mouth. The stunned expressions and open jaws adorning the faces of his friends confirmed this. He had reacted swiftly without thinking and sent a volley to a rather high-ranking official. All he and his friends could do was wait for the inevitable reaction.

"Son, you have a lot to learn!" barked the admiral. "Do you think that our history was any different than yours? Don't you think that our population is as diverse in ideology, culture, and religion? Well, we are, and it took many centuries to unite. This happened long before we ventured into space. It is a lot of work, but that is why we sent our best historians and negotiators on that ship to your planet in order to help seek common ground among your peoples."

"But I was told that the *Liberty* had to leave hastily in the final battle," Dan remarked. "It did not have its whole crew aboard. They weren't at optimum staff for their mission."

Janet decided to interrupt and hopefully calm the situation. "One thing that we cannot comment on," she gave Dan a stern glance to keep him from opening his mouth, "is what the crew of the *Liberty* are doing on Earth right now. They had no idea we came here. We only found out about Dan's grandfather once we got aboard that ship."

Grand Admiral Retenik pointed a bony finger at Dan. "You should listen to her. She is the smart one of you three. Unfortunately, if you do not know the true status of the *Liberty*'s crew, there is no way to determine Earth's readiness for attack."

"Captain Demenar said there would be an attack. Is that true?" asked Tom.

The admiral lifted his hand and waved to indicate his entourage should leave the room. They quickly filed out the door, closing it behind them.

"When Captain Demenar communicated your story to us, we sent a scout ship to the space not far from our home planet. It is the staging area for any Gaarich assault actions. A small station there is designated as a main rally point. A fleet is being formed. It will be sent to Earth—not to conquer just yet, but to destroy its defenses and pummel any larger population centers. The Gaarich would then come back every so often to do the same—to keep Earth in shambles until they are ready to invade."

"Then, sir," started Dan in a soft and serious voice, "as a representative of Earth, I ask for your assistance."

The admiral got up and started to pace, as if to help craft his answer. He gazed off into the expanse of the room as he mumbled to himself. "They just keep coming … and coming … they never stop … they are relentless … there are so many of them." He broke himself from his trance and turned to the three teenagers. "I am sorry. I cannot commit the fleet to any action without the permission of the Magnicieat. We live like vermin here—hiding so we do not get caught, while our home is overrun with— Forgive me, I let my personal feelings get in the way of my judgment."

"Shouldn't you let your personal feelings drive your judgment?" asked Janet.

"Not when it comes to the survival of our people," the admiral responded. "We have limited resources and do what we can to survive. The Magnicieat is the supreme authority, and any action like coming to the aid of Earth would need to be approved by them."

"You say that like you're disappointed that you can't make the decision," stated Dan, looking for the truth in Retenik's eyes.

"It is better that I don't make the decision. It is simply better that way." The admiral put on a brave smile as he deeply suppressed his own feelings. "The one thing I can do is offer you sanctuary. Consider yourselves welcome."

"Thank you, but if you cannot guarantee our planet, our families, and our people sanctuary, then we cannot accept your offer," stated Dan, as he rose out of his seat.

An expression crossed the face of Grand Admiral Retenik. It was the kind of glance a father gives to his son when he has made him proud. He could see the emerging leader in Dan—just as the Magnicieat had seen it in his grandfather so many years ago. The cycle was continuing. "From the legends we have of your grandfather, you *must* be his kin. I admire your strength, but understand the sanctuary I offer you three is all I can give."

"Then I ask to speak to the Magnicieat."

"And that will be arranged," the admiral answered in a softer voice. "It will be up to you then." He turned his glance to the door. "Lieutenant Tyril!" The lieutenant burst into the room. "Please show our new citizens to temporary quarters."

Icing on the Cake

MAJORS JENSEN AND VODNIKOV HAD SPENT the past day running through every safety and maintenance checklist they had. They were effectively cut off from NASA, and NETO did not have the same level of expertise and diagnostic equipment to ensure the station was safe. They had to do all the work on their own. Normally a minimal crew is four, so these two had to scramble to ensure their own safety. Tired, frightened, and cut off from Earth until a rescue craft could be readied, the two worked like busy beavers, sometimes running checks three or four times merely to keep occupied.

They were running the tests on the main solar panels for the fifth time when suddenly all power to the station was cut. The emergency lights came on. Major Jensen was in a different part of the ISS than his Russian crewmate, who was still in the command module. He quickly pulled his way through the zero gravity to get back to her, navigating by the dim emergency lights running off minimal battery power.

Jensen floated into the command module. "Major Vodnikov, what happened?"

"I don't know!" she screamed, shaking her hands. "Everything just cut out!"

Jensen grabbed for his headset. "I'll get NETO on the line."

"It will be no use. When I rigged the makeshift antenna through the water pipes, I used auxiliary power to help boost the signal. We will be lucky to have anyone hear us."

"Wait," said Jensen, as he held the earpiece of his headset, pressing it against the side of his face as if to get closer to the sound.

What he heard was a faint voice saying, "ISS, this is NASA. ISS, this is NASA. You must listen. You have a dangerous situation that you must resolve. If you can hear me, acknowledge by firing your stability thrusters for one second. Do not change attitude—fire simultaneously to indicate that you can hear. ISS, this is NASA. ISS, this is …" The message kept repeating.

Major Jensen, looking confused, glanced over at Vodnikov. "It's NASA. They say we have a major problem."

"They're right!"

"They want us to acknowledge by firing our stability thrusters in station keeping—for one second."

"Of course. We cannot answer, but they have links to our systems and can see if we fire the stabilizers."

"Major Vodnikov, fire the thrusters for one second—station keeping."

Vodnikov pushed herself over to the attitude control computer and fired the stability rockets. The station shuddered for a second and then stopped, her precision action keeping the ISS stationary.

"Wait," said Jensen, as he listened intently to see if there was a response. He flipped a switch to activate the speaker so Vodnikov could hear.

"ISS, we have your acknowledgment. I apologize, but I had to shut down your power to get your attention. You have a serious situation. The experimental solar panels mounted on the embarkation module are still connected to your power grid. The relays are fused. A severe overload will occur on one of your passes around the light side of the planet—expect catastrophic result. You must disconnect those panels from the grid as soon as possible. Please acknowledge you understand by firing your stabilizers again."

Major Vodnikov leaned over and fired the thrusters for a second time.

"Good. Now, you don't have much time. NASA out." The communication ended, and the power came back on.

Major Jensen adjusted the frequency to contact NETO. "NETO this is ISS. Do you copy?" He waited for a response. "NETO, this is commander ISS. Please respond." The response was only silence.

"I am sorry, Commander," apologized Vodnikov. "The power surge must have shorted out my makeshift antenna. We have lost communications."

"No matter," Jensen said, as he tore off the headset. "We have bigger problems. There's a manual release in the embarkation module, but it's almost out of air. There's no way we can get in there. How much time before we pass around to the light side again?"

"Five minutes. Commander, I think I can pull up the logs from the last several hours. We might be able to see how much time we have." Vodnikov pulled up the internal diagnostics for the past twelve hours, looking at the power fluctuations from each pass around the light side of the planet. "Here, each pass we have had an exponential boost throughout the system. Not enough to blow anything out, but …"

"But what?"

"When our power came back up, only 20 percent of our battery storage came back on the grid."

"Great. We'd have to travel outside the station to fix that. I wish the engineers who designed this thing got to work in here for once. They may have made the critical systems easier to access. So, tell me, what does this mean?"

"In four minutes and twenty-one seconds, when we pass to the light side, those panels, if still connected to the grid, will overload the remaining batteries, and—"

"Boom!"

"Unfortunately."

"What about the battery isolators?"

"Ah, Russian made. You know how we hate redundancy. The power grid is protected by the relays and breakers built into the solar panels themselves."

Jensen shook his head and let out a deep sigh. He began running through the design of the ISS in his mind, trying desperately to come up with a plan. Vodnikov punched up the schematics on the computer and began poring over them. Major Jensen moved to peer over her shoulder.

"Well," said Jensen as he pointed to the thruster controls, "this is totally hillbilly—"

"Hillbilly?" asked the Russian.

"Listen, never mind. Look here. Since the station is modular, each has its own set of thrusters. That way the bigger it gets, the more oomph you have to keep it in place."

"Oomph?"

"Listen—just bear with me," begged Jensen. "We can reprogram the thrusters to fire against each other and hopefully rip that damaged module free before it blows us to kingdom come."

Vodnikov looked at him like he was crazy, nonetheless being somewhat careful not to offend him. "Well, how do we know it won't rip the station apart, and we go floating off into space? The whole structure could fail."

"Or it could blow up in two minutes."

"Good point. I will reprogram the computer; you see if you can loosen some bolts or something."

Without another word, the two quickly went to work, Vodnikov intently pecking at the computer, and Major Jensen examining the hatch between them and the damaged module, looking for ways to soften up the connection.

Sixty seconds of their two minutes passed. "Commander!" called out Vodnikov.

"Yes."

"I got it, but we only have fifty-eight seconds."

"Grab onto something and fire those thrusters."

Vodnikov secured herself as she pressed the button. The station shook violently at full thrust, trying to rip itself apart. Metal creaked and crumpled as the seconds ticked by. Out of the window, the blue-and-white glow of the light side of Earth was coming into view. Soon the warmth of the sun would touch the station with its rays.

"I used to like my job!" shouted Jensen over all the noise.

The shuddering grew more violent, as lights burned out from the horrific shaking.

"Thirty seconds!" yelled the Russian, as she watched the position indicator.

A loud pop sounded right before the station ripped apart, the damaged module careening off into space. Vodnikov kept the thrusters firing to try to get as much distance from it as possible.

"What about the shockwave?" asked Jensen.

"This is about as far away as we are going to—" A brilliant flash interrupted her as the damaged embarkation module incinerated. The majors braced themselves as the shockwave hit, crushing against the ISS and pushing it well outside its orbital path.

Peering out the window, Jensen saw that the station was in an uncontrolled tumble. "Can we right her?"

Vodnikov looked at the controls. "No, thrusters damaged. Life support is okay, and we have power and plenty of active battery storage left in the remaining modules, but—"

"Oh, and there has to be a but."

"Sorry, Commander, but our orbit is decaying. Thirty-six hours from now we will burn up in the atmosphere."

Major Jensen put his hands against his face and shook his head. "I really used to like this job."

Insomniac

THE QUARTERS THEY WERE GIVEN were much more than adequate. Situated near the command tower, they were originally designed as accommodations for high-ranking officials, heads of state, or leaders from other worlds. Effectively a four-bedroom home, the space consisted of a small entranceway that opened up into a common area littered with a myriad of lounges for gatherings, receptions, or the private security guards of some big shot to pass the time. A dining room with an elegant table suitable for the most opulent holiday dinner sat surrounded by twelve very stately chairs, richly carved and painted with silver and gold accents. A fully stocked kitchen was not far away, holding everything an esteemed guest could need. The four bedrooms were identical in size, and each had its own sitting area, small office, and bathroom.

Janet and Tom had retired to their rooms for some much-needed rest. They felt safe for now and had had so little sleep over the past few days that this was the opportunity to get some. Dan, in contrast, could not. There was no question that he was sufficiently exhausted to fall away into dreamland, but the adrenaline pumping through his veins manufactured from the horror of knowing his world would be attacked was all the stimulant he needed to stay awake.

Dan spent time fidgeting around the kitchen, trying to see if there was any beverage resembling coffee. A nice pastry would have suited his palate well, but Dan did not have the knowledge or the will to experiment with the foreign appliances and interestingly colored food in the refrigerator. He much preferred to have something prepared for him.

A ship as large as the *Atera* must have had eateries of all kinds, possibly even a little store where he could buy something to satisfy his hunger. Grand Admiral Retenik had been kind enough to make Dan and his friends official citizens, even providing them with real ID cards. In addition, they each got a limited amount of credits—some small spending money Dan was eager to find out where to use.

Before Dan stepped out the door, he looked back to see if his companions were awake. They were most assuredly not. Their doors were closed, and he could even hear snoring coming from Tom's room. They were fast asleep, so Dan slid into the hallway.

The long corridors that snaked through the *Atera* would be intimidating if not for the well-placed signs. One was located right outside Dan's door, which made it very easy to head in the direction of the closest train station. It was to the left, off the main lobby below the command tower. Dan walked the several yards to enter the ostentatious command tower lobby. The conference room he and his friends had been in with the admiral only hours before was located across the great space. The lights were dimmed, seemingly to simulate night. Since there was no sun, the systems on the ship did their best to simulate the natural patterns of the day. The guards with the golden capes that ringed the elevators to the command tower were still at their stations. They acknowledged Dan with a nod as he passed over to a sweeping staircase leading down to the train platform.

The station was as extravagantly appointed as the lobby to which it led. The same gold-flaked marble covered the platform, which was flanked by two train tunnels traveling in opposite directions—in this case, fore and aft of the ship. A sculpture with the insignia of the *Atera* hung on the far end, with smaller versions dotting the walls.

Which way to go? Dan had already been forward, as that was where the *Liberty* and *Defiance* were docked. He decided on exploring the aft section of the massive star cruiser.

Dan and his friends used to cruise the subway in Boston, known as the "T," just to explore the city. They would ride it to the end of the line, buy a candy bar at some convenience store, and then hop the train home. This may have seemed lame to most, but to kids who could not yet drive, it was a wonderful taste of freedom. Exploring the trains on the *Atera* was a way Dan could draw on something familiar to make him feel more at home. It would give him time to think and maybe calm his nerves enough to allow sleep. The journey might even present him with the opportunity to buy a candy bar with that alien money in his pocket.

An aft moving train glided into the station. The doors opened, and Dan stepped into an empty car. He slumped down in his seat and rested his head against the window as the train sped off. The tunnels were dark except for the occasional light that raced by. Dan cleared his mind of all thoughts as the train continued from stop to stop. He did not have the will to get up and explore. He just wanted to sit quietly for a while and let the train do the exploring for him.

"Daerderus shuttle bay, next stop," announced the computer.

The words piqued Dan's curiosity. Daerderus was the asteroid where the bulk of the populace lived. He pulled his head away from the cold window.

As the train slowed, Dan stood up and exited once the doors had finally opened. He walked up the stairs into a terminal that could have been plucked from any airport back on Earth. About twenty people were sitting and waiting. A row of windows looked out into a long tunnel that ended abruptly at a force shield that led out into space.

Before Dan could fully get his bearings, a small shuttle appeared and came alongside the windows and docked. The people in the waiting area anxiously stood up as the door opened. Off came its load of passengers, the majority of them dressed in Daemerik military uniforms. Once the parade of arrivals ceased, those in the waiting lobby made their way into the shuttle.

One of the older travelers looked over at Dan, who remained entranced at the whole scene. "Better come if you're coming, son. This is the last shuttle for a few hours."

Not really thinking, and not really caring either, Dan followed the man into the shuttle. The interior was very plain, just row after row of seats. Dan grabbed one by the window. From his years of traveling on airplanes, he reached for a seatbelt, but the inertial dampers made them unnecessary. Instead, he turned his attention out the window as the shuttle pulled away from the landing and began to speed down the corridor, through the force shield, and out into space.

Besides the *Atera*, the space around Daerderus was teeming with ships of all sizes and shapes. Cargo vessels were ferrying supplies between the asteroid and the craft nestled in the nebula. Military ships remained anchored in formation, quietly waiting for some reason to act. Smaller craft buzzed about like mosquitoes on a warm and humid summer evening. Dan peered out the window, marveling at the wonders and getting increasingly frustrated with the realization that a people with this level of technology seemed reluctant to help Earth.

As the shuttle descended toward Daerderus, the curved domes on the surface came into view. Cities and farmland were domed to create artificial gravity and atmosphere on the small asteroid. The shuttle was destined for the largest, Primatt, which housed the most expansive settlement. The shuttle skimmed toward a structure connected to the city by a long tunnel. This was the docking area, kept outside of Primatt for safety. It was open on two sides, with shuttles entering in one way, depositing their cargo, and exiting out the other. A force shield kept the vacuum of space at bay.

The shuttle steered into the landing area, continually slowing until it stopped several yards away from the terminal.

"We have arrived at Primatt. Next shuttle back to the *Atera* in four hours."

The door opened, and the passengers began to file out. Dan remained in his seat. The crew left the helm and began to exit the ship, when the copilot caught a glimpse of Dan. The copilot stood by the door as he shouted, "Hey, you have to get off! They're going to clean this thing. Next shuttle leaves in a few hours."

Like awakening from a trance, Dan stood up and made his way to the door to exit the ship, the copilot having succeeded in getting him on his way.

Dan stepped down onto the floor of the landing bay and looked around. The area was deserted, as it was late in the evening. Several other shuttles were lined up, but they too were quiet, their crews getting a good night's rest. He looked to his left, where he could see out the force shield. The terrain of Daerderus looked like that of the moon—barren and gray. There was no way life could survive here without the artificial environment created by the domes.

Following the stream of passengers, Dan stepped through into the terminal. Again, the scene was reminiscent of any travel facility late at night. Rows of benches were empty; grates were pulled down over the shops; and, much to Dan's dismay, even the eateries were closed. As he watched his fellow passengers move off deeper into the facility, he caught a glimpse of a sign that read "To Trains." It pointed down to a descending stairway where the others from the *Atera* were headed. Dan followed, climbing down to the platform.

A train was waiting patiently to whisk off the passengers from the last transport of the evening. He quickly rushed in just as the doors closed, and the train began to move. He grabbed a seat as the rail cars skirted swiftly through the tunnel toward the city.

The train slowed as it entered the main station in Primatt. It was riddled with platforms that allowed access to any of the domed enclaves on Daerderus. Dan stepped out as the doors opened, and he walked up the stairs into the main part of the station. From what he had seen on the *Atera*, he expected a majestic space rivaling some of the most beautiful stations on Earth, like Grand Central Station in New York, South Station in Boston, or the beautifully restored Union Station in Washington, D.C. Yet, what greeted him was plain and utilitarian. Holographic signs held the train schedules, while the floor was dotted with benches where passengers could sit and wait. There was no marble floor or ornate artwork—no indication at all that any care had gone into building it, only haste.

Dan exited the station and stepped out onto the city streets of Primatt. The sunless sky and strange dim glow from the nebula blanketed the asteroid in an eerie permanent dusk. He looked up at the towering buildings and small transports that buzzed about, taking a deep breath to soak in the experience. When he inhaled, his throat constricted as he choked on the foul air, breaking into a coughing fit to clear his lungs. It was not sweet smelling, but stale, as if it had been created artificially and recirculated time after time. The overall mood in the city was dark and oppressive. Like the train station, there was no art, color, or beauty. The buildings, the streets, in fact everything his eye touched looked like it was built for utility—out of speedy desperation, rather than the pride of expression, almost to spite artistry itself. The contrast to the elegant ships on which he and his friends had spent the past several days was marked. Dan held his hand out to feel a breeze, but there was none. He closed his eyes to focus on trying to hear the sounds of life, but could only hear the low groan of survival.

Dan was compelled to move forward and explore to see if the dark atmosphere was just representative of this section of Primatt; he hoped in his heart it was. Dan did not want to see the Daemerae living so poorly. He wished that they still had the passion to resist the Gaarich menace. This he needed to know, because if a people so advanced as the Daemerae had had their souls ripped away, then what hope was there for the people of Earth? Fear kept him plodding ahead—fear of what he would see and what he would learn about the refugees from Daemerik.

Dan was on his own now. His friends did not know—in fact no one knew that he was wandering about on the surface. His head spun like a radar dish trying to take in all that was around him. There was not one plant, no ornamental vegetation at all, which made the city appear more dead than it actually felt. The streets were narrow, and the buildings were tall, creating an uneasy claustrophobia that made the already acrid air feel more weighty. Every few blocks an open square thankfully lifted the veil of the artificial canyons, situated not for any aesthetic purpose, but simply as a clearing where small transports could land and pick up passengers to whisk them off to other parts of the city.

Dan rounded a corner and could hear noises further ahead. A holographic sign came into view. It read "Irikiq's—Always Open." Dan walked toward it, his ear identifying voices and what sounded like music coming from inside. Insatiable curiosity propelled him to open the door and walk in. Sure looked like a bar to him, but he was too young—well at least on Earth, but he was hungry and thirsty, and maybe they had that coffee he was aching for.

At the center of the room stood a round bar with a tower of neatly stacked bottles filled with brilliantly colored liquids planted in the middle. Two very attentive bartenders took care of the six or seven patrons who were sitting about. Tables filled the rest of the room, except for one corner, from which the music was emanating. It was a trio, but Dan could make out neither their instruments nor their style.

Dan nervously took a seat at the bar, not knowing if he would be welcome or thrown out on his ear. He thought about standing up and leaving, but it was too late. The bartender, an older overweight gentleman, approached.

"Aren't you a little young to be out so late?" he asked. "Doesn't the academy have exams tomorrow?"

"Uh ... um ... ," muttered Dan, his lips quivering ever so slightly.

"Yeah, all that studying must have you a little wired," responded the bartender, quickly interrupting Dan's stuttering. "Well, you're too young for beer."

"Uh, you have beer too?" Dan asked, surprised that the Daemerae had such a thing.

"Of course. This is a bar, son. You must have been studying too long. Let me get you some catria and a plate of netrik sticks. That should get your senses back to you." The man walked away. Dan raised his hand as if to say something, but the words just disintegrated into his brain. He rested his hand back on the bar.

A few moments later the bartender returned with a steaming hot cup of catria and a plate of netrik sticks. Dan thanked him as he went back to his other duties.

Before indulging, Dan just stared at the food in front of him. He had no idea what the netrik sticks were, but they looked a bit like long, skinny chicken wings. He picked one up and tore off a piece with his teeth.

"It tastes like chicken!" he exclaimed.

"Yeah, kid, that's what they all say," answered the bartender, chuckling while attending to a patron several feet away.

Dan greedily attacked the netrik sticks, pounding them into his palate. He was so thirsty he picked up the hot cup of catria without thinking. He took a sip and pulled it away from his mouth. *Coffee!*

As Dan continued through his food, an older man sat down next to him. He was about in his midfifties, using Earth age standards, and dressed in grubby khaki pants, a black t-shirt, and a utility vest littered with as much grease as pockets to hold things.

"Bartender, beer, please," the man said as he took off his hat and slammed it down on the bar. He looked over at Dan, who was still gorging himself. "Are the netrik sticks good?"

"Freakin' great!" exclaimed Dan.

"Glad to hear it." The man took his beer from the bartender and pointed to the netrik sticks, indicating that he would like an order. "I could use them. This cargo running gets to be a pain in the rear sometimes."

"Cargo running?" asked Dan, still munching away.

"Yeah, if we're not running from the Gaarich, we have to deal with those Pyietri. Major pains they are. They got us almost back to the nebula. Jumped us in hyperspace and knocked out our drive. They stole just about everything, and we had to limp back on sublight power. Lucky we weren't that far away, but we had to wait to get through the shield. They only take it down once a week, and they make a big deal about it."

"How so?"

The man gave Dan a funny look. "What, you not from around here or something?"

Dan thought quickly to come up with a response. "Uh, no ... another colony ... place."

The man, satisfied with his answer, continued, as he was much more interested in complaining than finding out where his bar partner was from. "Well, anyway, they post some big ships out there, and they sweep the area for two full days. Then you have to have been in the event horizon of the nebula for three days prior to that. Heck, they don't want the Gaarich following and waiting for one of us," he said in frustration as he lifted his beer to take a swig. "Next they have to inspect your ship, and then after that, they open a small section of the shield for ships to pass. It's only open as long as need be for the ships waiting to get through. It's a major pain."

"Have there been any problems?"

"Well, here's the catch. If after all that they suspect any Gaarich, the orders are to power up the shield immediately. All warships that are supervising are to jump out of the area. We lost a ship several years ago. It was passing through the opening when the order came due to a scare. It cut the ship in half in an instant."

The man took another swig of his beer, downing at least half of it in one gulp. "But that was cake compared to the Pyietri."

"Who are they?" asked Dan, trying to get as much information as possible.

"Rogues is what they are! A ragtag group of deserters and rebels, they came out of a faction on Daemerik that wanted to hit the Gaarich hard back in the old days—real tough bunch. They hate the Magnicieat for ordering the evac of the planet fifty years ago— just hate them. When the order was given, commanders loyal to the Pyietri took their ships and headed off into space. Supposedly they made alliances with pirates and scoundrels. They even gathered up some remnants of the Votraxain military. Basically they have two purposes now. They do whatever they can to harass the Gaarich, for that I give them credit, and second, they steal our supplies, a lot of which we steal from the Gaarich anyway."

"So they're still fighting the war!"

"The war is over, son. We lost. If you look around, we lost big!" The man tipped the beer up and slammed down the last few drops. "We've been living here for decades. There's been no attempt to take back Daemerik, and for good reason. Those who live here barely made it out alive during the invasion. I remember those days as a young boy. It was hell. I don't see how we could go up against the strongest force in the galaxy now. So we just get by, day by day."

"Well, that's no way to live."

"Well, it's the way you live, and it's the way I live. That's just the way it is," the man said with a certain finality.

"Not if I can help it!" Dan stood up, put down a few credits, and headed out the door. He needed to get back to the *Atera*.

Call for Help

Captain Dillings burst into General Peters's office, jarring him from his review of the current situational status reports. "We lost contact with the ISS!"

"What?" exclaimed the general, jumping out of his chair.

"About five minutes ago. We thought it was a glitch on our end," she said, still breathing heavily from having run into the room.

"Are they okay? Have they been attacked?"

"We don't know. According to what we can pick up from our satellite network, there was some sort of explosion, and now what's left of the station is tumbling into shallow orbit."

The general's face darkened with concern. "The majors?"

"We ... we just don't know ... sir."

The situation had quickly spiraled out of control, and NETO did not have the needed access and expertise to handle the problem from here. The only agency that could deal with an incident like this with the ISS was NASA, an organization that Peters had quarantined with a fully armed tactical unit. He had based his decision in the fear that news of the attack by the aliens would leak out, causing widespread panic. In the end, it had simply cut him off from the only group that could save Majors Jensen and Vodnikov. Now, to save the lives of two dedicated astronauts, he would have to rescind his order.

"Fine. We're going to have to pull NASA into this."

"Good luck," answered the captain, knowing how NASA would react. "You just ordered them locked down, and they are not going to be very happy with us."

"I know, but we don't have a choice. I made the call to lock them down at the time because I thought we could handle it on our own. Well, we can't."

"Agreed," said the captain.

General Peters sat back down at his desk and let out a long sigh, prepping himself for the conversations ahead. "Get me Agent Wachovic on the secure line."

Dillings picked up the phone. "This is Captain Dillings, secure access code alpha one gecko charlie. Request contact with commander NSA quarantine team." A few seconds later, she handed the receiver to the general.

"Agent Wachovic, what's the status of our subjects?"

"They're locked in the cafeteria," responded the agent. "The rest of the building is clear."

The general wiped his hand over his face. "Wachovic … we're going to need their help here."

The agent was silent as he let the order sink in, finally answering, "Yes, sir."

"Get them back into the control room, and get Walters and yourself on the phone with me in a jiffy. Got it?"

"Yes, sir. Will call you back in five."

General Peters hung up the phone. "I shouldn't have quarantined them. Now Mark Walters is going to clean my clock and rub my face in the fact that we're in over our heads."

"General, you couldn't have taken the risk. You made the right call," encouraged the captain. "If there had been a leak—"

"That risk is still there—and I thought this would be a good retirement job."

Back at NASA, the control room staff was still locked in the cafeteria. Betty was leaning against the wall, longing for the taste of a cigarette, when Agent Wachovic walked into the room with two of his goons. He approached Mark and spoke softly for a few moments. It didn't take long for the fireworks to start. Mark's face turned beet red, which was a colorful contrast to his white teeth, which were gnashing about in anger.

"You gotta be kiddin' me!" screamed Mark, his loud outburst grabbing the attention of everyone in the room. The two agents with Wachovic took a step back to avoid the barrage. "So, after all of this bull, you need our help? Sir, I am going to make sure you are out of a job and that General Peter Pan freak boy either gets court-martialed or is stuck commanding some radar station in Antarctica!"

Betty dashed over to try to quell the situation. "What is it, Mark?"

"Agent Thugboy here wants us to help now. NETO's in over their heads."

"Mark, we have people up there that we're responsible for," said Betty, trying to help calm Walters. "Don't worry about this boy scout here. We need to complete the mission."

Walters folded his arms and looked down at the floor, nodding his head as he rocked back and forth. "You're right."

Mark clapped his hands to get everyone's attention, which he already had, thanks to his tirade. "People! I need you to go back to your stations and bring up a status on the ISS. Do it now and quickly. I will get with you in ten minutes." He turned to Betty and softened his voice to a whisper. "Get me a full status. I need to talk to the general."

The group noisily headed back to the control center and got to work, powering up their systems. Mark could hear screams of elation as the staff realized that their accesses had been restored. He continued through the room over to his office with Agent

Wachovic. Once they stepped inside and closed the door, the agent radioed that they had arrived. The secure phone rang a few moments later. Mark put it on speaker.

"Mr. Walters, let me start by—"

"Don't you even think about being sincere," interrupted Mark. "You treated us like prisoners when we trusted you to assist the ISS. You have zero credibility with me, sir."

"Understood, but we have a situation here," responded the general. "We lost contact with the ISS about ten minutes ago. There was some sort of explosion, and from what we can gather, she's tumbling into a lower orbit. We don't have the access to get status on the majors, but you do."

"Like we always have," Mark snapped.

"Can you give—"

Mark again interrupted the general. "Understand, sir, we are not giving you crap! That station and the safety of its people have always been the responsibility of NASA. We will assume full mission responsibility for the ISS."

"No, sir, you will not," responded the general angrily. "This is a joint military mission in response to a possible alien threat. You will answer to this command."

"We are a civilian agency. Write that down on a sheet of paper and shove it up your ..."

A long pause followed as the two contemplated their mutual hostility. Seeing this was getting nowhere, Captain Dillings took the opportunity to speak up. "Mr. Walters, this is Captain Dillings. I am in charge of operations here. I assure you, if I am able to work directly with your ops head, I do believe that we can give you clearance over the health and safety aspect of the ISS as long as it does not interfere with our larger military mission. You will have full authority over the ISS, as you request. We just need to work together."

Mark smiled. The blood that was ready to burst out of his cheeks receded; his color returned to normal. "General, she should have your job. Captain, agreed. Betty Tedesci is your contact. I'll tell her to call you once I speak with my staff and get a status. NASA will deal with you directly. I have no desire to speak with the general on this matter." Mark hung up the phone without another word and looked over at Agent Wachovic.

"As for you, stay out of the way and get out of my office." Mark stood up and marched into the control center. Betty rushed forward to meet him.

"Status?" he asked.

"The station is in critical condition. It looks like we got through to them. They were able to forcibly pull away from the damaged module, which exploded on the last pass around the light side of Earth. The shockwave hit the station, and it's now tumbling out of control, with the orbit growing shallower by the minute. Two-way communication is out, but we can access most of the diagnostic routines."

"Keep broadcasting. I hope they can at least hear us. Do we have vitals on the majors?"

"Yes. Their heart rates and blood pressure are up, as mine are right now, but they're alive," Betty said with relief.

"Excellent." Mark turned and began clapping his hands to get everyone's attention. The personnel in the room stopped what they were doing and turned to Mark. "Can I have your attention? Thank you. I apologize that many of you are now working well past your shift, and I much appreciate your attention and dedication—plus the goon squad wouldn't let us leave." The room chuckled. "On a more serious note, we have a situation here that is most critical. As many of you know, the ISS was attacked several hours ago by four unidentified objects. What we all saw did happen—I can confirm the rumors. The escape craft with four onboard was destroyed. Majors Jensen and Vodnikov are the only two survivors, and they are in trouble. We need to keep them alive. That is your top priority. I don't want to hear about experiments, this and that—you are to keep them alive. Understood?" The room responded with a "yes, sir" in unison.

The staff began to get back to work as Mark whispered a question into Betty's ear. "Where's Mr. Washington?"

The Magnicieat

Dan made it back to the *Atera* and was able to get a few hours of rest before he was awoken by Tom. His friend rudely barged into the room and turned on the lights.

"Get up, space boy!" Tom shouted, while clapping his hands. Dan leaned up and wiped the sleep from his eyes to see Tom standing in front of him, fully dressed—no, make that fully decked out in an intimidating robe.

"You look good in a bed sheet," Dan said, still groggy and unable to see clearly.

"Yeah, whatever. They just dropped these off about an hour ago. Supposedly they're some sort of formal ceremonial robe that you must wear when speaking to the Magnicieat."

Dan was able to muster enough strength to sit up in bed and examine Tom's outfit more closely. It was a simple black robe that covered the entire length of his body, completely obscuring his hands and feet. A hood draped off the back.

"They hung yours up over there," said Tom, pointing to a mess of red fabric dangling on a hook.

"Why is mine red?" Dan asked, a little concerned at the color distinction.

"Oh, I asked about that. Seems since you're the petitioner, you get to wear the red one. Janet and I are just backup singers."

Dan stepped out of bed and walked toward the robe. Tom noticed the bags under his eyes.

"Hey, you look like garbage. Didn't you sleep last night?"

Dan was fidgeting with the robe as he answered, "No, I went down to Daerderus last night."

"You did what?" scolded Tom. "Was that such a good idea? And how did you get down there, anyway?"

"Yes, it was a good idea, and how I got there is immaterial," Dan answered sternly.

"Sorry, I just think wandering about an alien world alone is not such a great idea."

"I don't disagree, but … whatever." Dan had no interest in going at it with Tom. He was much too tired and a little intimidated at having to wear the petitioner's robe. Best to change the subject. "How much time do we have?"

"Not much. They said they'd fetch us after breakfast."

Great. That did not give Dan enough time to get mentally prepared. What a trip to put on a sixteen-year-old. He had to go in front of the Magnicieat and plead the case for the defense of Earth. What class was there for this in high school?

"You know, this just stinks!" Dan shouted. "Why me? Why not someone else? The whole future of our world, our families, our way of life depends on me putting on that red robe and begging some aliens to come and give us a hand."

"Stop feeling sorry for yourself right now!" barked Tom, his eyes burning with anger. Dan was a little frightened, as he had never seen Tom get this upset with him before. Tom's blood vessels pulsed close to his skin, his ears fire engine red. "I have listened to you doubt yourself about this, and you just can't. Too darn bad that it's up to you; deal with it. You are the right person for this because fate put you here. It put us all here."

"I don't believe in fate."

"Well, neither do I, but fate, destiny, or whatever has brought us here right now to do this, and we *will* do it. Let me correct myself—*you* will do it. You will get showered, put on the stupid red robe, and meet us out there for breakfast. Then you are going to get up in front of that council and win one for the team. You got it?"

"Gee, I never saw you so animated before."

"That's because I have never been in a situation where my family and friends were threatened, and I have never believed in someone the way I believe in your ability to get us through this. Now enough said." Tom turned and left the room, closing the door behind him.

Dan stood silently in shock. His friend had never freaked out like that before, or said such nice things about him. It was definitely strange.

Dan's hand continued to fidget with the red robe. The material was silken soft, but did not shimmer like the silk he knew of on Earth. In fact, the richness was in the lack of luster—a matte look, beautiful in its simplicity.

Dan turned to get ready, showering, cleaning his teeth, and combing his hair. He put on an outfit from his closet—a simple white collarless shirt, blue pants, and boots. Next he draped the robe over himself and walked toward the mirror to examine his couture for the day. He sighed as he looked at his image, putting the hood up and down to see which was more flattering, or what was easier to mask his nerves.

After a few moments Dan got up enough courage to leave his room. He walked out the door into the common area. Janet was already dressed in her black robe, sitting at the dining table eating her breakfast.

"Little Red Riding Hood!" Janet exclaimed in jest. Dan answered with the appropriate hand gesture.

"What are you eating?" Dan asked, quickly turning the subject away from his outfit.

"Well, it tastes a heck of a lot like cereal, and I put this white stuff from the fridge over top, and it sure tastes like milk. Kinda weird that they'd have milk and cereal too."

"Is there anything else?"

"Oh, yeah, but it depends on how adventurous you are."

Dan didn't feel adventurous. He had enough pressure and didn't want the uncertainty of trying some strange alien food that might upset his stomach more than it already was from the nervousness of speaking in front of the Magnicieat. He could go with a cup of catria to wake him up, but that would be quite enough. Anything more would most assuredly guarantee some projectile vomiting.

"I'm not that hungry," he finally answered.

"Then go help Tom," she suggested.

The whole time Dan was speaking with Janet, he heard grumblings coming from the kitchen. Tom was obviously frustrated with something, and the constant banging and swearing made his chagrin apparent.

"What are you looking for?" shouted Dan.

"Coffee! I need some coffee!" screamed Tom, sounding like he was ready to explode.

"He sure is grumpy in the morning," whispered Janet.

"It's called catria!" yelled Dan.

"What?" queried Tom from the kitchen.

Dan went to assist but was stopped in his tracks by Janet. "How do you know that?"

"I went down to Daerderus last night," Dan said casually. "Also had some chicken wings." He left Janet sitting at the table in astonishment as he went in the kitchen to help Tom.

Tom was fussing about, opening cabinets, looking in the fridge, and just generally lost. His face was beet red, apparently caused by this very dramatic caffeine fit.

"Wow, slow down, Tex," announced Dan in a soft voice, trying to calm Tom. "Look—catria." Dan pointed toward a small appliance attached to the refrigerator that said "catria." He grabbed the cup out of Tom's shaking hands and placed it under the nozzle. He pressed the button, and beautifully pungent black catria flowed out—steaming hot. Dan handed the cup to Tom, who took a sip.

"Oh, that is good coffee!" Tom said, sounding much more relaxed, the red from his face disappearing more with every sip.

"What do you mean you went down to Daerderus last night?" Janet had snuck up from behind. Tom looked as if he'd just seen a hungry tiger enter the room. Dan slowly rotated to see Janet standing there with steam coming out of her ears. "You mean you couldn't wake me up?"

"It was sort of an accident," answered Dan in a futile attempt to explain it away.

"How is that an accident? What? Did you just fall out of the ship?"

"I went for a walk, and there was this shuttle, and—"

Janet interrupted Dan before he could finish. "You just can't go wandering off alone! You just can't." She began to cry. Dan walked over and embraced her as she sobbed. She tried to continue through the tears. "We have to stick together. We might be all that's left." She kept sobbing, and Dan held her tighter, trying desperately to ease her sadness. They were interrupted by someone at the door.

"They're ready for us," said Tom quietly.

Janet pulled away from Dan and wiped her eyes with the sleeve of her robe.

"Are you going to be all right?" asked Dan sympathetically. Janet simply answered with a restrained nod.

Dan continued toward the door, followed by his companions. He opened it and saw two guards, elaborately dressed in jet-black armor laced with gold, holding long ceremonial staffs. A now familiar face also greeted them outside.

"Commander Teitrik!" The commander was dressed in a black robe identical to the ones Tom and Janet were wearing.

"Being new here, you probably don't have a lot of friends," Teitrik answered as he looked over at Janet, still trying to pull herself together. "Thought you might need one right about now."

"I really appreciate it. Thank you," said Dan, reaching out with his right hand, the commander responding to the now familiar custom.

"Now, let me give you some words of wisdom as we walk," advised Teitrik as they moved through the corridor toward the command tower lobby. "These robes and everything about this experience are supposed to be intimidating. Don't let it be. Just be yourselves and speak with respect, but don't think you have to walk on netrik shells. Dan, you are the petitioner. They will specifically address you, and you alone. They have put this procedure in place so that groups coming to petition don't have folks speaking over one another. Just stand tall and look them in the eye. You'll do fine."

"What can you tell me about the Magnicieat?" asked Dan.

"There are four councilors. The reason for this is that there were four superpowers on Daemerik many centuries ago at the time we began to unite as a people. The original Magnicieat was formed of the leaders of these nations—one from each. Many years later, national distinctions vanished as our exploration of the galaxy advanced. It was funny how we found more in common among ourselves once we discovered others in the universe. The way the selection process for new councilors to the Magnicieat evolved was that when a position opened, the people nominated several candidates based upon their life accomplishments and overall effect on Daemerik's society. They then had to endure several trials to test their personal and moral resolve. Then the councilors would vote on the new member. It has worked well for centuries."

They entered the lobby of the command tower and walked toward an open space in the room, nowhere near the elevators or stairway to the train station. The two ceremonial guards moved forward and pounded their staffs on the marble twice. As they stepped back, a black rectangular shape rose out of the floor.

"Okay, here we go," uttered the commander.

The honor guards angled their staffs until they just touched the black box. Two doors slid open. The commander had Dan stand behind them, followed by those in the black robes. "This is how we must enter the chamber. Now let's go." Teitrik drove the group toward the elevator door.

The guards stepped inside, but as Dan was ready to enter, all he could see was darkness—no walls, no floor, no nothing. When he was sure that the guards in front of him were safely standing on something and not plummeting to their demise, Dan entered, followed by the rest of the entourage. This was obviously an optical illusion designed to intimidate, just as the commander had advised. When the doors closed he could see fine, but it was not apparent where the illumination was emanating from. He brushed it all off per Teitrik's advice.

The elevator moved slowly and quietly, not giving away the distance traveled or direction to anyone inside. The rear door finally opened into a room just as black and featureless as the elevator that had brought them there. The two guards in front of Dan were the first out. They fanned off to the side and motioned for him to continue into the room.

The chamber for the Magnicieat was pitch black, except for that same strange illumination as in the elevator. Dan could not see the walls or ceiling, yet he had a sense that this was an enormous space, again designed to intimidate and make the petitioner feel humbled. He walked forward into the blackness, not knowing exactly where to go or what to do.

Dan stopped as a light came on, illuminating a large curved pulpit, standing almost ten feet above the floor, forcing those standing in front of it to raise their chin and look up. Four golden thrones sat behind the pulpit, with backs extending far into the air, each ending in a sharp point. Each chair had the insignia of the Magnicieat emblazoned on it. This insignia consisted of four concentric circles situated at the four poles—north, south, east, and west. Two symbols unfamiliar to Dan were in the area where the four intermingled, the symbology alluding to the four councilors and four nations that originally made up the Magnicieat. On the front of the pulpit was a globe, strikingly similar to the one that made up the insignia of the *Liberty*.

Only one of the chairs was filled. In it was a very old man, dressed in a beautiful golden robe, again with the Magnicieat's symbol emblazoned on the front.

"Please step forward, Daniel Foster," the man said in a very authoritative tone. "My name is Councilor Etenar. I first want to thank you and your friends for your bravery and courage in saving the passengers and crew of the *Stoic 2*. I speak for the entire Magnicieat and the citizens of Daemerik when I express our sincere thanks. If it were not for your courage and quick thinking, their fate would not have been so fortunate."

"Thank you, sir," Dan said nervously. He looked at the three empty chairs and wondered why they were not filled. "Councilor Etenar, will the other members be joining us today?" Dan looked back at Commander Teitrik to seemingly get his approval and to ensure he did not cross the line. The commander continued to stare forward, expressionless. Dan turned back to Etenar.

"This session only requires the presence of one councilor. The other three are attending to additional matters."

"But sir, does not the Magnicieat need a majority to make a decision?"

"Yes, that is true, and I commend you for being so quick to learn our ways. A decision has been made, Mr. Foster, prior to this session, so the attendance of the others is unnecessary." Councilor

Etenar spoke in a matter-of-fact tone, like so many politicians getting ready to deliver bad news. His words danced around the truth and also appeared to camouflage his own feelings.

Dan, in contrast, could not hide his feelings, nor was he schooled in the intricacies of political verbiage. He knew enough to realize that the Magnicieat had already decided not to help Earth, and Etenar was the only one with enough courage to tell him to his face. Dan did not want to insult Etenar, but the growing cocktail of anger, hopelessness, and fear was clouding his judgment.

Dan took two determined steps forward. "Councilor Etenar, I want to thank you for your courage in coming out and meeting with me today. I wish the others had the same level of courtesy as you." The comment generated some tension in his team that he could feel permeate through the large dark space.

Councilor Etenar simply smiled. He admired Dan's courage and knew what this boy was saying in the most indirect way. The young man's attempt at diplomacy was charming the aged councilor.

Dan, seeing Etenar's reaction, continued, "Sir, I am here to plead my case. To plead for the people of my planet, which will be attacked by the Gaarich, I am told, very soon. We do not have the technological advances that you possess and, like the *Stoic 2*, need outside help for our fate to be—just as fortunate."

A grin crept across Etenar's elderly face. "For a young man, and for one from a planet as young as yours, you have a way with words. I am moved by your request, but the Magnicieat has already decided against intervention."

"May I ask why, sir?" asked Dan, punctuating the sir at the end, more of a jab than a notion of respect.

"We don't believe that we could be of adequate assistance. Our participation would not assure your planet any hope of resisting, but would most assuredly put our existence in great peril. If we would intervene, we would lose the battle dooming us and your planet to a level of existence that I would wish upon no one."

"How do you know that you would lose without trying?"

"Because we did before!" shouted Etenar, clearly agitated, his hands flying about, accentuating his frustration. "We had ten of these ships and a fleet that would darken the sky with its numbers, but we were no match. Eight star cruisers like this one were destroyed, and this, the *Atera*, almost also. Ninety-five percent of our fleet was wiped from the universe. What to you looks intimidating and numerous is but a drop in the pond compared to what we were, and then we could not stand up to the Gaarich." He stood up and yelled, "Recording off!"

Etenar fixed his robe and walked down from the pulpit toward Dan. "I was the newest and youngest member of the Magnicieat selected during the Great War to replace one of the councilors who was killed. I was involved in the discussion whether to stand and fight to the last, or run, take what and who we could and run." He paused and looked at Dan's other companions. "We were evenly split for weeks, discussing and trying to come to a consensus. As the time passed and as we got closer to the inevitable moment, the other councilor who was standing with me changed his vote—the decision was to run. I was the one dissenting opinion, the last voice calling for us to stand and defend our world. Fortunately, I was able to convince them to agree to send a ship, a single ship, to Earth to try to see if one day they could help us and the rest of the galaxy wipe the Gaarich from our space; or at the very least prepare Earth for their arrival, hoping they could be the one world that would stand against the Gaarich and win.

"I knew your grandfather from the academy, and I recommended him for the command of the *Liberty*. His exploits throughout the war made him the obvious choice.

"But the *Liberty* left hastily, as the Gaarich came upon us so quickly. The invasion was terrifying. Whole cities were wiped from the planet, military installations were annihilated in mere moments, and millions of people died in only the first several hours. It was like this on Votraxain, Mordula, Treibik, and countless other worlds with which we were allied. We tried to help them in their time of need, but they fell, as did we. Every world that stood against the invaders was overwhelmed by the relentlessness of the Gaarich."

"Then you must understand why we need your help," pleaded Dan.

Etenar started to pace back and forth, turning away as he spoke. "They will come to your world and soften it up. They are not ready to invade; our intelligence is rather certain of that. Yet they will do whatever they can to ensure that you are not a threat. One day, though, they will come and take your home, as they did mine.

"When we finally escaped Daemerik, all the other councilors were killed except me. We ran here, but lost many ships along the way. Several squadrons ran suicide missions to divert the Gaarich so they would not know where the *Atera* and the remaining fleet were going.

"Once we made it to this place, chaos reigned. We had to elect a new Magnicieat, which took some time." Etenar stopped speaking and moved very close to Dan. "It took us almost ten years to reach some level of security to where our people could exist."

As Dan listened to Etenar's speech, he could only imagine the same devastation on Earth. The councilor's words did nothing to calm Dan's emotions, but only enraged him. "Councilor, I saw the level of existence of your people. I went down to Daerdcrus last evening. There is no life there. You hide and cower from these monsters and have doomed your people to a half existence."

Commander Teitrik moved forward and put his hand on Dan's shoulder. "Dan, enough," he said, breaking protocol, but trying to help quell the coming storm. Dan simply brushed it away.

Dan continued, "How can you stand there, sir, knowing what you lost, and do nothing?"

"Because most of us that knew are gone!" shouted the councilor, spinning around and stopping only inches away from Dan. "Most of our people were born here. They know of no other life and are not willing to risk this half existence, as you say, for a chance of life on a planet where most of them have never been and none have ever lived. This is Daemerik now! The last hope, the last light of our planet was sent on that ship with your grandfather."

"And I am here with that ship to ask for your assistance. Do not let the last light in the galaxy go dim. Do not let Earth fall!"

Etenar turned and slowly stepped away. He began to speak in a softened tone as he walked up the steps to the pulpit. "The decision of the Magnicieat has been made."

"Then the *Liberty* has failed her mission! Your light has gone out too!" Dan shouted as he walked away.

Etenar, who was now standing behind the chair he had sat in at the beginning of the session, turned, staring deep into the eyes of the young man in the red robe. "No, Daniel Foster, the *Liberty* has not failed. You are here." With that, the light illuminating the pulpit went out, leaving Dan and his companions alone in the empty room.

32
Restlessness

NOT A WORD WAS SPOKEN as Teitrik and the three teenagers made the trek back to their quarters aboard the *Atera*. The ruling of the Magnicieat was final. The decision needed no discussion. The commander stayed with Dan, Janet, and Tom as they sulked through the hall. He respected their need for voiceless expression and simply put his hand on Dan's shoulder as a measure of support when he dropped them off and went on his way.

The three friends had their own individual means of dealing with their wracked emotions. Tom spent a lot of time banging around in the kitchen. Janet lay on her bed, staring up at the ceiling and weeping. Dan took a seat on one of the large couches in the common area and gazed off into the abyss, still dressed in the red petitioner's robe. He tried to clear his mind to grasp what had just happened, hopefully allowing his subconscious to make some sense of it all.

Hours passed, and while Dan's two friends moved on to other activities to distract themselves, he remained planted on the couch, eyes fixed forward. But then, as if awakening from a deep sleep, Dan's face came back to life. The color returned in a vengeance, changing his white complexion to blazing red, matching the flowing robe still covering his body. His brow crinkled as he sprang up, flailing about violently as he tried to tear free of the petitioner's garb. "No! No freakin' way!"

The abrupt end to the quiet roused Janet and Tom, who quickly bounded out of their rooms.

"Dan, you all right?" asked Janet, as she watched him tearing the fabric from his body.

Dan turned with a crazed look in his eyes, the red robe still hanging off one arm. "All right? All right? Are you crazy! Of course I'm not all right! Are you?"

"Sorry," Janet answered timidly "I was just trying to—"

"Janet, I'm sorry," Dan said, apologizing for his rudeness. "I'm so sorry, and I appreciate you trying, but that is what I'm so frustrated with."

"Okay, you wanna fill us in, chief?" asked Tom.

"We've been trying to do this and trying to do that. We started with trying to get home, and we're farther away than before. We tried to get help from these people and got nothin'!" Dan returned to his raving but paused to calm himself before he continued. "We didn't try to save the *Stoic 2*; we just did it. I suggest we stop trying and start doing. Every time we set out to do something we're successful, but every time we try, we come up dry. So right now, we stop trying and start doing."

"Agreed. That was a good speech," said Tom. "Now how 'bout you get your big laser gun, and I get mine, and then we kick the Gaarich ourselves."

"That's exactly what I suggest!" Dan exclaimed.

Janet sarcastically smirked at her friend. "What, you got us big lasers?"

"Sure do. We've always had them."

Janet and Tom looked at each other trying to figure out what he was saying. All of a sudden it hit Janet. "The *Liberty*?" she asked.

Dan smiled and nodded, leading to frustrated sighs from his friends.

"What, we're gonna jack a spaceship out of some bigger alien spaceship surrounded by a whole bunch more alien spaceships that aren't half as busted up as the *Liberty*—am I correct?" asked Tom, wondering if his friend had finally cracked.

"That is exactly what we are going to do."

Janet, realizing Dan was serious, grew troubled. "Uh, I don't like it. These people have been kind to us so far. I—"

"The heck with these people!" shouted Dan. "They're content with hiding here and living like vermin. Well, goody goody for them. I for one do not want the same for my friends and family. If the Daemerae want to cower here, fine, but I'm not going to let them have my grandfather's ship! It was sent to Earth for a reason, and she will complete that mission!"

"Dan, we can't defend Earth alone," said Tom.

"If we have to, we will, but I don't think that will be the case."

The two studied Dan, who was brimming with confidence. It was clear to them that he was set upon doing this, with or without them. One thing they both knew about Dan was that he would never let his friends down. The fact that he believed in the idea so much was enough for them.

"What's the plan?" asked Janet.

Dan continued, "When I was down on Daerderus, I talked with this surly cargo guy who spoke about the Pyietri. Supposedly they're a group of former military from Daemerik, along with mercenaries and some overall unsavory characters."

"Oh, yeah, they sound like they would be perfect," joked Tom.

"Just shut up a minute and listen. In the final battle, when the evacuation order was given, several ships in the fleet left and refused to go where the Magnicieat ordered. They were aligned with the Pyietri movement, whose core belief was that the Daemerae should stand and fight for their world. These military ships joined with rogue groups from around the galaxy to create a resistance. Their whole purpose these days is to make life as uncomfortable for the Gaarich as possible, and hope to someday take back Daemerik and the other allied planets."

"I think I'm getting this," affirmed Tom.

"I'm in—and so is Tom." Janet said, giving Tom a friendly nudge, happiness returning with the hope Dan was giving them.

"Good! I'm glad to see that you're hip to the idea, and it's nice to see you both smiling again." Dan sat back down on the couch, now completely free of the robe, and was joined by his two friends, who grabbed chairs across from him. "Now comes the question of how."

"Won't we need guns?" asked Tom.

"I doubt we'd get very far. I think we use our age to our advantage. Tonight, when the ship goes into its evening mode, and most folks are asleep, that's when we go. We'll dress in the clothes that they gave us on the *Defiance* and make our way out into the hallways. We'll just look like a bunch of teenagers wandering around; no one will see us as a threat."

Janet mulled the plan over. "You know, I've seen you two on a Saturday night terrorizing the drive-through."

"Hey, someone has to get you your fries," jabbed Tom.

"Listen, I just don't see it as a problem," continued Dan. "If they're suspicious or catch us wandering the halls in some strange area, I'm banking on them simply escorting us back here. Then we just go again."

"I like it!" Janet exclaimed, showing clearly that her enthusiasm was returning. "You're right. They'll think we're some punk kids out roaming around. It's so simple it's brilliant!"

"Yeah, until we get shot," added Tom.

"We're not gonna get shot," countered Janet, "not if we just look like we're aimlessly wandering."

"Right, which means no sneaking or James Bond stuff until we have to, and that won't be until we get close to the *Liberty*," Dan added.

Tom grumbled a bit before asking the next logical question. "Fine, so we make it to the *Liberty*. Then what? They're gonna have guards around it."

"Couple of options," suggested Dan. "First is we punch them out, which I vote against. Second is we sweet talk our way onto the ship, or third, you guys make out with the guards, and I make a run for it."

"Hey!" Janet and Tom exclaimed in discord.

"Just kidding," giggled Dan. "Sweet talking is my vote, but we're just going to have to think on our feet."

"Okay, now we're on the ship. Do we just fly it out of the docking bay?" inquired Tom.

"Exactly that. With the time of night, they'll scramble to see what's happening. If they try to close the door, we'll blast it open. Once outside the ship, we'll cloak." Dan seemed to have it all figured out.

"One thing you forgot, Captain." Janet had the scientific mind, which was needed to temper some of Dan's excess enthusiasm. "Remember that barrier? We need to calculate a slide into hyperspace exactly to make it through."

Dan smiled, as he had an answer. "When I was down on Daerderus talking to that guy from the freighter, he told me all about how they bring down a portion of the shield every few days to let disabled or sublight ships pass through. We'll cloak ourselves, wait with the others, and sneak out when they open the shield. Since we'll be cloaked, they won't be able to see us. We'll just glide on through."

Janet clapped. "Bravo! But how long do we have to wait?"

"Does it matter?" asked Tom. "We need to do something to save Earth, and if we have to wait a month, we'll wait."

Dan reached over and patted Tom on the shoulder. "But we won't have to wait long to get started. We go tonight."

Chickens

President Thompson sat in his office going over the joint speech he was supposed to give to the nation at the same time his counterparts in Russia and China were to give that speech to their countries. The conference call he had with the leaders had gone well, although they were a bit skeptical about the true threat. However, a treaty is a treaty, and at a minimum it was a good exercise for their militaries, which outside of fighting the war on terror were not allowed to fully interact with their larger weapons platforms.

This was the seventh iteration of the speech. The international leaders could not universally agree. The president sat at his desk in the Oval Office, liberally using his red pen to change the verbiage one more time. He was interrupted by Secretary of Defense Sandra Jackson, who casually walked into the room and sat down in front of Thompson, still going over the document.

Without taking his eyes off the paper, Thompson began to speak. "We keep going over this speech. We can't even agree what tense it needs to be in, and the problems with translating into three distinct languages—"

"There is not going to be a speech, sir," Sandra Jackson said as she interrupted him.

The president pulled off his glasses, slammed them on the table, and lurched upright in his chair. "What do you mean no speech?"

"Well, both the Chinese and the Russians say they are better at keeping secrets from their people than we are. They admit that there is a concern and will keep their forces on alert, but they do not want to tell their people a thing until we know more."

"Fine," said the president bluntly, as he grabbed the speech and threw it in the trash. "We weren't going to agree on the language anyway. Glad the former president negotiated this treaty. I wouldn't want to have my name on it."

"Mr. President, we still have all of our forces on alert."

"That's the other thing. They're all being told to wait for a speech from me." Thompson sat for a moment and then continued. "Let's just 'tell' everyone that this is a drill, if they push it, but not go any further." The president hit his intercom. "Get me General Peters."

"What are you going to tell him?" asked Sandra.

"I was going to try the truth. We still have a situation, whether we admit it or not, and I need this guy."

The intercom buzzed. "Sir, I have General Peters on the line."

The president activated his speakerphone. "General Peters?"

"Yes, sir."

"I'm here with the secretary of defense. What's our current status? Have we seen any other unidentified ships approach the space station?"

"Mr. President, we have linked systems with NORAD and our counterparts in China and Russia. We are in constant communication and have an excellent view of the near-Earth situation, but at this time we have seen no other unidentified craft. As for the ISS, there was an explosion, and we lost communications. The majors are still alive, but we continue to work the problem. We have NASA assisting."

This confused the president, since as far as he knew they were still quarantined. "General, I thought NASA was under lockdown and not to be told of our current situation."

"Yes, sir, but we do not have the technology here to assist the ISS. The explosion caused a decay in the orbit of the station. We need NASA to help with this one. We anticipate your speech to the American people to be forthcoming and are confident we can keep a lid on the situation until then."

"General, there will be no speech." Thompson waited for the reaction.

There was an uncomfortable silence before General Peters answered. "Sir?"

"Until an imminent threat can be confirmed, my counterparts do not feel comfortable communicating this to their people."

"Mr. President, what type of proof do they need? This could escalate quickly."

"General, you still have access to the Defense Pact. Officially it will be considered a drill and will stay live for a while. You can turn it hot in a moment's notice. Got it?"

"Yes, sir," answered the general, sounding unconvinced.

Thompson hung up the phone. "Well, he's not happy, but we had no choice here."

"Agreed," answered Sandra. "I only hope the escalation you just spoke about does not come."

We'll Take It to Go

THE DOOR INTO THE LONG HALLWAY of the *Atera* opened. Dan carefully peered out, inspecting the area to make sure that there was no one in sight. The lights were dimmed for the evening cycle, and most personnel were sleeping, except for those few who had night duty.

"Remember, we just look like we're wandering. Don't look suspicious," Dan reminded them.

They exited their room and walked casually toward the lobby of the command tower. The guards paid them no notice as they moved to the elevator. Traveling down several levels, they boarded the train back to the fore section of the *Atera*, where the *Liberty* was docked. The car they sat in was empty except for a maintenance person, who was minding his own business. He eventually exited at a stop halfway through their journey.

Once reaching the great station outside the docking bay for the corvettes, the three friends got off the train. The area, which was piled with people when they first arrived, was now completely empty, which was what they had hoped.

Janet pulled Dan close and whispered, "The *Liberty* was two ships down from the *Defiance*. Say we go to the top gangway, which will be closer to the bridge." Dan nodded.

The trio made their way through the station to the escalators near where the *Liberty* was located. They traveled to the fourth level, being now up so high they could look around the great room. It was deserted. They had picked the right time of night.

Dan led the way toward the embarkation ramp. He figured that if there were any guards, he would be the first to try the sweet talking, since it was his plan. As they climbed through the ramp to the entrance of the ship, they saw no guards—none at all.

"This makes me nervous," said Tom.

"Everything makes you nervous," Dan responded.

"Okay, tell me where the guards are?"

Janet intervened with a whisper. "Stuff it, you two. No guards equals no problem. So just shut up and keep walking."

They continued up the ramp and into the *Liberty* herself. Many of the lights were turned off, but they could see a clear pathway to an elevator and made their way toward it. Dan selected the bridge. The doors opened, and they stepped inside.

"This is too easy," remarked Dan, echoing what the others were thinking.

The door to the elevator opened onto the landing above the bridge. Before venturing out, Dan peeked around the wall, half expecting some guards to jump out at him, but the coast seemed clear. He quietly exited the elevator and motioned for Janet and Tom to follow. The three smiled triumphantly, relishing the fact that they had made it this far. Boldly they continued toward the landing above the bridge, then suddenly froze.

"Mr. Foster," boomed Commander Teitrik, who was standing on the bridge flanked by several other people. All in all there were about twenty uniformed officers.

Dan tried to think quickly—time for the sweet talk. "Oh, hi! We just ... uh ... came to pick up some stuff." Dan could tell from the commander's smirk that he was not buying it, but he continued to try anyway. "Tom here, well ... he left his teddy bear, and—"

"Teddy bear!" shouted Tom.

"Uh, I mean—" Dan tried to finish his thought, but the commander interrupted him.

"Really," Teitrik said, as he laughed and looked over at his comrades. "I thought you might have come to steal this ship."

"Ha, ha!" laughed Dan, trying his best to shrug off the comment. "I didn't think you were so good at comedy. I mean, three teenagers stealing a starship. Funny."

"I agree," answered the commander. "That is why we are here to help."

This jolted Dan, almost knocking him to the floor. "Are you kidding?"

"I have seen your commitment to saving your people. That performance in front of Councilor Etenar was powerful. No one goes up in front of the Magnicieat like that, but you, who are just a kid, did so with grace and conviction. After that I knew what your next step could only be."

"But why help us when your leaders seem happier to keep their heads in the sand?"

"First, realize that many leaders do not, Etenar being one of them, but you cannot underestimate the fear and reticence of my people. They are terrified, and many of them think staying well clear of the Gaarich is the only way to survive." Teitrik motioned to the others he had with them. "We do not. We believe that one day we will need to fight and take our world back and help eliminate the Gaarich from the galaxy. We are not content to live like this or doom our descendants to a life of hiding or servitude under the Gaarich. That is why we are here. We will start that fight with you and with this ship. We will draw the line that should have been drawn many years ago at Daemerik. Today, we will begin to take back the galaxy, by helping you."

Dan and his friends were moved by the outpouring of support. They were not alone after all, but Dan still needed to know more. "But again, why us? Why now?"

"Because the *Liberty* was sent off to establish the groundwork for the fight against the Gaarich through your people. She was the last hope of the Daemerae. This one ship is the spark that will start the fire. That is why she was sent away, and that is why you are here now. By your words and actions, you have started the fire, and we," he again motioned to his companions, "are the flames."

Dan did not know immediately how to react. He was so moved. Looking over at Tom and Janet, he could see that they were also.

"Now, can we go kick some Gaarich booty?" joked Tom. The whole room chuckled.

"Captain, what are your orders?" one of the men shouted below, looking right at Dan.

Dan noticed all the attention directed toward him. "What?"

"Suck it up. You're in charge!" Tom exclaimed.

Dan surveyed the room as those in it continued to stare at him, waiting for his response. "Uh, Commander ... um ..." There were a lot of friendly faces, but his gaze affixed on one, that of Janet. She gave him a wonderful smile that conveyed much more than mere words. It gave him pause to consider that some things happen for a reason, and he needed to deal with the deck life had handed him, and today that deck had handed him being captain of this ship.

With this Dan got the courage to give the order. "Commander, let's get out of this parking lot." The crew quickly moved to their assigned stations.

Dan stepped down onto the landing. Commander Teitrik motioned for him to take the captain's chair. Dan walked over and ran his hands across it, contemplating its shape, texture, and obvious importance, including the incredible burden he would assume by sitting in it. He turned and lowered himself in. "Commander, can we plot a slide through the barrier?"

"Consider it done," answered the commander.

"Excellent! Then undock the ship," ordered Dan. "Janet, take the helm. Tom, you take the weapons station; hopefully you won't have to shoot at anyone just yet."

"Release umbilical!" ordered the commander. "Retract ramps!"

The *Liberty* shuddered a bit as the mechanicals began to pull away from the ship.

"Look!" shouted Janet as she pointed toward the screen. The docking bay came alive with red flashing lights. Alarms were going off. Their crime had been noticed.

"Janet, get us moving before they shut the door! Tom, if they do, blow it open!"

"Cap," said Janet, "it's close quarters, but I'll do my best not to hit anything."

Commander Teitrik leaned down and whispered into Dan's ear. "I hope she doesn't hit anything."

The *Liberty* moved forward out of her docking station into the center of the bay. She rotated and faced the force shield that led into open space.

Back in the command tower of the *Atera*, Grand Admiral Retenik had just made it to the bridge. The alarms had rousted him from his sleep, and he quickly rushed up to the command deck to get a full report.

"What is happening?" Retenik asked his duty commander.

"Someone's stealing the *Liberty*!"

The grand admiral's eyes widened in amazement; then the corners of his mouth began to curl upward in a slight smile. "Did we check to see if our guests were in their quarters?"

"Just did. They're not there. Sir, we're ready to shut the door to the docking bay."

"Commander, we haven't shut that door in years. I want you to run a check on the systems to make sure we can close it safely."

The commander looked perplexed. "Sir, that will take about four minutes. The *Liberty* will be long gone by then."

The grand admiral got very angry. "I will not give an order that will cause any additional damage to the *Atera*! Check the door to make sure it will close and not rip a hole in the side of this star cruiser. Now get to it!"

The commander saluted and went to run the check. The grand admiral stood there listening to the chaos, trying to hide the slight grin that kept running across his lips.

"They're not shutting the door!" shouted one of the crewmen aboard the *Liberty*.

Dan looked up at Teitrik, who said, "Looks like we have some friends in high places."

"Still, I don't want to take any chances. As soon as we're clear of the *Atera*, cloak the ship." Dan wanted to stick with the plan, which had worked well up to this point.

Janet nudged the throttle to try to get some more speed, and the *Liberty* sprang out of the *Atera*. Immediately her cloaking device was activated, and to the naked eye or any other tracking system, she vanished.

"We're clear, Captain," uttered Janet from the helm.

"Great job! Tom, clear away from the navigation console. The commander is going to plot us a slide through the barrier."

Tom stood up as Commander Teitrik rushed over and started plotting a course.

"Where are we going?" asked Tom, watching over his shoulder.

"Someplace safe," the commander said, then turned back toward Dan. "We have a course plotted. Ready to slide."

"Transfer power to the hyperdrive," ordered Dan.

The crewman at the engineering console acknowledged and routed power. "Captain, cloak is dropping. Power is transferred. We are ready to slide."

The *Liberty* emerged from her protective cloak. Immediately the small ships searching for her pounced and darted toward the corvette.

"Helm, slide! Do it now!" screamed Dan.

Janet pulled back on the lever, and the *Liberty* slid away from her pursuers, through the barrier, and into her hyperspace wormhole. They had escaped.

35
Fubar

General Peters delicately replaced the hot phone in its cradle. Bureaucrats were always so predictable, always backing down from controversy at the last minute. He did not blame the president. He knew that the Russians and Chinese had their own local concerns. He had to remind himself that the Global Defense Pact was more lip service than substance. The guise of a simple drill would not last long. If no action happened, they would stand down—but what about the truth? Would the greater population ever know what had truly happened?

What to tell the public was happily out of his hands. It was someone else's problem. He only had two to worry about—the ISS and keeping the supposed "test" of the Global Defense Pact in play as long as he could just in case more unpleasant visitors returned.

The general again called Captain Dillings into his office.

"Captain, change of plans. The Russians and Chinese have cold feet. They want to officially call this thing a 'drill.' The spinmeisters in Washington are working on what to tell the public about this. I need you to keep this 'drill' going as long as possible."

"Yes, sir." She saluted and left the room.

Farther south, in Houston, Marcus Washington was still sitting at the terminal in the training room, keeping an eye on the systems of the ISS, when he felt a tap on his shoulder. He jerked in fright to turn around and see Mark Walters standing there with one of the NSA agents.

"Good job, Marcus. You must have gotten the word to them."

Marcus was very careful in how to answer, seeing the NSA agent standing close to his boss. "Uh, what do you mean, Mark? I was just doing some training sims ..."

"Cut the bull. We're back in the game. We need you downstairs," grumbled Walters.

Marcus stood up. "Hey, I've been in the game! I've been up to my skivvies in taco meat to stay in the game!"

"Fine. Let's get going—Merv," Walters joked referring to the name on the overalls Marcus was wearing. "And take a shower on your next break. You smell bad."

Marcus Washington put his head down in disgust. He knew it was hard for Mark to pass out compliments, but the indignity of swimming around in a garbage bin should have bought him something. Yet he knew that although Walters had the reputation of being a tough person, he was also smart and fair, which was enough for Marcus. He followed Mark Walters and the NSA agent out of the training room and down to the main floor of the Houston control center.

Betty was waiting for them. "Oh, hi, Merv." She began to giggle, but held her nose at the same time to try to ward off the smell.

"You know, some semblance of respect would be nice," suggested Marcus.

"No time for that!" barked Walters. "Tell him."

"Have you heard of the Global Defense Pact?" asked Betty.

Marcus looked puzzled. "You mean that silly treaty we signed with the Chinese and Russians a couple years back? Yeah, I know something about it."

"Well, our friends at Cheyenne Mountain have worked with the president and invoked the thing."

"What?"

Betty continued, "There are thousands of nuclear warheads pointed straight up at something. Officially it's being called a drill."

Marcus looked at them like they were crazy. "Ah, I can't work here anymore. It is way too whacked."

"Whacked or not, Mr. Washington," uttered Walters, "we need your special skills right now. You are clear to hack into any system anywhere that will get you a better look at the overall picture in space—telescopes or whatever—have at it, but be quick about it. If something else is coming, I, along with that jerk General Peters, would rather have the jump on it before the Russians and the Chinese. That way we can call the shots."

"Okay, I get it. It's a game of who gets to blow up the aliens first sort of thing. Whatever, I'll go do it, but just remember that bonus. I deserve to get hooked up." He walked away and sat down at his terminal, placing his headphones in his ears as he got to work.

Walters turned toward Betty. "How is the ISS doing?"

"Fine. We've established some very basic communication. We can speak to them, but they're broadcasting back in Morse code. They were able to get enough of the systems back so that they could flatten the spin. Problem is the orbit is too shallow. We bought a few more days, but only five. The Russians are refitting a rocket they had for a commercial satellite launch. It should be ready in four. Barring anything else going wrong, the majors should be all right."

"But are they safe?" asked Walters.

"As long as the Russians get that rocket up there before the ISS tumbles through the atmosphere, they'll be fine. My counterpart over there has high confidence."

Walters looked pleased. "Great job, Betty," he said proudly. "You and Mr. Washington really made this thing come together. Fine job."

36
Planning

WITH A FLASH the *Liberty* slid out of hyperspace, emerging near a dense asteroid field, her cloaking device switched on to ensure that she was invisible to any hostiles in the vicinity. Being alone, and now hunted by even their own people, they needed to find a secure place to hide. Not only would the Gaarich be unfortunate to come across, but also the Daemerik fleet was hot on their heels.

"We will be safe here," noted Commander Teitrik. "Even if they do find this place, it would be like trying to find a draynot in a mastenier."

"I assume you mean needle in a haystack—right?" asked Dan.

Teitrik gave him a surprised look. "I guess you could say that."

The *Liberty* pulled into the asteroid field, stopping near the edge. They did not want to go in too deep, only far enough to hide among the rocky debris. It gave them a quick escape route just in case there was a need to slide out of the area in a hurry. Ramping up to light speed with a bunch of space rocks around was not such a wise idea.

"Now we have a ship. What's the plan?" carped Tom.

Dan waved to Teitrik. "Probably best if we go in the conference room to discuss this."

The commander motioned for three of his people to follow Dan, Tom, and Janet into the executive conference room. Dan nervously sat down at the head of the table. He was obliged to as captain, yet it still felt extremely awkward. "Commander, I cannot thank you enough for your help."

"No time for thanks," Teitrik answered. "If our intelligence is correct, we only have about two days until the Gaarich attack Earth. That is not a great deal of time to put a fleet together, and we cannot do this alone."

"Commander, I've learned of the Pyietri." Teitrik's eyes widened, and he shook his head as Dan continued. "If they hate the Gaarich so much, they would be perfect allies."

Looking down at the table as he spoke, Commander Teitrik tried to dissuade Dan from his thoughts. "Listen, these are not the types of folks you want on your side. The ones who aren't traitors are pirates and criminals at best."

"Commander, be honest," challenged Dan. "Were they traitors, or did they simply have a different opinion than the Magnicieat? You can't call anyone who's willing to fight for his world a traitor."

"He has a point," said one of the crewmen who had come in with Commander Teitrik. She was very tall, with long black hair, and luminescent blue eyes. Her long fingers and olive skin would have made her an instant modeling success back on Earth. In fact to Dan, it looked like she might have just emerged from the cover of a fashion magazine.

"Let me introduce Lieutenant Mahdara," said the commander. "She is one of the best in the fleet and has much the same passion for freedom as you young ones."

"Pleased to meet you," said Janet, extending her hand.

"Lieutenant, you were going to make a comment about the Pyietri?" asked Dan.

"Yes, thank you, Captain. They may be unsavory characters, but they love freedom and continue to fight for it, while the Daemerik fleet sits hiding, doing only what it needs to survive." Dan could see the fire in her eyes when she spoke. There was a passion there that she was desperately holding back. Dan sensed that this lieutenant had much more to offer their mission.

"Lieutenant, do you believe there is any chance that they may help us?"

"No ... I am sorry, I do not know," the lieutenant answered. "Perhaps they may—"

"Captain, Admiral Tantera commands the other star cruiser, known as the *Besenti*. Maybe we would be able to get his help. He's a hawk in a political sense, and he was my first commander. I may be able to help sway him," offered Teitrik.

Dan sat and thought for a minute, holding his chin with his two fingers while the gears in his brain meshed to come up with how to proceed. "Only problem I see is that if they don't go for it, we're caught. There's no way we could pull that escape again."

Janet piped up. "We could definitely use the firepower of a star cruiser, but Dan, you're right. The only way I could see us getting in and out of there is if we had a negotiating advantage."

"Go on."

"Let's say we try these Pyietri types. If it goes down badly, we have a better chance of fighting our way out of the situation. If it goes badly with the star cruiser, we're toast."

"Is there any time when we won't be toast?" griped Tom. "I could use one scenario where we know we'll come out on top. Just one would be fine." Commander Teitrik tapped him on the shoulder and chuckled.

Janet continued, ignoring her friend's whining. "My thought is if we get the Pyietri on our side, we take our little fleet to visit the

Besenti. Then we have a much better chance of getting away from the star cruiser."

"Janet, you rock, as usual!" exclaimed a pleased Captain Foster.

Commander Teitrik grumbled. "You are forgetting one thing. The Pyietri are going to want something besides the opportunity to battle the Gaarich. That will not be their only motivation to join the fight."

"The cloaking device," added Tom.

"One more time?" asked Dan.

"The cloaking device," repeated Tom. "Didn't everyone say that this is the only one? Well, we let them copy it, if we don't all die first."

"You know, Tom, that is the type of brilliant bull that keeps you on the dean's list," remarked Dan. "Now, if you just spent as much time coming up with great ideas like that instead of whining all the time, we would have won the war by now!"

Teitrik protested, "We can't give them the technology for the cloaking device!"

"Why not?" asked the lieutenant.

"It would give them an unfair advantage."

"What, against the Gaarich? Why is that bad?" she asked, the tips of her ears beginning to turn red.

Teitrik looked puzzled, as to him this was obvious. "Well, Lieutenant, not only do they harass the Gaarich, but they also steal from the Daemerae to survive."

"And you steal from the Gaarich to survive, if I'm correct," added Janet, jumping into the middle of the conversation.

Commander Teitrik folded his arms and sighed with frustration. "Okay, what is your point then?"

"Both factions are trying to survive by scavenging off the Gaarich because they took your homes. You're both in the same boat, and you forget the greatest thing we can offer the Pyietri and the Daemerae."

"What's that?" asked the commander.

"Earth—a new home. Food that you can grow, air to breathe, and a place to mount the liberation of your home world."

"Janet, that's a noble idea, but I don't think that our world is ready for aliens running around rampant building ships and stuff," added Tom. "I mean, people freak out at the coffee place when they don't have enough caramel on their fru-fru-latte."

"Tom, you have a point, but we owe it to these people. They can't continue to live the way they do and expect to thrive as a civilization. So I think we have it—sanctuary on Earth and a cloaking device. Sounds like a good deal to me." There was not unanimous support at the table, but Dan was acting captain, and what he said was the final word. "Now, where do we find the Pyietri, Lieutenant Mahdara?"

The lieutenant was taken aback. She glanced at all the people at the table, who were now looking directly at her. "Why do you think I know where they are?" she asked, her voice quivering from nervous laughter.

"Let's just say your reaction when you spoke about them gave you away as a Pyietri. Am I right?" asked Dan.

The room was very still, waiting for an answer, no one more intently than Commander Teitrik, who had served side by side with the lieutenant and recommended her for her current assignment aboard the *Defiance*.

"Yes, I am a member of the Pyietri." The room gasped at her answer. "I feed them information, and they feed me information. Commander, it is one of the reasons why we have been able to stay one step ahead of the Gaarich for the past few months."

The commander grumbled. "It is still no excuse! How could—"

"Before this gets out of hand into a game of who betrayed who, may I point out that you both helped us steal this ship?" Janet articulated. "That gets pretty much everyone in this room in deep trouble. We're all rebels now."

Commander Teitrik nodded his head in agreement. "You are right, Janet. I am just surprised—"

The critical alert siren interrupted their planning session. A voice came over the intercom from the bridge. "Captain, we have a proximity alert. Looks like a Gaarich patrol."

The table cleared without another word as they ran onto the bridge and took their places.

"Can we get a look at them?" asked Dan.

A magnified picture of four ships appeared on the screen. They were long and diamond shaped, with four triangular engine nacelles emerging from the aft of the vessels. The size of each appeared comparable to the *Liberty*.

"Gaarich destroyers," remarked Teitrik. "They're very fast, very nasty, and packed with all types of weapons. We should get out of here."

"No," answered Dan. "How's the cloaking device functioning?"

Lieutenant Mahdara, who was seated at the engineering console answered, "It's 100 percent."

"Good! Then let's give it a try. What use is a cloaking device that doesn't work?" Dan's little plan made the stress level rise considerably on the bridge. He glanced over at Tom, who was seated at weapons. "Tommy boy, keep an eye on those ships. If they so much as blink, get those weapons ready. Janet, get ready for that emergency slide thing. We may need to use it again."

The crew watched the screen as the four Gaarich destroyers continued their patrol of the asteroid field, searching for any signs of life. They would destroy any Daemerik military vessel they happened across. The four ships remained in a consistent formation as they slowly crept along, searching for any signs of movement. The enemy ships inched closer to the *Liberty*. On their current course they would pass less than one hundred meters off her bow.

Tom put the tactical view up on the screen next to the actual zoomed visual.

Commander Teitrik leaned down and whispered, "Captain, they are going to get really close."

"Exactly," Dan answered, keeping his voice down so only the commander could hear. "If they don't pick us up after almost tripping over us, we know this cloak works as well as we need it to."

All eyes on the bridge were glued to the viewscreen, intently watching the Gaarich overtake the *Liberty*'s position. The destroyer on the outer flank would pass closest to them, just a breath away if what the computer projected was correct. The magnification of the viewscreen switched off, as it was no longer necessary; at this close range they could almost see into the Gaarich windows. The hulls of the destroyers were a deep black with an interlocking diamond pattern that was cold and mechanical. This pattern was what filled the screen—the dark void of the hull now so close, it seemed to wipe away the stars themselves.

The nearest destroyer began its pass over the *Liberty*'s hull, seemingly oblivious to its enemy that was so near. The proximity alarm wailed on the bridge of the *Liberty* as the indicator counted down the distance. The crew held its breath as the Gaarich continued to float by, maintaining their current speed. The cloaking device had proved itself. The *Liberty* truly was invisible.

The crew breathed a collective sigh of relief and broke out into thunderous applause. Commander Teitrik patted Dan on the shoulder to congratulate him.

"Lieutenant, you and Janet work out a course to get us to the Pyietri. I need to go speak with the captain in private," said the commander.

Dan looked surprised and wondered what the commander could want, but he stood up and followed Teitrik into the conference room. They continued toward the locked door that was opposite the captain's office.

"There is one more reason why I want to help you. You see, my grandmother was your grandfather's older sister," uttered the commander, with a proud smile on his face. "We're cousins. The same blood runs in our veins."

Dan was moved. This whole time he had felt like an alien among aliens, but now he had found a member of his own family. The realization shook him as he tried to grasp the enormity of it all. He had focused on his family back on Earth, but his grandfather was from Daemerik. It would only make sense that he would have alien relatives. Some might be aboard the *Atera*, down on Daerderus, or worse, enslaved on their homeworld of Daemerik. It gave more purpose to his mission. He had to succeed, not only for those he knew, but also for the family he was just beginning to meet.

"I don't know what to say. Why didn't you tell me sooner?"

"With all that you had been through the past several days, I don't think it would have been wise."

"And it's wise now?"

Commander Teitrik looked Dan directly in the eyes. "It is, because for us, there may be no tomorrow."

Dan felt no need to answer. He knew what Teitrik was trying to say. This moment might have been the only time he could have told this to Dan. They might not survive the battle ahead. He tried to wipe the thought away, digging deep inside to find the confidence he needed.

Teitrik pulled down the panel on the door and began to play with the wires. "Now let's see if we can get you some proper clothes. Those won't do for the negotiations that are before us." Sparks flew, and funny noises abounded, but after a few moments the door opened. He motioned for Dan to step inside.

"All captains and admirals have their quarters right by the bridge," the commander pointed out. "This was Captain Jostak's room."

As Dan stepped through the threshold, the lights came up. The quarters were elegantly understated. It might have been expected that someone with the responsibility of a captain would have rich hardwoods, gold leaf, and expensive artwork, yet the room was simple. A sitting area with a couch and some chairs greeted Dan and Teitrik as they entered. An intimate dining room table that could seat four was against the far wall, directly in front of a window with a breathtaking view of the space outside. A small galley kitchen was nearby. Most likely the captain had had his food brought up, but the kitchen was adequate enough to make small meals if the need arose.

The quarters were meticulously kept. Even after over fifty years there was barely a speck of dust, partly thanks to the excellent ventilation system on the *Liberty*. Dan turned to his left, where there was a beautiful entrance table with more pictures scattered about. The faces were similar to the ones he had seen in the captain's office, but there were others he did not recognize. The commander walked over and pointed to them one by one.

"This is my mother," the commander said, pointing at a young woman in her late teens. The picture had the backdrop of a tree on a beautiful sunny day. "She was a little bit older than you in this picture. This was her first day at the academy, where she studied propulsion." He put the picture down and picked up the next, which had a young man under the same tree. "This is your grandfather at his first day at the academy." The commander looked over at Dan and then down at the picture. "Wow, you almost look like identical twins!"

Dan walked over and looked at the picture. There definitely was a resemblance, but he was not about to think that they were twins.

The commander took Dan into a modest room off to the left. This was the sleeping suite. Teitrik made a beeline for the closet and pulled out an intensely formal uniform. It was deep blue with golden armbands and stripes flowing down the arms. The shirt was white and collarless, the fasteners cleverly hidden inside the fabric. The jacket was three-quarter length and spoke of authority even resting quietly on the hanger. The insignia of the *Liberty* graced the lapel.

"Try it on," suggested the commander, thrusting the outfit toward Dan.

"What?"

"Try it on."

This was too much. Acting as captain was one thing, but if Dan put on that uniform, it would be the real deal. Not only that, but he would very literally have to fill his grandfather's shoes.

"Hey ... I just don't think it will be a good idea," Dan said timidly.

Teitrik sighed. "Listen, you're the kid who wants to save the universe, starting with your planet, right? Well, you need to look the part. You have to turn your words into actions and become the person you need to be to pull this off. By putting on this uniform, you make it real." The commander shoved the uniform into Dan's hands. "I'll wait in the seating area."

Teitrik waited for several minutes until Dan emerged from the room. He stood up in amazement. "You look like a captain now. Let's go and meet your crew."

Dan smiled. Wearing the uniform definitely felt good, and Teitrik was right. It would help communicate his station to the Pyi-etri and hopefully assist in the negotiations. More important, it made him feel the part. Like the commander said, it made it real.

Dan emerged back onto the bridge. As everyone turned and got a glimpse of him, they stopped what they were doing and stood up one by one, until the entire crew was standing at attention facing Dan. Janet's jaw was almost to the floor. Her eyes sparkled with the surprise of seeing her friend looking so elegant and authoritative.

"Dan, is that you?" asked Tom. "You look serious!"

"Lieutenant, Janet, are we ready to roll?" asked Dan.

"Yes, sir," responded Janet with a quick salute and a wink.

"Then let's do this!"

37

The Pyietri

THE SHIMMER OF THE WORMHOLE filled the screen of the *Liberty* as she raced toward her meeting with the Pyietri. Lieutenant Mahdara had plotted the course with Janet. Since Janet was operating the helm, it was very important that they be completely aligned on the approach. Coming in too hard and fast would make the Pyietri react aggressively, and the *Liberty's* crew did not want to pick a fight with probably the only group they had a chance of convincing to join them.

"Lieutenant, how did you ascertain their location?" asked the captain.

"Many months ago I devised a way to track the Pyietri transmissions I was receiving. I noticed a pattern and could approximate where they liked to hide. Based upon their pattern over the past few months, my bet is that they're near the planet Tresti 2. It's a barren world, with no life and little atmosphere. The Gaarich have no use for it, so they stay clear, but they come by once in a while to make sure the area is secure. As for the Daemerae, well, they simply don't venture into the Tresti star system. There is nothing there for them."

"How sure are you?" asked Teitrik.

"Commander, relax, it's the best we've got," interrupted Dan.

"Ten seconds until normal space!" shouted Janet from the helm.

"Captain, we should cloak as soon as we come out of hyperspace," recommended the lieutenant.

"Go for it. Any advice you have, feel free to give it. You know these people."

In a brilliant flash, the *Liberty* slid into normal space and decelerated from light speed. With a move of Lieutenant Mahdara's hand, the cloaking device was activated, and the ship shimmered into nothing.

"They saw something!" exclaimed Tom. "Some smaller ships are moving this way."

"If the cloaking device works as well as it did before, they should sail right past us," remarked the commander.

"Still, let's keep our distance," ordered the captain.

The *Liberty* swung out of the way as it bounded toward the orbit of the bluish red planet Tresti 2. It resembled an enormous version of Mars, with an orange red surface, but was also covered in veils of blue wispy clouds in its thin and shallow atmosphere.

"I have multiple contacts," announced Tom. "Wow! I have a whole lot of contacts. At least fifteen large ships and a bunch more smaller ones."

"I told you they would be here!" announced Lieutenant Mahdara, smiling proudly. "Captain, I recommend that we get as close as possible to the largest vessel, which is a Daemerik dreadnaught called the *Eclipse*. That is where Captain Tyreal will be. He's the current leader of the Pyietri."

"Go ahead and take us in, Janet," Dan ordered.

The *Liberty* closed in on the ragtag fleet. Its numbers were strewn with capital ships, armed transports, and even some Votraxain warcraft, whose hulls glowed green from the exotic alloy used to construct them. Votraxain was one of the sister worlds to

Daemerik and populated by humans. The Votraxain and Daemerae were once the closest of allies. These two ships, members of the Pyietri, were all that remained of their once grand fleet.

Besides the *Eclipse*, there were three battleships, four destroyers, and three corvettes. The smaller ships were so varied in design and size that distinguishing their exact types was almost impossible.

"Lieutenant, how would they feel about us pulling right up to their bridge and decloaking with gun ports opened?" asked Dan.

Mahdara turned around and looked at Dan with amazement. "Good guess. I was just about to suggest that. They respond to strength, plus being that close, they won't attack us."

Janet responded by directing the *Liberty* toward the dreadnaught. The Pyietri flagship was at least ten times the size of the corvette-class vessels, with a curved hull that met in a point at the end. The signature command tower that seemed a theme on Daemerik vessels was toward the very aft of the ship and rose arcing forward as if trying to leap ahead, urging the ship to follow. It was in front of this structure that Janet positioned the *Liberty*.

Game on, Dan thought to himself as he gave the orders. "Tom, fire up weapons." With that Tom armed the weapons on the *Liberty*. The turrets rose from the hull, the sliding doors revealed the one functioning supergun, and indicator lights showed that all beltline defense armaments were ready to go. Tom gave the thumbs up.

"Decloak!"

Lieutenant Mahdara deactivated the cloaking device. The *Liberty* appeared to a startled Pyietri.

Aboard the *Eclipse*, Captain Tyreal and his bridge crew jumped as their viewscreen filled with an appearing ship, guns at the ready. Instantly they went to red alert.

"What is that?" shouted Tyreal's second in command.

"Only one ship I know of has a cloaking device like that," Captain Tyreal remarked.

Back on the *Liberty*, Dan ordered, "Open a channel." A green indicator on the viewscreen noted that ship-to-ship communications were active.

Dan cleared his throat before he began. "Captain Tyreal of the Pyietri, I am Captain Foster of the *Liberty*. We come seeking your assistance."

Captain Tyreal's bridge appeared on the viewscreen. He stood as a stocky, elder man, almost completely bald except for clumps of hair protruding over his ears. "Captain Foster, when most people come seeking help, they do not do it with a gun pointed at your head."

"Captain, that was a demonstration of one of the things I have to offer you in return for your assistance. The cloaking technology of the *Liberty* will give you a distinct advantage in your battles with the Gaarich. No one else in the galaxy has this technology, and as you've just seen, it is absolutely undetectable."

"I could just take it from you," answered Tyreal.

"Not before we decapitate your vessel, with you being in the less fortunate part of the bridge."

Captain Tyreal maintained the scowl on his face for a moment before breaking out into a chuckle. "Fine, you have my attention, but what's the second thing you have to offer?"

"A place to hang your hat, as we say on Earth," Dan offered. "A planet where you can raise your children, grow your food, and mount a fight against the Gaarich to take back your home world. I offer you sanctuary on Earth."

Again Captain Tyreal broke out into laughter. "Earth!" He continued to chuckle. "That backwater planet. Not even the Gaarich are interested in it yet."

"Well, they are now," answered Dan. "They're amassing a force to soften up Earth in advance of an invasion. We need to stop them once and for all. They can have no more of our galaxy. I'm asking you to join me, and in return for your service, I open my home to you."

Janet turned around and smiled at Dan with her eyes gleaming. She could not believe the words that were coming out of his mouth. He was a natural at this; that or the uniform was boosting his ego for the time being. Nonetheless, it was impressive.

"And if we fail?" asked Tyreal.

"That's not in the plan. Yet even if my planet falls, and if we survive, I will honor my word and give you the cloaking device. In addition, I will serve you in the cause of continuing to fight the Gaarich until we can drive them from this place."

"You have big delmecks for someone so young," complimented Tyreal. Delmecks did not translate, but Dan could guess what the word meant. The snicker from Tom confirmed his suspicion.

"Uh, thank you … I guess."

"Before I agree to anything, I need to know who you are. My spies know of no Captain Foster in the Daemerik fleet. They would tell me if there was some young hot shot coming up the ranks, as that person would be a prime candidate for recruitment. Tell me, Captain Foster, who are you really?"

Dan was waiting for that question and had practiced the answer in his head over and over just in case. All he had to do was speak it. "I am the grandson of Captain Meikre Jostak, former commander of this ship."

Captain Tyreal's eyes got wide as he sat down in his chair. The surprised looks of everyone on the bridge of the *Eclipse* also told the story.

"Jostak," muttered Captain Tyreal. "How is he? Why is he not with you? I knew Jostak from back on Daemerik. We served together on many ships early in our career."

"Sir, he died about six years ago."

A cocktail of grief and disappointment crossed Captain Tyreal's face. "I have lost friends, loved ones, my home planet, and my son, but it always feels the same when you hear about death. It never gets easier.

"Jostak was a fiery youngster, like yourself. His courage and final mission are the things that we rally upon. It is the legend of your grandfather and the ship you are standing on that gives us hope and is why we fight, knowing that we are not alone—that there are other forces at work, forces of fate. Did fate bring you here today, Captain Foster? This I need to know before I commit the lives of my small fleet to defend your planet."

"Thank you for considering."

"I need to meet you in person. Please bring yourself and a small party aboard the *Eclipse*," directed Tyreal, "and I think I recognize Lieutenant Mahdara, which explains the reason why you found us so easily. Bring her along also. I look forward to our meeting." With that the communication ended, and the image of Captain Tyreal disappeared from the screen.

"Going aboard that ship doesn't seem to be the brightest idea," remarked Tom.

"I still don't trust these people," added Teitrik. "Once you are aboard that ship, they can do whatever they want to you."

This got Dan a little concerned. He was so flattered that Captain Tyreal wanted to meet that he had not considered the implications of going onboard that ship. If he boarded the *Eclipse*, they might take him and his party hostage, using them to bargain for the *Liberty*. "Then we must be careful," Dan ordered, after giving the situation some additional thought. "Lieutenant, it's just you and me. Everyone else stay behind. Commander, you're in charge."

"Wait, I want to come too," requested Janet.

"Janet, you're not going to like my next order."

"Then give it. If I don't like it, then I'll just stay here and torment Tommy boy."

Dan turned to Teitrik. "Commander, I'm not important. The mission and the safety of my friends, my family, and my world are. If they hold us hostage or try any funny games, blast the heck out of the *Eclipse* and get your butts out of here. Do you understand?"

"I do," Teitrik answered. "Let us hope that I do not have to follow your order."

"I'm still going," added Janet.

"Are you sure?" asked Dan. "Do you know what this could mean?"

"I do, but you're important to me—as a friend," Janet quickly added.

Tom stood up, about to throw in his hat. Dan stopped him. "Tom, we need to have at least one Earthling here. You need to stay."

Tom, disappointed, plopped down into the chair at the console. "I understand. I don't like it, but I understand."

"Tom, you don't like anything, so how is this any different?" jabbed Janet.

Tom turned to address the commander. "If someone needs to blow them up, I volunteer to press the button."

"Don't worry. We won't be turning into hostages if I have any say." Dan had given the order as a last resort; he had no intention of getting killed.

Janet, Dan, and Lieutenant Mahdara made their way down to the docking bay to board a shuttle to the *Eclipse*. It would not be a long trip, as the *Liberty* was practically sitting on the larger ship's hull. Dan's final order was to maintain their current position just in case this was a ruse, so that the *Liberty* was in the best position to fire and escape quickly.

The shuttlecraft, piloted by Mahdara, exited the *Liberty* and skimmed along the flat upper hull of the *Eclipse* and then down the smooth curved sides until she lined up with a modest docking bay. It did not run the width of the ship, as did the massive docks on the *Atera*. It was clearly intended for smaller craft, but could comfortably hold several shuttles or a larger cargo vessel. This bay was specifically used for visits from admirals or other leaders, as it was located directly below the command tower. Mahdara directed the shuttle through the force shield and landed delicately on the bay floor.

The starboard door opened and revealed two security guards waiting to greet them. They were fully armed with pulse rifles and looked none too friendly.

Janet saw them through the open shuttle door. "Wow, they sure know how to make a girl feel welcome."

The lieutenant was the first out the door and challenged the guards. "Are those absolutely necessary?"

"Captain's orders," one of the guards said blankly.

The lieutenant sighed and motioned for Janet and Dan to come out of the shuttle. "I'm sorry for this. They evidently don't completely trust you."

"That's not what I'm worried about. Why don't they trust you?" asked Dan.

Then Dan addressed the guards. "Take me to your leader," he said, trying to be a bit obnoxious. Janet chuckled at his use of the cliché.

They followed the guards across the bay toward the elevator that would take them to the command tower. After a brief ride, they exited the lift into a lobby area directly outside a large conference room with a frontal view of the *Liberty*, which was just outside the window ahead of the command tower.

"Wait here," said one the guards. The two reentered the elevator and left Dan, Janet, and Mahdara standing alone.

"They don't trust us enough to even let us up to the bridge!" grumbled Janet.

Lieutenant Mahdara walked toward the conference table and sat down in one of the chairs. Janet and Dan entered the room, but did not sit down. They were far too nervous.

"You two need to relax," suggested Mahdara. "If they wanted to kill us, they would have done that already."

"No, but is torture on the menu?" asked Janet.

"Listen, girly, you calm down."

"Who you calling girly?" screamed Janet. She did not like being called names by a complete stranger.

"All right, both of you, relax! How 'bout that?" yelled Dan.

Janet plopped down and gave him a pouty look, not unlike the one that Mahdara was projecting at him. Dan sat down at the end of the table, where he could get a clear view of the elevator. "Now I am going to sit down here and play captain, and you two play whoever the heck you want to play, but just relax."

Just then the elevator door opened. The two guards reemerged and stepped to the sides, flanking the door. Out walked an old man dressed in a captain's uniform, followed by four others. This was Captain Tyreal—average height, stocky, and well along in years.

Tyreal bounded into the conference room. "Captain Foster, welcome aboard."

"Thank you. This is Janet and Lieutenant Mahdara," Dan said, introducing his companions.

Captain Tyreal did not acknowledge them or introduce his entourage. "Captain, why is your ship still out there pointing its guns at my bridge?"

"Captain Tyreal, can you tell me why we had armed guards escort us to the secured conference room and not the executive room on the bridge?"

Captain Tyreal huffed. "Well, seems like you cover yourself like a pro. I like that. Shows that you think through situations."

"And have you thought through your situation?" asked Dan. "Are you going to help us?"

Captain Tyreal sat down at the opposite end of the table. His companions filled in seats near him on either side. "Look at me. I'm an old man. Do you think I have the time to fidget around? I am sick and tired of living like this. We're scavengers. We neither build nor create any more. My people simply survive. It disgusts me!

"I commanded a corvette during the final battle of Daemerik. When the order to flee was given, I lost all respect for our so-called Magnicieat. They were nothing but cowards. Even if we failed to defend our world, we should have died trying! Instead we scattered like scared vermin. I would not have it. As soon as I got the order, as my blood boiled, I was able to contact several commanders who felt as I and we separated ourselves and our ships from those cowards. We dedicated our lives to making life for the Gaarich difficult and deadly. As long as they infest our world and the galaxy, we will try to kill every last one of them."

"So do you speak for the Pyietri?" asked Dan.

"Ha! Speak for whom? We're just a band of ticked-off rebels trying to hopefully annoy the Gaarich enough so they just leave. We're a mix of military, pirates, scofflaws, and even a few Votraxain warcraft that escaped their world's invasion. We're a loose confederation that is only bonded in the hate we have for the Gaarich and our passion to wipe them from existence."

The tirade solidified Dan's initial impression of the captain as a hothead, but he was just the type of hothead Dan needed.

"So, we have an alliance?"

"Alliance, ha!" exclaimed the captain. "First you stole the *Liberty*, were able to inspire enough people you met on the *Atera* to get together some sort of crew, fought the Gaarich and won—and yes, we have spies who find this stuff out, thank you, Mahdara. Plus the antics you pulled in getting our attention do not warrant an alliance. No, they require more—much more. You have proved yourself just as passionate and somewhat misguided as the rest of us. Just the type of material we need."

"What exactly are you asking?" Dan was a little concerned with where the conversation was leading. He had offered much in the hope they would join up in the defense of Earth, but now Tyreal wanted more.

Tyreal leaned across the table. "You said that if we lost the battle of your planet, you would pledge your allegiance to the Pyietri. That is not enough. I need to know that you are in this thing not only for the defense of your world, but also for the hope that my world and the worlds of our allies may one day be free. I need to know that the passion I see in you right now will not stop after your home is defended, because, Captain Foster, until the Gaarich are wiped from our galaxy, no place is safe."

Dan was a little taken aback by the request. The tone was not condescending, but nonetheless, Dan had a difficult time swallowing Tyreal's words. "Captain, you may look across this table at a boy—a boy who a few days ago only cared about good grades and not wrecking his car. Well, that boy and those petty concerns died when I stepped aboard that ship," he said, while pointing out the window at the *Liberty*. "If I am to pledge my allegiance to the Pyietri, let this be the last moment you doubt my commitment."

A smile broke across Tyreal's face. "I perceive your grandfather's attitude in you. Glad to see that chip on your shoulder comes from somewhere. Welcome to our band of misfits, Captain."

Dan was pleased. He now had allies and friends. The reactions from his companions were equally as jovial, and the proud glance that Janet was projecting at Dan only confirmed that he had done well.

"Now, down to business," continued Captain Tyreal. "I hope you've thought this battle with the Gaarich through."

"We have, but as you know, the more firepower the better. If we can stand our ground, I'm told that the Gaarich will go away until such time as they're ready for a full invasion."

"Generally that is the case," added one of Tyreal's unnamed companions. "They will not move to another world until they spawn a queen. It is a very ritualistic process and takes much time. We will have fair warning, but they will try to keep the planet soft for future invasion."

"I think we need some more ships, and a really big one would be a welcome addition to our fleet," added Dan.

Captain Tyreal immediately knew what he was implying. "You're crazier than I thought! You want to try to recruit the *Besenti*?"

"She has big guns and lots of ships in escort, and we could use every last one of them."

"Ha! He's the worst of them. Admiral Tantera talks tough, but he just follows that cursed Magnicieat and chooses to harass us from our mission," barked Tyreal.

"What exactly is their current mission?" asked Janet.

"Well, the *Besenti* is the only intact star cruiser capable of putting up any sort of fight. Her mission is to basically be bait for the Gaarich. She jumps from sector to sector, makes a presence, and bugs out. It keeps the Gaarich busy. The Magnicieat believes that by doing this it will keep the Gaarich from discovering Mahtri," said Tyreal. "Oh, yeah, and their other mission is to oversee the supplies smuggled to Mahtri and to kick us around."

"Well, then, how would joining us be contrary to their mission?" asked Janet.

"Because they would actually have to fight for something, which is way beyond anything that ship has done for the past fifty years."

"We should still give them a shot," recommended Dan. "We have nothing to lose. If we go in right, we can get out in a hurry. If we play it safe and smart, we could come out with a very powerful ally."

Tyreal thought for a minute. "What is your plan?"

38
Spin

Captain Dillings walked into General Peters's office to give him the hourly update and found him on the red phone speaking with the president. She could only hear one part of the conversation. The general just kept repeating "yes" and "I understand" as the conversation continued. The captain stood and waited for him to finish. She should have left the room, but judging from the look on the general's face, it appeared like he could use someone to swear at after he slammed down the phone.

As Peters continued to listen to the president, a buzzer went off. The captain turned her attention to the lights that indicated their alert level. They had dropped from Defcon 2 to Defcon 5, their previous peacetime setting before the situation with the ISS had flared up.

The general slammed down the phone and rubbed his hands across his face. Captain Dillings thought she should say something.

"Bad news?"

The general pulled his hands away from his head and placed them on the desk. His face was adorned with a goofy sarcastic smile. "Oh, just that they're pulling the plug on our little drill. The Russians and Chinese don't want to play anymore. They don't think there's an actual threat, and if there is, they'd rather deal with it their own way than have to answer to anyone else. Look, we're back at Defcon 5."

"Do you think the danger has passed?" the captain asked.

"You know, I have no freaking clue—maybe so, but maybe not. The official word is that there was a severe structural flaw on the station. Jenkins and Vodnikov stayed to try to repair it and save the ISS, but the rest of the crew died trying to escape when the module rapidly lost pressure and exploded."

"Well, that will hold the *X Files* fans for about thirty seconds," snapped Dillings.

"Doesn't matter," the general said hopelessly as he shook his head. "That's the official word, and we'll stick to it. There are some 'crisis managers' coming down here to talk to our people. They're sending some to NASA also. This will just be reported as a horrible malfunction on the news tomorrow—nothing more."

"What do we need to do for damage control?" asked the captain, anticipating the wave of inquiries that were bound to follow.

"You have nothing to worry about," answered Peters. "I on the other hand, will be offered early retirement, and that's that." He looked proudly at Dillings. "I want to thank you for your help. I will put you in for major before I go. You deserve nothing less."

"Thank you, sir, but my career is not the focus of our conversation."

"But you are the only one in this room with a career left—Major."

In Houston, Walters was speaking with Betty Tedesci when about ten people waltzed into the command center. They were NSA but looked an awful lot like politicians, well dressed and carrying briefcases with their black laptops. One of the men approached.

"Can one of you tell me where Mark Walters is?" asked the gentleman.

"Who are you, the Easter bunny?" joked Walters, which got a good laugh out of Betty.

"No, sir, we're from the NSA Communications Division."

"Ah, communications, but you guys only communicate spin and rumor," jabbed Walters.

"Sir, you may call what we do whatever you please, but we have a job to do here. I assume that you are Mark Walters? I need to speak with you in private."

Mark turned and started to walk toward his office. "You know, I've been dragged into the office more in the past two days than in my whole career as a schoolboy—and I wasn't a well-behaved schoolboy."

Upon entering his office, they sat down. Mark motioned for Betty to join them.

"Sir, I need to speak with you first," the man insisted.

"Listen, I am tired and hungry, and I smell foul because I have been stuck here for days without a shower. You can shove your protocols right up your butt, mister. Whatever you can say to me, you can say to her."

The agent swallowed nervously and waited for Betty to enter the room. "Good, now that you're here, let me begin," he muttered. "Our government, along with the Chinese and the Russians, have come to an agreement on how to deal with this situation. They are standing down from alert; this has already occurred. I'm here to communicate to you and your staff, through one-on-one interviews, the official internationally aligned approved communication.

"Officially, the incident aboard the ISS will be called a structural failure. Majors Vodnikov and Jensen stayed behind to potentially correct the problem and save the station. The other scientists were attempting to escape when something went wrong with the escape pod, killing all inside."

Betty interrupted him. "You know that will kill the funding for any future station."

"We understand that, but the political situation is much more important now," the agent answered.

"Fine," said Walters. "Fine, whatever they want us to say." Mark crossed his arms, completely disgruntled. This politicking would bind up the program for years, again slowing their development of space exploration. This agent who had walked into the command center signaled to him the beginning of the dark ages for NASA.

"What do you need from me and my people?" asked Mark.

"We'll first need to speak with them one on one. We will also have to commandeer all files and recordings from the past several days."

Mark threw up his hands. "Fine, go ... go ... enjoy yourselves."

The agent stood up without saying a word and left the room. His body language indicated that he was very glad that his conversation with Walters was over.

"You know, it's just a load of bull!" snapped Betty.

"This has all been a load of bull—" Walters stopped speaking as he saw Marcus Washington dart into his office.

Partly out of breath from sprinting, Marcus dragged out a few words. "Hey ... hey ... who are these people?"

"We're finally going to get out of this," said Walters.

"What do you mean?" asked Marcus with a furrowed brow.

"It was all just a catastrophic structural malfunction of the station," Walters said with a hint of sarcasm.

Marcus just looked more confused. "Structural ... what ... are they ... nah ... nah ... this is a load of bull!"

"We were just saying that," added Betty.

Marcus took the liberty of sitting in the chair next to Betty and lowered his voice, leaning forward for Walters to hear him better. "We have no idea if those ships will be back. We can't just cut and run now—go home and put our guard down. Did you see those things?"

"Yes ... yes, we all did, Marcus, and I agree we have a problem, but we're not going to solve it today. Let's just be done with this situation and go home."

That did not calm Marcus one bit. Walters could read it in his eyes. There was a great deal of concern there. "Listen, it will be several hours until they can set us loose. Until then, keep up your vigil, and when the next shift comes in, get your buddy Teddy Spenelli to keep an eye toward the stars. How about that?"

"I'll take what I can get, Mark, but you keep that cell handy. If anything happens, it'll be ringin'."

Are You In?

Admiral Tantera sat on the bridge of the *Besenti* going through his daily reports. The star cruiser and its fleet were constantly on the move to stay one step ahead of the Gaarich and to ensure that the Daemerae at Mahtri were getting the supplies that they needed to survive. The fleet had just jumped into this open part of space, well between any important solar systems, in order to regroup. They did not remain in one place for any longer than a few hours. Hyperdrive was their lifeblood and the key to their defense strategy. The fleet that traveled with the *Besenti* was small, but extremely formidable. In all there were about thirty capital ships, along with many other corvettes and blockade runners that were available for fast attack. Seven enormous battle cruisers fifteen miles long, whose only purpose was to carry weapons, flanked the *Besenti*.

A single ship exited hyperspace in the middle of the formation of warships.

"Report!" ordered the admiral.

His tactical officer answered, "A single ship has exited hyperspace. Designation and marker have it as a Daemerik corvette. Sir, it looks like it could be the *Liberty*."

"Good," remarked the admiral. "At least we've found our little lost ship. The Magnicieat will be pleased. Open a channel, and when they're in range, get a tractor beam and pull them into the docking bay."

"Channel open, sir."

"Rogue corvette, this is Admiral Tantera of the *Besenti* battle group." There was no response or visual communication. "Please respond."

A crackle came over the loudspeaker on the command deck of the *Besenti*. "Admiral, this is Commander Teitrik of the *Defiance*. We have successfully retrieved the *Liberty*."

Tantera raised his eyebrow. "Commander, from our reports you were a party to the theft of that ship."

"Incorrect, sir. I took a small contingent knowing that the Earthlings would try something like this. It took us a while to overpower them."

The executive officer of the *Besenti* whispered in the admiral's ear. "Sir, this doesn't feel right. I think they're stalling. Could be a trap."

"Captain, it's just one corvette, and an old one at that. How can they be a threat?" Tantera whispered back.

The admiral directed his conversation back to the *Liberty*. "Commander Teitrik, can you establish visual?"

"No, sir. The ship is badly damaged."

Multiple flashes appeared all around the battle group as numerous craft emerged from hyperspace right in the middle of the fleet. The invaders quickly picked a mark and moved in at point-blank range, catching the Daemerae by surprise.

"The Pyietri! It's a trap! Arm all weapons and launch fighters!" ordered Admiral Tantera.

"Sir," interrupted the tactical officer, "they're at point blank range to many of our most critical craft. The dreadnought *Eclipse* is targeting this command tower. We are at the disadvantage, sir."

The admiral sighed in frustration and anger. The *Liberty* had slid in as a distraction, probably broadcasting the location of each one of the ships so the Pyietri could quickly move into a dominant position and catch the *Besenti* by surprise.

"Order the fighters to hold one thousand meters off our bow. No reason why we shouldn't look threatening."

"The *Eclipse* wants to open an channel," announced the communications officer.

"This ought to be good. Give me visual," ordered the admiral.

The image of Captain Tyreal filled the viewscreen. "Admiral, we did not come here to fight. You can tell your fighters to stand down."

"And how do you know that we don't want to fight, Captain, after that little stunt?" asked the admiral. "What could you possibly want?"

"We've been fighting the same war for many years," stated Captain Tyreal.

Admiral Tantera exploded. "No, sir, we have not been fighting the same war! We have been fighting to survive while you're off stirring up the Gaarich and making our survival more difficult!"

"What survival?" shouted Captain Tyreal. "You have the most powerful fleet that humanity has left, and what do you do? You play cat and mouse—and you are the mouse!"

"Unlike you, we have millions back at Mahtri to think about. Their safety and survival are our top priorities. What are yours, sir?"

"Freedom—freedom from these cursed creatures; freedom to live in the galaxy in peace and not run and hide at the sign of a scout ship or marauder; the ability to breathe fresh clean air and to walk on the grass or in the sand. We deserve better than this existence. We are not slaves!"

"And what, you expect to do it with your pathetic group of rogues? Oh, and the *Liberty*—that old broken ship. Thank you for bringing it back to us. It saved me the search."

"They did not bring the *Liberty* here. I did," said a young voice, the communication covering that of the *Eclipse*. The screen on the *Besenti* now showed Captain Dan Foster. "I am the one who took the ship. I am the one who went to the Pyietri looking for help after the Magnicieat denied it. I am the one who comes to you now asking for yours."

The admiral broke out into a laugh. "You're just a boy. I don't follow boys. I lead men!"

"Then lead your men in the defense of my planet!"

"I have been before the Magnicieat many times, and they have denied my requests many times. One thing they do very well is explain themselves, so I am sure you understand why we cannot help your planet," added the admiral.

"No, I do not," answered Dan. "We are the last outpost of humans in the galaxy who have not been enslaved by the Gaarich. Doesn't that mean something?"

"Yes, it means you're next, so get ready, and I highly recommend that they send someone much older than you to lead the charge," snubbed the admiral.

"If we fail, you will not have any refuge in the galaxy that is free of the Gaarich."

"You have already lost!" shouted the admiral. "The fate of your planet has already been decided, and there is nothing that you or I can do about it. Go, if you choose to die."

"We do not choose to die. We choose to live! That is why we are going back. You sit there in your grand ship and criticize us for trying to save our world. Well, we may do it with sticks and stones, but we will continue to fight until the last stone is tossed."

"Then go. We will not stop you. By taking the Pyietri, you are getting rid of another of our problems—so go! You do not have much time. Our operatives say the Gaarich are ready to head to

Earth." The admiral's tone began to soften. "You do not have much time. They will be there soon."

Without another word the Pyietri fleet, with the *Liberty*, moved away from the battle group and jumped into hyperspace, heading for Earth and the conflict with the Gaarich.

40
Reflection

"WELL, NOW, THAT DIDN'T GO WELL," said Tom, noting the obvious. His trademark sarcasm spoke the truth about their encounter with the *Besenti*—tense, unpleasant, and unproductive.

"I thought you did very well, Captain," encouraged Mahdara, trying to boost Dan's confidence.

"I agree," added Janet.

"Well, I appreciate it," Dan stated, his voice a little somber. "All we did back there was yell and preach at each other. A minute more and I would have asked that guy to take it outside."

Teitrik was very quiet. He had not said a word after the encounter. "Hey, Commander, what do you think?" asked Janet, trying to gauge his feelings.

It took Teitrik a while to craft his words, as if he hadn't spoken in years. "Well, Mr. ... I'm sorry ... Captain Foster did very well. I just never realized how cowardly the leaders of my people were. I was always under the illusion that we had no hope. The fact of the matter is that they had no guts. They robbed hope from us for so many years, and I followed them blindly."

"Until you stole the *Liberty*, may I add," interrupted Mahdara. "You made a choice to make a difference when you helped steal this ship. You turned the tide, sir."

Teitrik smiled. "Thank you, Mahdara, and I'm sorry I criticized you for working with the Pyietri. You have more courage than I."

"Okay, folks," said Tom, trying to get everyone to regroup, "we're going to battle for the future of our planet in a few hours. Can we get some focus here? I for one want to win. Up to this point I'm still alive and would like to keep it that way. Plus, if I die, Dan, I'm coming back to haunt you."

"Thanks for that fresh dose of reality," added Mahdara. "Dan, your friend has a biting sense of humor."

"No, he's just a jerk," uttered Janet.

The discussion was broken up by an incoming transmission. Mahdara listened in and relayed the information. "Captain, I got word from some of my contacts. The Gaarich fleet is on its way to Earth. We should just beat them there at this speed."

"Send a message to the fleet. We'll jump in so that we're behind the moon. Let's be ready with that plan that we worked out with Tyreal. We have to be tight with this."

Commander Teitrik offered an observation. "Captain, what is Earth's largest structure? Do you have a space station, base, what?"

Dan thought for a minute. "Uh, could be that telescope or—"

"The International Space Station, silly." Janet felt the need to correct him.

"Well, I would trust her judgment."

"Then that is what they will attack first. I recommend we form up in front of the station," advised the commander.

Tom turned to offer his perspective. "But that's going to majorly freak people out. I mean, that is really close to Earth—and what about those folks on the station?"

"They're going to find out sooner or later. There's going to be a space battle for Earth, and it's going to be hard to ease them into it," counseled Dan.

Tom shrugged his shoulders and went back to manning his console.

"Lieutenant, send word to the fleet. We will form a blockade in front of the International Space Station."

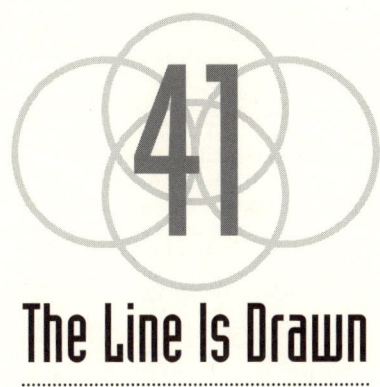

The Line Is Drawn

MARK WALTERS'S HEAD HIT THE PILLOW. Finally he'd been able to go home and get a shower and was now headed off into a very long sleep. Thoughts of the past few days rolled through Mark's mind as he drifted off into dreamland.

Just as Mark's brain began to release the exhaustion from his ordeal, the beeping of his cell phone did its best to cram the stress back inside him. He wiped the sleep from his face and sat up in bed. After turning on the light, he gave the cell phone the appropriate hand gesture, just to make it clear how he felt about whoever was calling him, and picked it up. He instantly recognized the frantic voice on the other end of the phone. It was Marcus Washington.

"Mark … Mark … you are not going to believe this. We have multiple contacts heading toward the ISS, and some of them are huge!"

Walters jerked up from his slouched position. "Do they look like the other ones?"

"No, they definitely look different, but there are a whole boatload of them heading toward the ISS. Some are big enough that people on Earth will be able to see them with telescopes."

"I'll be there in twenty minutes. Get Betty in there too."

Walters hung up the phone and jumped out of bed.

Majors Jensen and Vodnikov were waiting in the ISS. It was their rest cycle. They tried their best to sleep, but all that they had been through the past several days created enough spare adrenaline that relaxing was difficult. Still, they took the opportunity to try to calm themselves, even though sleep was not really possible. Yet even the uncomfortable quiet would not last. The proximity alarm went off, jolting them from their thoughts. They peered out the portholes and saw what they could not believe.

An incredible collection of spacecraft closed in on the ISS. Their wonder at the number and size of the fleet ripped the oxygen from the majors' lungs, robbing them of breath. The ships rotated, facing out into space, awaiting the imminent arrival of something.

"Commander," asked Vodnikov, "is this a good sign or a bad sign?"

"Well, they're not shooting at us and are turned the other way. So I would say it's a good sign in one way. The bad thing is that they're obviously waiting for something, and whatever they're waiting for has to be the bad news."

Back on Earth, Mark Walters made it into the command center at NASA after a swift drive through the Houston streets. Betty and Marcus were already waiting for him. They were frantically discussing the situation. He looked up to the view panel to see the external of the ISS. It showed numerous ships forming a blockade facing out into space.

"What the ..." Walters mumbled as he joined Betty and Marcus.

"They don't seem hostile," remarked Betty. "In fact, it looks like they're here to protect us."

"Yeah, but who are they?" asked Walters.

"Aliens," offered Marcus.

"Well, I can see that! How are the majors?"

"They're punching up the fastest Morse code I've ever seen. They're obviously scared," said Betty. "Also, General Peters called.

His team has also seen this. He's informed the president, but needs to speak with you immediately."

Mark hustled into his office and picked up the phone to call the general. After a few seconds he heard Peters's voice.

"Mr. Walters, it seems we have a situation on our hands."

"That's an understatement, General. There is a whole alien fleet out there facing away from Earth. They're apparently waiting for something, and I don't want to find out what it is."

"Well, I do not intend to wait, and the president agrees. The Global Defense Pact was a joke. Now, with the current situation, the Russians and Chinese are scrambling. This looks like it will go down in a few minutes. It will be up to us."

"What do you have?" asked Walters.

"Thanks to the navy, I have several submarines at my disposal."

"General, do you honestly think a few nuclear missiles are going to have any effect on ships like that? I'm sure that whatever they're waiting for is going to be just as large."

"Well, do you have any other suggestions?" asked the general. "This is all we have, and it will have to do. Hopefully our newfound friends will ensure that we don't have to launch anything." The general paused for a moment. "Walters, no doubt the past few days could have been handled better, and you should have not been left in the dark. I need your help on this one."

Walters was pleased to hear the general ask for help and offer some level of apology. It was much better than the threats and intimidation Walters had received from the NSA during the past several days. "Agreed."

Moments

ABOARD THE *LIBERTY*, the crew was silent. Everyone was busy at his or her respective station keeping watch for the Gaarich fleet. Many ran endless checks to remain occupied. Unfortunately, Dan did not have the expertise to look busy aboard this ship, so he simply stared at the viewscreen, his eyes fixed in such a way as if to detect the approaching enemy.

"This waiting thing really stinks," Dan said.

"Well, I'd rather be bored than all blown up," noted Tom.

"Thank you, Mr. Hunt. You always bring a dose of reality to my day."

"It won't be long," added Commander Teitrik. He was standing by Mahdara's shoulder, looking at her console. "That beacon we dropped in hyperspace is going crazy. They're only a few minutes out."

"Lieutenant, get me the *Eclipse*," ordered Captain Foster.

"Yes, sir." Mahdara's fingers danced across the console until the image of Captain Tyreal appeared on the main viewscreen.

Tyreal was the first to speak. "Well, Captain, the Gaarich will be here in a few moments. I hope you are prepared for this. I hope we all are."

"Ready or not, we have a job to do," Dan responded.

"Good to know you haven't lost your backbone, son. Just make sure you don't lose it in the coming moments." Captain Tyreal's words echoed the gravity of the situation. This was serious, and not everyone was going to make it out in one piece. "We are ready to launch fighters. I'm giving the order now. They will form up in front of us. Go to red alert, Captain."

Captain Foster waived his hand to Mahdara, who did the honors. The lights turned red, and the siren pulsed three times to indicate general quarters.

"Captain Tyreal, the International Space Station looks to be damaged." Dan was concerned about those onboard, since in its current condition the ISS would not survive an attack.

"We see that. Our friends have already paid Earth a visit and left their mark." He turned to give some orders to his assistant. "I'm sending a craft to retrieve any survivors."

"Thank you," acknowledged Dan.

"One more thing, Captain," added Tyreal. "From what I knew about Jostak, he would be very proud of you on this day."

Dan blushed as Janet turned around and smiled at him. Whether Jostak would be proud of Dan or not, he still had to put his money where his mouth was. He needed to protect Earth.

Before Dan could thank him, Tyreal ended the transmission.

The larger ships in the Pyietri fleet launched their fighters. The swift craft moved in squadron formation in advance of the fleet. A smaller shuttle from the *Eclipse* flew the opposite way, bound for the International Space Station. Onboard, Majors Jensen and Vodnikov saw the small alien ship approaching and frantically communicated the situation via Morse code down to NASA.

In the operations room in Houston, an analyst brought the message over to Betty and Mark as they watched the ship approach on the tactical view.

"Sir," said the analyst as he handed the paper to Mark, "they're asking what to do."

Walters grabbed the nearest headset and put it on while motioning to have voice access. "Commander ISS, this is Houston. We understand your situation. Craft do not appear …" Mark stopped himself. The majors had experienced much over the past several days. They were tired, hungry, and probably scared, even though their military training would not let them show it. "David, it's up to you. You as well as I know we have nothing to counteract these aliens. Either the ship moving toward you has hostile intentions, or it does not, but at least we're looking at a possible first contact situation. No one asked you to be a diplomat, but it may just come to that. I trust you, your country trusts you … heck, the world trusts you, if that helps any. You make the call, son. You make the call. This is Houston, out."

There was a long pause before the answer came back. The analyst read it and chuckled.

"Care to share?" snapped Walters.

The analyst nervously handed him the paper, and Mark broke out into laughter. "No problem. Will get pictures."

Aboard the International Space Station, the majors peered out the window as the shuttle positioned itself over their heads. A loud shudder followed, and the station shook.

"Well, they are here." Vodnikov grabbed the handgun she had taken out of the emergency locker and held it behind her.

There was a flash as a hole was cut in the hull of the ISS. Sparks flew, and both majors stood back as the work continued. When the bright glow reached a complete circle, the severed portion of hull thrust to the floor in a gust of smoke. A ladder extended down from the shuttle. Major Jensen stepped forward, grabbed it, and looked up. He was greeted by—a human! He was very surprised, and the elated look on his face showed it as he glanced back to Vodnikov, who continued to clutch the gun.

"Major, they're human!"

"*Ytretisi! Bolanat tednekis dreit.*" The Pyietri crewman was trying to communicate, but the crew of the ISS did not have the translators needed for comprehension.

Major Jensen tried anyway. "I am Major David Jensen, commander of this station. I bid you greetings from Earth." The speech was straight out of a 1950's science fiction movie, but it was all he could muster at the moment.

Major Vodnikov had to reply. "Commander, I will embellish that a bit for the history books."

The crewman on the shuttle looked confused and again motioned for them to board the shuttle. "*Ytretisi! Ytretisi!*"

"Let's go, Vodnikov. They cut a big hole in what was left of this station. We can't stay anyway—and—leave the sidearm." Major Jensen climbed up aboard the alien craft. Vodnikov discreetly put down the gun and followed.

Arrival

"Here they come!" screamed Tom as his targeting screen lit up. His fingers frantically scurried across the terminal, attempting to attend to all the enemy alerts that were flooding in.

An enormous blast of light shone off in the distance. It was the Gaarich fleet exiting hyperspace. The glow would have been brilliant enough to be seen from Earth in the night sky.

Janet started to panic. "Dan … I … there are so many of them … they …"

"Janet, you'll be fine." Dan needed to keep her and the rest of the crew focused.

"They're launching fighters!" shouted Mahdara.

The fighters poured out of the Gaarich craft like swarms of bees ready to attack that which disturbed their nest. The Pyietri fighters that were lined up ahead of the fleet accelerated away to meet them. The two enemies converged halfway between the moon and Earth. Flashes of light like fireflies in the night sky indicated the death of one fighter or another. The Pyietri were clearly outgunned. There were ten Gaarich fighters for every one of the Pyietri.

"Captain Tyreal is on the line," barked Mahdara.

"Captain Foster," said Tyreal, "we're losing fighters quickly. We're making a good dent, but we are losing badly!"

"Can you pull them back?" asked Dan with concern.

"No ... they will not make it back."

The reality of their situation finally sunk in. There were people dying for Earth who would not return home. Their commitment to the survival of humanity had driven them to this battle, and for the defense of their race, they were giving their lives.

Janet spoke up from the helm. "How many Pyietri did we send out there?"

"Over a thousand," answered Mahdara, her voice trembling from knowing so many were dying.

"Well, let's not make their sacrifice be in vain. Let's go!" ordered Dan.

The *Liberty* lurched forward toward the attacking ships. She was the first off the line leading the charge, followed closely by the rest of the Pyietri fleet. Swiftly they closed on the remaining Gaarich fighters. Several of the enemy ships swarmed around a Votraxain warcraft, battering it with shot after shot until its hull blew apart. Many other of the lesser Pyietri ships, those not specifically designed as military vessels, were quickly destroyed.

The beltline laser turrets of the *Liberty* fired continuously, trying to take out as many craft as possible. The weapons effectively cut many of the enemy into pieces before they could get any substantive hits on the *Liberty*, yet the larger medium fighters and fighter-bombers were having no problems hitting their mark. The blasts pounded the *Liberty*, and although the shields absorbed the hits, every subsequent attack chipped away at the ship's energy.

The *Liberty* shook violently from the onslaught, but her shields still held. Many others in the Pyietri fleet were not so lucky. By the time the ragtag battle group made it through the fighter screen, half of the smaller ships were destroyed, one corvette was gone, two of the destroyers had sustained heavy damage, and one of the battleships was burning.

In front of them now lay the main bulk of the Gaarich fleet. Ten marauders were bearing down on them, joined by fifteen or so smaller corvette-class attack ships. The simple wedge shapes came at the Pyietri ahead of the marauders in groups of three.

Captain Tyreal sent a broadcast to what was left of the attack force. "Fleet, the battleships and the *Eclipse* will concentrate on the marauders. The rest of you take out those corvettes!"

"Janet, punch it!" ordered Dan.

Janet pushed the *Liberty* toward the attackers, followed by one Pyietri corvette and a Votraxain warcraft.

"Tom, give it everything you've got!"

Tom proceeded to fire the main turrets at the closest Gaarich corvette. The enemy ship responded with its main guns, which cut through the *Liberty*'s shields and ripped the forward turret from the hull.

"Holy crap!" shouted Tom.

"Just keep shooting!" ordered Dan.

Tom continued to fire at the ship as it closed in on the *Liberty*. The other two craft in their attack formation were having better luck. The Pyietri corvette and Votraxain warcraft ganged up on one of the Gaarich and quickly dispatched it. Next they turned their attention to the other, leaving the *Liberty* to fend for herself.

Commander Teitrik ran down to help Tom. He looked over the console and turned back toward Dan. "Captain, we're down to one forward turret and the defensive belt."

"Just keep shooting with whatever we have. Target the bridge!"

"Yes, Captain," answered Teitrik.

All the weapons on the *Liberty* concentrated their fire on the bridge of the Gaarich ship. After several seconds of bombardment, the *Liberty* was able to punch through the shields and decimate the bulkhead that protected the command deck. The Gaarich ship ceased firing and listed like a dead hulk in space. The

Liberty continued to strike until the ship started to crumple. Quickly the *Liberty* moved away to avoid the shockwave as the enemy corvette exploded.

Dan now turned his attention to the *Eclipse* and the three battleships trying desperately to fight off the marauders. The *Centat* had an extreme amount of damage from the first wave of fighters; the glow of fires and explosions pockmarked the hull. Dan quickly requested a channel to be opened.

"Captain of the *Centat*, this is Captain Foster of the *Liberty*. You've done enough. Get your ship out of here!"

A badly distorted transmission carried the response. "Your kindness is acknowledged, Captain, but we will run no more."

With that the *Centat* powered up its engines and plowed at speed into the Gaarich marauder she was attacking. The enemy's hull crumpled as the battleship disintegrated into the Gaarich ship, the force pushing both of them closer to another marauder that was in near formation. The resulting explosion annihilated all three ships.

"Holy crap!" shouted Tom. "Did you see that?"

Whether or not Dan saw it would not change the outcome of this battle. They had stood well against the fighters and the corvettes, but most of the Pyietri fleet were quickly being beaten. They were badly banged up and still had five marauders to deal with. Another corvette was gone, and one of the destroyers was dead in space, a bright explosion signaling her final demise.

A transmission came in from the *Eclipse*. "Fleet, concentrate on our target. We will try to punch through their reinforced hull to get at the reactor. It's our best shot. Link your targeting computer through us."

Tom stood up to let the commander take the weapons control. He had no idea how to link anything. Targeting and shooting were all he had learned. Commander Teitrik did the honors and connected the *Liberty*'s targeting computer with that of the *Eclipse*.

The eight remaining ships focused their firepower on the reactor of the nearest marauder, while the other four Gaarich ships moved to intercept the Pyietri at point-blank range. In unison the Pyietri fleet fired, tearing into the side of the Gaarich ship like a can opener. The plan worked, and their success was greeted by the total destruction of the enemy craft.

The other four Gaarich ships were now right in the midst of the Pyietri, so close that neither they nor the defenders could concentrate their fire on a single vessel. Each ship picked a mark and continued the fight.

"Captain, we have contacts that have just jumped into normal space," said Mahdara, who was frantically trying to make out who or what they were. "Oh, no ... sir, we have ten more Gaarich marauders on an intercept course." She looked up at Dan with a bleak frown on her face.

Dan felt hopeless too. There was no way they could stand up to those ships. The *Liberty* was already damaged and was taking more with every passing moment of the battle. The good news was that the four marauders from the original attack group had moved off to regroup with the ships that had just arrived.

Down on Earth, Mark Walters sprinted into his office and picked up the secure line to General Peters. "General, looks like our friends are getting their butts kicked hard, and we just picked up more of the bad guys on their way in."

"Mark, this is all over the media. Geeks with telescopes—heck, you can see the flashes with the naked eye! Is Major Jensen okay?"

"Don't know, General. No life signs have registered aboard the station since that ship pulled away. I hope they're fine."

"It's time we help our new friends. The Russians and Chinese are freaking out and for once are looking to us for some advice. Plus, all of this is going on over our heads right now, thanks to the rotation of the planet."

"General, I'm up for suggestions," offered Walters.

"I say we use the missiles on the subs I have at the ready. They've been reprogrammed to fly off into space."

"Won't their fuel cut out? How will you aim? Won't they just be dumb bombs?"

"Dumb, yes, but twenty missiles with multiple warheads will cause quite the ruckus. Let's hope our friends know to get out of the way."

Walters hung his head down and thought for a moment. "Do we have any other options?"

"No," the general responded, adding no more explanation.

"Then let's do it. They're not going to last long, and those other ships probably will be headed for our cities or something next. I should have watched more *Star Trek*." Walters hung up the phone.

On the *Liberty*, Mahdara announced, "Sir, we have contacts coming in from the planet!"

"Wait! We don't have anything for space defense. The only things we have that would ... uh oh ..." Janet's voice trailed off.

"They're nukes! Get me the *Eclipse*!" ordered Dan.

Captain Tyreal's voice was coming over the loudspeaker in short order. "Seems your planet is taking an active role in this. I hope they're not aimed at us."

"Captain, I don't know if they can aim. My guess is they just lobbed them up here hoping they'd hit something."

"What are they?" asked Tyreal.

"They are thermonuclear weapons." The comment had folks on the bridge jumping with concern.

Tyreal responded, "Then it doesn't matter who they're shooting at. The shockwave from those weapons will be a problem for all of us."

"Well, Captain," said Dan, "I don't know if we can handle the rest of those ships. The missiles seem to be our only chance."

Captain Tyreal thought over the problem. "Follow my lead. We'll retreat toward the planet and those missiles, and hopefully the Gaarich will take the bait. I will coordinate a jamming field so the Gaarich cannot make out what they are. Hopefully they will play right into this."

"And if they don't?" asked Dan.

"No plan B here, son. This has to work, or the battle is lost." The transmission from the *Eclipse* ended.

There was silence on the bridge, which was quickly broken by a chuckle from Mahdara, who was reading the orders uploaded from the *Eclipse*.

"What is so funny, Lieutenant?" asked Teitrik.

"Sorry, but they want us to plot a jump to behind the moon. As soon as those marauders get close enough, we'll jump and hopefully leave them to their demise with those missiles."

Tom decided to speak up. "Dan, you haven't killed me yet, but you're sure as heck trying."

Janet barked a simple "shut up!" from the helm.

"Mahdara, plot us a course behind the moon. We go on Tyreal's signal," ordered Dan.

The Pyietri fleet slowly reversed toward the planet and the oncoming missiles. The Gaarich marauders took the bait and closed in on the Pyietri. The stress level on the bridge of the *Liberty* kept building as they watched the enemy ships advance on their position. The Gaarich were now near enough to launch fighters.

"Here they come!" shouted Dan as the swarms of small attack craft converged on the Pyietri fleet, picking away at the hulls of the remaining ships. One of the corvettes that was already damaged succumbed quickly to the relentless onslaught. The marauders began to volley shots from their large cannons.

The *Liberty* was being rocked violently by these attacks, her structure straining from each devastating hit. Lights on the bridge were exploding, and structural pieces crashed to the floor. One beam fell on two crewmen and killed them instantly. An exploding electrical panel caught another on fire, badly burning her face. She was quickly assisted by two others, who extinguished the flames covering her body.

Dan looked up at Teitrik for any type of comfort. All he noted was the confirmation in his cousin's eyes that the *Liberty* might not survive the next few moments. Emotions cascaded down to his stomach and rested inside like a knot. He had known that this battle might result in his death, but now that it was approaching, the fear and disappointment were paralyzing. Moreover, he felt like he had failed his friends, which hurt considerably more than the fear of his own demise.

"Captain, the engines on the missiles have failed," announced Mahdara.

"Correction," added Janet. "They're not designed for firing off into space. They've used all of their fuel."

"Which means they'll blow soon," said Dan. "Get me the *Eclipse*." A channel opened a few seconds later. "Captain Tyreal, my dollar says those missiles are set to go any moment."

"Agreed," Tyreal answered, "but we need about thirty more seconds. We have to make sure the Gaarich are close enough and don't have time to run."

Thirty seconds was a long time considering the damage the *Liberty* and the rest of the fleet were taking. Dan peered up at the main screen, eying the tactical view. The missiles seemed to be moving perilously slowly, but Tyreal was correct; it would be at least thirty seconds until they would be in sufficient range to destroy the rest of the Gaarich fleet.

A blast from one of the marauders hit the *Liberty* hard, blowing the remaining gun turret from the bow of the ship. Debris hit the bridge, and the console Tom was sitting at exploded, severely burning his hands. The commander rushed over to help him, followed by Dan, who flew out of his chair.

Tom was in a tremendous amount of pain, but managed to get off a few words. He looked pointedly at Dan, who was leaning over him. "No, we're still good. I'm not dead."

As Tom said this, a beam from the ceiling fell down and tumbled to the floor, crushing the captain's chair. That would have been Dan's life. Captain Foster looked back and could feel that knot in his stomach getting tighter. This was becoming all too real.

"Ten seconds!" shouted Mahdara. "Five … four … three … two … slide!"

The Pyietri fleet quickly accelerated away and disappeared into hyperspace. The Gaarich tried to react and began to turn their ships, but it was too late. Almost in unison the missiles from Earth exploded in a brilliant flash, disintegrating the last of the Gaarich. The destruction was total. When the blackness of space returned, nothing of the invaders remained.

The *Liberty* emerged from hyperspace to join the rest of the fleet behind the moon. Ironic, as this was where Dan and his friends had started their journey several days before, but they were no longer alone. The Pyietri were now with them—much fewer in number, but victorious nonetheless.

Cheers and hugs were the order of the day aboard the *Liberty*. Although victory was at hand and Earth was safe, they had lost many friends and numerous ships. Only seven Pyietri craft remained, and countless thousands of people had given their lives to defend Earth—a planet where none of them had ever been.

Captain Tyreal hailed the *Liberty*. "Captain, we won! Your planet is safe. This is one for the history books. It may turn everything around for us!"

Mahdara looked at Dan, not with the joy that was gracing everyone else's lips, but instead with hopeless disbelief. "Uh, Captain. They're not done."

"What do you mean?" asked Dan, his words grabbing Tyreal's attention.

"Look!" Mahdara put a tactical image on the screen and piped it through to the *Eclipse*. What they saw was an enormous Gaarich ship that had appeared on the opposite side of Earth, escorted by thirty or more marauders and other minor craft. It was now obvious that the other ships had been a diversion. This was the main Gaarich attack fleet.

"We call it a star killer," said Tyreal. "The purpose of that ship is to wipe a civilization from a planet. They will pound your people back to living in tents and caves." Despair crossed his face. "I fear this battle has turned for the worst."

"Um, I think we have another problem," added Janet. "Two of the reactor thingies are flashing red."

"Captain Foster, the ship is lost! The reactors are damaged! We must make it to the escape pods," recommended Commander Teitrik.

Dan thought hard. He could not just abandon the ship before the battle was over. That star killer was going to devastate Earth. They had made it this far and emerged victorious. He would not yield his home planet to the Gaarich.

Dan's reflections were interrupted by Tyreal's voice. "Captain, two of your reactors are critical. Abandon ship. We'll engage the star killer."

"No! I have an idea. You'll be no match for that fleet, and I do not wish you to die in vain. If my plan works, you and my people can go home."

Janet made her way out of the helm and stood in front of Dan. "Well, let's hear it."

"Now bear with me here. One of the issues with traveling through hyperspace is not emerging inside a planet, sun, moon—you get my drift."

"Yeah, hyperspace 101. What about it?" asked Janet.

"What if we came out of hyperspace inside of a ship?"

Commander Teitrik shook his head. "We have fail-safes in the system. It just is not possible—"

"But it is," interrupted Mahdara. "This ship uses old sliding technology. It doesn't have the same safeguards as the newer jump drives. All I have to do is make the right calculations. We *can* slide inside the star killer."

"Mahdara," ordered Dan, "make the calculations."

Janet gave Dan the thumbs up. "You da man!" She went back to the helm to help Mahdara set the *Liberty* up for the slide.

Tom, whose hands were badly burned and was retching from pain, eked out a few words. "So ... we need to slide through Earth and come out of hyperspace inside a Gaarich star killer. So I am going to die."

"Relax! We'll set the ship on autopilot and be outta here before she slides. Right?" Dan asked tentatively of Commander Teitrik.

Not looking absolutely confident, the commander answered, "Right ... that is what we hope."

Dan punched up communications with the *Eclipse*. "Captain Tyreal, we're going to slide the *Liberty* into the star killer. Will the explosion be enough to destroy the rest of those ships?"

"Wait ... what ... you ... Captain Foster, you are out of your mind, but it probably will work. A star killer is one big weapon. If it goes up, it will take out the rest of the ships protecting her and cause a big light show for your friends back home."

"Good. We're going to escape from the *Liberty* before she slides, so be ready to pick us up. Foster out."

"We're good to go!" announced Janet as she stepped out of the helm toward Dan. She got a glimpse of the destroyed captain's chair, which pushed a cold shock straight down her spine. She gazed at Dan and gripped his arm. "That could have been you."

"Yeah, but it wasn't," Dan said, trying to brush it off as nothing.

"We have forty-five seconds!" announced Mahdara as she made her way toward the extremities of the bridge.

Dan observed the crew opening small hatches and climbing in, two or three at a time. Commander Teitrik motioned for them to follow. Dan and Janet ran toward one of the hatches and opened it. First Janet slid inside. Dan waited until he saw Mahdara, Commander Teitrik, and Tom climb into another. The bridge was clear. He took one last look around. Panels were on fire, sparks flew from many terminals, and his grandfather's command chair was destroyed. In a few seconds the ship would disappear, and Dan would lose another part of his grandfather, but he had gained many things over the past few days, and hopefully, if this worked, he would gain the safety of his family. Dan climbed into the tight quarters and closed the hatch.

"What do we do?" Dan asked frantically.

"Hey, the blue button has never served us wrong." Janet pushed it, and the small pod rocketed out of the ship. It cleared the hull just as the *Liberty* accelerated away.

All alone, the *Liberty* slid into hyperspace and disappeared. Aboard the *Eclipse* Tyreal watched his tactical display. The seconds ticked away like hours, but the waiting was rewarded with a great flash that emanated out of the hull of the star killer. Resultant explosions continued to ripple through the structure as the menacing Gaarich ship exploded. The shockwave engulfed the remaining Gaarich fleet, wiping them from the sky. When the blast cleared, all the enemy ships had been destroyed.

Captain Tyreal contacted Dan's escape pod. "Captain Foster, your plan worked! The Gaarich fleet has been destroyed! Your planet is safe! We are victorious!"

Janet hugged Dan in celebration. "We did it! We really did it!"

Dan didn't respond. He had to take it all in. He was emotionally and physically exhausted and felt like he could sleep for a whole week straight. All he could do was smile back at her.

Janet responded by kissing him. Their lips locked for a moment before she pulled away.

"What was that for?" a startled Dan asked a smiling Janet.

"Well, I wanted to be the first to kiss the hero. Plus, I have a thing for military guys."

Their celebration was interrupted by the flash of another group of ships leaving hyperspace. An enormous hull raced past them, completely filling the view out of their small porthole in the escape module.

"Is that what I think it is?" asked Dan.

An incoming transmission came from the *Eclipse*. "Captain Foster, we have the *Defiance* on the line for you."

A moment later a familiar voice crackled over the radio. "Mr. Foster, this is Captain Demenar of the *Defiance*. We have come to assist. We will be sending a shuttle to pull you aboard."

"Thank you," answered a confused Captain Foster. "I thought the Magnicieat voted against—"

"Correct," interrupted Demenar, "but Councilor Etenar revisited the issue with the other councilors. He convinced them otherwise, albeit using rather unorthodox tactics from the rumors I heard."

"Unorthodox?"

"Let's say the old man can be convincing and just leave it at that."

"No problem." Dan needed no explanation.

"We brought the *Besenti* Battle Group. They will be stationed here at Earth until further notice."

Dan smiled. "That would be much appreciated, Captain."

Janet again gazed into his eyes, her proud smile making Dan feel a little uncomfortable in the small space.

"What?" he asked.

"You were right. We didn't try, we just did—and now look. We have a star cruiser protecting Earth."

Dan mulled the thought over as he looked out the window at the *Besenti*, the massive structure reaching far off into space. The Daemerik were here, and Earth was safe from the Gaarich. The *Liberty* had completed her mission.

44
Never the Same

DAN STOOD STARING OUT OF HIS HOTEL ROOM at the Willard InterContinental. The view of the *Defiance* hovering over the Mall between the Capitol and the Washington Monument was a sight one had to see to believe. So many around the world had witnessed the battle in space, either through seeing the intense flashes of light or by watching through telescopes. There was no keeping the lid on this event, and the governments around the globe had to own up to what was happening.

Full disclosure along with exposés from just about every media outlet on Earth over the past several days helped prepare the world for this moment. At the upcoming ceremony, not only would Dan and his friends be honored as heroes, but new friends from a far-off world would begin to join the family of Earth.

There was a soft knock at the door. Dan went to open it. "Mom!"

Dan's mother gave him a big hug, her familiar perfume filling his nostrils—the scent always made anyplace feel like home.

"Where's Dad?" asked Dan.

"Oh, he's already down in the limo. I just wanted to see you before the ceremony." She stepped back to look at his outfit, gasping at how elegant her young son looked. "My, don't you look handsome! Is that really my father's?"

Dan nodded. He was wearing the captain's uniform. "They wanted me to wear it. I guess to give an Earthling face to the whole thing."

"Is it clean? I mean, it's been sitting—"

"Yes, Mom," interrupted Dan. "Don't worry, they cleaned it up. It was pretty ripped up after the battle."

Dan's mother walked to the window, gazing out at the *Defiance*. "This is still all too much for me to grasp. It's going to take some time. I wish he had told me. I wish he would have said something."

Dan moved toward his mom, grasping her hand. "Me too. I don't think he had the chance. I just feel bad because everything I touch of his seems to get destroyed—the car, the *Liberty*, the filing cabinets—"

"What about the filing cabinets?" asked Dan's mom.

"Uh—"

"Later. I'm just glad to have you back safe."

"But I still feel we've lost everything of him."

She shook her head. "Look out the window, son. Look! We haven't lost anything."

Dan looked out at the *Defiance*, but pulled his gaze back to see the reflection of him and his mom in the window. She was right. His grandfather had left behind much more.

There was a pounding at the door, and in walked Janet and Tom, all dressed up. Tom's hands were heavily bandaged, but otherwise he was none the worse for wear. Janet looked radiant, in an elegant black dress and coat. The outfits made his friends look older, and no doubt they were. The experience they had shared did more to thrust them into adulthood than high school or college could have ever done. Innocence was now replaced by confidence and maturity.

"Don't you two look nice," said Dan's mom.

"Thank you, Mrs. Foster," they both acknowledged in unison.

She kissed Dan. "I should get going before your father has at the minibar." She smiled at the three as she left the room.

"You guys look great!" exclaimed Dan.

"Thank you," answered Janet. The two joined Dan over by the window.

"You're wearing the captain's uniform," said Janet, a bit surprised.

"Yeah, they want me in it. Plus, technically I'm still a member of the Pyietri. I pledged that to Tyreal, if you remember."

"It's amazing," added Tom. "Because of a goofy turn of events, this all happened. Look, there is a freaking spaceship hovering above the city! The world, heck, the universe will never be the same, all because of us. If we'd never tried to go to the lake … oh … it's creepy."

"There's something to say about fate … to say about legacy, Mr. Hunt." The irony was true, but everything happens for a reason, of this Dan was now sure. "Time to go."

Tom and Janet turned toward the door.

"One more thing, Janet." Dan handed her a box, which she quickly opened.

"A digital music player!" Janet looked at Dan a little puzzled.

"Now you can lay off the eight-tracks."